I0585329

Angels of the Prairie Coteau

This is a work of fiction. With the exception of Fr. Arthur Belknap and Fr. V. S. Majer, the names, characters, business, events and incidents are the products of the author's imagination. Any resemblance to actual persons, living or dead, or actual events is purely coincidental. The opinions expressed are those of the characters' and should not be confused with the author's.

All rights reserved. No part of this book may be reproduced or transmitted in any form or by any means, electronic or mechanical, including photocopying, recording, or by any information storage and retrieval system, without the written permission of the copyright holder.

Cover design by James E. Lewandowski

Copyright © 2018 James E. Lewandowski
All rights reserved.

Hardcover ISBN 978-0-9821084-5-1
Paperback ISBN 978-0-9821084-4-4

Published by Prairie Hills Publishing
www.prairiehillspublishing.com

Angels of the Prairie Coteau

J.E. Lewandowski

Prairie Hills Publishing

Angels of the Prairie Coteau

Contents

Introduction

Chapters

for

Donna

Introduction

Do not go in search of the sleeping cross scarred upon the vacant hill, but be content in your knowledge of its existence. I remember, as a small child, traveling on weekend family outings from my home in Webster, SD to the surrounding area lakes. The Chevrolet Impala sailed the paved surface of Highway 12 while my siblings and I squabbled over the imaginary finger-drawn lines evenly dividing the vehicle's backseat. "Can you see the cross?" My mother's words always ended the dispute and pushed our faces against the side window glass to search the tall grass tufts of the steep hillside, and be the first to spot the instrument of our Savior's demise.

In the thoughts of a child, a cross on a hill symbolizes the crucifixion of Jesus on Calvary. As time passed, I came to understand the true meaning of the cross partially concealed within the hillside pastureland – that in the summer of 1925, during the second birth of the Ku Klux Klan, comprised primarily of community leaders, the powers that be cut a mutilating gash upon the earth that teared the eye of God, and bled a hateful fire stemming straight from the pits of hell below and touching the star filled heavens above.

I have traveled that stretch of highway countless times over the years. Approaching the cross, I hear its haunting cry taunt at my senses, it beckons me to look upon its face and remember the ghosts who carved it generations ago. I can not turn away. I always look. I always find it, and I always feel foolish in my act of doing so.

As with Webster, many towns and cities throughout the Upper Midwest were home to their very own klavens. If you are curious as to the Klan activity in your community, search the local newspaper archives, or the area church council minutes. Pay attention to missing editions, sections, pages, or in considering the church minutes, missing pages or those with the appearance of a rewrite.

Angels of the Prairie Coteau begins with the murder of Father Arthur Belknap in Lead, SD during late October of 1921. A young priest, originating from Dubuque, IA, he performed duties as pastor of Owl Creek, SD and Belle Fourche, SD before accepting his final position as rector of the St. Patrick Cathedral in Lead, SD. His murder was never solved to the full satisfaction of the general public.

As stated in the disclaimer, the story is a work of fiction. With the exception of Fr. Arthur Belknap and Fr. V. S. Majer, the names, characters, business are the products of the author's imagination. Any resemblance to actual persons, living or dead, are purely coincidental. The opinions expressed are those of the characters' and should not be confused with the author's.

Chapter 1

STOIC shadows swayed. Upon the four walls they slithered and reeled to the taunting flicker of a burning kerosene lamp. As the undiscerning flame churned the darkness within its light, hasty fingers, uninhibited by the erratic morphing flow, grazed the steel-nib of a fountain pen over an abrasive paper surface. The light scratches echoed within the room. Glossy wet ink tracks, reflecting in the lamp's soft, amber glow, wove a series of cursive characters in revealing a thoughtfully constructed expression.

Boom! Startled by the sudden backfire discharged from a motor vehicle creeping along a nearby side street, the writer froze, and glanced at the open window facing him from across the room. Squinting through the lightly flowing draped curtains, he nudged a pair of wire-rimmed glasses up the bridge of his nose, and scanned the darkened outdoor landscape beyond the small opening's lacquered wooden frame. As his eyes strained to focus, he began to identify a scattering of dried, silver leaves gently dancing as they rustled across the late autumn, moonlit treetops. Their gentle, synchronized motion gradually induced a rhythmic chant from the darkened silhouette of a great horned owl. *Hoo-hoo-hoo! Hoo-hoo!*

He held his breath in anticipation. Slightly tilting his head, he aimed an ear toward the open window. His heart raced. Its increasing tempo gradually flooded the canals of his inner ears and eventually overpowered nature's autographed medley, with the exception of the owl's late night mantra. *Hoo-hoo-hoo! Hoo-hoo!*

The taboo phrase, *spirit of the owl*, crossed his weary thoughts and teased at his receptive imagination.

Many of the natives recounted stories about the supernatural realm ruled by this tiger of the night sky. He recalled a conversation

1

with one of the locals who explained how the yellow-eyed raptor was a carrier of the elders' spirits. His people believed the mysterious dark hunter possessed the power to seek out lost souls of the dead, and guide them back to their predestined paths.

Others became worrisome of the bird's haunting cry, in fearing the foretelling of death. In the remote villages south of the U.S. border, the inhabitants reverenced the influence of the owl with an ill-omened adage – *when the owl cries, an Indian dies.*

He rubbed the soreness from his tired, red eyes, pulled his hand down his face, and cupped his chin. "Get a grip on yourself, Belknap. There's nothing out there. Nothing, but God's creatures of the night. As long as you're inside the sanctuary of these four walls, they cannot hurt you." He glanced once more through the rolling sways of the burlap curtain. "Yes. Yes, that's right. They would never enter here."

Ending with a final short stroke, he laid the pen at the head of his desk. Gently pealing the paper's sides from the desktop with both hands, he attempted to expedite the evaporation of ink solvents with a few light puffs of air. The wooden armchair creaked as he leaned back and began to read aloud the freshly scribed words.

October 25, 1921

My dearest Sister,

I hope this letter finds you and your family in good health and spirits. It has been over a month since I last wrote, and must apologize for my tardiness in returning correspondence. Please know that I am content in wearing the robes of a Catholic priest, and walking in the footsteps of our Lord and Savior, Jesus Christ, in teaching his lessons to the immigrants toiling the deep mines here in Lead, South Dakota, and especially to the natives in the outlying areas, when the opportunity arises.

In writing this letter, I hope to ease a few of your concerns regarding my wellbeing. The first is my safety in what you refer to as a wilderness land as harsh and desolate as the Dakotas. I will agree with you that during General Alfred Sully's campaign through the Dakota Territory in 1864, he did scornfully describe a portion of this land as

"Hell with the fires out", but I believe he referenced a specific region known as the Badlands, which is located a reasonable distance from where I reside.

In all fairness, I wish you could witness this beautiful country with its overflowing sea of rich, green tall and short grasses, covering an endless rolling prairie spread for hundreds of miles beneath the foot-hills of the majestic Black Hills. In my personal thoughts, I often attribute this land to a comforting refuge where many millenniums ago, weary angels once slumbered. Without a doubt, you would certainly find the openness quite breathtaking.

You also seem somewhat concerned with my safety in dealing with the natives. I must confess that it is not the natives I fear, but the secret klavens of the hooded men known as the Knights of the Ku Klux Klan. I am sure you have read in the newspapers back in Dubuque of how, in recent years, this group has grown in large numbers and gained much power throughout the country. Their push to eliminate immigrants, minorities, and Catholics in an effort to remove what they see as a threat to their traditional American way of life is nothing short of a misguided agenda profiting from blind fear.

Draped in white sheets, these ghosts parade openly down our small town main streets with the intent of recruiting the like minded and intimidating the rest. Local businessmen, church leaders, miners, farmers, and both men and women alike, proudly enlist as if joining a community social organization. Their gatherings include family picnics and suppers where the klavens and their women's auxiliaries sew the seeds of hatred and bigotry under a false banner of patriot-ism. On more than one occasion, they have burned large wooden crosses within plain view of our own picnics and outdoor gatherings.

Before the foundations of this earth, a third of the souls in Heaven followed Satan in his attempt to overthrow the Almighty. In all probability, a third of the people on this very planet at any given time could likely be some of these same foolish beings. I find it interesting in observing the actions of my fellow man in discerning whom these people may have once been, as their hatred and prejudices permeate the essential blindness, affixed by God to all living, and bleed out into their present day lives.

Do not let this upset you in a concern for my welfare, for many across our great nation bear the brunt of this organization's questionable activities. Their strength lies in fear, and the fear resonates from ignorance. We must continue to stand tall against this hatred and help free them from their darkness in showing that we are like them, equal in the eyes of God, but more importantly demonstrate that we are unlike them in our actions.

Please understand that there is a plan for my presence here. Every sunset, I am one day closer in discovering what that may be. Please take care and give my best wishes to all as the holidays approach.

Your loving brother,

Fr. Arthur Belknap

Relishing in the pleasant thought of his family living fruitful lives back in Iowa, he folded the papers, slid them inside a yellowed envelope, and placed his boyhood home's address upon its front. He reclined back in his chair and stared at the flame flickering within the confines of the lantern's glass funnel, and pondered the next day's chores, to include the letter along with the various pieces of parish mail during his stop at the local post office.

The long day wore close to an end as the wall clock's hands ratcheted toward a rendezvous at the face's summit. He covered a long, quiet yawn with the back of his hand as he reached to dull the lamp. Out of the corner of his eye, he noticed a dark profile of a man standing just outside the open window. Startled at sight of the strange shadow, he glanced toward the opening as the shape disappeared within the haunting flow of the draped curtains.

Jumping to his feet, he reluctantly moved toward the window. "Who's there?" He called out.

Spreading the curtains apart with both hands, he cautiously leaned down and stared out into the darkness. "Who's there?" He called once again, this time forcing a sternness to his voice in hopes the intruder would not sense his apprehension. "Is there anyone out there? Is there something you are in need of?"

While listening for a response, the increasing tempo of his heart beating from within his chest became quite apparent, until distracted by the distinct sound of breaking twigs and rustling leaves.

"If you are in need of help," he hesitated, "if you are in need of help, speak up or approach the front door." He listened attentively as the solitary rush of the wind raced through the pine needle branches of the spruce trees. Eventually, the night provided its own final answer in the form of the owl's cry. *Hoo-hoo-hoo! Hoo-hoo!*

Upset by the intrusion, he pulled the metal pin holding the open window in place, and allowed it to crash against the sill. Looking out through the glass into the midnight darkness, he turned the locking clasp tight, securing the opening. Reaching up and grasping the shade's dangling cord, he drew the fabric covering over the window, concealing himself from the outside world.

Sleep tips the balance as a valuable commodity for those whose vocations demand a constant watch. The call to service can be very unpredictable in presenting itself at any moment of its choosing. A priest is certainly not immune from this uncertainty, but in fact is a profession considered by all a testament of such selfless service.

Ring, Ring! Ring, Ring! The telephone's unmistakable reverberation shook the slumbering priest into consciousness, pulling him from a deep sleep, and robbing him of his soothing dreams.

Ring, Ring! Ring, Ring! Opening his eyes, he gasped for air as his chest tightened and his heart began to pound rapidly. Sitting up in bed, he hazily oriented himself to the dark surroundings of the cool bedroom quarters.

Pulling a woolen blanket over his shoulders, he stepped onto the cold, maple wood floor and rushed toward the beckoning sound. *Ring, Ring! Ring...* He knocked the receiver from its pronged switch hook, fumbling it in the darkness, and finally placed the cold metal tight against his ear.

"Yes, this is him," he cleared his throat while speaking into the telephone's mouthpiece in answer to the frantic caller's question.

"How sick is he?" He began shifting his weight in rotating one bare foot on top of the other in an attempt at maintaining the warmth of both.

"Where is he at?"

"Benders Park. Yes, I know where that is. I'll be there as soon as I can."

Ending the call by returning the earpiece to its hook, he rubbed his eyes and slowly ambled back to his quarters. He struck a match against the nightstand and ignited the saturated wick of the kerosene lamp, slowly illuminating the small room. Sitting motionless on the edge of his mattress, he stared blankly across the room until his eyes focused on the image of a wooden crucifix, garnished with several dried woven palm leaves, hanging on the all but bare walls. The mechanical ticking of his alarm clock aroused his attention and pulled him to the concerns at hand. He reached for the clock. "Three a.m., I should know better than to stay up so late."

Dressed in a black cassock and pulling his wool coat over his arms, he quickly left the rectory with his bag of essentials in hand. Dried leaves swirled from freshly raked piles, crackling and scratching against one another in the frigid early morning wind. A constant bark of an angry neighborhood dog echoed through the trees as the confused hound chased the dark shadows and unfamiliar sounds of the night.

Grasping the handle of the shed's wooden, folding doors, he pulled it open, causing the worn hinges to screech loudly with the retracting folds locking solidly into place. As always, the remaining door refused to move without a slight coaxing. Damaged from a prior resident's frustrated attempt to open the door, its upper rollers no longer moved freely within the track, and the assistance of a brick propped against its base now pinned the door closed.

Retrieving the brick from the ground and heaving it into the nearby grass, he lifted the heavy folding door and carried it open, dropping it along the outer wheel track, fully extended from the building's opening. He hesitated for a moment at what sounded like murmurings–quiet whispers in the night. A chill went down his spine. He scanned the darkness looking for the source, but observed nothing to indicate a valid concern. Shaking his head, he entered the small shed and found his automobile waiting.

An older Model T, the motor vehicle displayed a few random dings and scratches, but for the most part, the black Tin Lizzie transported him to a vast number of out of the way places. The honest parishioner who sold the vehicle to him claimed that by owning it, he strengthened his convictions and became more of a religious man for the experience. He explained that every time he started the vehicle, he prayed it would take him to the next destination without a breakdown in between.

The long narrow shed, originally constructed for storage and the housing of maintenance equipment, proved a tight fit for the wide vehicle. His heels clicked against one another as he sidestepped through the narrow space along the driver's side. Reaching into the cab, he checked the handbrake, making sure the lever remained engaged. Flipping the ignition switch to the on position, he raised the left timing lever on the steering column, and pulled the throttle upward the standard five notches. Searching with his bare hand along the backseat floorboard, he located and retrieved the angular hand crank before sidestepping back to the front of the vehicle.

After adjusting the engine's choke rod, protruding through a hole in the front of the radiator, he bent down and inserted the hand crank, engaging the engine's crankshaft. The cold temperature of the night air, and the sting of the auto's metal pieces, slightly numbed the skin on the tips of his fingers. Standing up, he blew a warm breath into his cupped hands while rubbing them together. He retrieved a pair of gloves from his coat pocket, covered his hands, and began the series of cranks to start the automobile.

Chugga-chugga-choo. Where the engine normally sparked to life, it now failed. He bent over and continued cranking, following the usual routine, and once again, it refused to start.

"Oh please, Lord, not now." He groaned.

A third, fourth, and fifth attempt produced the same disheartening results. Tapping his heels once again, he sidestepped along the driver's side and unlatched the engine compartment's side cover. Lacking even a hint of light, an attempt at repairs seemed hopeless. The smell of gasoline vapors filled the air. The engine likely flooded during the process, but the loss of spark continued to puzzle him. Repairs would wait until daylight, as for the time being, a deathly ill man urgently needed his assistance elsewhere.

He replaced the brick at the foot of the shed door and brushed the soil from his gloves. Standing on the narrow wheel path, stretching from the building to the street, he anticipated the long, frigid walk through the darkness. Leaves swirled within the air while the massive limbs of the tall trees gently bowed with the push of the high mountain winds. In the distance, a lone wolf called into the night. Lifting his coat's woolen collar to cover his neck, he raised his shoulders and began the dismal trek.

The wind pulled and twisted the cassock around his legs and confined his stride. Traveling on the shoulder, along the street's edge, he measured his progress by moving from one gas lantern streetlamp to the next. The darkness between the dull lights concerned him. If not for the appearance of the shadowy figure in the window earlier in the evening, he would think nothing of it.

The snapping of twigs paralleled his movements. Echoes of footsteps followed close behind and increased speed as he did. Attempting to prevent the noises of the dark from toiling with his imagination, he struggled to affix his mind on the task at hand.

Catching and passing a stranger walking in his path, he hurried along the street with thoughts focused on arriving in time to assist the ill man. The telephone directions began to spin and merge with his own cognate map. Becoming unsure of the house's exact location, he glanced over his shoulder in hopes the stranger still trailed. Finding him just a short distance away, he slowed his step and stopped under a streetlamp to wait for the unknown person to catch him.

As the man approached, the priest extended a hand. "Excuse me. I'm Father Belknap from St. Patrick's. I'm on my way to answer a sick call in Benders Park and want to be sure I have the correct information."

"Father?" The man stopped and nodded his head. "I was wondering who would be out this time of night. I'm Arthur Miller, the assistant mine foreman at the Homestake. I usually don't see many out this late when I'm on my way home from work."

"One need not be out here long to understand why." Belknap chuckled as he pulled the ends of his woolen collar to block the wind from is neck. "The directions given stated the third house in Benders Park. Does that sound like a familiar address to you?"

"Yes, I believe I know the people who live there."

"Is the house located near the Standard Oil Company tankers, near the city limits? It sounds correct, but I can't be sure."

"Yes, that's right, but I don't know why they would have requested a priest. I was just there the other day, and no one was sick at that residence."

"Are you sure about that?"

Miller nodded.

The priest shook his head. "This could be just another wild goose chase."

"Wild goose chase?"

"Yes, I've taken a number of these calls over the past few weeks, and when I arrived at the homes, nobody knew anything about it. I stood there looking like a fool for an unknown prankster."

"Who would do something like that?"

"It's hard to say. Someone with a warped sense of humor I would guess."

"Father, I think you should go home and try calling these people. It doesn't sound right. It may save you some steps."

"No. I'm over halfway there. Besides, I may have heard the directions incorrectly. When I get close, I'm sure I will see a light on, or find someone there to meet me. I wouldn't want to add to an ill man's suffering because of some idiot's antics."

"Suit yourself, Father. I can walk with you for a ways, but then I'll have to turn off."

"Yes, the company would be very much appreciated."

Trudging through the cold and darkness, the two men continued movement from one lighted lamppost to the next. Each deserted street intersection came and went without hindrance, until eventually the two bid farewell in their departure. Estimating the final length of his journey at less than four blocks, the determined priest readjusted his coat in curbing the infiltration of frigid air, and continued with his task, as he followed the scarcely lighted route.

Approaching the next lamppost, Belknap noticed the distinct silhouette of a large man suddenly appear opposite the circle of light's fading edge. Taking one last quick leap, he nearly lost his balance as he reached out and grabbed at the tubular pole to steady himself. Stopping, he waited for the shadow to move toward him, but the dark figure remained out of sight.

"Can I assist you with something?" The priest's voice quivered.

Standing motionless, the man continued his awkward silence.

"Come now, I know you're there. Is there a reason for all of this?"

A match ignited outside of the tight boundary of the light's dull perimeter as a cupped hand scooped the flame toward the stranger's face. Lighting a freshly rolled cigarette, drooped between his lips, the flickering match partially illuminated an unshaven face and sparked a reflection in its dark eyes. Without hesitation, the stranger flicked the match toward the street roadbed, extinguishing before it struck the ground.

"Who are you?" The priest demanded, as he squinted into the darkness. "Do I know you?"

The cigarette's cherry glowed bright orange as the man took a long, slow drag. "Yeah, I talked with you on the telephone a short while ago." Attached to each slurred word, dark wisps of smoke, snaked from his mouth.

"Good, I'm glad you're here. This has been a very strange night, indeed. At one point, I wondered if this was all just a charade—a terribly bad joke."

"Oh, I can assure you, this is no joke." He pulled a familiar shaped bottle from within his coat, twisted the cork from its opening, and drank two large gulps. "Yeah, this is no joke." He replaced the cork and returned the bottle to his pocket.

"Very well, let us continue on our way. I would appreciate it if you would take me to the sick man. I am concerned that I may not have heard the location correctly over the telephone."

Rubbing his gloves together in hopes of warming his hands beneath the fabric, the cold, nervous priest exited the circle of light and moved into the darkness with the man trailing closely behind. They moved in and out of the next streetlamp's glow, maintaining a quick, steady pace. Questions as to the specifics of the ill man's condition and his exact whereabouts went unanswered.

Glancing behind, every few steps, at the man trailing at his heels, the extreme sense of unease quickly deteriorated to a gut wrenching fear. This did not feel right. There were too many uncertainties. No, this did not feel right at all. With an unknown man waiting at death's door and the strange actions of his shadowy acquaintance, the town police officer should be involved.

Pausing at the street corner's edge, in hopes of persuading the man to return with him to the parsonage, the black night suddenly erupted into a brilliant torrent of white as a piercing pressure crushed against his fragile skull. Time stopped, as warm, peaceful colors stirred about his inner being. Images of love and peace soothed his spirit as it attempted emancipation from its earthly host.

Roused to consciousness by an excruciating pain radiating from the back of his head, Father Belknap found himself kneeling upon the ground. As he struggled to regain his vision, sparks of brightness transformed into the yellowing rays of approaching lantern beams. Staring at small bits of flesh and fine strands of hair covering the marred, steel face of a large hammer that lay near the stranger's feet, all doubts as to what happened, quickly vanished.

"You got him! You got him!" Enthused voices applauded through the sound of snapping branches from a small group of men rushing from the tree line.

"Yeah, I told you I would." The man impassively replied.

The priest reeled and swayed upon bended knees, his shaky voice finally calling out in a slur of painful cries and moans.

A stocky man stepped from the group and tugged the confused priest back up onto his twisting feet. Pinching the priest's face with a set of soiled fingers protruding through the ends of a cut-off woolen glove, he slowly leaned in, nose-to-nose, and stared into his misaligned eyes. "You don't look so good, priest. You got yourself a headache?" His foul breath caused a slight stir in the priest's senses. "I'll bet you'd like a cure for that headache of yours, right about now, wouldn't you."

Winding back, the man unleashed a driving force in his free hand, and connected solidly against a vulnerable, bleeding ear. The crowd winced at the loud, nauseating smack, but their intense craving for sadistic torment and humiliation spawned a muffled round of ridicule and laughter. Spinning in a semicircle, the priest dropped to the ground as his eyes disappeared under fluttering lids.

"What are we going to do with him now?" A voice inquired as they began to argue quietly among themselves. "We'd better think of something quick before another damned immigrant decides to walk home from work."

"Yeah, let's wrap this up." Another demanded. "I've got to open the store early tomorrow. Tar and feathers?"

"Just wait, we can do better than that." The man stared intently at the priest's face, as if studying the blood trails originating from both ears and nostrils, and pooling upon the ground directly below him.

As nervous bodies began edging back toward the dark tree line, he raised his hand into the air. "Hold on! Hold on! I know. I know what we'll do." A sinister smile crawled across his worn face as he reached into his coat and pulled out the bottle. "We'll just put a cure to that bad headache of his." He took a large swig and passed the uncorked bottle for the others to partake.

Fishing again, deep within his coat pocket, he soon revealed a .45 caliber semi-automatic pistol, its cold, dark steel reflecting the lanterns' dim flickering glow. "You know what they say?" He swirled the barrel of the pistol above his shoulders. "Yes, of course, we all know what they say." He dropped the .45 to his side. "The only way to cure a Catholic…is to kill him."

The sporadic appearance of satisfied grins and slow nodding heads provided a final verdict of the defenseless, wounded man wearing a blood stained, white collar. Gathering in a tight circle, secret verses and sacred chants rhymed within the ceremonial assembly as all repeated the words in unison – an accepted systematic process, justifying insufferable deeds, under a false banner of patriotism.

Directing the others aside, with the barrel of his .45, the man stepped in front of the priest, and with a sure and steady hand, calmly aimed his pistol.

Light crystal snowflakes gently drifted from above, as a frigid northwest wind quietly moaned through the dense forest spruce trees of the northern Black Hills. In the small mining community of Lead, the creatures of the night paused in fear, at the haunting echo of a well-known demon. Perched within the crook of an old, twisted bur oak tree and hidden by the cover of darkness, a lone great horned owl gave a solemn final cry. *Hoo-hoo-hoo! Hoo-hoo!*

Chapter 2

S OUTHERLY winds blew. Their invisible gusts swept the thawing, northern plains and engulfed the emergent prairie life with its unseasonable warmth. In full bloom among the clumps of bleached, buffalo grass, wild pasqueflowers played host to a rabble of newly awakened sweat bees attempting to dance each lavender edge. The bright purple hues accentuated a series of pale red, quartzite monuments, aligning the once disputed Seventh Standard Parallel. Seven hundred-twenty in number, the seven-foot tall stelae, erected at half-mile intervals, effectively defined the border that split the last remnant of the Dakota Territory into two separate states.

The churning, dark waters of the wide Missouri River separated the land once again. Its unforgiving nature divided the southern state into nearly equal distinct parts. The land's inhabitants identified those occupying the drier west as ranchers, and those dwelling in the more fertile east as farmers.

Countering the mountainous Black Hills of the state's southwest corner, the northeastern terrain provided a likewise rise in its landscape. Carved by slow moving glacial masses, some 11,500 years ago, the seemingly out of place, 100-mile wide by 200-mile long plateau towered above the shortgrass prairie flatland. Its continuous waves of rolling hills harbored numerous freshwater lakes, in nurturing a plethora of migrating wildlife. French explorers, and fur trappers and traders arriving from the north once referred to this distinct land mass as the *Coteau des Prairies* – Hills of the Prairie.

Crisscrossing the coteau, a maze of dirt roads and twisted trails branded a woven pattern that separated, as well as connected, the many farms and villages. As observed from a distance, a small cloud of dust rolled upward before slowly dissipating along one of these well-traveled paths. Sparrows scattered and ground squirrels scrambled in clearing the roadway as the fearsome scream of an Indian motorcycle raced past.

Reaching down, Jacob repositioned the twisted twine, tied around the necks of two, square, Ball Mason jars, saddled over the red fuel tank. Inside the glass containers, the clear liquid danced to the engine's vibration. Occasionally, when the wheels struck a dried mud hole, the corn liquor leaped against the underside of the lid as the jars struck against the side of the frame.

The rushing wind pinned Jacob's dark brown hair against his head. Squinting through round goggles, he spotted the sharp rise in the road's slope that always beckoned him to test his bike's abilities. The rolling hills around the many lakes offered numerous opportunities for those odd few who craved a brief moment of weightlessness, but this one was superior to the others. Striking the base of the hill at rapid speed, a rider could launch his bike high into the air, before landing a great distance on the other side.

Imagining himself the pilot of a biplane attempting to break from the earth's grip, he glanced at the speedometer. The needle wound to the far right, hovering slightly above the stenciled 70 mph mark.

"Is this all the better you can do!" He yelled, as if coaxing the demon harbored within the machine.

Twisting the handlebar grip to its very end, in an effort to squeeze every ounce of horsepower from the deafening engine, he smiled as the bike suddenly lurched forward. Centering his torso over the motorcycle as it initiated the swift ascent, he held his breath at the final moment when the rubber broke contact at the hill's peak.

Turning from a side road, an automobile drifted directly onto Jacob's intended path. He yanked back on the handlebars in an attempt to avoid a collision with the vehicle's rear end. As the bike's wheels touched the loose dirt behind the accelerating auto, Jacob squeezed the brake lever with all of his might while laying the bike on its side. The motorcycle slid, caught a large tuft of dried grass, and threw Jacob clear as it rolled along the roadside in a small cloud of dust. The automobile, followed by another, continued its course of travel without attempting a stop.

Slightly dazed, Jacob moaned as he pushed himself from the ground. Rubbing the soreness from his wrist, he wondered as to how

he survived the mishap. He slid his goggles above his eyes as he staggered toward the bike, and gave a quick exam of the wingless wonder. The twisted front fork and the seeping of oil from around the
cylinder heads indicated it would be some time before he would
attempt the jump again.

As he circled the bike, his boot hooked a small piece of debris hidden within the tall, brown grass. He gently kicked at it, exposing a
long piece of twine connected to a jagged shard of glass. Giving
another tug to free himself, he exposed its completely intact companion, still tied to the opposite end. Raising the glass jar against the
bright blue sky, he slowly shook his head. "It seems that you and I
share something in common today. We should both be shattered into
pieces like your twin."

"Go, Kettie! Why are you stopping? Keep going or they'll be in
the water before we even get there."

Jacob turned his head toward the voice as a dark screen of road
dust overtook him. The gradual settling of the fine particles slowly
revealed two young girls sitting in an idling maroon roadster parked
at the path's edge. The driver propped herself up on one knee, and
raised her sunglasses in examining the wreck, while her passenger
sharply scolded her for the delay.

"Can't you see he's fine? They're getting too far ahead of us. Let's
go!"

"Relax, Brina. I told you before, it isn't a race." The reluctant
driver slid down onto the seat and set the vehicle in motion.

The passenger gave a quick glance toward Jacob. Without making
eye contact, she stuck her nose in the air, and gave a quick laugh as
she flicked a cigarette butt in his direction.

Lifting the goggles from his forehead, Jacob wiped the sweat from
his brow as he watched the vehicle race over the next hill to join the
others. Crackle! Snap! Jacob turned suddenly to identify a series of
strange noises repeating from behind him.

"Oh no!" He yelled as he dashed to the roadside.

The burning cigarette ignited a small puddle of spilled corn whiskey and adjoining dried grass. In a chaotic dance of stomps and kicks,
he quickly extinguished the flames before they reached the bike.

On one of the many gradual sloping hills overlooking Pickerel
Lake, a man paced the farmyard near the front porch of his house.

Stopping momentarily in the flickering shadow of rotating wind wheel sails, he watched as Jacob pushed the disabled motorcycle along a meandering cow path within the pasture.

"That boy. What has he got himself into now?" The Polish words mumbled from his lips. "Ah!" He snapped the side of his pant leg with the back of his hand and marched toward the water tank.

"Peter, how much longer are you going to be? We don't want to be late." A concerned voice called from the porch.

Peter rinsed his mouth, spit, and hung the tin cup on a wire hook fastened to the windmill's angle brace. He pointed down the hill at Jacob and raised his hands into the air.

"Come. Come and sit. You've been pacing in the driveway for the past twenty minutes. It's not good to worry like that."

Peter approached the house and rested on the top step. "I'm not worried, Maria. It's just...it's just sometimes, I don't understand that boy."

"What is there to understand that you don't already know. Jacob is Jacob. He is different from you, just like you are different from your father."

"Yes. I know we are all different, but he should be doing so much better. He should have more to his name by now. It's this damned poor farm economy – that's what it is. A young man just doesn't have a chance these days."

"You can't blame Jacob for the low grain prices and overvalued land."

"No. I don't blame him for that, but he should take things more seriously. This is not the time to wander aimlessly. He should know what he wants to do by now, and be darned smart about going after it."

Maria knelt behind Peter and rubbed his shoulders. "I may be just his stepmother, but in raising him, I think I know him well enough. Let Jacob be himself. Things will work out for the best. Besides, he will be leaving us and going off to Chicago in the fall."

Peter chuckled. "He will be the first of the brood to leave the nest."

"That's right. Please try not to spoil these remaining months with unwarranted feelings."

Peter rested his head against Maria's hand. "Yes Mama. You are right as usual. I'll try and watch myself from now on."

As Jacob laid his bike onto the rough, hoof-beaten ground to open the pasture gate, Maria gave Peter a slight nudge.

"What?" Peter returned a puzzled look.

Maria nodded toward Jacob.

"Oh. Oh yes." Peter jumped to his feet. "Wait a bit, son. I can help you with that."

Maria opened the screen door, paused, and watched through the fine mesh as the two men worked the pasture gate open and close. In her thoughts, she could still see the proud young father with his eager little boy. Smiling, she turned to enter the house in finalizing preparations for the afternoon outing.

Thud! Jacob's bike landed against the tool shed wall. Kneeling down, he re-examined the damage.

Looking on, Peter scratched his head. "From the shape of that turned fork, you endured quite a spill on that contraption. You hurt?"

Jacob stood up, walked past Peter, and began picking through an assortment of odd wrenches in the toolbox. The metal pieces sang and rattled until he finally located the correct sizes. Moving in front of Peter once again, he returned to the bike, placed the open end of a wrench over a bolt head, and applied pressure.

"Ah!" He screamed as his wrist burst into pain.

"Here, let me help you with that." Peter reached for the wrench in Jacob's hand.

"I got it!" Jacob growled as he pulled away. "I can fix it myself."

"Yes, of course you can." Peter shook his head while searching for the words to spark an agreeable conversation. "Was Anton home?"

Jacob retrieved the broken chunk of glass from his coat pocket and tossed it into the air.

Catching it, Peter rubbed his thumb across the raised numbers molded into the translucent round base. "One, three – thirteen?" He sighed. "Maybe there is something to those silly superstitions."

"Ah!" Jacob screamed once more as he attempted to free the bolt locked tight within the frame. Defeated, he stood up and wiped a run of sweat from his forehead.

"He sells the number thirteen jars to people who stop by. The others he saves, to carry with him on his delivery runs. He said he doesn't take unnecessary risks – doesn't want to end up paying a large fine, or being sent to federal prison at Leavenworth."

"Well, if he's the one taking the chances, I suppose he can determine the rules as he sees fit." Peter bounced the glass bottom in his hand. "That's too bad. It sure would have gone down well at the baseball game this afternoon."

Jacob reached inside his coat, pulled a half smile across his face, and handed a sealed jar to Peter. "Thirteens are half-price, so I bought you two."

Peter's eyes lit up. "Now, that's my boy." He looked at the clear liquid within the container clenched in one hand, and then at the broken piece of glass in the other. "Although under the circumstances, we can't rightly call you half price now can we? But we'll gladly take you just the same."

He turned the lid free, sniffed the corn liquor, and took a small sip. "Whew!" He blew a quick breath as he squinted one eye. "That'll bring 'em running to the confessional." He returned the lid and gently set the jar in a safe location on the workbench. "You'll need to finish your repairs another time. We're running late as it is. They won't start the ballgame without you, but it wouldn't be right to keep them waiting."

"Ballgame? No, not today. Don't you remember? We talked about this. I made plans to ride Pickerel Lake. I can't miss the spring run-off."

"Ride the lake? But they're counting on you to play. You'll find time for that nonsense another day."

"The water's already begun to pour through the spillway. Now is the time – not later. Besides, the game is between a couple of small, cow patty teams. It doesn't mean anything. Someone else can take my spot this time."

Peter hesitated and then grinned. "Telka will be there."

Jacob rolled his eyes.

"Oh, come on now. There's nothing wrong with that girl. She's available and comes from a respectable Catholic family. Looks to be a good strong worker, too."

"A girl with marriage on her mind?" Jacob laughed. "I value life more than that, especially my own."

Peter shook his head. "But you don't understand. You have a responsibility to play, at least for the people watching. Some folks travel a good distance just to see you hit. You don't want to disappoint them."

Jacob raised a swollen wrist into the air, and then slapped the wrench into Peter's hand. "I don't think I will be hitting any balls today." He turned and walked out of the shed doorway.

Peter rubbed the back of his neck, and then grabbed his chin as he watched Jacob walk toward the house. "I don't understand that boy." He looked down at the wrench in his hand and gave it a quick toss toward the toolbox. *Crack!* Broken glass fell from the bench as clear liquid streamed between the boards and pooled upon the dirt floor.

As the compliant paint stepped forward, it exhaled, releasing just enough air from its massive lungs to allow Jacob to readjust the saddle's girth around its firm midsection. The unusually warm day would provide for a comfortable ride around the lake.

Jacob led the horse over the straw-covered, barn floor, thinking of the specific areas that interested him the most. The mild winter offered little in snowmelt, surmising expectations that the runoff would be much less than measured in previous years.

"I won't be here when you return, Jacob," Ben stretched his arm in offering a dark brown, calloused hand. "I'm catching a ride with your folks to the ballgame, and then hope to hitch a ride on south from there."

"Are you sure you can't stay on for another week?"

"No. I need to get back home. Mama's still feeling poorly – it's that damned cough again. Kids are doing what they can for her, but they have families of their own to tend with. It's not fair to them."

Jacob grabbed Ben's hand. "We'll be thinking of you and your family while you're away."

"I appreciate it. Though your pa seems a might upset." Ben gave a quick shake of his head. "I explained there was nothing I could do. I feel bad about leaving him with the spring work, but I have to get home."

"Don't pay any mind to him. We should be able to find temporary help to handle the workload until you return for harvest in the fall."

"And I'll be here as soon as I can."

Jacob hesitated. "Tell me, Ben. Why is it that each summer you always leave your home and family, and travel up here to work for Pa? Don't get me wrong. I for one am glad to accept the help, but it seems like an awful long way to go just for work."

"I was born up in this country, Jacob. My pa was a buffalo soldier at the fort, back when there were no fences strung across the prairie."

"At Fort Sisseton? That's less than twenty miles from here."

"Yep, we moved to the southern end of the state when I was still in diapers. My pa always spoke highly about living on the coteau. He could never stop talking about the deer, the fish, and the continuous rolling hills. After he passed, I began talking with the missus about experiencing it for myself – seeing if it really was like he said. I guess I talked about it just once too often. One spring morning, she pushed me out the door and told me to stop talking and start walking. I've made the trip back here every spring since."

"You ever thought about bringing your wife and staying?"

Ben laughed. "Quite often, Jacob. Yes, quite often. But I don't think there's room up here just yet for a full-time colored man."

The view down the hill and across the pasture painted a summoning sparkle to the crystal blue lake. Anxious to begin, Jacob cradled a bandaged hand close to his chest as he kicked his boot into the stirrup and pulled himself into the saddle.

"Wait! Wait for me!" A young voice called.

Jacob gave the horse a slight kick as Aggie jumped from the front steps of the house and dashed across the yard.

"Did you forget?" She reached up and grabbed the bridle to stop the horse.

Confused, Jacob stared at her.

"You promised I could go with you and watch the fish swim over the spillway."

Jacob looked down at the lake and then back at his siblings preparing to leave. "Come on, sis. Don't you want to go to the ballgame with the others? Your friends will be there."

"No. I don't want to go with them. Besides, Pa said I could go with you."

"Oh, he did, did he?" Jacob scanned the buildings and discovered the silhouette of a man watching from the barn. "I know I said you could come along, but there's not enough time to saddle another horse. How about we do something next week, or the following?"

"Please, Jacob. I want to see the fish running through the spillway. I don't need my own horse. I can ride with you."

Jacob hesitated. Out of the corner of his eye, he could still distinguish the dark shadow observing from the barn. "All right, come on." He reached down and grabbed Aggie by her arm. "Maybe I can use your help." The horse staggered to the side as Aggie slid behind Jacob.

The lake rested less than a half mile below the hill, where the farm overlooked its deep spring-fed basin. The horse trotted along the dirt road and knowingly veered onto a narrow path that led them directly to the water's edge. Adjacent to the shoreline, a small resort stood open for business. Providing a limited assortment of groceries for the area farmers during the deep snow months, it now readied for the steady stream of vacationers and summer anglers.

While Aggie searched the beach for a flat rock to skip across the water's surface, Jacob found Frankie, the resort's owner, kneeling in the grass while spreading the final coat of white paint over the wooden hull of an inverted rental boat.

"Anyone give up their secret fishing spots?" Jacob reached down and released a fly caught in the tacky finish.

Frankie looked over the top of his white speckled glasses. "I haven't heard of any. Why don't you go out and catch yourself a monster. It'd give me a real good story to tell people when they get here."

"I'll wait a while longer. It just wouldn't feel right without Stach coming along."

"I understand. Sorry to hear about your dog. Good ones like that are hard to come by."

Jacob looked up the shoreline at a small group picnicking in a clearing beyond a scattering of one-room cottages. A few lay upon plaid blankets absorbing the warming rays of the midday sun, while others swam in the cool, shallow water. One couple, having a small dispute, paced back and forth next to the parked automobiles as the young man attempted to make amends.

Frankie laid the thick brush across the paint can's wide opening and pushed himself from the ground. "Kids are staying at the south end of the lake. From Webster I would guess. Drove over this after-noon. Just out having fun."

"Yeah, I recognize some of them from last summer." Jacob com-mented as he remembered a brief altercation with two of the boys. "I think we'll try riding in the other direction, down by the spillway first. Maybe check out the fish entering the creek."

With Aggie seated directly behind him, Jacob gave a slight kick to the horse's ribs, leading a course along the lake's meandering shore-line. Nearing an adjoining slough, they slowed to investigate the returning fauna. The small wetland's still waters echoed the raspy calls of a yellow-headed blackbird flock and wove their hoarse cries through the encircling dried cattail reeds. Amused by a vegetation gathering muskrat, they watched as it dived and surfaced, until an overprotective tern directed them to continue on their way with a series of intimidating swoops.

The gradual movement of runoff water through the narrow spill-way was unlike the roar and rush of prior years, when the spring snowmelt filled the lake to capacity. Now, the shallow, rocky mouth of the outlet became somewhat of a challenge for the fish attempting to make their escape.

A line of bright rainbows appeared and dissipated above the creek as a northern pike splashed its glossy tailfin against the flowing sur-face. Aggie knelt down and reached her hand across the water to feel the smoothness of the northern's exposed, shiny scales. "Where are *you* going little fish? Ah!" A quick splash sent her tumbling backward as the fish darted over the moss-covered rocks and disappeared within the creek's darkening flow.

"Be careful, or you may find out, firsthand." Jacob chuckled.

Aggie wiped the water droplets from her face. "You could have warned me." She knelt back against the water's edge in searching for the culprit that splashed her, while keeping a keen eye on those con-tinuing to swim through.

"Most will follow the flow of the creek as it winds through the hills, and drains into Waubay Lake, near Grenville. That's unless someone with a pitchfork spears them from the water before they can get there." Jacob opened his journal. "Do you think you can count them for me?"

As Aggie began tallying aloud, Jacob unbuttoned his shirt pocket and retrieved an old mercury thermometer. Forcing it through a piece of cork, he fastened it to a long piece of string and set it afloat within the moving water. Hopping among the smaller stones, the soles of his boots skidded against the wet, green moss, as he made his way to a flat, oblong boulder protruding from the center of the stream. Inserting a notched stick into the water, he took note of the creek's depth.

"That's good, Aggie. You can stop." Jacob penciled additional marks within the pages of his book.

"What are you doing with that?" Aggie moved closer to look at Jacob's fresh notations.

"It's my journal." He retrieved the thermometer from the water. "I keep a record of the lake."

"Why do you keep a record?"

"I don't know. I got started when I was about your age. Watching the wildlife. Seeing how it changes each year. I guess it just interests me."

As Jacob explained the different variances he noted over the years, he lifted Aggie into the horse's saddle. Brushing his foot within the twines of bleached reeds and tallgrass, he found a midsized dried cottonwood twig. Placing the stick in the water at the lip of the spillway, he marked the time on his pocket watch, and began tracking the branch's movement with the creek's current.

They pushed through the light brush, along the water's edge, following the creek as it moved away from the lake. As Aggie kept an eye on the twig, Jacob examined the foliage on the overhanging tree branches and peeled apart a scattering of newly sprouted buds adorning the various shrubbery and bushes.

"The twig stopped." Aggie pointed at the creek's far bank."

Jacob glanced at his watch and entered notes in his journal, estimating the volume of spring runoff flowing from the lake.

Aggie watched as the small stick pulled loose and returned to the flow. "There it goes again. Floating all the way to Waubay." It swirled within the current. "What will happen to it when it gets there?"

"It could continue on to Bitter Lake, but it won't go any farther than that. All of these lakes are part of a closed basin. The water can't escape. Unless it evaporates or is absorbed into the ground, it'll stay trapped on the coteau. You could say it's stuck here, stranded." He watched the twig drift out of sight. "Just like me."

Grabbing the saddles horn, Jacob pulled himself up onto the horse. "The water's too deep here to cross. We'll follow the creek to the road, cross over the bridge, and continue around the lake from there."

A startled hen pheasant leaped into the air and glided above the tall, dried prairie cord grass, as the horse stepped through the brush in moving toward the bridge. Following the movement of large shadows roaming about an open field, Jacob pointed directly overhead, where a flock of white pelicans circled with a slow, majestic grace against the bright afternoon sun.

Reaching the bridge, Jacob stood in the stirrups and turned an ear toward a distant firing of an automobile engine ignite into action and then choke to a stall. Directing the horse onto the road, he discovered the dark maroon roadster that slowed during his wreck earlier in the day. Leaning in front of the vehicle, a young woman attempted to start the engine, which ran momentarily and then stopped.

"I don't recognize that car. Do you know who that is, Jacob?"

"No, not personally." Jacob returned to his saddle.

"She needs help. Let's go."

Recalling the disagreement the girl contended with her boyfriend near the cottages, Jacob wondered if she became upset and left before the others. Considering last summer's painful confrontation with two of them, he thought it best to keep his distance. "Her friends will be along shortly. She'll receive help when they arrive."

Aggie looked over her shoulder at the quiet, empty road. "I don't think her friends are coming, Jacob. We can't just leave her without at least asking."

Jacob turned in his saddle and looked down the vacant road. The sky lacked any obvious signs of rising trail dust. He glanced at the girl lifting the engine's side cover, and then back down the road again. "Okay, Aggie. You win. Let's go see how much trouble we can get ourselves into today."

The vehicle rocked from side to side as the girl worked within the engine's compartment. A series of metallic chimes alternated with an occasional grunt of desperation.

Halting the horse behind the roadster, Jacob hesitated as he watched in disbelief as she attempted to resolve repairs on her own. He cleared his throat. "Could you use some help?"

A string of profanity echoed from beneath the hood as the girl's long reach pulled her feet off the ground.

Sliding his foot over the saddle, Jacob jumped from the horse, and walked to the front of the vehicle. Her short auburn hair bounced across the side of her face as she tinkered within the engine's compartment. Its shimmering reddish brown tint reminded him of the color of his favorite spice. "Excuse me, miss. Do you need help?"

A smudged face appeared from the engine well. "You must be the idiot asking all the intelligent questions." She stepped away from the vehicle.

Jacob stopped in his tracks. "I…"

"I, what?" She pointed at him. "Before you even start, I think you should know that I'm fully capable of taking care of myself. I make my own decisions and have been successfully doing so for some time now."

"But I…"

"But I, what? You think just because I'm a girl, I don't know how to fix one of these…," she pointed at the open engine compartment, "one of these things?"

Jacob threw his hands into the air. "I don't need this abuse. I'm going." He turned and walked away.

"Good! Then at least I won't waste my breath in telling you where to go. You men are all alike." She stepped to the front of the vehicle.

Winding the hand crank, the engine sparked and burst into life. A content smile appeared between the grease smears and then slowly faded as the engine choked and died. As the hand crank bounced in the dirt, she rested her arm upon the radiator, and hung her head.

Jacob grabbed the saddle horn and inserted his boot into the stirrup. "Tell me where to go? Ha! I know where she's going – nowhere." Pulling himself up, he felt his balance tip as Aggie pushed him from the saddle. She poked a finger in the girl's direction. Jacob hesitated, and then shook his head. Aggie countered with a nod, and then gave him a slight nudge toward the vehicle with the bottom of her foot.

"All right, all right, I'll try one more time." He looked at the girl and wiped his hands down the front of his shirt. "If you find anything left of me, be sure to scrape it off the ground, and take it home."

Jacob took a deep breath and returned to the front of the automobile. He knelt down and retrieved the hand crank. "It sounds like it's not getting enough fuel. Is there gas in the tank?"

"Do you honestly think I would be standing here cranking on this contraption if it were out…" She stopped, took a long look down the road and then at Jacob. "Listen, I'm sorry. It hasn't been a very good day for me. My friends…well, anyway, my name is Kettie." She extended a soiled hand.

"I know you would prefer not to be here, but most times, it's less about what you want, and more about what you're actually stuck with." He smiled. "I'm Jacob, and that's my little sister, Aggie." He shook her hand and leaned in to scan around the engine. "Buick Sport Roadster – Special Six." He looked up at Kettie. "Very nice."

Aggie gave a slight wave from atop the horse.

"Your brother seems to know what he's doing." She found a towel on the vehicle's floor and wiped the motor grime from her cheek. "So, did he rescue you today as well?"

Aggie nodded. "Yes, but he didn't know it at the time."

"Ah!" Jacob screamed as he stepped back and gripped his wrist.

Kettie raised his arm and tugged at the bandage. "Looks like a bad sprain. Are you sure you can make repairs with that wrapped hand?"

"Jacob wrecked his motorcycle today." Aggie explained.

Kettie looked at Jacob. "That was you? The rider in the ditch?"

Jacob yanked his arm away. "Thanks for stopping. Even if it was for just a moment." He continued under the hood.

"If I were you, I wouldn't read too much into it. I was only checking to see if you were dead. I had plans to take the bike."

Jacob looked at her. "Sorry I disappointed you."

"Don't worry. If you can get this thing started, maybe I'll forget about it." She smiled.

A stream of liquid splattered upon the ground beneath the vehicle. "Ah. Water."

"What?"

"There's water in your fuel tank." Jacob retrieved a pair of pliers from his pocket. "It settles beneath the gasoline. I'll drain it off from the bottom of the tank through the fuel line."

"Then will it run?"

"It should." He slid the pliers back into his pocket.

"How in the world would I acquire water in…"

Ahooga! Ahooga! An automobile's horn blasted while a cloud of road dust overtook them. As the piercing screech of wheel brakes faded, the fine dirt particles settled before squinting eyes.

"Well, look who we have here." The passenger door swung open. "If it isn't our friendly neighborhood Polack. And it looks like he's getting sweet on your girl, Dob." He poked his elbow into the driver's arm. "What do you think, Milt?" He turned toward the rider in the backseat. "Is it about time we teach this troublemaker another lesson?"

"Knock it off, Casey!" Kettie crossed her arms. "I can take care of myself. He fixed my car, so just leave him alone, and speaking of leave…please do."

Casey stepped from the vehicle. "Fixed your car?" He walked toward the front of the roadster, stared into the engine compartment, and smirked. "Now, just what could have happened to your precious automobile?"

Jacob looked at Kettie. "Who's asking the intelligent questions now?" The tin, engine cover rattled as he slammed it down across the opening and glared at Casey. "Your reputation precedes you, but I'll admit, you make a damned good fool in more ways than one."

Casey's knuckles whitened as his fists tightened. "Milt!" He shouted, taking a step into Jacob.

"Buick Sport Roadster – Special Six." An inquisitive voice interrupted from beyond the group. "Very nice."

Heads turned in discovering a black wool suited elderly man gliding over the road's wheel tracks in approaching the automobile. The deep crevices in his reddish-brown hand filled with road dust as he wiped a path in the thin layer coating the vehicle's fender. Tipping his dark bowler hat, he leaned down and stared into the glossy finish at the distorted reflection of his teenage companion, who appeared at his side. A smile extended across his face as he raised his head, looked at the youngster, and nodded. "Yes, very nice indeed."

With one eye glued on the stranger, Casey made quick steps in joining his cohorts, who sat motionless in amusement at the intruding native circling the auto. "Hey, you knotheads!" His fingers snapped before vacant faces.

"Huh?" Dob focused his eyes on Casey's hand.

"Your old man still keep that revolver under the seat?"

"Revolver? Yeah." Dob's attention drifted back toward the man entertaining his young sidekick. "Yeah, the handgun is there, but there are no bullets."

Casey grabbed Dob by his shirt collar and pulled him through the driver's door opening. "What the hell do you mean no bullets?"

"Wait a bit, Casey. It's not all my doings." Dob jerked loose from the tight grip. "After hearing about the road signs shot full of holes, Pa suspected it was us. He took the shells out of the gun and locked them in the drawer."

"That idiot." He shoved Dob onto the car seat and stared at the unwanted visitor. "We've got to get rid of this bum – and fast." He looked at Dob. "Get the gun."

"But Casey…"

"Listen! It doesn't matter if it's loaded or not. He won't know the difference."

"But Casey, the judge…"

"Don't you tell me about my old man." He jabbed a finger into Dob's face. "It's like the judge says, if you're afraid to pull the trigger on an empty chamber, at a worthy man, you can't be trusted to pull the trigger on an opposing man when it counts. You're not worth a damned red cent to anyone, including yourself. Now, don't argue with me, and get the gun!"

Dob hung his head. Stretching his arm under the seat, he swept an assortment of rags and tools, and grasped the angled handle of his father's revolver. Concealing it behind the door, he stood waiting for Casey's instructions.

"Hey, chief! Scram!" Casey stopped midway between the vehicles. "There's nothing around here for you to beg for, so why don't you be a good injun and beat it."

The man paused and then turned. Void of any emotion, he began walking toward Casey with the young man at his side.

"Dob!" Casey stepped backward.

Hesitant to display the handgun, Dob remained motionless and watched as the strangers stopped at Casey's toes.

The young man stepped to the side as the elder handed him his derby and stared into Casey's eyes. "Uncle says he does not beg for anything." He glanced at the old man and then back at Casey. "Uncle says he will take what he wants."

"Take what he wants?" Casey snickered. "What does he want?"

The young man hesitated. "Uncle says scalps." He pointed his lips at Casey. "Uncle says he wants yours."

"Dob!" Casey took another step backward and then looked at the native teen. "Wait. How do you know what he's saying? He's not even moving his lips."

The young man glanced at Kettie. "Uncle says we'll also take the pretty redhead girl for his nephew."

The old man glared at the boy.

A smile pulled across the young man's face as he raised his shoulders.

Dust overtook the small group as the automobile transporting Kettie's girlfriends stopped next to her vehicle. Her roadster popped to life. "You men are all alike." She yelled as she slammed her door and speeded away with her female companions trailing close behind.

Dob ducked and backed away in avoiding Casey's missed backhand swing.

"Didn't you hear me yell your name? Twice!" Casey screamed as he followed Dob around the vehicle. "Why didn't you pull the gun like I told you?"

Dob stopped. "Oh, that was when you wanted me to pull the gun?" He scratched his head. "I guess I don't remember discussing signals."

"Don't give me that." Casey shoved him away.

Milt repositioned himself within the rear seat. "I've never seen anyone get scalped before." He looked at Casey. "If I asked, do you think he would show me how?"

"Shut up!" Casey slid onto the passenger front seat. "I don't even know why I call you my friends." He pointed at Dob. "Just start this damned thing so we can get back to town."

As the final automobile disappeared over the far hilltop, the two native men stepped toward Jacob and Aggie. To a round of applause and cheers, both men bowed.

"I trust our performance didn't frighten you, Miss Aggie?" The old man smiled.

"No. I wasn't scared."

"Excellent. As my good friend William S. Hart would say – all the world's a stage, and all the men and women merely players. He claims to have been a Shakespearean actor on Broadway at one time." He chuckled. "You wouldn't expect that from a screen cowboy."

"Thanks for stepping in when you did, Samuel." Jacob shook his hand. "Things might not have gone so well if you hadn't."

"I was never afraid. The altercation ended the way it was meant to. Besides, I knew if something went wrong, you would have my nephew's back."

The young man expelled a quick snort.

"What brings you back to the coteau?" Jacob asked. "Don't tell me you've tired of the Hollywood lifestyle already."

"No. Acting in moving pictures fits me very well. But for now, the wacipi calls me home – time for the annual pow wow. There are getting to be fewer and fewer of us who actually lived back when the plains were truly free for my people to roam."

Jacob nodded. "They are fortunate to be gifted with your knowledge of the past to draw from."

"I am also recruiting actors for my good friend Bill Hart." He glanced at his nephew.

"Recruit actors?"

"Yes, he told me to bring back as many Indians as I could find, but not just any Indians. They must be *reel* Indians."

"You shouldn't have a problem filling that request around here."

Samuel chuckled. "It's more difficult than you would realize." He grasped Jacob's arm. "I hope you will accept my invitation this year to join us at the wacipi."

"I don't know." Jacob shook his head. "From what I've heard, those things can get a little spooky."

"Perhaps for some, for others there is great wisdom to be gained in the experience." As Samuel and the young man turned to depart, he pointed his chin at Jacob. "You will be there my friend. I've dreamed it so – many times."

The late afternoon sun continued its gradual descent to the horizon. Glancing at his watch, Jacob decided to postpone the remainder of their journey around the lake for another day. With a light kick from his heel and a sharp click of his tongue, he persuaded the horse into a steady trot.

"You could have beaten that boy if you wanted to, Jacob." Aggie affirmed as she hugged him from behind.

Thoughts of his odd but favorable encounter with Kettie shaped a slight smile on his face. He shrugged his shoulders. "This time, I just may have."

* * * *

Carrying a small pack filled with personal belongings, a dark skinned man trekked the vacant road's edge. As the sun touched the coteau's rolling skyline, the patches of perspiration disappeared from his shirt with the cooling of the evening breeze. Tired, the words to his song began to weave with a short whistle and a light hum. The sound of an approaching vehicle aroused his spirits. As the truck stopped, a flannel covered arm reached from the open window and pointed a disfigured thumb to the rear bed. Hesitant at first to accept, the man glanced at the fading sunlight and then hopped onto the flat-bed as it began to accelerate away.

Chapter 3

TRUST him? I trust him about as much as…" The judge wiped the sweat from his palm as he exchanged the telephone earpiece with its receiver base in his other hand.

"Yeah, I know, but there's not a whole lot we can do about…" He spun in his chair, turning his back toward the desk, and looked through the stenciled glass at the people moving along the sidewalk on the opposite side of the street.

"Because I need him! That's why! Frankly, I don't see how it can work without him. Once it's over, I don't care what the hell happens to…" Pressing the side of his face against the window, he attempted to peer around its raised frame in eyeing the pedestrian traffic strolling the walkway adjacent to his building.

"Well, that's your own damned fault." He rocked his chair back to the desk. "Maybe next time you'll use your head before you…"

"Listen, you've seen the important names that have committed to attend July's Klan meeting – the klonverse. At this point, we'd be foolish to do anything different than what was originally planned. This Klan gathering is going to be one of the biggest ever convened this side of the Mississippi. As you have said yourself, this event is going to put…" The mechanical bell sounded as the outer door to the judge's offices struck against the clapper.

"I've got to go. I believe that's him now." He planted the receiver on the desk.

"I said I would! I've got to go! Yeah, I'll see you tonight at the lodge meeting." The earpiece bounced on the receiver hook as he slid the telephone across the desktop.

"Tom Wesley?" He leaned to the side in scanning the reception area in an attempt to identify the visitor. "Is that you out there?"

"Yeah…it's me." Wes poked his head from the side of the open doorway.

"Come right on in, Wes." The judge gave a quick motion with his hand. "You've got to forgive me. I'm short my secretary this morning. She's having her hair done or some crazy thing." He shook his head. "Women aren't like they used to be. No sir. There was a time when having a job meant a satisfaction in completing an honest day's work, contributing to society. Now, it's more important to socialize, while flaunting what you do have, and more often than not, what you don't."

The leather soles of Wes's shoes produced a soft swoosh as they brushed against the carpet's grain. Tipping the dark gray fedora from his head, Wes dropped the felt hat onto the corner of the desk. Prying the buttons from the holes in his jacket, he eased himself into an overstuffed chair, and sank deep within its cushions.

A low rumble rolled from the judge's throat as he glared at Wes while making sudden glances toward the offending hat.

"Oh!" Wes lifted the hat and flung it onto the adjacent chair. "I do apologize."

"How is business down at the hardware store?" The judge rested his elbows on the armrests of his chair, and propped his fingertips against one another.

Wes gave a quick look around the room. "Fine."

"That's good. That's real good. I remember when you took over for old man Anderson after he passed away. You've done a marvelous job maintaining what he built."

Wes nodded his head as he continued to scan the room.

The judge cleared his throat once more. "Say, I was talking with Whittson on the phone a bit ago."

Wes's face snapped forward. "Oh yeah? Which one?"

"You know full well which one. The mayor, Dayton Whittson."

Wes shook his head. "I haven't seen him at any of our meetings since he took office."

"And you won't. He's playing things low keyed, which is a good strategy. He needs to show he represents all of the citizens in this community, and that includes the Catholics. He needs to avoid placing himself in a situation where he publicly would have to choose sides. It's a no win. And besides, I hear it cuts down on the phone calls coming into city hall."

Wes laughed. "Working on his reelection campaign already?"

"Don't you forget." The judge pointed his finger at Wes. "It was Whittson, in his capacity as mayor, which allowed for the smooth organization of this summer's Klan gathering."

Wes slowly nodded. "Parades, picnics, concert bands...I heard they're even having a tightrope walker from the visiting carnival troupe."

"It will be the biggest event ever to hit this town. Yes, sir. One that will not be soon forgotten."

"As long as Whittson remembers, that without the Klan, he wouldn't be in such a prestigious position to make those decisions."

The judge waved his hand. "Ah, he continues to put in his effort where he can. There are still some very vocal individuals in this community who oppose the Klan."

"Hugh Langley? Huh, Hugh Langley's a loudmouth. He's a know-it-all. To tell you the truth, I don't know which of those traits is worse."

"That may be so, but if push comes to shove, he could organize the Catholics and cause problems for all of us, maybe even get this whole thing stopped."

Wes shrugged his shoulders.

"Listen, all the mayor is asking for is that we halt any...let's just call them...late night engagements, until after the Klan gathering."

"No. No, just the opposite." Wes shook his head. "We need to stay visible. We need to maintain a strong presence, right up to and following the meeting. The members expect it. Our supporters expect it. And I've got a few ideas in mind that will demonstrate just how anchored into the community we truly are."

"No!" The judge raised his hand. "With the death of that priest, out in the hills, still fresh in their minds, the Catholics across the state become somewhat nervous when the Klan proposes a large event such as this, including those living right here."

Wes tapped his finger against the armrest. "That was never actually proven to be a Klan related activity. The best they could come up with was some damned drifter got himself liquored up and tried to rob the poor bastard."

"That may be so, but the fact is that a priest was killed in an area that's home to a large Klan membership."

"You're giving it too much weight, Judge. People have forgotten about the whole thing already. They've moved on."

"Forgotten about the death of a priest? Moved on?" The judge's chair creaked as he rocked back. "Please explain to me just how you came about with this reasoning."

"You're not seeing the true picture, Judge." Wes leaned forward in his chair. "A priest is not like a normal person just walking down the street."

"Oh, really?"

"No, he's not. He wears a uniform, and in that uniform he represents something larger. The fact is, when that priest was killed, the people mourned his death up until his replacement arrived." He sunk back into the soft cushions. "See, it's the position, and not the person. They figured he did his duty and died for the cause. Now, if a regular person were to be murdered, that would sour in folks' bellies for a long time. They consider themselves to be regular too, and if it happened to him…well, it could happen to them, and that is just not acceptable."

"So, you're telling me that a member of the clergy is not like the rest of us? He's lesser of a person than you and I?"

Wes laughed. "Oh, I would not consider him to be alone in that category. Why, it would be no different for a cop, a soldier…or a judge."

The judge cleared his throat. "I'll consider that last remark as made in jest. Just keep in mind the wishes of the mayor. Trust me, things will go a whole lot smoother for everyone."

Wes stared at the judge. "If that's all you wanted to see me about, passing along a request from the mayor, who could have spoken directly to me, himself, then I believe we're done. I've got new stock to uncrate and inventory." Wes retrieved his hat and pulled himself to his feet.

The judge sprang from his seat. "No. No, that's not the reason I was wishing to speak with you." He spun a Spanish cigar box around on the top of his desk, and lifted the cedar lid. "Please stay."

Wes hesitated as he looked upon the even row of tightly wrapped Cuban Larranagas. "Sure…why not." He rolled one from the line and inhaled the strong tobacco scent as he slid it under his nose. "I guess I have a few extra minutes before I actually need to return to the store." He dropped his hat onto the edge of the desk and plopped back into the chair. "So tell me, Judge, what did you have in mind?"

Glancing at the hat, the judge sat down and folded his hands across the desk. "The reason I asked you to meet with me, is that I have a proposition that might be of some interest to you."

Wes nipped the end of the cigar and waved it toward the judge. "Go on."

"It's no secret that you've been eyeing the Grand Dragon position in leading the state Klan. I think you would be a good choice, and I just might be able to help you achieve that goal."

"I appreciate the support, Judge," he struck a match on the edge of the desk and drew a few breaths through the cigar, "but I'm not seeing where you would possess that kind of pull."

The judge straightened his posture. "As you know, I've been tapped to speak at the Webster Klan gathering in July."

"Yes, you're on the list. You, along with some of the other big hitters from across the state and region."

"Well, it is my intention, that during my speech at the meeting, I will announce my candidacy for the U.S. Senate in the '26 elections."

Wes pointed his cigar at the judge and smiled. "Senator Conrad Barker? That sounds mighty ambitious."

"Not at all. Not at all. In fact, it seems a natural progression for someone with my experience in public service, and unique ability in dealing with people in solving their problems."

"So, you're looking to take Norbeck's seat in the Senate. I don't know. Governor, senator, the people seem to like voting for him."

"He's been in politics long enough to garner a substantial amount of mistakes. The way I see it, he'll be ripe for the picking."

"But it's not how you see it, Judge. It's how the voters see it. It seems that once a man is initially voted into office, they're in for a long time. Most would look the other way until their heads twisted right off the ends of their necks, before they would vote for someone new."

"Yes. Yes, they would, but it's my plan that when the voters begin to look the other way, the direction in which they are looking is toward me."

"So, if I'm reading between the lines correctly, you, as senator, would throw your support behind me to become the Grand Dragon of the state realm."

"Yes, in a manner of speaking."

"Now Judge, I know I've done nothing to end up at the top of your political gift list." He pulled a puff from the cigar and blew it into the air. "So I'm sure you'll understand if I ask the question. What's the catch?"

"There is no catch. Just one small favor."

"Oh, here it comes."

"No, not at all. I simply would like you to introduce me as the speaker during the July gathering. As a well-known, decorated, war veteran, the people trust you. It's that simple. You support me in my bid for senator, and if elected, I support you in obtaining the position as head of the state Realm." The judge stood up and stepped toward a tall bookcase next to the window. Gently repositioning an assortment of military souvenirs, he picked up an expended, shell casing. "Actually, it would be like one veteran helping another, an officer providing a hand to a fellow officer."

Wes blew a long steady stream of smoke into the air, and slowly nodded his head.

A streak of shine appeared within the tarnish as the judge rubbed his thumb across the smooth brass. "We wanted to go to France." He returned the brass piece and pulled a framed photograph of a group of soldiers from the wall. "Oh, how we wanted to kill the Hun. You know where they sent us?" He turned to Wes. "Arizona, for God's sake. Why would they do that? You don't train men for war, and then have them spend the duration guarding an army base in the middle of nowhere, Arizona." He raised the picture and stared into the faces. "Oh, how I pleaded with the generals. I begged them, 'Let my boys go to war'. 'You'll go where you're needed,' was their reply." He turned back toward Wes. "You see, it wasn't my fault. I tried. I tried my damnedest to get these boys in the fight."

Wes examined the tobacco seam as he rolled the cigar between his fingers. "All your boys came home in one piece. It beats the alternative."

"They came home in one piece, but unfulfilled, to live a life pondering what should have been. So, you see, you and I need to help each other fulfill what should be. It would be a tragedy to allow this opportunity to pass us by." The judge draped the picture's wire over a nail head on the wall and walked to his chair. "So, what's it going to be?" He stretched an open hand toward Wes. "Can we count on each other for support?"

Wes stood up and spread his hands across the edge of the desk. "You'll make a damned good politician all right." He laughed. "However, let's be truthful about this. You don't *want* my support because I'm some forgotten war hero. You *need* my support as the voice of the Klan." He straightened up and took a puff from the cigar. "What's the matter, Judge? Don't tell me you've lost faith in the party to carry you to victory."

A reddish glow moved over the judge's face. "No. No, that's not...well what I mean to say is..."

"The Klan is very particular about which candidates they endorse for political office. The person's ideals and beliefs need to match with the Klan's philosophy." Wes sat down and crossed his legs. "Tell me, Judge. What is your platform?"

The judge sank to his seat. "I don't have an official statement prepared as of the moment, but I can tell you I am against Romanism and its steady creep throughout the country, we need to keep the Pope's control out of American politics. We also need to decrease the number of immigrants we allow into this country each year, especially those from Southern and Eastern Europe. Their ideas and loyalties do not align with what we consider to be truly American. We need to better control what is taught in our public schools to build a strong patriotism in our young people, with that said, I'm for the complete elimination of parochial and private schools. I think it goes without saying, I'm for one hundred percent Americanism."

"Excellent." Wes gave a few slow claps of his hands. "Almost as if quoted straight from the literature of the Ku Klux Klan itself. Now, tell me again, but this time, try to be more persuasive. Put your heart into it. Speak to me as though you were attempting to convince Hiram Evans, the Imperial Wizard himself."

"All right, damn it!" The telephone rattled as the judge smacked his fist against the desktop. "Enough with the goddamned games. I'm going to be straight with you. The truth is, after the war, this country lost its sense of direction. The people didn't know who to trust. The

Klan just happened to be there, at the right place, at the right time. With the Klan, people found something in common to believe in. It pulled them together. It united them."

Wes blew a quick puff of smoke into the air and watched as it dissipated above his head.

"Within a few short years," the judge continued, "the Klan has grown to represent a large portion of conservative America. They are 6 million members strong and increasing by leaps and bounds every day. That means fifteen percent of the white males in this country are Klansman. A number that significant carries a tremendous amount of weight."

"Wes spit a piece of loose tobacco from his lip. "And you plan to use this weight to manipulate your campaign for Senate?"

"I would be a darn fool not to. During recent elections, the Klan has been very influential in removing from office those who did not adhere to their standards, and electing those who did. When it comes right down to it, a man couldn't get himself elected dog catcher without the backing of the Klan. Like every other politician in this country, I need the Klan's support. I need its membership to push me over that line to win."

"Thank you, Judge. That's the first truthful thing you've said to me since I walked through that door. I'll tell you what." Wes stood up and retrieved his hat. "I'll get you Klan support in your run for Senate. Not because I need your help in becoming the Grand Dragon. And certainly not because I believe you're the best qualified candidate. I'll support you because I think you are right in knowing that Norbeck can be beat, and if so, I would like someone in that position who understands and works well with the Klan."

"As adverse as that sounded, I'll accept the backing." The judge extended his open hand.

Wes looked at the judge's hand and laughed. "Don't kid yourself, Judge. This is a shady deal. Do you really think a handshake is going to matter?" He placed the hat on his head, turned down the front of the brim, and walked away.

"Don't worry about preparing my introduction, Wes." The judge called out as Wes pulled the door closed behind him. "I'll assemble one for you and have my secretary type it up."

Stepping toward the window, the judge watched as Wes mean-dered through the street traffic and stepped up onto the far sidewalk. "You just wait you arrogant bastard." The judge spoke to himself. "Your time at the top just might be very short lived." He picked up the telephone and spun the dial. "Yeah, this is Judge Barker. Get me Whittson."

Chapter 4

THE urban creep advanced without relent. Devoid of prejudice, it engulfed a small, weathered bungalow, as the house struggled to maintain its identity within the bright, fresh colors of a newly developed neighborhood. Lacking an odd board here and there, the dwelling's white picket fence encircled an overgrown lawn and hid its weed-infested flowerbed. Rusty chains rhythmically creaked to an early morning breeze as it gently swayed an empty swing across the open front porch. Perched on an electrical wire, suspended high above a nameless mailbox, a lone mourning dove cooed endlessly in hopes of finding its absent mate.

Not long ago, Jonn Reese appreciated the privacy offered by the property's remote location. Those living within the community of Webster, and the farmers residing about the surrounding townships of Day County, rarely passed his way. With the exception of an occasional cry from an arriving or departing train whistle, the irksome birthing pangs of a crowning metropolitan society seemed somewhat nonexistent, but as with all else in his life, that soon turned and twisted with change.

Tink! Tink! Tink! A stiff bristled shaving brush created a dull rattle as its handle tapped the inside of a cracked ceramic mug. Churning a white sudsy lather, it tossed and rubbed the small remnants of the once rounded soap block, which lined its bottom. While scooping a sizable amount of the frothy mixture with the bristles, Jonn squinted into the mirror through a stream of rising cigarette smoke. Trying to remember when he last shaved, he began to spread the foam across his hair covered chin. After pulling the lather up his neck, he removed the smoldering cigarette from his lips, and gave a final quick swipe just below his nose.

Replacing the shaving mug on its chalky, water scale ring near the edge of the glass, bathroom shelf, he picked up the burnished silver, safety razor, lying adjacent to it, and stood motionless as he stared into the mirror and contemplated where to begin. Lifting his chin, he placed the razor at the base of his neck and pulled upward, against the growth of rigid stubble. The sharpness of the new carbon blade quickly cleared the foam-covered whiskers, revealing patches of soft bare skin. Always advised to shave with the direction of the hair's nap, he preferred the closeness achieved by performing the opposite in shaving against its grain.

Multiple dips of the safety razor, deep into the water-filled, porcelain basin, soon produced a thick floating layer of soap lather and dark, facial hair. The slight tremor, once noticeably apparent in both hands, was now nonexistent. The tense anxious feelings replaced by a steady hand and determined thoughts as if he experienced a miraculous healing.

The image of the traveling evangelist he watched with skepticism the night before came to mind. While sitting in the back row of a gathering tent, he observed the preacher place his open hand upon the heads of those with various ailments. With a cry in his voice the clergyman commanded, "Jesus, heal you!" while slapping his palm against their foreheads.

The Reverend Alfred P. Gallagher from somewhere out of Illinois, he remembered. It's possible the town didn't even exist. That night the reverend left with his pockets full of cash. The next day, when the aches and pains returned, many followed him to the next county waving fists clenched with hard-earned greenbacks.

He shook his head and thought to himself. People refuse to believe in anything unless they can shove money at it. The more they give. The more they believe. I don't know, maybe they consider it an investment. He gently tugged at the stopper chain and watched the water slowly funnel down the sink drain, and end with a loud gurgle of air sucking through the pipes.

Rotating the cold-water lever, he cupped his hands beneath the faucet's stream and rinsed the residual lather, mixed with a few scattered blood splotches, from his face. After blotting the remaining water droplets with a soiled hand towel, he retrieved his comb and ran its fine teeth through his hair with his right hand, while gently holding it into place with his left.

Dressed in his underwear, he stood in front of the mirror and gazed at his reflection. A half smile appeared as he began to recognize the resemblance of a man he once knew many years ago. A man with hopes. A man with dreams. A man with the courage to see them through. "Yes, Jonn, old boy." He stared into his dark blue eyes. "I do believe you are right. Today is a good day to make that trip home."

Entering his bedroom, he opened the closet door, knelt down, and pulled out a dark brown footlocker. He pushed the heavy box across the linoleum-covered floor and into the dining room, where he positioned it next to the table. Sitting down, he stared at the chest. "This is the third time I've seen you since I returned," he muttered. "Three strikes, you're out. Right?" He quietly laughed.

Unlatching the metal buckles fastened at the front of the box, he slid their worn leather straps to each respective side and gave a tug at its brown, wooden cover. A soft cry emanated from the dry hinges as he slowly opened the case. Hesitating for a moment, he scanned its hidden contents. Reaching inside, he retrieved the uniform jacket worn by a returning doughboy some six years prior, fresh from the World War.

"A.E.F. - American Expeditionary Force," he said as he slowly shook his head. "I remember you like it was yesterday."

Unfolding the olive drab, wool coat, he reached over and gently placed it on a wooden hanger suspended from the coat hook mounted on a nearby four-panel door.

Brushing the soft material with his hand, he pulled on the overlapping folds to straighten its appearance. Five black, rimmed eagle buttons, spaced from the collar to the bottom waist hem, centered the coat. Commonly called the "walking out" uniform, each soldier received a new set to return home with when the war ended. Some, he recalled, felt dissatisfied with the cut of the standard issue and paid French tailors to sew custom-made uniforms, or waited until they arrived back in the States and sought out big city clothing shops to fabricate the same.

Every soldier's uniform told a story of the man who wore it – where he went, with whom, and what he did while there. Standing in front of the jacket, he began eyeing each attachment. Two gold embroidered V-shaped overseas service stripes rested above the left cuff. Each one corresponded to six months of overseas duty. Arriving in France during the latter part of February 1918 and departing at the beginning of May 1919 earned him the twelve months worth of stripes.

The handmade felt image of a red arrow piercing a line highlighted the top of the sleeve. The patch represented the 32nd Division, a National Guard unit comprised mainly of soldiers from Michigan and Wisconsin. The likeness symbolized their record of shooting through every line the Boche placed before them.

Prior to the war, Jonn and his best friend A.J., transferred to the 4th South Dakota Infantry Regiment with a little coaxing by A.J.'s uncle, who claimed insight into a possible call up. Fearing they might miss the chance to participate in the action along the Texas border, they begged to switch units to assure they would go.

When the nation activated its guard and reserve units for the World War, he and A.J. remained with the 4th South Dakota Infantry and traveled to Camp Greene, North Carolina where they fell under the newly formed 41st Division encompassing National Guard units from the northwestern states. With the likely need for additional artillery units, the Oregon National Guard provided specialized training to the South Dakota troops whereby transforming them into the new 147th Field Artillery Regiment. After arriving in France, the commanders split the 41st Division to provide much needed replacements for other units, and attached the 147th to the 32nd Division where they remained for the duration of the war.

The uniform's stiffened standing collar held a darkened bronze, round insignia at each tip. The emblem on the collar's left side exhibited two raised crossed cannons representing a field artillery unit. The insignia on the right side displayed the letters "U.S." with a smaller "N.G." at its core, signifying a United States National Guard entity.

Centered on the upper middle section of the right sleeve, three gold chevrons, sewn vertically adjoining one another, indicated the rank of a sergeant. Prior to the war, regulations stated that both sleeves carry the stripes, but with a sudden explosion of new troops during the war, a shortage of non-commissioned officer's rank occurred within the army. New regulations came down the line requiring the removal of the rank from the left arm, and returning it for distribution to new soldiers.

Farther down the right sleeve and attached just above the cuff, a single gold embroidered stripe indicated a wound received while in action with the enemy. Not knowing the exact details of how he became injured, he certainly knew when it happened – during the battle of the Argonne Forest. He awoke in the hospital weeks later with a bandage wrapped around the outside of his head, and a painful feeling as though a sledgehammer beat against an anvil on the inside. As he faded in and out of consciousness, he vaguely remembered a young nurse explaining how a bullet grazed the side of his skull, and that the war ended on the eleventh hour, of the eleventh day, of the eleventh month.

Observing some of the patients attempting to function with lost limbs, and others experiencing the horrid effects of mustard gas and phosgene, he felt the wearing of the stripe inappropriate. A group of elderly French women, comforting the sick and wounded, picked up his coat one afternoon and attached the stripe without his knowledge. In a show of appreciation for their altruistic assistance to the soldiers, he left the stripe on.

As he ran his fingers over the stripe, bitter memories resurfaced relating to the egotistical commanding officer who oversaw the hospital's operation. A major, stemming from a National Guard unit out east, like many others, seemed promoted well above his abilities. Had he run into the officer on the troopship during the return trip home, he may have thrown him overboard into the freezing waters of the North Atlantic Sea.

Above the left chest pocket flap, hung two medals. Normally represented by two small rectangular shaped silk ribbons, he replaced the symbolic pieces of cloth with the actual medals to coincide with the uniforms of the other veterans, who he noticed wore them as they marched up Main Street while participating in the local parades.

Looking at the emerald green and golden yellow striped ribbon of the first award, he reached down and gently lifted the attached bronze medal. Rubbing his thumb across the raised feature of a sheathed sword, he read aloud the inscription. "For Service on the Mexican Border."

Deployed to the southern border of Texas nine years prior by order of the then President Woodrow Wilson, his unit joined with many others from across the country in protecting the numerous small towns and villages from Mexican raiders. He remembered how he and A.J. trained and stood watch as they waited for the Villistas to attack. "Dust, tumbleweeds, and rattlesnakes." He spoke to himself. "If it weren't for the tequila, we would have gone nuts." As they spent their days enduring the heat and monotony on the border, the U.S. Army's Mexican Expedition, under the command of General John J. Pershing, trudged through the rugged Mexican countryside in search of the revolutionary, Poncho Villa, and his men. "They never did find him." He laughed.

Hanging beside the award, a silk rainbow colored suspension ribbon supported the bronze medallion of the Victory Medal. A winged figure of victory covered its front. Turning the decoration over, he read aloud the inscription. "The Great War for Civilization." Upon its multicolored ribbon rested four bronze battle clasps stating service in the major operations of the Aisne-Marne, Oise-Aisne, Meuse-Argonne, and Defensive Sector.

The Meuse-Argonne, called the Battle of the Argonne Forest, was the final offensive which ended the war. That is when he received his wound and when his old friend, Wes, received a Citation Star for his actions of heroism. Wes refused to speak of the incident, and Jonn noticed that Wes never wore the small silver star on his Victory Medal while marching in the parades.

Detecting a slight bump protruding from beneath the coat's fabric, he reached his hand inside the front pocket and retrieved a single red chevron. "Honorable discharge chevron." He said as he straightened the V-shaped woolen stripe. Normally sewn onto the middle of the upper left arm, the stripe indicated to the public and the military that the wearer of the uniform received an honorable discharge and no longer remained in the service. Others proudly displayed their scarlet colored stripe, but Jonn refused to attach it to his uniform. Not after learning of the events in the Argonne Forest. Not after what happened to A.J. No, he would never let himself wear the stripe.

"I wish that I could remember what happened that day." He beat his fist against the hardwood tabletop. "Come on, think. It's got to be in there somewhere."

Wiping his hand down his face, he shook his head. "I don't know. Maybe it's all for the best. Maybe my mind can't handle the painful images. All that I know, is that it is my fault that my friend is dead. It is entirely my fault."

Reaching down into the footlocker and pulling out a neatly folded pile of clothing, he donned the matching trousers, flannel shirt, and ankle boots. He wrapped the woolen puttees around his lower legs, beginning at his ankles and ending just below his knees. Notwithstanding the strong, pungent odor of mothballs, the uniform appeared intact and seemed to fit comfortably.

Clearing a pile of yellowed newspapers from the table, he pulled again from the wooden box and laid out a collection of photographs, an overseas cap, gas mask, Brody steel helmet, .45-caliber semi-automatic pistol fastened within its leather holster, and an assortment of odd French souvenirs.

Sorting through the rigid pictures, he stopped at one of him and A.J. standing in front of the headquarters tent erected near the Mexican border. Another photo showed him, A.J., Wes, and few French soldiers drinking wine in front of a small village café along the Marne River in northern France. "The Three Cannoneers." He chuckled at the title bestowed upon them by the inebriated Frenchmen, referencing the musketeers from the Alexandre Dumas novel. Others from their company quickly picked up on the name and it became their trademark. Where one went, the other two followed – "one for all, all for one".

The next photograph was that of Sarah, his fiancée. Slightly faded, with torn and jagged edges, it displayed the coarse effects of a soldier's weathered march through France. He lightly moved his index finger over the black and white image as if gently stroking her long, silken hair, then touching the slender curvature of her nose, and soft lips.

Sarah suggested abandoning her dreams of a large, church ceremony in favor of a small, quaint service prior to Jonn sending off to the war. Jonn cared for her like no other and felt that it would not be fair to her if he were to become maimed or even killed while serving in France. A glistened tear rolled down the smooth skin of her cheek as he declined her eternal commitment of love. His selfless courage crushed them both.

His eyes welled up as he gently kissed her photo. Slowly reclining in the chair, he closed his eyes as pleasant memories of her affectionate nature overtook his tangled thoughts. Recollections of intimate moments released gradual amounts of endorphins within his brain and brought about an artificial euphoria, which soothed his inner being.

"No!" He forced his eyes open and jumped to his feet. "Stop doing this to yourself. It's not real. She's gone – gone forever."

With a light toss, the pictures fanned across the tabletop. Pulling his jacket from the hook, he shoved both arms through its stiff sleeves as he walked toward the dining room window.

"One thing about it." He sniffled as he split the curtains by lifting one drape to the side. "When I'm gone, I'll finally be rid of all those damned ghosts." He stared through the streaked glass window and into the open yard at a young boy, dressed in the field grey uniform of a German soldier, roaming through the tall, uncut grass.

Bearing the markings of a lance corporal upon his torn, buttonless collar, he held to an even path spanning the width of the property, as if standing watch. Missing a wool cap or steel helmet, his unkempt blond hair flowed with the light morning breeze. Seemingly unarmed, with the exception of a twisted trench bayonet dangling in its sheath below a chewed, jagged stump resembling the remnants of a left arm, he slowly paced with a gaze fixed in his eyes as he peered into nothingness.

Within a few short months of returning home from the war, the first one appeared during a noon meal at the Peterson's Café. While finishing his lunch with a piece of the diner's renowned fresh, apple pie, Jonn glanced up into the wall length mirror, mounted behind the cash register. Within its reflection, he noticed what he thought resembled a German soldier sitting directly behind him by one of the booth tables.

As Jonn stared through the mirror in disbelief, the soldier slowly turned toward him, revealing an exposed, mangled, open head wound, and then raised a cup into the air as if beckoning Jonn to join him. Jonn's guts wrenched as his heart raced uncontrollably. Quickly spinning on his stool in total surprise of the gruesome sight, he found no one sitting there – soldier or patron. He convinced himself his eyes played tricks on him. It must be the movement of shadows caused by the sunlight reflecting off the glass door as customers walked in and out of the establishment. That's what it was, just a figment of his imagination.

Attempting to remain composed, a sudden tremor in his hand tumbled the flaked piecrust from the end of his fork as he reluctantly forced the remaining few bites.

"Jonnie, you feel okay?" Susan smiled as she slid the check toward him through a ridge of spilled coffee. "You look a little peeked, as if you saw a ghost or something."

The fork crashed onto the plate, causing some of the noon guests to stop and stare. Jonn quickly pulled his hand beneath the counter, and shoved it into his pocket. "Yeah, I'm fine."

"I'll see you tomorrow, meatloaf special?"

Jonn returned the stares, forcing the onlookers to mind their own business. "Yeah, tomorrow, okay."

Susan wrinkled her brow at the odd behavior and moved to the outer tables in assisting a newly seated couple.

Jonn clenched a bill and some odd change within his pocket and dropped it onto the coffee stained, customer check. As the rolling coins circled the receipt, he noticed his hand continued to shake. Pulling it closer to his face, he watched with crushing anxiety as spastic fingers randomly danced at the end of his trembling hand.

Jamming the disobedient appendage beneath his armpit, he gave a quick glance over each shoulder, hoping no one noticed its unseemly movements. A painful heave extended his belly outward. "I must be coming down with something. Yeah, that's it." He reached up to wipe the perspiration forming on his forehead as he struggled to force down the contents of his churning stomach. "I must be getting sick."

Jonn cupped his nose as an overwhelmingly familiar odor of sweat, damp wool, and decaying flesh emerged from the buried past and seared through his nostrils. He jumped to his feet, turned around, and found the disfigured soldier standing directly behind him. This time, it did not disappear, but remained motionless within Jonn's reach.

Jonn's heart raced as fractured memories of the trenches flooded his head. Taken aback at the inexplicable appearance, he instinctively swung at the soldier numerous times. His tight fists met no resistance. Losing his balance, he found himself upon the floor realizing he provided the noon entertainment as a one-man show for the entire restaurant, lunch crowd.

Since then, others sporadically appeared, numbering twenty-three different soldiers in all. He undertook everything he could think of to rid himself of the unwanted followers. Ignoring them did not work so he tried talking, which led to yelling, but that only irritated the gray mangled ghouls as they responded in kind with shouts of incoherent German.

Those who unintentionally witnessed his screams into the wind became upset with what they felt unacceptable behavior, but he did not care. He poked, stabbed, and shot at the soldiers. He even tried burning one of them by locking it in his backyard tool shed and setting it ablaze. All of this did nothing but upset the townspeople, many of who demanded his confinement to the local county poorhouse, or if possible, psychiatric treatment at the Yankton State Hospital.

He almost lived his remaining days fitted in a size 42-long straitjacket if it were not for the caring and compassion shown by one man. From the first murmurings of detest over his bizarre behavior, Gust defended Jonn's actions as a symptom of shellshock - hidden inner wounds resulting from his war experience. He convinced those rallying to send Jonn away, that he was not a threat to himself or others. Deep down, Jonn denied the layman's diagnosis. The ghosts were all too real, but as long as it pacified the public, he said nothing to contradict Gust.

Watching the young boy march through the tall grass stirred the smoldering coals of anger that kindled deep within Jonn's core. Day after day...the same damned thing...dead German soldiers. They never left him in peace.

"Don't you worry, Fritz. I see you out there." He spoke in a reserved tone. "Where are all your Hun buddies hiding now?" The boy stepped an even pace, not straying from his intended path. The window glass shook and rattled as Jonn's clenched fist beat upon the frame. "Hey you! Fritz! Hey, I'm talking to you!"

The soldier stopped in mid-stride, turned toward the disruptive racket, and cast a blank stare. Jonn recognized the crown buckle fastened to the young boy's belt and the inscription pressed upon its face – GOTT MIT UNS.

"God with us?" He chuckled. "No. No. God was never with you or anyone else. Apparently, even in death, he is still absent."

The window frame shook once more. "Gott mit uns!" he smiled. "Gott mit uns!"

The boy hesitated for a moment, displaying no sign of emotion, and continued his seemingly meaningless, determined walk.

Jonn slowly shook his head and fastened the remaining buttons up his coat. "No sense in putting it off any longer. It's time to go."

He pulled the dining room chair under himself as he sat down, stopping just at the tables edge. Retrieving the pistol from its leather holster, he slowly rubbed its smooth metal surface against his clean-shaven cheek. The coolness of the blued steel and the penetrating scent of oil and sulfur produced a heightened feeling of awareness, invigorating his senses.

Releasing the encased magazine from the handgrip, he paused for a moment as he watched it bounce against the photos on the table-top. The methodical instinct of a seasoned veteran surfaced as he prepared to perform the standard function tests of the weapon.

With quick, precise movements, he jerked the slide back and engaged the slide stop. Looking into the empty chamber, he inserted his pinky finger to reassure it was clear of shells.

Easing the slide forward, he confirmed the location of the thumb safety situated in the off position. Clutching the pistol in his right hand, he pulled the trigger. Snap! The hammer struck against the firing pin.

Retaining pressure on the trigger, he again jerked the slide back and allowed it to spring forward. Releasing and pulling the trigger one more time, the hammer fell once again against the firing pin. Snap!

Rotating his hand from right to left, he examined the pistol's exterior finish. "Perfect." He said to himself. "You are perfect."

Grabbing the magazine from the table, he pressed his thumb down on top of the .45 caliber ACP shells stacked one on top of the other within its confinement, finding little movement. "Seven. All there. All seven."

With a quick thumb-flicking action, he counted to himself as he began ejecting the cartridges, in succession, directly onto the tabletop. "One, two, three", each shell danced on the hardwood surface before rolling in random half circles. "Four, five, six..." He hesitated for a moment, staring at the last round suspended within the guides of the magazine.

Briefly scanning the assortment of photographs scattered about the table, he reached down and separated Sarah's picture from the others and pulled it before him. "I love you Sarah." He gently kissed the black and white image and slowly bowed his head.

Slap! The magazine locked into the bottom of the pistol grip. He jerked the slide back and forth allowing the lone shell to ram into the empty chamber. "And to the rest of the world. Enjoy your time in hell."

He pulled the pistol to his head, placing the barrel next to his right temple and took a long, deep breath. Closing his eyes, he envisioned himself with Sarah as his index finger began slowly exerting pressure upon the trigger.

Knock! Knock! Knock! A fist beat upon the front porch door. "Jonnie, you in there?"

His eyes popped open. "No. No, not now. Go away, Gust. Go away." He angrily whispered to himself. Taking another deep breath, he again closed his eyes. Do it now. Do it now. Do it now. The determined thoughts ricocheted like a mad demon within his head.

Knock! Knock! Knock! The unwanted visitor continued the intrusion. "Jonnie, if you're there, I need your help with a project this afternoon. I can't do it myself. I need you to climb up onto the high places. Jonnie, you there?"

Do it. Do it. Do it. The chant seemed to echo within Jonn's mind. His eyelids squeezed tighter and tighter as he placed more tension upon the trigger.

"Jonnie!" The man gave a final shout before turning to leave.

"Ah!" Jonn screamed as he threw the pistol across the room. It bounced off a padded chair cushion before sliding across the floor. This was the third time he began this final routine and the third time he failed. Why? Why couldn't he do it? It seemed easy enough. Place the barrel of the gun to your head and pull the trigger. No, not for

Jonn. For him there was always something or someone who pulled him back at the final moment. The end would never come that easy.

"Damn it! Damn it! Damn it!" He continued to shout as he placed his head in his hands.

"What's wrong? You okay in there?" Gust shouted as he dashed to the window, cupping his hands to the clear glass while attempting to distinguish patterns through the curtain's sheer fabric. "Did I wake you? You stub your toe or something?"

"Yeah, yeah, I can help. I can help." Jonn shouted in a quieting voice.

"Thanks Jonnie. You're a lifesaver. I've got to make another stop and I'll be back in less than an hour to get you." Gust shouted through the glass, turned, and quickly stepped off the porch toward his truck, left idling in the street.

"Yeah, okay, Gust." Jonn said quietly to himself. He pushed the bullets and pictures to the side with a trembling hand, laid his head upon the table, and began to weep. "Oh, Sarah, I miss you so much…"

Chapter 5

THE house sparrows darted. Through the upper, truss web maze, they dashed and chased, from one end of the lumber storage building to the other. Chirping and hopping, they danced around Jonn's feet, as he slid the asphalt shingles onto the wooden, truck bed.

"Clean shaven? Fresh shirt?" Gust scratched his head. "It ain't Sunday, so I know you're not going to church."

Jonn gave a quick look as he threw the last of the roofing materials onto the truck, and pulled a handkerchief to wipe the sweat from his forehead.

"No, I would definitely guess that you aren't going to church."

The lumberyard attendant pulled a pencil nub from behind his ear and handed Gust a clipboard. "Here you go. Put your John Henry on the sheet as usual."

"Thanks Arch." He scribbled a quick signature on the bill and tapped the clipboard against the man's protruding belly. "I'll be in to pay as soon as I collect from the job."

"No hurry, Gust. You're not a customer I worry about."

"You know, Arch?" Gust cracked open a roasted peanut and stripped the fruit. "That's why I keep coming back."

Arch smiled. "Because I trust you?"

"Well, it sure ain't because of these damned stale peanuts." He tossed the shell fragments upon the floor, where the sparrows wrangled to carry them off.

"Get out of here before I change my mind." Arch waved the clipboard toward the open doors.

Laughing, Gust tipped his hat and slid into the driver's seat, while Jonn crank-started the truck, and crawled in through the passenger side.

Idling down the busy street, the truck lurched as Gust released the clutch in shifting gears. "I noticed you worked yourself into a pretty good sweat back there." He depressed the clutch peddle and shifted once more. "Are you trying to exorcise some liquid demons through your pores or something?"

Staring through the glass windshield, Jonn remained silent as he watched the on-coming traffic pass by.

"You know what you need?" Gust rapped on the steering wheel.

Jonn turned his head and raised an eyebrow.

"You need yourself a girl. Someone who will care for you, but more important, someone you can take care of. See, a man has to have purpose. He needs a reason to build his life into something tangible, something respectable. A good woman will give him the meaning to do just that."

Jonn turned back and continued watching the traffic. "I have one."

"You do?"

Jonn rested his arm upon the doorframe and watched the people walking along the sidewalk.

"I know it's tough, boy. We all lose people we care deeply for, but even for those who are married, the vows state 'until death do us part'."

"It wasn't that way with Sarah and I. We felt something greater than that. She's waiting for me. I know she is."

"I'm sorry if I overstepped my bounds." Gust slowed the truck and downshifted as he turned the corner. "It just seems like something is bothering you more than usual today. Like something is weighing you down."

Jonn watched the houses begin to accelerate by as Gust stepped on the gas pedal.

"Is it the war?" Gust hesitated. "Because if it is, Jonn, you know you can talk with me about it. I may not know France, but I know the Philippines. Now that's one they're trying to bury in the history books. When they mention the Spanish American War, they talk about Cuba, San Juan Hill, but not the Philippines. We killed thousands of those little Filipino bastards in an attempt to liberate them from Spain, and we still haven't given them their independence yet." Gust shook his head. "I guess it's not something people want to hear about. The more they can ignore it, the more it never happened."

Gust switched off the ignition and coasted the truck to a stop in front of a large two-story house. "So, what do you think?"

Jonn looked at Gust. "I think you're right."

Puzzled, Gust stared at him. "How's that?"

"It just may be a touch of that liquid demon reminding me of last night's overindulgence." Jonn opened the door and stepped out.

"Some people," Gust mumbled. "I just don't understand."

As Gust and Jonn surveyed the house in assessing the damage and discussing repairs, a sudden cool breeze chased a scattering of loose dried leaves about their feet. Glancing to the west, they noticed a long, dark bank of towering clouds forming upon the horizon.

"We should have enough time to get a good start or possibly even finish." Gust rubbed his chin. "You never know about these cloud formations. It may just fizzle out by the time it arrives."

An automobile turned into the dirt driveway and rattled to a stop as three young men stepped from the vehicle. Bags and blankets flew over the sides, and then collected from the ground, as two of the boys hurried off with their arms full.

"Dob." Jonn stopped one as he rushed toward the house. "You still palling around with that same bunch?"

"Sure, they've been my friends for so long that I wouldn't know what to do without them."

"Just be careful." Jonn warned. "Keep in mind, if trouble should happen, they have the means to walk away without even so much as a scratch, and you don't."

"They would never do that to me."

"For your sake, I hope you're right."

"Robert, you're back from the lake sooner than I expected." Mrs. Radson dried her hands upon an apron as she stepped from the backdoor. "Your father won't be home until this evening, so you go change your clothes and see if you can't assist these gentlemen with the roof."

"Oh, that won't be necessary, Mrs. Radson." Jonn patted Dob upon his back. "We can handle it ourselves."

"Nonsense, as long as Robert is here, he can help. Beside, he may even learn a thing or two."

Gust finished checking the unloaded materials from the truck. "Jonn, this looks like a small job. There's not much more I can do around here, but stand on the ground and watch you work upon the roof. If you don't mind, Mae asked if I could pick up a few things. I should be back shortly."

"Sure thing, Gust. If I need help, I'll put our new assistant to work." Jonn chuckled. "Wish Mae well."

"You're a good man, Jonn. Just make sure he doesn't break anything." Gust stepped into the truck.

"Gust," Mrs. Radson approached the vehicle. "Would you please tell Mae that we miss seeing her at our Ladies Aid? She was always such a great help and a cheerful soul to have around."

"Yes ma'am, I will."

"And Gust, let her know that if she needs help with anything, we'd be happy to stop by."

"Yes ma'am, I will." Gust started the truck and waved, as he set the vehicle in motion.

Mrs. Radson returned the wave as he pulled away. "He's going to need to do something about her, and soon. If he doesn't, I'm afraid it's going to take an awful toll on the both of them."

Jonn tightened his work gloves over his hands. "They've managed this long. I'm sure they'll be fine."

"I pray they will." She watched as the truck turned the corner. "Oh, how I pray they will."

Pea sized hail rained from the sky and danced across the narrow hood, as the truck brakes squealed to a stop in front of a small yellow house. Reaching the front porch, Gust found the entrance door standing wide open. Inside, Mae's chair sat empty with the exception of a neatly wound length of rope draped across the armrest.

"Mae!" Gust called out as he ran through the house. "Mae, where are you!"

As he glanced through the rear window, he spotted Mae standing in a colorful beam of sunlight with a shower of sparkling hail raining down upon her. "Mae!"

The screen door slammed against the frame as Gust leaped from the back porch. Sliding through the grass, he reached Mae as she buckled to the ground. Standing over her, he attempted to shield her body from the bruising hailstones. "What happened? What are you doing out here?" Streams of melting hail turned red as it dripped from her hair. "Oh my, you're bleeding, Mae! You're bleeding!"

"You did it Gust." Mae looked up at him with a smile. "I never thought it would happen, but you did it."

"What's that Mae? What did I do?"

"You said one day diamonds would fall from the sky for us." She waved her hand around the yard. "You did it."

"Come on, Mae, you're hurt. We've got to take care of these wounds." Gust wiped a tear from the corner of his eye. "You really did it this time."

Mae reached down and raked a handful of the hailstones from the grass. "What's happening? The diamonds, Gust. The diamonds are melting."

"Mae, it's hail. It's a hail shower. Come now. Please." Gust lifted her to her feet as the hailstorm gradually ended. "We've got to bring you inside."

"I'm sorry Gust. The diamonds are melting. I guess they just weren't meant for us." She leaned her head into Gust's shoulder. "Help me. Take me home."

"I've got you, sweetheart. I've got you." Gust held Mae tight as he walked her to the porch. Noticing multiple scratches and bruises upon their arms and hands, he attempted to wipe away the small trickles of blood seeping from the slight skin tears.

"The wife and I are wondering if everything is okay over there!" A voice called from the neighbor's rear doorway.

Gust glanced over as he lifted Mae onto the porch. "Everything is fine, Bill. Everything is just fine. Go about your own business."

"Are you sure, Gust? It looks like you could use a little help." Bill hesitated, and then stepped down the porch stairs. "I'm coming over."

"Stay where you are. There's no need. I said everything is fine."

Bill stopped in his tracks. "We know what's been going on over there. You can't keep hiding it, Gust. Mae needs help."

"Don't stick your nose where it doesn't belong. Someone just might take a whack at it. Now, leave us be."

"Sooner or later, you're going to have to face it. Mae needs help. More help than you can give her. There are places that can care for her, like the county poor farm or the state hospital in Yankton."

"Those places are for crazy people. She doesn't belong there. As long as there's blood pumping through my veins, Mae is staying right here with me."

"I'm only trying to help. Next time I see her outside wandering about, I'm calling the authorities. If you can't figure out how to do the right thing, then maybe the court will."

Gust opened the screen door and helped Mae inside. "If you're thinking about starting trouble with me, it will be the last thing you ever do. Now, I'm not going to tell you again. Mind your own damned business." He stepped inside the house and slammed the door.

Singing and humming a Swedish hymn, Mae picked at the strings of the white bandage cloth wrapped around her arm. Grasping a fine thread, she stopped the rocker's motion as she liberated the cotton fiber from its weave. Aligning the piece on top of the armrest with the previously freed strands, she pushed against the floor and continued rocking.

"A limb fell on the Radson's roof last night during the wind storm. You remember how the wind came up, don't you?" Gust placed the coffee cups onto the kitchen shelf and hung the dishtowel to dry.

"Of course, I'm no good on the roof anymore." He walked into the living room. "The doctor told me to stay off. You know, my heart. It just upsets me when I'm not able to do the things that I used to."

Gust straightened Mae's bandages and cleared the pile of thread. "Jonn agreed to help. I felt bad about leaving him to finish up. He's a good man. You can't find help like that anymore. I don't know what I would do without him."

Mae lowered the volume of her tune to a whisper as she continued to sing.

Gust removed a newspaper from his chair and sat down as he placed it on the lamp table between them. "Mae, you've got to be careful when you're here by yourself. You need to stay in your chair. If something like this should occur again, I'm afraid they just might take you away. If that happens, you'll have no one to blame but your-self. There won't be anything I can do about it. Do you understand? There won't be anything I can do."

Mae ended the hymn as she stopped the rocker, looked at Gust, and smiled.

"There's my smile." Gust chuckled. "Even with all the bruises and scrapes, you are still the most beautiful woman I have ever seen. I wish those really were diamonds falling from the sky this afternoon. I would scoop them all up and give them to you, and it still wouldn't be a fraction of what you deserve."

Mae tilted her head and puckered her brow. "Do you know who my sister Ellen is? She is supposed to give me a ride. Can someone tell her that I am here? I don't want her to worry. She is supposed to give me a ride home."

"Mae," Gust shook his head. "Ellen is no longer with us. She died of the influenza eight years ago."

Mae leaned back in her chair. "No, that must be someone else. I just spoke with her today. She is going to be worried. Can someone tell her I am here?"

"Mae, why are you like this?" Gust reached across the table and lifted her hand into his. "Think. Think really hard. How about the apple trees? Do you remember the apple trees? Your father's grove?"

Leaning forward, Mae stared at Gust as she attempted to speak.

"Sure you do." Gust continued as he brushed her hand with his thumb. "You remember, don't you? The blossoms?"

"Yes, the blossoms." Mae smiled. "They were beautiful."

"There you go. What about them? Come on?"

"Daddy loved those apple trees. And…and, oh Gust, we swore we would never tell anyone."

Gust smiled. "And we never did."

"That was our first time. The blossoms. It was like…like Heaven."

"Oh, no. No. Heaven could never compare." Gust shook his head.

The Swedish words of the hymn returned, as Mae sat back in her chair and continued rocking.

"See, Mae. You can do it. You just have to think harder. It's all there. You just have to try." Gust squeezed her hand.

Mae halted the motion of the chair and stared at Gust. "Who are you?"

Hanging his head, Gust looked up and patted her hand. "Just a bruised soul, sweetheart. Just a bruised soul."

Lifting the newspaper from the table, Gust retrieved a black book from beneath. As he opened the thin pages to a tasseled marker, he began reading a series of underlined verses in reassurance to himself. Flipping through the chapters to the final page, he stopped and stared at a handwritten paragraph, signed and dated by a young couple beginning a new life together. Gust swirled his finger over the smooth ink tracks. Having read them countless times before, he knew the words by heart. He knew they were not as much of a promise, as they were an instruction.

"I'm so sorry, my dear Mae. I don't know if I can do it." A tear rolled down his cheek. "I know we made a promise to each other those many years ago, but I just don't know if I can do it."

As the Swedish words of the hymn sang within his heart, Gust closed the book and looked at Mae. With her eyelids pressed shut, the words softened to a quiet hum with the gradual slowing of each sway, which eventually exposed a welcomed silence hosting the steady echo of the ticking wall clock.

Retrieving a cushioned pillow from the sofa, Gust stood hovering above Mae with trembling hands gripping the frayed trim on each side. He stared at her in determining if the young woman he fell in love with a lifetime ago remained present in the body sitting before him. The body he cuddled next to him each night in their bed as they slept. Was he being selfish in not following through with their promise? If their positions were reversed, what would he expect of Mae? These same questions gnawed at his mind without reprieve. Day after day, night after night, they consumed his thoughts with what he considered a true test of one's love.

"I'll see you again one day, my dear love." He raised the pillow next to Mae's face. "Please forgive me, Lord." He tensed the muscles in his forearms and began to lean in.

Feeling a sudden pressure of the wooden rocker push against his foot, Gust jumped back, as the sound of the hymn once again sang from Mae's lips. Lowering the pillow to his side, he discovered her staring up at him.

"Who are you?"

Gust looked at the pillow in his hand and then at her. "It's...it's just me, Gust." He dropped the pillow upon the floor and shook his head. "I think...I think it's time I go check on Jonnie." Wiping the perspiration from his forehead, he knelt next to her chair, and steadying his shaking hands, he tightened the rope knots around her waist.

Chapter 6

Dark grounds swirled within the dregs. Resting the empty cup upon the saucer, the young pastor chimed the porcelain against the silver spoon as he slid it upon the coffee table. "He stalked your father right off the steamship?"

"Yes, like a predator, the thief tracked him through the streets, beat him unconscious, and stole the artifact." The Reverend Woodard dropped his head in reenacting the motions.

"I believe I enjoy hearing that story more than Rolf enjoys telling it." Genevieve gathered two saucers with empty cups onto the silver tray. "If you will excuse Noelle and me, we will leave you two gentlemen to talk, while we engage in our own conversation in the kitchen."

"Perhaps we should be leaving." Evan brushed the crumbs from his shirt as he rose to his feet. "I still need to make a quick visit with one of the parishioners. Besides, we wouldn't want to wear out our welcome."

"I'm sure you can spare a few more minutes." Genevieve motioned to Noelle. "We shouldn't be long."

Evan lifted his shirt cuff and looked at his watch. "Sure, a few more minutes will be fine." He placed the crystal against his ear and wound the crown. "Noelle and I really appreciate what you are doing for her. The women from our congregation are most helpful in making her feel at home since our move, but it seems to me that it is somewhat beneficial to hear from another pastor's wife as to how things really operate."

Noelle raised the coffee decanter, while supporting it with a pad, and topped off the two remaining cups on the table. Smiling at Evan, she followed Genevieve through the swinging door and into the adjoining room.

"I hope Noelle brought her notebook." Rolf laughed as he blew into his cup while taking a sip. "Gene is involved in quite a range of activities within the community."

Evan sat down and crossed his legs. "You seem very comfortable here, yourself. Are you originally from around these parts?"

"You haven't picked up on the accent?" Rolf raised an eyebrow. "Born in New York, moved around some, but actually I spent most of my childhood in Benson, Minnesota."

"Benson. That's just a short ways over, on the other side of the border. What brought you from New York to Benson?"

"That would be a continuation of my father's story. After regaining consciousness, he was dead set on recovering the artifact, so he returned to the steamship and talked the ship's purser into allowing him to transcribe a copy of the passenger list. As a young boy, I remember moving from town to town, where my father worked as a minister in various churches, but his main objective was in searching for the individuals whose names were on the list."

"Did he eventually find the scoundrel?"

"No. The search caused a strain on our family. My mother finally put her foot down, and it landed in Benson."

"So, he gave up the search?"

"I asked him that, once. He looked at me with a determination set deep within his eyes and said, *never*. He said the artifact belonged in the hands of learned men for safekeeping, not some poor, ignorant immigrant. It was the Lord's decision and not his to continue the search. He eventually suffered a stroke and passed soon after. In looking back, I think the stress of coming up empty handed, time after time, eventually took a toll on him, thus ending his life. In retrospect, the search was most likely his decision and not the Lord's."

"I'm sorry to hear he never found it."

"Oh, he gave me the old passenger list and wanted me to continue the search. To tell you the truth, I wouldn't know where to begin. At least my father knew what the man looked like. They're just names on a piece of paper to me. It makes for a good story, and that's about all it will ever be."

"And an excellent one, indeed." Evan nodded his head and then took a steady sip from his cup. "I understand your niece will be finishing her training at the Peabody Hospital this spring. Does she have plans upon completion?"

"Yes, we are excited with Kettie becoming a nurse. They offered her work at the hospital, but she is unsure where she would like to go. That one is somewhat of a dreamer, always looking for a new challenge. I remember my brother being the same way when he was younger. It drove our father nuts. My brother owns a factory now in Minneapolis, so I imagine Kettie has the luxury to ponder her next move and go where she likes."

"Maybe one of the young men around here will catch her eye. Sometimes, that's all it takes to motivate one to settle down and begin planning for their future."

"There are some very good suitors within the congregation, but she's just too picky. I've told her on several occasions that it doesn't have to be love at first sight. Love can grow with time."

"Yes, that has been known to happen." Evan chuckled as he returned the cup to the table.

"Say," Rolf rotated in his chair, "have you been approached to join any of the fraternal organizations?"

Evan gave a slight shrug of his shoulders. "Only a few of the luncheon clubs, Kiwanis and the Rotary."

"I'm sure you will have your pick once the businessmen in town come to know you." Rolf sat back in his chair. "The mayor boasts there are more fraternal organizations per capita in Webster than in any other city in the state. They are extremely proud in showing how they support their community. I'll put the word out that the new Reverend Thomas has an interest. You'll be contacted shortly by some of the various group members."

"Thank you. You have been very helpful." Evan turned a sip from his cup. "That *is* very interesting though?"

"What is that?"

"The number of fraternal organizations – interpreting how it may relate to the characteristics of a community."

"What do you mean? How it supports a community?"

"No. In hosting that many different fraternal organizations, one could say it shows a great division among its people."

Rolf lowered his brow. "How is that?"

"Generally, people tend to associate with those who they feel possess similar beliefs as they themselves do. You know, birds of a feather flock together. With so many different fraternal organizations, or flocks, in one community, it would cause one to assume there may be more here that divides rather than unites. In the great assortment of plumage, they are unable to find even one feather in common. Or maybe they just refuse to…or are not allowed to."

Rolf shook his head. "That may be the case elsewhere, but you will find things are quite different here. The people are friendly to one another and work well together."

"Yes, I've heard that said about many of the small towns dotting the upper Midwest." Evan chuckled. "It must be the strong Christian values."

Rolf smiled. "Of course, what else could it be?" He leaned forward. "Evan, I know of a fraternal organization that you may have an interest in becoming a part of."

"Oh, which one is that?"

"It's quite secretive, and only admits new members who are of a high moral character."

"Secretive? What causes do they champion?"

"Those the others fail to address. It's a very patriotic group as well. They stand for all that has made this country what it is today."

Evan tilted his head as his eyes recognized the distinct book cover imprint of the Kloran. The bound handbook of the Ku Klux Klan lay partially hidden on the lower shelf of the bookcase. Taken aback, he quickly turned away. "Tell me, Rolf, do you know much about this big Klan meeting to be held sometime during the summer? What do they call it, a klon…klonverse?"

An odd array of clatter erupted as Genevieve placed the dishes into the sink. "The Klan ladies auxiliary is sponsoring a picnic in the park next weekend. You and Evan should make plans to attend. It's open to anyone who has an interest."

Noelle shook her head. "Oh, I don't think that would be a good idea."

"Why is that? It will be an excellent opportunity to meet other good people from outside of your congregation, and you'll receive a chance to listen to some brilliant speakers."

"No. Evan does not fully agree with how the Klan has operated. He would never attend one of their events."

"Oh dear. I'm sure he has just been misinformed. The Klan supports public schools, prohibition, and womanhood, and they're against adultery and prostitution. Why, they stand for everything that true Americans believe in."

"Yes, I'll admit they have accomplished some good, but he believes the Klan's efforts are unfairly directed against the Catholics. He feels the Catholics are only exhibiting their right to freedom of religion, and should be allowed to continue to do so."

"Oh, I don't know. It can become confusing at times." Genevieve shook her head. "But I was never so proud to be an American, as when the local Klan members visited our church during service that one Sunday. Rolf nodded to the ushers to begin the offering, when four Klansmen walked in through the rear narthex doors. I can still picture their white robes. So bright and pure. Almost as if they were sewn from the cloth woven by the hands of God himself."

"Weren't you afraid?"

"Oh, no my dear." Genevieve patted Noelle's hand. "Not in the least bit."

"What did they do?"

"Without saying a word, they marched straight up the aisle, carrying our beloved flag, and laid a gift of money before Rolf's lectern. The church was in need of extra funding to repair the parsonage, and there they were, like shining knights straight out of a fairytale." Genevieve rubbed her hand across her forearm. "Look at that. I'm getting goose bumps all over again, just talking about it."

Noelle tilted her head toward Genevieve. "How did the members of the congregation feel about that?"

"Immediately following the service, the church council held a special meeting, and cast a unanimous vote to allow Rolf to become a member of the Klan. You know, their organization seeks educated, community leaders, and they provide free membership to clergy. Well, Rolf, and nearly every male in the congregation joined and became part of the Invisible Empire that day." Genevieve shivered. "Look, there go the goose bumps again."

"Oh, my. Nearly every man in the congregation?"

"Well, no, not every. Only those of stature – those with the means to contribute the fee."

The hinges squeaked as Evan poked his head in from around the door. "Gene, I apologize, but Noelle and I really should be going." He handed Genevieve the remaining cups.

Genevieve smiled. "Of course. We should do this again sometime." She placed the cups in the sink. "If you don't mind, I'll let Rolf show you two out."

Genevieve took hold of Noelle's hand as she stepped toward the swinging door. "Work on Evan, dear. See if you can change his mind, that is, to attend the picnic next weekend. There will be good food, music, and lots of friendly company."

Noelle smiled and nodded as she left the kitchen.

Genevieve spun in her tracks at the jiggle of the doorknob and slow creak of the hinges. Stepping back, she watched as her niece quietly folded around the door's edge and latched the handle's catch behind her. "Kettie, is there a reason you are attempting to sneak in through the backdoor?"

"Aunt Gene!" Kettie jumped. "I wasn't expecting anyone in the kitchen." She slid her bag across the countertop. "I noticed you still had company and I didn't want to interrupt."

"The Reverend and Mrs. Thomas were here for a visit. You know you don't have to worry about interrupting. We've talked about this before. You are a part of the family. The next time you notice we have company, feel comfortable to join us." Genevieve pulled a dry bath towel jutting from the bag's opening. "How was the lake outing? Did you and Brina have fun with your friends?"

"Uh." Kettie frowned as she shrugged her shoulders.

"Oh, I see." She scanned Kettie's outfit, from head to toe. "Anyway, you better change out of those trousers before your uncle sees you in them."

Kettie looked down at her legs and smiled. "To be honest, that's the reason why I came in through the backdoor. I didn't have time to change in the car."

"You know what your Uncle Rolf has said about wearing such things."

Kettie flared the material on both sides of her legs. "I know, but this is today's style. It's in *Vogue* magazine. It's what all the smart, young women are wearing nowadays."

"No, not all. Just because it's in a magazine, doesn't make it right. Why, I have even heard from some of the mothers that their daughters have been begging to wear them. I'm worried they might blame you. If that happens, just think of what they would say about the reverend."

"Auntie, trousers are very comfortable." Kettie swayed her hips from side to side. "Let me find you a pair. If you would only try them on, I'm sure you would like them."

Genevieve shook her head as she began to organize the dishes in the sink. "No, I'm afraid not. It's too boyish. I would prefer to remain more ladylike, and so should you."

Kettie hung her head as she pulled the bag from the countertop and tossed it onto a nearby kitchen chair. "Aunt Gene, why do boys always have to be that way?"

"What way is that, dear?"

She shrugged her shoulders. "I don't know. It seems like whenever I'm around them, they act as though they need to take care of me. As if I'm their property or something. Well I'm not, and I don't like it."

"I don't see anything wrong with a boy taking an interest in a girl." Genevieve shook the rinse water from one of the saucers and placed it onto the dry rack. "Some girls actually prefer it. It's much better than if the boys were to shun you."

"I don't want to be shunned, but I don't want to be owned. I just want to be treated normal, as an equal."

"My, you sound really upset. Did something happen while you were at the lake?"

"Well, yes. I mean no, not really. Oh, I don't know." Kettie picked up a dishtowel from the countertop. "It's probably just me."

"It wouldn't have anything to do with Robert would it? I think he is a very nice young man. His parents have managed to do very well for themselves."

"Who, Dob? Yes, he is nice, but we're just friends." Kettie lifted a cup from the stack of dishes and wiped the water from inside. "I did meet someone else today…another boy. It was the strangest thing. I mean, it felt…different."

"Oh Kettie," Genevieve smiled, "do his parents own one of the cabins on the south end of the lake?"

"No, I actually met him on the road. You see, my automobile broke down and he showed up, as if out of nowhere, to help."

The dishwater splashed onto the sink's edge as Genevieve pulled her hands from the water. "Kettie, as a young lady, you need to be very careful about strangers you meet on the road. There are many drifters out there, let alone the Indians. It could be very dangerous."

"I'm sorry, Aunt Gene, but at the time, I wasn't really given a choice." Kettie placed the cup upon the shelf.

"Well, I suppose not." Genevieve continued washing. "I'm just happy you made it home, safe and sound."

"Aunt Gene, if I ask you a question, will you promise to keep it to yourself, and not bring it up to Uncle Rolf?"

Genevieve stared at Kettie. "This young man you met on the road today, he wasn't just passing through was he?"

Kettie hesitated and then slowly shook her head.

"He's from the Pickerel Lake area isn't he?"

Kettie hung her head and nodded.

"Please don't tell me he's Catholic?"

Kettie looked up and shrugged her shoulders. "I didn't think it was the polite thing to ask at the time. Anyway, why does his religion matter? If he happened to be a Catholic, so what."

Genevieve shook her head. "No. No. No. Kettie, Protestants and Catholics do not mix."

"Why does everybody say that? I just don't understand."

"That's just the way it is. We never have gotten along and we never will. You need to forget about this young man. Forget that you ever met him. Believe me, if your uncle found out that you gathered an interest in this boy, a Catholic boy…well, I just don't know what he would do. People would not approve. No, young lady, trust me, they would not approve at all."

The dishtowel flew across the countertop. "You don't need to worry, Aunt Gene. I'm never going to see him again. Beside, I don't plan on sticking around here for much longer anyway. I'm leaving when my training is through this spring. I don't want to take a chance on getting stuck here. It's a place where only narrow minded people can thrive. Life has more to offer than this. Its just got to have." The kitchen chair rocked, as Kettie grabbed her bag and pushed through the swinging door toward her bedroom.

"Why is Kettie upset?" Rolf stepped into the kitchen.

"It's nothing to worry about. Just boys. You know."

"Oh, well, I'm glad she has you to talk with." Rolf chuckled. "By the way, my conversation with Evan veered off course, so I ended up changing the subject. Were you able to talk with Noelle?"

Genevieve nodded. "Evan is definitely set in his ways, but Noelle and I enjoyed a very encouraging conversation. With a little convincing on her part, we just may see them at the auxiliary picnic next weekend."

Chapter 7

WOODEN spoke wheels pulled dust from the well-traveled Yellowstone Trail. The fine sediment swirled into the drifting wake of the black Buick as it negotiated the road's concealed potholes. Anticipating the next sudden drop, Jacob occasionally tightened his grip upon the door's metal frame, as his Uncle Roman spun the steering wheel in rhythm to the sporadic shadows appearing in the vehicle's path.

"Are you sure he's not going to be there?" Roman's voice competed with the mechanical chatter of the 4-cylinder engine.

Jacob nodded as he cast a vacant stare ahead. Within the windshield's rectangular assembly, a steady stream of coal black smoke began to snake the green prairie horizon against a deep blue, morning sky. A wide grin pulled across his face as he leaned forward on the bench seat. The steam driven engine of the Chicago, Milwaukee, St. Paul & Pacific Railroad thundered toward them on the glistening, twin beams that paralleled their route.

The east-west running line, known as the Milwaukee Road, originated in Chicago, and stretched its creosoted timbers and forged steel rails across the upper Great Plains, through the Rocky Mountains, and ended at its last stop in Seattle, Washington, an awe-inspiring trip of some 2,000 miles in distance.

As the bridled behemoth split the ocean of rolling tall-grass, Jacob imagined himself riding the various passenger trains in the magazine articles he enjoyed reading. Traveling the East Indian Railway as it crossed over the spectacular two miles of its Grand Chord line's Nehru Setu Bridge, suspended above India's rolling Son River, as well as zigzagging the staggered descent through the switchback of the Devil's Nose, on the Guayaquil and Quito Railway as it wound through the snowcapped peaks of the Ecuadorian Andes Mountains.

The intense percussion, generated from the massive steam engine, liberated a small covey of sharp-tailed grouse from their late morning lekking, as the sound shifted with the locomotive's pass. Jacob watched as the mighty piston's back and forth movement forced the main rod to spin the enormous driving wheels, which he remembered each stood practically as tall as a man did.

While listening to the clickety-clack of the wheels passing over the rail splices, he counted each passenger car and pondered as to whom the riders were, where they may be going, and if one day, he would join them in their travels. He pictured himself lounging in the lavishness of the dining car among the company of fellow adventurers, while uniformed servers topped half-empty cups as vivid tales of far off lands wove through the fabric of meaningful conversation.

Including the observation car, positioned at the train's rear, the engine pulled twelve pieces in all. Within the final car's multiple panes of window glass, Jacob detected a dozen sets of eyes studying him as he admired their impressive mode of railway transportation. Feeling slightly uncomfortable, as if thrust upon a stage as an unwilling character for their traveling entertainment, he maintained his grin while extending his arm in attempting a sociable half-wave. The stoic faces rotated in unison as they continued to watch his uneventful performance. If it were not for a young girl returning his gesture from her father's lap, an average person would have thought them all store window mannequins.

As Jacob stretched his upper body out from the moving vehicle in following the train as it faded into the rolling hills of the coteau, the distinct, heavy smell of steam, burning coal, and hot grease gradually filtered into his nose and overwhelmed his pallet, leaving a pleasant, slight sulfur taste upon his tongue. Closing his eyes at the delightful euphoric touch to his senses, he emptied his lungs and drew in a long, deep breath.

"Must be the Columbian."

"What?" Jacob opened his eyes and slowly pulled himself back onto the seat.

"I said, the train, it must be the Columbian. It's heading east, so that would designate it the number Eighteen...end up in Chicago by tomorrow. The Seventeen, on the other hand, runs in the opposite direction, to Seattle."

Jacob nodded his head in agreement to his uncle's observations.

"Now, if it's speed that you want, the Olympian is the train for you. Yes sir, speed and luxury for all who can afford it." He looked at Jacob. "Which would you prefer?"

"I wouldn't know." Jacob shrugged his shoulders. "I've never ridden on a train."

"I thought you were planning on traveling to Chicago in the fall."

"Yeah, Pa thinks it's a good idea. He made arrangements so I can board with a family he knows. They have a job waiting for me at a paint factory."

"Old Stanislaus?" His uncle laughed. "He still mixing paint?"

"He's a supervisor. He told Pa that it's tough finding workers. They pay good wages."

"Yes, paint is not a glamour job and it can be dangerous, but it's a good way to earn a buck. If you're going to be living with Stan, then you will be in a good Polish neighborhood, too. It'll be safer for you there. We take care of our own."

Jacob shrugged his shoulders and remained silent as he turned and stared out of the side window.

Surprised at a lack of enthusiasm, his uncle continued. "I sense that you are not pleased with the arrangement? Is it possible that you don't want to go to Chicago?"

Jacob hesitated. "If I had my choice…if I had my choice, I would travel. Maybe see some of the places that I've read about."

"And where is it that you would want to see?"

Jacob's face began to brighten as he sat up and turned toward his uncle. "I'd like to hop on the Columbian or follow the Yellowstone Trail up the road and see Old Faithful, then maybe go south and ride the Colorado River as it cuts through the Grand Canyon, travel to Mexico and Central America, maybe stop in Panama and see the canal, then maybe the Hawaiian Islands, Japan, Australia, India, there is a whole world to explore."

"Tell me Jacob, after you have seen the world, then what?"

"Maybe come back home and go to school, or buy some land and farm. I'll know then."

"You sound like a man who has done some serious thinking. Does your pa know about these plans of yours?"

Jacob slouched into his seat. "Yeah, he knows."

"Then I take it that he does not completely agree with your ambitions."

"He says, with land prices high and grain low, times are tough for farming. He thinks that I should go to the city, work in the factories, and build a savings. If the farm economy improves, I can use the money to buy land for farming. If things stay the same or take a turn for the worse, then we may need the money to keep the farm afloat."

"As much as I know you would like to see the world, I tend to agree with your pa. Farms are going under every week and their unpaid loans are taking the banks with them. They say the country is in a boom, but we're not seeing it on the farm. It's not just farming. As you know, even the Milwaukee Road filed papers for bankruptcy. If the railroad can't make it…" He wrinkled his forehead and shook his head. "Yes, Jacob, these are strange, uncertain times we are living in, it's best not to stray too far from the beaten path."

"And *paint* is the beaten path? I don't see the connection." Jacob gazed out into the passing fields. First his pa and now his uncle, it seemed as though no one really understood how important it was for him to be out on his own – to see for himself what the world had to offer. His whole life centered about the farm and the expectations to contribute in making it work. He gave without question and treasured the experience for it, but now it was time to move on. It should be up to him in deciding the next step.

Sensing great frustration, his uncle spoke up. "Chicago isn't so bad. You could look at it as that first step in beginning your travels. The big city, many different peoples, *the girls*." He reached over and gave a quick slap to Jacob's shoulder with the back of his hand. "Oh yes, Jacob. Chicago could be the beginning of big things for you."

Jacob leaned his head a little farther out the window in pretending not to hear his uncle. He thought for a moment, half smiled, and pulled back inside. "You know, Uncle. You're right. I think you're on to something. Chicago could be the start of something big."

"That's the spirit. Now you're talking, kid." His uncle nodded.

"It's perfectly clear. I'll go to Chicago and begin work at the paint factory – make a little money, meet a few girls. If I'm still needing excitement and adventure after a few months of living the big city life, I can track down Al Capone and ask him if I can join his Chicago Outfit. Yes sir. The money will flow like water. I should be able to earn enough to buy land and travel, all in just a fraction of the time it would have taken me at the paint factory."

"Al Capone!" The tone in his uncle's voice rose. "No. No, Jacob. You need to stay away from those people. They're a nasty bunch. They would just as soon kill you as look at you. You stay away from…" An unexpected sound of laughter interrupted his thoughts. Confused, he looked over and discovered Jacob sporting an amused smile upon his face. Realizing the absurdity in the notion to join the Chicago Outfit, he shook his head. "Very funny. Very funny. I suppose I had that one coming."

As the old, black coupe churned a long cloud of dust behind them, Jacob observed a sign suspended between two square posts, dug in just off the road, indicating the town of Webster lie four miles ahead. Across the fields he recognized the skeletal remains of weathered cultivators and dilapidated automobiles scattered through a wooded shelterbelt. As he pondered a search through the used equipment for the parts to rebuild his wrecked motorcycle, the faint sound of a distant train whistle engulfed his thoughts. Surrendering to its overpowering lure, he closed his eyes once again, and listened to its haunting cry as it beckoned him to follow.

A cascade of barks and howls intensified as the vehicle slowed and followed two dirt, wheel paths stretching up a long, narrow driveway. The diverse dog pack tripped over one another while wrestling to nip at the spinning road wheels in welcoming the unexpected guests.

"Woof! Woof! Woof!" Roman added to the harmony of the a cappella hound choir. "My God! He must pick up every stray mutt he comes across." He laughed and turned toward Jacob. "Did Emil mention where he was off to today?"

"He was going to the ballgame. Webster plays Redfield this afternoon." Jacob opened his eyes. "Said if I found anything I needed, we could settle up later."

"Yes, he sure is a trusting fellow isn't he? Always has been."

"Then why don't you two get along? Pa said you used to be the best of friends before the war."

Roman shrugged his shoulders. "It's not that we don't get along. I suppose you could say we just don't talk."

"Don't talk? Why?"

"It's just an understanding between the two of us. Nothing further needs to be said."

Jacob stared at Roman in forcing a long uncomfortable silence.

"Okay. Okay, the short story." Roman repositioned himself within his seat. "Quick and to the point. I went to France. Emil stayed home. The girl who said she was going to wait for me...well...she wound up in the family way."

"You're kidding me." Jacob shook his head. "Was it Emil's?"

"It sure as hell wasn't mine. And I don't believe it was Emil's either, but he evidently thought it was, so he did what any trusting young man would do. He married her."

"Huh. I didn't know they had any kids."

"They don't. At least none living." He looked at Jacob, then back at the road. "The Spanish flu took it."

"This was before you knew Aunt Sophia?"

"Yes. I met Sophie after I returned." Roman slowed through the farmyard to miss a brood of chicks scattering from the path. "As far as I was concerned, there was nothing left to go home to, so after the ship docked in New York, I made it as far west as Chicago, and stayed."

"You were a Chicagoan? So that's how you know so much about the city."

"Yes. Things were very much different back then. Work was hard to come by. There were just too many returning veterans, so I took what I could. The money was good, but the people weren't. You could say I fell in with the wrong crowd. When I wasn't on the job, I was boozing. I didn't care about anything. That is until I met Sophie at a dance. My life changed in a heartbeat. That beat and all that followed belonged to her." Roman reached down and pulled the old Buick's handbrake, stopping the vehicle just before the closed pasture gate. "Anyway, she wanted to experience the west, so here we are — living on the coteau of the Dakotas."

"If everyone is content with how things are, then why do you and Emil still not speak?"

"Like I said, there is nothing that needs saying." He pointed through the windshield at the post wire securing the gate.

Dried wormwood and budding ash shoots wove through the orange rust of the scattered plow, disc, and harrow pieces. A line of disassembled tractors and assorted haying equipment filled the spaces between the buildings, and blended into a tree line of sun bleached automobiles and outworn truck chassis. Resembling a contemporary graveyard of modern fabrication, the sorted layout narrowed Jacob's search to a small section reserved specifically for the two-wheeled denomination.

The entangled grass slowed Jacob's progress as he freed similar bike frames and aligned them for comparison. Each Attempt to remove a stubborn bolt or corroded nut proved a subtle reminder of the incident that brought him there. Caressing his bandaged wrist, his thoughts drifted to the determined girl he met along the road, and if he would ever see her again.

"Go on, git!" Roman shooed a dog as he kicked a half-buried, gear assembly from the soil. "Any luck in finding a piece that'll work?" He studied the beveled design within its dried grease.

"No." Jacob wiped the sweat from his brow and stared at the row of partial bikes. "What I did find looked to be in worse shape than what I'm replacing."

Roman slid the iron, scrap piece across a wooden, truck bed. It tumbled from the platform and sent a spooked dog yelping through the tall grass. "We can stay as long as you like. I'm in no hurry to get to town."

"We can leave now. I believe I'm through here." Jacob brushed the dirt from his pants. "I'll keep asking around, something's bound to…" He hesitated as his eye caught the wide, faded red, white, and blue vertical stripes of a rear airplane rudder protruding above the automobile rooftops.

"You all right, Jacob?" Roman watched as the boy leaped over the field machinery and disappeared within the rows of motor vehicles. "Jacob!"

A flight of pigeons whirled between the buildings as the stiff canvas snapped in shedding its protective cover from the hull of an all but forgotten biplane. Pulling the remainder of the tarp from the wings, Jacob squinted through a haze of molted feathers and fragmented bird droppings in confirming his hopeful expectation. "A Curtiss JN-4. By God, it's a Jenny!" He ran the palm of his hand along the jagged edge of a splintered propeller. "I don't believe it. Where did Emil ever pick up a Jenny?"

Roman emerged from the yard and circled the aircraft in examining large holes in the wing's fabric. "This must be the air circus plane that crashed in Emil's field." He reached into the rear cockpit and moved the control stick back and forth, while observing the up and down movement of the wing's ailerons. "I wasn't around at the time, but I heard about it." His fingers pushed against the dash gauges in clearing a coating of fine sediment. "The airplanes were flying through the area, and for some reason, the pilot of this one lost control." He brushed the dust from his hands and looked at Jacob. "The poor bastard didn't survive."

"He died?"

Roman nodded. "The family wanted nothing to do with the plane, so they gave it to Emil to cover any damage the wreck caused." He shook his head. "It's a damned shame he did nothing with it. People would pay good money for a plane ride around the lakes."

"Around these lakes?"

"Sure. A flyer stopped in Sisseton last summer, and I saw people standing in line just to hand over five bucks for a short flight over the town. During the winter months, an enterprising person could travel south and make good money giving rides, all while seeing the sights this country has to offer."

Jacob's mind raced. Discovering the Jenny seemed like the answer to his prayers. Why waste even one minute of his life working at a paint factory in Chicago when he could earn ten times the amount of money, and see the world on top of it. Far off places, exotic people, an abundance of adventure, it was all very clear to him now. "What do you suppose Emil would take for the Jenny?"

Roman laughed. "No Jacob, you don't want anything to do with this aircraft. It's been neglected for too long. It would most likely fall to pieces just taxiing down the dirt road. Besides, it's a death plane. I'm not superstitious, but I certainly wouldn't feel comfortable in flying it."

The loose cowling tumbled to the ground as Jacob reached into the nose to check the engine. "It doesn't look like there is anything wrong under here, at least on the outside. If there is, I'm sure I can fix it."

"No Jacob, you're not listening to me."

"Come on Uncle. I can't do it by myself. You know Pa. He would never let me keep an airplane on the farm. If it doesn't benefit the cattle or the crops, then he thinks it's a waste of valuable time and good money."

"Jacob. That's another thing, your pa. And what about your plans to go to Chicago in the fall?"

"Don't you understand? To hell with Chicago!" Jacob threw his hands into the air. "Chicago was never my idea. It was always Pa's. He said it would satisfy my yearning for travel, and also guarantee money would be available for the farm." He slapped his hands upon the airplane's hollow shell and stared into the coated fabric. "This...this is my idea. I can make it work. I know I can." He looked up at Roman. "Don't you see? I really want this...I need this."

"I don't know, Jacob." Roman rubbed the back of his neck. "You don't even know how to fly the damned thing."

"You could teach me, Uncle. You were a pilot in the war. We could be partners."

"I've never flown a Jenny. I flew a few French trainers, but no, not a Jenny." He stepped back and scanned the plane from nose to tale. "If the engine runs, flying this one shouldn't be too difficult. They are basically all the same." As he stared at the plane, a smile appeared upon his face and he chuckled. "They used to say 'Any dumb idiot can fly an airplane. It's the smart ones who have trouble'." The smile quickly faded. "No. No. What am I saying?" Roman shook his head. "No, Jacob. Let's get the hell out of here before we talk ourselves into something that will get us killed."

Panting sounds grew louder as a pair of dogs appeared from around the corner of a building and circled the plane. Each stopped briefly to sniff Jacob and Roman, and then vanished within the junk assortment.

"I heard the vehicle drive through the yard, but wasn't presentable enough to just come right on out." A feminine voice followed. "Jacob, are you finding..." She paused at the discovery of an additional visitor. "Well, I'll be damned, if it isn't Roman. I haven't seen you in, oh how many years has it been now?" She pressed two fingers to her lips and drew a breath through the long ash of a store bought cigarette.

"Hi, Tess." Roman pulled at the brim of his hat. "Yes, It's been quite some time."

Elongated streams of white smoke exited from both of her nostrils. "Emil said Jacob might be stopping by, but he mentioned nothing of you." Wisps of smoke danced on each word.

Roman glanced at Jacob and then back. "Oh, ah, yeah, I have business in town today, so Jacob asked if he could ride along and stop by."

She laughed. "Business in Webster? I see." She staggered slightly as she turned toward Jacob. "Please tell me you found what you were looking for. Maybe you can help relieve us of some of this abandoned...treasure."

"No. I'm sorry, ma'am. There didn't seem to be anything that would work."

"No? Nothing at all?"

"That's right, Tess. Jacob struck out, so we we're just about to leave." Roman tipped his hat and nudged Jacob toward the vehicle.

"You mean, out of all this...," she waved her hand about the yard, "junk, you can't find even one thing to take with you?" She drew another breath through the cigarette and blew the smoke above her head. "Oh, you must take something. That idiot brings home more each time he leaves. I've warned him repeatedly. How do you expect to operate a reputable farm when you treat it like a junkyard? How are you going to get your work done when every step you take you're tripping over piles of shit." She grasped the airplane's strut to steady herself. "And where is he now, when he should be here helping you?" She hesitated as if expecting an answer. "Well I'll tell you where he's at. He's off watching some goddamned kid's ballgame. That's where he's at."

"Well there might be one thing, Mrs. Dodson." Jacob moved away from Roman. "What can you tell me about the Jenny?"

Roman glared at Jacob and gave a quick shake of his head.

"The Jenny?" Tess held a puzzled stare.

Jacob pointed at the aircraft. "Yes, the Jenny."

"Oh. You mean this damned thing?" She stepped away from the plane and took a long drag from her cigarette. "You know, I would be extremely pleased if you would just take it. Go on, take it. He hasn't looked at it since it crashed and they pulled it from the field to the barn. I told them I didn't want that damned thing anywhere near the farm, but here it sits."

"No, we can't do that, Tess." Roman reached for Jacob's arm. "We really should be going."

Jacob returned the glare.

"I insist." She swung her hand in the air. "Go on, take it. It will teach that goddamned fool a lesson. Always running off when there's work to be done."

"Tess, we're traveling to town anyway. How about we let Jacob stop by the game and talk with Emil. It won't hurt if the plane sits here another day or two."

"Yes Roman, you're right." Tess smiled at Roman. "That's what I miss about you. You always had the right answers for everything."

Roman returned the smile and pulled at the brim of his hat as he pushed Jacob toward the vehicle.

"It was sure nice seeing you again." She called out as the Buick's engine sparked to life. "Stop back when you have more time. We can catch up."

Jacob tossed the hand crank onto the floor and slid into the seat while closing the door. "Uncle Roman. I…"

Roman stared through the windshield as he gripped the steering wheel, and set the car in motion. "Don't say a word. Not one word."

Chapter 8

THE colors blurred. As its red and blue stitching wobbled back and forth, the baseball rolled into a shallow rut following the edge of the dirt, wheel path. Feeling its slight tap against his shoe, Jacob retrieved the ball from the ground and gripped his fingers over its bulging seams. Once baring a smooth, ivory finish, its brown tobacco stained, horsehide cover revealed a roughened texture, forged by sneaky pitchers throwing countless spitballs.

Ahooga! Ahooga! The startling bellow of a motor vehicle horn sent Jacob leaping from the edge of the street.

"Get out of the road or become it!" The driver screamed, followed by an encouragement of laughter from his fashionably dressed passengers.

"Hey, mister! Can you throw me the ball?" A youthful request called from within a jumble of parked automobiles.

Bouncing the ball against his palm, Jacob spotted the young boy waiting with a baseball glove spread open to the sky. He watched the boy's head bob with the rhythm of the ball, then freeze as he cocked his arm in readying to throw. The ball loosened within his sprawling fingers, as a burning pain engulf his wrist – a sobering reminder of his recent brush with misfortune. Rolling the ball in his hand, he walked over and dropped it into the impatient boy's glove.

"Thanks, mister." The boy ground the ball into the worn leather to reform the pocket.

"I cut my teeth on a ball like that, but I haven't seen one in years." Jacob remarked. "Nobody uses dead-balls anymore. They get too soft. The pitchers liked the handling, but if you're standing at the end of a bat, it's difficult to get any distance out of a hit at all. That's if you're lucky enough to even see the discolored ball against the dark soil."

"It works for us." The boy declared. "We can hit it far enough."

"Yeah, we can hit it far enough." A smaller version of the first boy stepped from within the cars. "The team gave it to us as a reward for returning foul balls." He peeled a wire-laced glove from the end of a well-used, wooden bat, propped against a vehicle fender.

Jacob smiled. "Yes, I'm sure you can hit it just fine." He nodded toward the spectators entering the bleacher area. "Do either one of you know Emil Dodson?"

The older boy pointed at a parked vehicle. "That's his car right over there. He's one of our customers."

"One of your customers?"

"Yeah. He gives us a nickel to keep the foul balls from hitting his car. Kind of like insurance I suppose. All the big shots pay us the same. He's not like them though. He just likes to pretend he is."

Jacob's heart skipped as his eye spotted a familiar looking two-seater standing next to Emil's vehicle. Glancing inside, he caught a hint of the pleasant scent he associated with assisting a young lady in distress on the edge of the road. He picked up a strand of auburn hair from the leather seat and smiled. "Did you happen to notice who drove this?"

"Yeah, that's Kettie's. She's the Reverend Woodard's niece. She moved here from Minnesota."

"Yeah, she gave us a special deal." The smaller one added.

"A special deal?" Jacob looked at the youngster. "Now, just what would that be?"

"She said she would pay us ten cents, but only if we actually stopped a ball from hitting her car. Don't tell any of the big shots. They might want the same thing, and that would be bad for business – no dough, let go."

"Yeah, no dough, let go, dent show." The young boy giggled.

As Jacob made his way to the ball diamond bleachers, he chuckled at the young boys' scheme to turn a buck off the fear of broken windshields, and dented fenders. Behind him, he heard the sound of a ball striking a glove, followed by the distinct thud of a missed catch.

"That's okay! It's not one of ours!"

The rows of freshly painted wooden benches arced a scattering of assorted spring hats, protecting fair complexions and squinting eyes from the bright, overhead sun. Scanning the arriving spectators, Jacob spotted Kettie's lake companions seating themselves near the home team dugout, but she was nowhere to be seen.

"Fancy seeing you here." Jacob felt a tug upon his shirtsleeve, and turned to discover Emil smiling as he twisted one end of his neatly waxed moustache. "Are you playing ball, or are you sitting this one out and watching?"

"Well, I..."

"Here," Emil rose to his feet as he finished forming the stray hair ends, "let me introduce you to some of the local businessmen." He stretched an arm toward a row filled with tailored, pinstripe suits and straw, boater hats. "Gentlemen, I would like to introduce you to one of the most powerful sluggers I have ever had the privilege of watching play."

Jacob smiled and nodded as a name and corresponding occupation returned a firm handshake or an acknowledging wave.

Smack! Jacob's head spun toward the wicked slap of a baseball striking the worn pocket of a catcher's mitt.

"Lighten up, Casey!" A coarse voice barked from the dugout. "Save your best for the game."

"So, young man, you're quite a hitter, are you?" The judge tapped the thick ash from his smoldering cigar, and watched it fall and scatter upon the ground. "Have you had the opportunity to bat against my son?"

"Your son?"

"That's the judge's boy out there warming up on the pitcher's mound." Emil pointed.

"Yes, Casey's starting off to a good season, Judge." Mayor Whittson chimed in. "The most any opposing player has been able to hit off of him is a double, at best. He's going to take the team far this season, and that equates to good business for the town."

Scanning the ball field, Jacob noticed Milt scooping ground balls in center field as well as Dob squatting behind home plate. "Sure, I recognize Casey. You could say I was a recipient of more than one swing of his arm."

"Is that so?" The judge grinned. "What team do you play for?"

"Well, I don't play for an actual organized team." Jacob cleared his throat as his eyes lowered to the ground before his feet. "Just the church parish."

"Church parish?"

"Yes sir." He looked back at the judge and smiled. "We, more or less, get together and pick up odd games from the local ball clubs. They get to practice against a fielded team and we get a chance to play ball."

"Oh, yes, rural church ball." The mayor turned to the others. "They've been known to become very competitive within the congregations themselves." He looked back at Jacob. "Who is your coach, I mean, pastor?" He chuckled.

"Father Majer."

"Father Majer?"

"Yes sir. From the St. Joseph Parish in Grenville. He's been with us about a year now."

"Oh, I see." Disinterested eyes rolled as the conversation turned to local affairs and wagers on the game.

Emil cleared his throat. "Yes, well, umm…say, were you able to find what you needed?" He grabbed Jacob's arm and stepped away. "I believe I had a good assortment of motorcycles for you to look at."

"I went through the bikes, but no luck."

"Nothing at all? Oh, that's too bad." He patted Jacob's shoulder. "Well, you've seen what I have on hand. If there is anything I can help you with in the future, just let me know"

"Well there is one thing." Jacob stopped mid-step. "I actually came here to ask about the Jenny."

"The Jenny?"

"Yes sir. The biplane sitting in the middle of your yard."

"Oh, yes, the Jenny." Emil smiled. "You don't look like the type who sits around dreaming about flying. Tell me, what set the fire in your thoughts to generate an interest in my airplane?"

"Well, my uncle and I were talking…"

"Your uncle?"

"My uncle, Roman."

"Roman?"

"Yes sir. We just might be able to take that broken down airplane off your hands."

"Roman, huh?"

Jacob nodded.

"I'm sorry, son, but I don't think I could part with the Jenny." He looked toward the ballplayers while keeping Jacob in the corner of his eye. "My wife wants me to fix it up and take her flying." He extended his elbows and dipped from side to side. "I wouldn't want to disappoint her."

Jacob laughed. "That doesn't sound like the same conversation she had with us."

"Oh, is that so?"

"Let's just say she may not share the same fondness for the Jenny as you do. She insisted we take it with us, but we managed to convince her to let us talk with you first."

"Ah, yes. Charming woman." Emil rolled his cigar from one corner of his mouth to the other. "So, what did you have in mind?"

Jacob retrieved a small roll of bills from his pocket. "I've got twenty dollars cash with me. The way I see it, a Jenny in good to new condition can be purchased for fifty, so considering the damage to the one in your yard, twenty would be more than a fair price."

Emil looked at the cash in Jacob's hand, and then glanced toward the gentlemen arranging odds on the players.

"For that price," Jacob continued, "we'll tow it away, and you will never need to worry about it again. Is it a deal?"

"You know what I think?" Emil pulled the cigar from his mouth and spit a tobacco fragment from his lips. "I think you came all this way for nothing. Sorry, Jacob, but the Jenny's not for sale."

"But Mr. Dodson, it's not doing you or it any good just rotting away under that tarp. I can put life back into that old engine. I can make it fly again."

Emil took a puff from his cigar and studied the tobacco wrap as he blew the smoke into the air. "You say a new one goes for fifty?"

"Yes sir. There are quite a few out there. Asking price for near new is around just that."

He pointed the cigar at Jacob. "There might be quite a few out there, but my Jenny is the only one in this county. You double the offer to forty, and it's yours."

"Forty dollars! For the Jenny? Oh, but Mr. Dodson, lets be reasonable, besides this is all the money I have. Do you know how long it will take to earn the rest?"

Emil placed his hand on Jacob's shoulder. "There is one thing about money, boy. If you want it bad enough, good or evil, it will eventually find you." He smiled and extended his hand toward the row of seated, pinstripe suits. "Now, if you will excuse me, these gentlemen are waiting."

With each weighted step, the chatter of the crowd's voice muffled, until the beating of Jacob's heart was all that remained. Thoughts of the airplane, and the freedom it provided from his shackled life, flickered to a blur within his mind and faded away. Chicago, a factory, and paint seemed his inevitable fate. Who was he to ever believe there may be a grander life somewhere out there waiting for him? The stories he read of far off places in books and magazines were all just a tease. It was all a lie.

"Jacob!"

He felt a slight tap on the back of his shoulder, and turned.

"I thought maybe you were trying to ignore me." Kettie smiled.

"Oh. No, I was just leaving." Jacob lifted his hat and looked inside while wiping the sweat from the band.

"You can't leave now." She pointed toward the playing field. "The game hasn't even started."

"Game?" He glanced back at the players scooping balls and returning throws. "Oh. Oh, yeah. The game." He positioned the hat on his head. "No, I didn't come here to watch the game. I was looking to buy an airplane – a Jenny to be exact."

"Buy an airplane? At a baseball game?"

"No. No, the Jenny isn't here. The fella that I was going to buy the plane from is though." He nodded toward Emil, who stood chatting with passing spectators.

"Oh. Well, did you buy it?"

"No. He's being ridiculous. I offered him twenty, as if the piece of junk is even worth that. The darned fool won't take it. He actually thinks it's worth twice that."

"An airplane, huh?" Kettie looked at Emil and realized the seriousness of Jacob's intent. "Would you pay him the money if you had it?"

Thoughts of soaring over snow capped mountain peaks brought a slight glow to his face. "You know, Kettie, as crazy as it sounds, I probably would."

Kettie extended an open palm. "Let's see your money."

"My money?" Jacob stared at her hand. "Why?"

"Don't ask questions. Come on. Just show me what you have."

Jacob dug into his pocket and displayed his roll of tightly wrapped bills.

"Wait right here." Kettie snatched the cash from his hand and darted down the aisle toward Emil.

"Stop! What are you doing!" Jacob nearly stumbled in reaching for her.

Kettie turned and smiled. "I'm going to buy an airplane."

Jacob cupped his hands around his mouth. "You can't do that! It's not enough, he won't take it." He dropped onto a bench and watched Kettie approach Emil with his cash in her hand. "Just when you think things are bad, someone comes along and proves you wrong by making them worse." He leaned back and tilted his hat forward to cover his face. "I'll never be able to speak to him again."

"Excuse me, sir." Kettie spoke into Emil's back as he tipped his hat to a parting acquaintance. "I'd like to talk with you about buying your airplane."

"My airplane!" Emil spun a half circle on his heel. "That's two in one day. No one has ever asked about the darned thing before." He took a puff of his cigar and blew the smoke into the air. "Tell me, young lady, did they forget to lock the door on the nut house today?"

"I know this may seem odd, but we're interested in purchasing that plane of yours."

"We?" Emil's eyebrows pushed together.

"Yes. Me and my partner, Jacob." She nodded up the row of benches, where Jacob attempted to conceal his face behind the brim of his hat.

"I see. Well, it's like I told *your partner*, the price is forty dollars." He smiled. "I take it, as a partner, you are investing the amount he was short."

"Well...no."

"Then we have nothing to discuss, young lady."

"But sir, don't you think you are being a little unreasonable? It's a piece of junk. It may *never* fly again." She grabbed Emil's arm as he began to turn away. "Just wait a bit. Please." She wound another bill around Jacob's roll. "Let's split the difference. How about thirty? You know you'll never get a better offer on that plane." She pushed the roll into his hand and wrapped his fingers around the money.

Emil stared at the bills, while through the corner of his eye he observed the group of businessmen laughing as they made wagers on the ballgame.

"Tell me, miss," he placed his cigar between his teeth, "would you consider yourself a betting person?"

Kettie stepped back in allowing others to pass between. "I wouldn't admit to it." She moved closer. "Why, what did you have in mind?"

Giving a light push to Kettie's lower back, Emil followed along. "I'd like to teach these stiff-necked windbags a thing or two. If you can convince Jacob to hit a fastball off their pitcher, and land it deep into the outfield, I'll take the thirty dollars, and the Jenny is yours."

"Hit a fastball? Jacob?"

Emil nodded. "Now listen carefully. I'll get him three strikes. If he fails by three, the Jenny stays with me, and you lose the thirty. You and your partner walk away with nothing. No cash. No airplane."

"Lose the money and the plane?"

"That's the bet." He replaced the cigar in his mouth. "Three strikes to knock one deep into the outfield, and the plane is yours. Take it or leave it."

"Can Jacob do it?"

Emil looked at Jacob, who sat hiding beneath the brim of his hat. "That's up to him."

"How are you going to arrange for this to take place? They're getting ready to host a ballgame."

"Don't you worry about that, young lady. These gentlemen will make it happen."

Smack! The sharp impact into the catcher's mitt grasped Kettie's attention. She watched Dob peel the ball from the palm of his glove, then toss it back to Casey, who showed no lack in furnishing disparaging remarks from on top of the pitcher's mound. Glancing for a moment at Jacob, who sat angling his body in an eagerness to leave, she turned toward Emil. "All right, let's teach them *all* a thing or two." She held out an open hand. "My partner will be right down."

One by one, the row of straw, boater hats tipped upward as Emil sidestepped his way to the center of the group. Gaining their attention, he pulled the roll of bills from his pocket.

"I have two hundred dollars cash that says the young man, whom I introduced to you earlier, can hit a fly ball off one of Casey's pitches." He made a cracking sound with his tongue against the bottom of his mouth. "And land it into the outfield." He whistled through his teeth as he drew an arc with the tip of his cigar in following the imaginary ball, as it started from the batter's box and ended at the outer edge of center field. "He gets three strikes to accomplish it."

"What was his name again, the young Catholic boy, right?" One gentleman chuckled as he crossed his legs and leaned forward.

"Jacob." Emil replied.

Sure, I'll place an even bet with you on that." He folded his arms and reclined against the wooden seatback.

"Why not." Another agreed.

"An even bet? Oh, come now." Emil hung his hands on his jacket lapels. "Casey has acquired an unbeatable reputation as a pitcher, whereas Jacob's experience solely lies with a rural *Catholic* Church team. In our discussion regarding today's game with the opposing team, we've determined maybe three to four players, at best, who could possibly even touch the ball, and that's with most of the team considered well seasoned ballplayers. In all fairness, the odds should definitely reflect the skill levels." He looked into each one's eyes. "Let's say four to one."

"All right, then I'll go two to one." The gentleman increased the odds.

Emil shook his head. "Like I said, he's only ever played on a few cow patty teams, nothing organized."

Another raised a finger. "But there is always that chance the young man might get lucky and connect with the ball. I remember you did say he was quite a slugger on the church team."

"Impossible." The mayor replied. "It's Casey. No one ever gets lucky off of Casey."

"Okay," a second spoke up, "maybe three to one."

"Sure, I'll go three to one." The gentleman increased once again. "What about you, Whittson?"

"Three to one?" The mayor thought for a moment. "I don't know. What do you think, Judge?"

The judge drew a long breath through his cigar and then blew a steady stream of white smoke into the air. "Gentlemen, as with all games, we've spent a good part of the hour discussing the abilities of each player on the visiting team. Their strengths, their weaknesses, and how it will affect play. These are solid ballplayers we analyze in an effort to determine appropriate odds. Now, to waste any amount of time at all calculating odds for…we'll just call him a non-player, when four to one has been asked, I feel is simply absurd." The judge looked at Emil. "Dodson, if you are feeling anxious to part with your money, I will most definitely honor your four to one request."

The ledger cover slapped against the hardwood railing. As Mayor Whittson began recording the bet entries, he halted his pen and stared at the others. "Someone needs to tell Red."

The judge pointed. "Bill, you go inform Red of the three strike competition." He waved him toward the dugout.

"Why me?" He hung his head as he turned to leave. "Coach isn't going to like this one bit."

"One thing about Red," another commented, "you can poke him on just about anything and he'll never flinch, but don't mess with his baseball."

As Whittson continued writing in the ledger, one of the businessmen in the group nodded at Emil. "Count it out."

Emil's eyes widened. "Count it out?"

The man tipped his head.

"What do you mean, count it out?" Emil pointed his chin around the assemblage of pale yellow hats. "Since when have any of us ever needed to count out cash to place a friendly wager?"

Detecting a slight nervous strain in Emil's voice, the others turned and stared.

"Well, gentlemen, this will certainly set a new precedence." Emil retrieved the roll of bills from within his pocket.

"No one's counting anything here." Whittson spoke up. "Put your money away. We have always operated on an honor system and will continue to do so."

Emil nodded in agreement as the others shifted their attention to adding their entries into the ledger. Taking a step toward the playing field, Emil pulled a handkerchief from his coat pocket, and blotted a sheen of perspiration forming above his brow.

"What the hell are you talking about? Three strike competition?" Red's clipboard skipped across the dugout bench seat and landed in the loose gravel. "Bill, if they haven't guessed by now, we're getting ready to play a game here. I don't have time for this horseshit nonsense."

"Sorry, Red, but you don't have a say in this one. Its already been decided." He pointed at the group of businessmen. "Just make it happen. You'll be taken care of later."

"This is baseball, not some damned three-ring circus." Red kicked at the ground. "Last thing I need is a bunch of red nosed clowns trying to play ringmaster in this big top." He leaped from the dugout and scanned the crowd. Getting the judge's attention, Red shook his head in defiance of the group's directive. A slow nod from the judge to comply released a string of foul words from the coach's mouth. Red shook his head again. The judge stared and then looked away to ignore any further protest. Tearing the baseball cap from his head, Red threw it down, and stormed onto the infield.

Jacob faced the exit. "Are you out of your Mind? These guys play serious ball." He slid his hat back. "I toss around to my brothers and sisters in the pasture during the week, and we piece together a ballgame on the weekends. And don't forget this," he extended his bandaged wrist, "which more than likely makes swinging a bat physically impossible. All in all, I'd say I don't have a chance."

"Mr. Dodson seems to think you do, and so do I." Kettie stepped between his gradual departure and the egress gate. "Come on, Jacob, you won't know unless you try."

"Trying is one thing. Losing thirty bucks on the deal is another." He rolled his fingers. "No, just give me my money, so I can leave before this whole thing gets out of hand."

"Your money. Well…"

"Excuse me, ladies and gentlemen. May I have your attention, please?" The crowd quieted as the announcer screamed through a large megaphone. "Today, I have the unique pleasure in announcing a special three strike exhibition provided for your pre-game entertainment. A chosen member of the audience will attempt to hit a home-run given the opportunity to do so in three strikes."

As the crowd supported a light applause, Jacob pulled his hand down his face. "Oh, it's a homerun now!" He angled once again in readying to flee the park. "I thought you said I just needed to land one in the outfield, now it's over the fence."

Kettie clutched his arm. "Jacob, you can leave if you want. A bit ago, you said you were willing to pay twice of what the plane was worth. After talking with Mr. Dodson, I don't think the bum would have even accepted that. The way I see it, you can walk away with nothing, or you can do what you came here for – to attempt to get the airplane."

"But, you don't understand, Kettie." He looked at the players huddling about the coach. "They're the ones who will be calling the balls and strikes. Do you really think they're set on being fair about this?"

Kettie watched as the coach directed each player. "No, not fair by any means, but still beatable. You can do it. You just need to outwit them."

The loose soil churned beneath the steel cleats as Casey stepped up to the pitcher's mound. Tossing the ball into his glove, he scanned the gathering crowd of spectators in search of the annoying rival seeking to challenge his superiority once again.

"Where do you idiots think you're going?" Red yelled at a scattering of players attempting to leave the outfield. "This won't take but a few minutes. You boys keep warming up." He waved them back onto the field as he looked at the opponent's vacant dugout. "Redfield will be here shortly, and you boys better be ready to play."

"Dob!" He spun toward home plate.

"Yes Coach."

"Get the rest of your pads on, pronto." He tore a chunk of tobacco with his teeth and stared into the crowd. "Let's get this harebrained sideshow over with, before the powers that be decide they want to try thinking again and shit out another idea."

"Casey!" The coach took a step toward the mound.

"Yes Coach."

"Three, do you understand me!" He pointed at the extended digits on his hand. "Three good ones, and only three."

"Don't worry about me, Coach. I know this chump. It'll be my pleasure to teach him he's got no business swinging a bat anywhere near my pitch."

Red looked into the filling bleachers and rubbed the beard stubble upon his face. "Truth is, it's not you that I'm worried about." He murmured to himself.

Jacob remained silent. With Kettie following directly behind, they maneuvered through the congestion of spectators to the infield opening. About to step out from the stands, he felt a hand press upon his shoulder.

"Do you understand it's all or nothing?" Emil pulled his hand back from its reached over the adjacent row of benches.

Jacob looked deep into the outfield, scanned the far fence, and gave a slight nod.

"Okay, then, let's show these uptight bastards what a good Polish Catholic farm boy is made of." Emil chuckled as he stepped to the opening to observe the competition alongside Kettie.

As Jacob walked out to the casual applause of the crowd, he glanced back at Kettie. Her confiding smile produced a slight grin upon his face, and a soothing warmth within. The conspicuous expressions amused her teasing girlfriends who rushed to her side. He shook his head as he spoke to himself. "Jacob, what did she get you into?"

Adjusting the head strap on the catcher's mask, Dob looked up and watched Jacob approach the batter's box. Over Jacob's shoulder, he noticed Kettie's eyes follow every movement that Jacob made. A half smile pulled up the side of his cheek upon realizing an inner fondness existed between them.

"Here." The coach shoved a weathered and beaten baseball bat at Dob.

"Huh?" Dob rubbed his hand over the rough, separated grain of the old grayed ash. "But Coach."

"Just give him the damned stick." Red grumbled.

As Jacob stepped up to the plate, he reached and caught the bat tossed by Dob. Examining the coarseness of the barrel, Jacob shook his head. "I see you weren't expecting company. Didn't have time to pull out the good silverware, did you?"

"Wasn't my decision." Dob pulled the catcher's mask over his face and squatted behind the home plate.

Red swept the plate and then stood behind Dob to call balls and strikes. He hesitated, and then took a long serious look at the increasing crowd. "I don't like this one bit. No, not one bit at all."

"What's that, Coach?" Dob leaned back.

"Shut up and catch." He growled. "Everyone ready!" He observed the bill of Casey's cap dip. "Gentlemen, let's play…ah hell, just throw the ball!"

Jeering erupted from the outfield, as well as along the dugout foul line, by the players who withdrew from their warm-ups to follow the contest. The murmur of conversation within the stands also quickly turned to shouts and taunts of pitching and batting abilities.

Agreeing to a hand signal displayed by the catcher, Casey turned, lifted his left leg, and stepped forward. The ball bolted from his right hand and smacked against the leather pocket of Dob's mitt.

"Strike one!" Red screamed.

Jacob stepped back in awe at the tremendous speed of the ball. He never experienced a pitch like that – straight down the middle and extremely fast. Although, one thing bothered him, the ball should have been easier to spot, even at that velocity.

"Can I see the ball?" Jacob extended an open palm.

As Dob placed the ball into his hand, Jacob rotated the dark brown stained sphere in examining the many scuffs and tears about its surface. This one, in particular, looked familiar. "I can't believe you're using a dead-ball."

"A ball's a ball." Red snatched it from Jacob's hand and threw it back to Casey.

Jacob shook his head as he stepped up to the plate and readied his bat.

An arc of spittle spewed from Casey's lips. Disagreeing with the finger signs Dob displayed between his legs, he continued shaking his head until a satisfying pitch request presented itself. Preparing to throw, his eyes shifted to Red, who counter-signaled behind Dob. Casey shook his head. He hesitated as he stared at the coach, and then shook his head once more. A look of disgust appeared on his face as he stepped to throw.

Released from his hand, the ball shot straight toward home plate before curving around its far side.

"Strike two!"

The crowd roared in disagreement with the unscrupulous call.

"What are you trying to pull, Red?" Emil shouted. "That's a ball. Even a crooked neck monkey could see that was no strike."

Dob looked back. "Coach, are you feeling okay? That was way off the plate."

"Dob," Red scanned the numerous rows of objecting spectators, "you ever question my call again," he pulled the wire mask over his face, "you're going to be looking pretty damned silly wearing my shoe up your ass."

Jacob stepped away from the batter's box. "Your boy's throwing spitballs."

Red raised his brow. "Is there a problem with that?"

"Yes, there is." Jacob planted the tip of his bat on the ground and pointed his finger at Red. "Everyone knows that spitballs have been outlawed from play since 1920. You've got a pitcher throwing spitballs with a dead-ball the color of mud. That's how Ray Chapman got killed – struck in the temple. That's why the league made the changes."

"Thank you for that interesting piece of information. Next time we play a ballgame, I'll remember that." He pointed at Casey. "Meanwhile, this is no ballgame, and you've got one more pitch coming down the keyhole. After that, you can go back into the bleachers and whine to your girlfriends all you want."

Jacob rolled his eyes as he returned to the batter's box. His thoughts raced. One more strike was all that remained. Outwit them came to mind. That's what Kettie suggested. He must outthink them. The next pitch would more than likely be out of the strike zone, and away from his reach as well. They got away with it once, they would surely try again. This was no longer about winning a chance to buy the Jenny. He needed to prove to himself and those watching, that he was every bit the ballplayer these jokers were.

"One more, come on, let's wrap this up." Red shouted to Casey.

Confused as to why the crowd slowly turned, Casey gave a few short chews of his tobacco and then spit. Following Red's signal, he turned, lifted his left leg, and stepped forward.

The ball fired from Casey's hand with a curve aiming beyond the far edge of the plate. Anticipating the pitch, Jacob stepped forward and onto the plate, swinging the bat in a plane just outside the strike zone, where the ball's path should travel.

Crack! The bat connected with the ball. Wood splinters scattered about the ground as the barrel of the bat separated from the handle and bounced along the third base line.

Wired masks flew to the sides as heads turned upward in watching the ball soar high over the crowd and into the adjacent parking area, where breaking glass could be heard. No one made a sound in awaiting the official call.

Red shook his head. "Foul ball."

A deafening roar exploded from the stands. Jacob handed the remnant of the bat to Dob and then gripped his wrist. The excruciating pain from his previous injury was paralleled by a tingling sting of his hands from the unexpected hit.

"You're done." Red gathered the shattered wood pieces from the ground. "That was your third pitch. It's over. We can't have you wrecking good equipment. We don't have that kind of money to throw away." He pointed toward the Redfield players filling the visitor's dugout. "Besides, our opponent has arrived, and it wouldn't be polite to keep them waiting, now, would it."

Surprised by Red's decision to end the competition, Jacob glanced at Kettie, who remained by the infield entrance, standing before the crowd of grumbling spectators.

"Three strikes! Three strikes! Three strikes..." Kettie began to chant, with the mass of agitated people quickly following suit.

"I have a spare bat in the dugout." Dob approached Red. "He can use that. I don't care if he breaks it."

"No!" Red threw the wood debris against the spectator fence line. "I said we're done with this."

"Give me one more throw, Coach." Casey pleaded. "I've never seen anyone do that before. It was a fluke, just luck."

"It's not worth it. He's better than you think." Red looked back at the chanting crowd. "We've got damage enough to repair."

"You don't understand." Casey continued. "I can't leave it like this, not knowing. I've got to finish him off."

Red shoved a finger into Casey's face. "No, it's you that doesn't understand. One more pitch and he just might finish *you* off."

"I found a bat." Jacob spoke up.

The three turned to discover Jacob propped against a baseball bat over home plate. Next to him, the two young entrepreneurs from the parking area stood with crossed arms and smiles across their faces.

Red spit and then wiped the tobacco juice from his chin. "Yes, you did. Yes, you did, all right."

Scanning the rows of chanting spectators, Red located the judge within the group of businessmen, who all sat with expressionless faces, in contrast to the enthusiastic energy that surrounded them. A lengthy stare produced a dip in the judge's head as indication to continue.

"Come on. Let's finish this damned thing." Red walked over and retrieved his mask from the ground. "Then we can move on to the real ballgame."

Pleased with the decision to resume the contest, Jacob massaged the pain from his wrist as he thought of a strategy to manipulate Casey into throwing the pitch over home plate. That was his only chance in connecting with the ball. He knew the coach's strategy was most likely the same as before – throw around the far side of the plate and then erroneously declare it a strike – game over. He might not be as fortunate as he was before, if he attempted to step forward and make contact for a hit.

"Looks like you're having a tough time steering the ball over the plate." Jacob caught Casey's attention. "You may have spent your only good pitch of the day on that first strike."

"Watch your mouth, Polack. I can beat you any day." He pointed at Jacob. "You're nothing."

"Is that why you're using a dead-ball?"

Casey laughed. "It's a poor player who blames the equipment."

"I'm not complaining. Use any crutch you need." Jacob lifted the bat in examining its barrel. "You have to give the kids all the breaks you can when they're playing with the adults."

"Why, I'll snap your neck, you…"

"Ladies!" Red shouted. "If the two of you are through sneering at one another, maybe we can execute this pitch, so we can get on to the real reason we are here today – to play an actual baseball game!"

Chew spit splattered beyond the pitcher's mound as Casey prepared to throw. Interpreting Red's signals, Casey shook his head. He hesitated as he stared at the coach, and then shook his head once more. Turning, he lifted his left leg, and stepped forward. The ball leaped from his right hand. At lightning speed, it sizzled toward the catcher's mitt pocket.

Crack! The borrowed bat set the ball high into flight as the outfield players rushed toward the fence in an effort to intercept the projected course aimed beyond the wooden barrier. Leaping into the air, a tall, lanky Milt stretched his long arm to extend his glove in anticipation of snatching the ball from its intended escape out of the park. As the ball descended into the leather glove, it rolled off the fingertips, bounced onto the board's edge, and dropped over the back side.

The crowd roared, with the deafening explosion of sound echoing for miles beyond the ball diamond.

Absorbed in the moment, Jacob turned toward Kettie to join him in his victory, but she was no longer there. The infield entrance held only Emil, who stood laughing uncontrollably.

"Scram!" Dob pushed Jacob toward the exit. "I'll try to hold them off until you get out of here."

As the team charged from the field in an effort to corral Jacob, Dob dove into their path, tripping the players on top of one another. Granted a fraction of time to escape the angry mob, Jacob passed the bat to the young boys and sprinted for the park gate.

A hand clenched Jacob's arm as he entered the stands, and another shoved a roll of bills into his front shirt pocket. "Here, take your money." Emil chuckled between cigar puffs.

"What about the Jenny?" Jacob grabbed Emil by his jacket lapels. "I still get the Jenny, don't I?"

"It's yours." He laughed as he pointed at the ballplayers rushing toward them. "That's if you survive."

Leaping from the egress gate into the parking area, with Milt leading a half dozen baseball uniforms on his tail, Jacob darted through a series of manicured neighborhood yards and narrow single-lane alleyways in an effort to gain an increasing lead on their pursuit, or preferably lose them altogether within the emerging obstacles and sudden sharp turns.

As Milt closed the distance, Jacob hurdled the last hedge of the block and rolled into the street, stopping just before a braking automobile.

"Well, don't just lie there." Kettie stretched her neck to look at Jacob from over the top of the hood. "Hurry up and jump in. I don't have room for everyone."

Pulling himself around the front of the automobile, Jacob caught the passenger door as it swung from the latch. He jumped and slid across the seat as the door slammed shut with the accelerating spin of the rear tires. Watching the players fade into the trailing road dust, he took a deep breath and looked at Kettie, whose amused laughter blended with the chatter of the roaring engine.

"Why did you do that?" Jacob lifted his hat and wiped his forehead with his shirtsleeve.

"It was the only thing I could think of to keep those lug heads from getting your blood all over my car." She glanced over her shoulder, and then straight ahead, maintaining a constant speed.

"Yeah, thanks. They seemed a little upset with my performance at the ball diamond." He shook his head and then looked at Kettie. "I thought maybe you deserted me."

"I did." She teased. "But my guilty conscious got the best of me, so I thought I would return and save you once again."

"Once again, huh?" Jacob held on as Kettie slowed to turn a corner. "Why did you go out of your way the first time, you know, to help me get the Jenny?"

"I don't like being in debt to anyone."

"What are you talking about? You were never in debt to me."

"Yes I was. The way I treated you on the road, you had every right to just leave me there and ride away, but you didn't. So, I wanted to return the favor by helping you today."

"You didn't owe me a thing, and I specifically told you I didn't want your help."

"That's not what you said at all. If I remember right, you told me, most times, it's less about what you want, and more about what you're actually stuck with." She smiled at Jacob.

"Oh, I almost forgot." Jacob pulled the bills from his pocket. "Here, this belongs to you." He peeled her money from the roll. "Besides giving me the plane, Dodson also returned the money."

"Keep it. You said our plane was in need of repair, didn't you?"

"Yes, but...hey, what do you mean, *our* plane?"

"Well, if I own a portion of the plane, it's only fair that I pay for my share of the repairs."

"Own the plane? How did this happen?"

"It's very simple. I worked the deal, and you swung the bat. Like it or not, we're partners."

"Why would you want to own part of an old, broken down airplane? It may never make it off the ground."

"I have confidence in your mechanical abilities. Remember, I've seen your work. Besides, the idea of flying intrigues me."

"Intrigues you? Intrigues you?" Jacob laughed. "What's Roman going to say? I don't see how we can possibly make this work between the three of us."

"Who is Roman? I didn't see anyone else with you at the game."

"Roman is my uncle. I caught a ride with him to town. He's a pilot, or at least he was one. I'm supposed to meet him on Main Street when I'm through." Jacob watched as her auburn hair swirled within the churning airflow of the open convertible top, and how she lightly moved it from her face with her fingers, and smiled at him.

"You'll have to thank your boyfriend for me." Jacob grinned. "If it wasn't for him, they would have torn me to shreds right on home plate."

Kettie looked at Jacob. "My boyfriend?"

"You know, the guy catching, Dob."

Kettie chuckled. "Yes, he's quite sensible. He's kept the others out of trouble on more than one occasion, but he's just a friend." She slowed and then parked the car along the side street before the intersection of Main. "Here you go. You should be safe now. I'm sure they've given up on you and returned to the ball diamond."

"I'm sorry, I didn't mean to... Well, who am I to assume. I don't have a girlfriend either." He looked at Kettie.

Kettie smiled as she turned toward Jacob. "Thanks for sharing, but I didn't ask."

The outer world fell silent while they gazed into each other's eyes. Conceding to a burgeoning desire, Jacob leaned toward Kettie, who quickly met him halfway, and then stopped within a fraction of touching. Both stared, sensing the warmth of one another's breath upon their lips. Their acceding bodies trembled and their young hearts raced. As their lips met, their souls entwined within the intoxicating flow of the twinkle in the constellation of their new being.

Adrift in the alluring softness of Kettie's sweet lips, Jacob felt the quick tap of a cool water droplet splash upon his pant leg, and soak through to his skin beneath. Another soon followed, combined with the metallic snap of a bottle cap releasing from its sealed grip, and bouncing upon the automobile's carpeted floorboard. Under a raised eyebrow, Jacob popped an eyelid open and discovered a row of condensation beads dripping from the bottom of a cola bottle suspended near his head.

"I'm not catching you at a bad time, am I?" Roman waved the bottle toward Jacob.

"Roman?" Jacob pulled himself from Kettie's embrace. "Oh, this is Kettie. She's a...she's a..."

"Slow down, boy." He chuckled. "Catch your breath."

Jacob's eyes drifted back into Ketties. "She's a friend of mine."

"A friend? Yes, somehow I surmised at least that much." Roman pried another cap loose against the windshield frame, and then handed the bottle to Kettie. "It's a pleasure to make your acquaintance, Miss Kettie."

Kettie nodded as she tipped the bottle in acceptance.

Swallowing a gulp from his soda, Roman pushed his hat up above his hairline. "Strange." He watched an elderly woman saunter past the alley entrance. "The streets practically emptied about twenty minutes ago. That must be some ballgame playing at the diamond today."

Kettie laughed. "Yes, the crowd was definitely on their feet." She stared into Jacob's eyes. "It's amazing how the appearance of one person can change the whole direction of the game."

Jacob brushed the back of Kettie's hand. "Amazing, indeed."

"So," Roman tilted the neck of his bottle toward Jacob, "did we get ourselves an airplane?"

Raising his bottle to Roman's, Jacob hesitated for a moment as he glanced at Kettie.

A smile appeared across Kettie's face as she tapped her bottle into theirs. "Yes we did, Roman. Yes we did."

Chapter 9

EMERALD sparkles dotted the high treetops. Fluttering with the light breeze, the covering of oval elm leaves filtered the midday sun, and projected random specks of light onto the rows of monuments aligned below.

Lying upon his back, in the fresh cut, prickly grass, Jonn followed the movement of shadows and light, as it waltzed its way through the block lettering imprinted on the dark, wrought iron cross. The words remained painful to read. The urgent but grim task to forge the marker seemed but a blur in his memory. After many tearful hours of labor, now, he could barely bring himself to look upon the cross and its somber inscription.

Jonn closed his eyes. Thoughts of a distant, warm, summer day surfaced in his mind. The brilliant glitter of clear, cool water in a secluded bay, clothing scattered upon the grass shoreline, and two bare bodies at play in the gradual roll of fading ripples. The seasonable air resonated with a mixture of songbird notes and lighthearted laughter. Oh yes, there was always an abundance of laughter.

"Shhh. We don't want to draw a crowd." Sarah reached her hands from the water, splashing a stream across Jonn's face, as she attempted to cover his mouth.

Jonn wiped the droplets away and turned an ear toward the tall cottonwood trees and thick shrubbery bordering the remote setting. "We're safe. Very few people know of this place. We should be able to hear anyone approaching from a mile off."

"I hope you are right. I don't want to lose my job. The hospital wouldn't look very fondly upon one of its teaching nurses performing peep shows for the general public."

"I'll make sure the attendance is kept to one." Jonn smiled. "You wouldn't want to let down your biggest fan now, would you?"

Sarah pulled Jonn's head into hers, stared into his eyes, and gently kissed his lips. "No, I would never disappoint my biggest fan." She returned the smile, glided toward the water's edge, and stepped out onto the grassy shore.

Jonn followed as they climbed onto a large, flat boulder overlooking the bay. Sitting in the sun, they felt its warming rays dry the remaining droplets upon their skin.

As Sarah watched the gulls skim the water's surface, Jonn couldn't help but notice the gradual curves of her body, the scattering of freckles upon her nose, and the shaded tint within her eyes. He wanted to tell her of the overwhelming passion she stirred within his heart, but any attempt at words would never express his actual feelings.

"This is one of my most favorite places." Sarah leaned into Jonn's shoulder. "It's so peaceful here. I wish we would come here more often."

"Sarah, I love you more than anything." The words stumbled from Jonn's mouth.

"I love you, too." Sarah smiled and kissed him.

"No. What I'm trying to say...what I'm trying to say is, sometimes, when I'm with you, I experience this powerful feeling inside of me. It's as if...it's as if all were to suddenly end, I would leave this earth content in knowing that my life was complete." Jonn looked deep into Sarah's eyes and kissed her. "Will you marry me?"

Sarah smiled. "Yes. Yes, I'll marry you." She returned his kiss. "Why do you keep asking?"

Jonn placed his arm around her waist. "I like seeing the smile in your eyes. I like hearing you say yes."

"One of these times, you may be surprised if you hear no."

"Would you really do that? Would you really say no?"

Sarah shook her head. "Not for the world."

"Do you want me to stop asking?"

"Please don't. I like hearing the words float from your lips. They make me weak, and at the same time strengthen my heart"

Jonn smiled and rested the side of his head against Sarah's. "Good, because I don't think I could stop."

"Oh, one day the words will fade." Sarah turned and looked at Jonn. "One day, many years from now. One day, when I'm gone."

"Please don't talk that way, Sarah."

"Jonn, everyone dies sooner or later. They always have. They always will."

"Yes, I know." He looked at Sarah. "If you should happen to leave before me, I'll still keep talking with you. I'll still ask the question."

"You will?" She laughed. "Now, just how will you go about that?"

Jonn hesitated as he looked out into the bay. "I'll visit each day with a picnic basket, lay next to you upon the grass, and carry on a conversation as we are now."

"And what will you talk with me about?"

"I'll tell you about our children and grandchildren. How they are growing. How they remind me of you, and," Jonn brushed the side of her cheek, "how I still love you."

A tear welled and rolled down Sarah's face. "I love you so much." She wrapped her arms around Jonn, and kissed him as they lay back onto the flat rock.

Jonn opened his eyes and stared at the twinkling leaves of the overhead tree branches. The vivid memory faded to black. The empty, painful realization of being alone, without Sarah, remained. He pondered at the notion of whether loneliness was his punishment for loving Sarah so strongly. The powers that be may allow the touching of souls, and the sensation of pure love, to exist only on the other side. The stumbling upon this forbidden pool may have caused their separation with her untimely death.

Feeling the sharp blades of dry grass poke the skin through the thin material of his worn shirt, he sat up and rubbed the irritation from his back. Along the outer edge of the cemetery's fence, two of the grim German sentries paced back and forth. He thought himself rid of the persistent ghosts for the day. They did not follow him as usual. Although, when they did, they stopped abruptly at the gated cemetery's opening, and never entered. He reasoned they must have a definite concern of stepping onto God's acre, a fear of possibly returning to hell, from where they most likely came.

"Go away you rotting bastards! You'll get no pleasure from tormenting me today."

The soldiers stopped mid-step and turned toward Jonn.

"Yes! I know you can hear me! No schadenfreude for you today!"

"I see you brought your lunch." A voice interrupted.

Jonn spun around and discovered A.J.'s mother, standing at a guarded distance, and attempting to conceal a confused expression.

"If I would have known," she continued, "I would have put together a little something for the both of us." She nodded at the unopened basket sitting next to Sarah's marker.

Jonn pushed himself to his feet. "Oh. No ma'am. I have no appetite for lunch today. You are welcome to take it if you would like."

"No dear. I am fine." She stepped a little closer, acting as though she did not hear Jonn's earlier absurd outburst. "It's such a nice day. I thought I would visit Albert's grave."

"Yes ma'am. It's a beautiful day."

"If you have time, I wish you would stop by and visit with him, too. I'm sure he would appreciate your company. He probably gets tired of listening to his mother all of the time. He's just right over there." She pointed to a white, sandstone marker aligned with the others.

"Yes ma'am. I know where he is."

"Good. I'll let him know you will be along." She turned and walked away.

Jonn sat down upon the grass and watched as Mrs. Sweeney pulled a few stray weeds that sprouted near A.J.'s headstone. The fresh cut flowers she assembled in a makeshift vase during the prior week's visit lay strewn about, wilted and apetalous. Jonn dropped his face into the palms of his hands and shook his head. Was she doing this to torture him? It didn't make sense. A.J.'s body was not there. They buried him in France during the war. She was well aware of this, but she continued to tend to the empty grave week after week. Was it possible that someone discovered the circumstances surrounding A.J.'s death, and told her?

Rocking back and forth while shaking his head from side to side, Jonn attempted to thwart the bleeding of painful memories that began to seep from the dark corners of his mind, and overpower his thoughts. The foul urine smell, the desperate cries of anguish, and the dry dirt taste deep within his throat.

"Water. Please. Please, may I have some water?" Jonn forced the words from his parched throat as his vision began to focus on the mildew stained landscape painted upon the ceiling above.

"Here you go, pal." A hand elevated the back of his head, while another pressed a tin cup against his lips. "Be careful now. You don't want to overdo it."

Each small gulp provided a soothing relief in extinguishing the dry burn in Jonn's mouth. "Thank you."

"I'm the neighbor to your left." The man reached up and grabbed Jonn's hand. "Gordy Altmann is the name."

"Pleased to meet you. I'm..."

"Save your breath." The man interrupted. "I read your chart hanging at the foot of your bed. Sorry. But there's not much to do around here."

Scanning the elongated room, Jonn was unable to count the large number of patients jammed into both sides of the aisle. "No. I suppose not." He agreed. "A.J., Wes. Have you seen either?"

"No. I haven't heard of anyone going by those names around here." The man shook his head. "Friends of yours?"

"Yes. Yes they are. We were retrieving a French artillery piece from the British in helping to stage a planned offensive. We must have lost track of time. The German shells started to rain down on us before we hit the halfway point on our return. The horses were getting nervous, but we managed to keep them on the road. That is, that is until we hit a crater and broke an axle."

"So, do you think this A.J. and Wes may have gotten themselves killed during the bombardment?"

"No, I remember we took cover in an abandoned trench line. A girl..."

"A girl?" The man leaned closer.

"Yes, I seem to recall a young girl with us. I don't know why."

"Now you have my attention. What happened next?"

Jonn shook his head. "That's all I can remember."

"Some lousy storyteller you are. You get to the best part and then you can't remember." The man chuckled. "Oh well. No use in getting too excited in here."

Jonn swallowed a few more sips of water. "How long have I been here?"

"I can't help you with that. You were here when they brought me in, and that's been over a week ago."

"Do you know what day is it?" Jonn asked.

"Yeah. It's Monday. No. No, Tuesday. That's right. Tuesday, the thirteenth of November."

"I vaguely remember one of the nurses telling me the war was over. Is it true?"

"Yeah. It's been over for a few days now. Parties and celebrations everywhere." The man looked up and down the filled ward. "Well, everywhere except for here."

"It does seem to be a might congested in here. Where did all these men come from?"

"With the exception of you, me, and a few others, these soldiers are all casualties of the eleventh hour charge."

"The eleventh hour charge?"

"Yeah. Even though they received word of the armistice hours before the end, they fought up until the very last minute."

"My God. Why in the hell would they do that, if they knew it was all going to be over?"

"Officers. The commanders in the field wanted to solidify their next promotions. They sent these men screaming into enemy machine gun fire in order to take every inch of ground they could, before the ending bell sounded. Ground, that minutes later, they could have turned cartwheels on without fear of even a scratch. One fella, over there, told me the Germans were trying to wave them back, but they were under strict orders to keep pushing ahead. The Germans finally opened up and clipped them down as clean as a fresh haircut." He shook his head. "Senseless slaughter. That's what it is. All for what? Blood promotions. Of the thousands of casualties, you can bet the church offering money that not a one of them was an officer." He laughed. "Now, just how could they be promoted if they were dead?"

The soldier's eyes widened as he recognized a gold colored oak leaf entering the ward. "Speaking of officers, looks like you may be having a visitor. The Major's been in here sometimes two, three times a day, kicking at your bed, trying to rouse you." He grimaced as he set his wheelchair into motion. "I've got to be going for now. It might be good strategy to play as though you're unconscious, and hopefully you'll still be here when I get back."

A chorus of antiphonal groans and cries alternated the aisle, as the major walked between the tight bed rows of oozing bandages and wooden splints. "Hold your heads high, boys. You're heroes. Every damned one of you. You will be remembered for generations to come, by your country, your hometowns, and your loved ones. They, as I, are extremely proud of you for your last minute effort to kill the Hun. He needed to be taught that lesson. The German's needed to understand that they should never attempt to do this again, for the resulting consequence will be an unimaginable hell."

In the wake of the major's verbose rhetoric, a scattering of obscene gestures appeared from otherwise motionless bodies. The empty words continued to stack high upon themselves and eventually oppresssed the unfeigned wails of the enlisted trench soldiers.

The major stopped at the foot of Jonn's bed and turned toward the rows of bedridden wounded. "Magnificent. Absolutely magnificent. I'm so damned proud of each and every one of you. I wish you were all my sons."

With eyes held closed, Jonn felt an uneasy stare pierce through his entire being. The rough sound of the major's throat clearing of mucus repeated twice, but Jonn remained defiant. The bed suddenly shook from the quick blows of the officer's boot heel striking the wooden leg post. "Say, you. I know you're awake. I saw you speaking with one of the men."

Jonn squinted through one eye. "Sorry, sir. I'm having trouble keeping my eyes open."

The major surveyed the beds in the immediate area and spotted a nurse in the far row leaving a patient's side to care for another. He took quick steps to retrieve her folding chair and placed it next to Jonn's bed.

Sitting in the chair, he crossed his boot over his knee. "You don't belong here, do you?" He looked up and down the rows of mangled soldiers. "No. You definitely don't belong here."

"Sir?"

"You don't know me, but my name is Major Frank Norville. You could say I kind of run things around here. Nothing gets to the colonel, unless it passes through me."

As Jonn angled his arm to retrieve a drink of water, the major intercepted the glass and set it out of Jonn's reach. In its place, he tossed a torn, soiled envelope.

"You see, I have access to privileged information, meaning, I know your little secret." He glared at Jonn. "Oh yes, I know what you did, and it sickens me."

Jonn shook his head. "I don't understand. What are you talking about?"

"In my eyes, sergeant, *you* are a coward. But you are different from the other yellow scum that I have had the displeasure of meeting here in my ward. I would say that you are the lowliest form of a coward. Anyone responsible for intentionally killing one of their own men, my God, their own friend, should be skinned and hanged."

"Sir, I think you have me confused with someone else. I don't know what you are talking about."

"Don't play games with me, damn it! I will not be toiled with! You are Sergeant Jonn Reese of the 147th Field Artillery, am I correct?"

"Yes, sir."

"And you are telling me that you retain no recollection as to what I am referring to?"

With a puzzled look, Jonn shook his head.

A slight smile appeared below the major's piercing eyes. He hesitated for a moment and chuckled. "Well, maybe you are being truthful. It is quite possible that the wound to your head did in fact relieve you of this recent knowledge." He gave two belly laughs. "Oh yes, the pleasure of this visit could be doubly satisfying."

Jonn stared in silence.

"Well, sergeant. Allow me to provide the details." He cleared his throat. "According to the report assembled by headquarters, a Private Albert Sweeney…"

"A.J. You know where A.J. is?"

"A.J.? Oh, yes. I have a good idea where he ended up. You see, it appears Private Sweeney, A.J. for the sake of the conversation, was taking advantage of a young French girl in the trench, during the Meuse-Argonne offensive."

"No! Not A.J. Never!"

"Calm down. Calm down. Who of us hasn't, on occasion, welcomed the services of our French host's blossoming flowers? Like fresh lilies in the field, they are eager to be picked. But you see, some-how, the young lady wound up dead."

"Dead?"

"Yes, dead. Now listen very closely. This is the point of the story that will be of great interest to you. According to the report, you and A.J. had an altercation over the matter, whereby you took it upon yourself to bestow unto him the same fate as he offered the young French whore."

Jonn stared at the major.

"You killed him, sergeant." The major shook his head. "You killed Private Sweeney."

"No!" Jonn screamed. "That's not true. I don't believe A.J. is dead, and I certainly will not believe that I had anything to do with it."

"A likely response. Then, can you explain to me, how your bayonet wound up in Private Sweeney's, excuse me, A.J.'s, chest?"

"It couldn't have happened. I would never hurt A.J."

"The report explains that it was at that moment, or shortly there-after, that enemy fire, possibly from a German soldier's rifle, grazed your skull and subsequently put you in here," he waved an open hand about the room, "in my ward."

"No! No! I tell you it's not true."

Oh yes. It is quite true. You see, you are nothing less than a filthy murderer of a fellow soldier, an American. If it wasn't for Lieutenant Wesley…"

"Lieutenant Wesley? You mean Corporal Wesley. Where is Wes? He'll tell you. He'll straighten this whole mess out."

"Lieutenant Wesley provided a full disclosure of the incident. It was all in the report. In fact, dozens of eyewitnesses from a British unit corroborated the facts. You see, while you and Private Sweeney were preoccupied with the whore, the Lieutenant was heavily engaged in the offensive. Unlike you two, acting as though you were two dogs in heat, he was fighting the war. It was his brave actions that held the Hun at bay, and allowed the British unit to advance, possibly saving hundreds of lives."

"Wes?"

"Oh yes. For his actions on that day, he received a field promotion to an officer, a first lieutenant to be exact, and will be awarded the Silver Citation, among others."

"Lieutenant?"

"Well now, you don't expect the army to give the Silver Citation to a simple enlisted man, do you?" The major laughed.

"I don't believe it. I don't believe a word you are saying. If it were true, I would be locked up somewhere, being questioned by a judge advocate, instead of here with you."

"As I was saying, before I was so rudely interrupted, if it wasn't for Lieutenant Wesley, there is no doubt you would have been hanged. But with the involvement of the British, the colonel did not want such a heinous act to tarnish Lieutenant Wesley's heroic feat. They decided the best thing to do was to make it go away – just like it never happened. They burned the incriminating statements, hid you in my hospital, and hoped you would die."

"How can this be true? I should have at least some recollection. I swear, I don't remember any of this."

"You see, normally, if a questionable soldier enters my ward, I would separate him from the others, or if possible, removed from the building all together. I don't care how sick they are. Send the trash back to their units...anywhere but here. You, and those like you, should never be allowed to pollute the air breathed in by these men, these heroes." The major closed his eyes and shook his head. "The thought of it makes me ill. I refuse to let that happen. Individuals like you are not fit to eat the nuts from their bedpans."

A crescendo of labored moans echoed from the bandaged hole of a patient lying two beds away. The major opened his eyes in following the quick steps of an orderly who rushed to assist. "Be tough about it, soldier!" He barked at the disfigured man arched in the bed. "You've been through much worse than this!"

The major nodded across the aisle. "His family will forever be proud of what he did here." He watched as a nurse drew a white sheet over a soldier's face. "For the rest of us, our families will eventually forget our service during the war, but he is privileged. His descendants will always remember his sacrifice, and speak his name with great honor."

The major's sharp words swirled within Jonn's head and scrambled his thoughts. He killed A.J.? Someone made a mistake. Files were inadvertently mixed. The horrible incident belonged to two other soldiers, not A.J. and him. Soon, A.J and Wes would come to visit him, and he would tell them of the wild incident the major described. This will make for many laughs on their long ocean voyage home.

"Oh, I almost forgot. There is a reason why I was waiting to speak with you." The major moved the envelope from the bed stand to Jonn's pillow. "You received mail from home. Considering the circumstances, I wanted to deliver it myself."

Jonn focused his eyes on the letter, and then snatched it into his hands. Soiled and creased, its severed flap displayed the careless handling of the postal sensors.

"I'll save you the time in reading it." The folding chair creaked as the major reclined. "It appears Sarah, your fiancée from what is written among the sentences, has died. A casualty of the Spanish influenza I'm afraid. As a nurse in the hospital, she contracted the illness from those she was caring for. Well, it's probably for the best. She would have eventually discovered the type of low lying beast you really are, and may have done away with herself anyway." He laughed.

The envelope exploded as Jonn ripped the pages from within. Studying each letter, he mouthed the words over and over, hoping to make sense of the gut wrenching news, until finally accepting their inevitable painful meaning. "No!"

"Oh yes, it's all right there in the letter. You know, one might relate this to karma. You took a life, and one was taken from you. It's all quite profound, don't you think? Oh well." The major stood up and straightened his jacket. "Just one more thing. One day, you will be held accountable for what you did to that soldier. You may think you have gotten away with this because of the war, but God knows what you did, and vengeance is his." He leaned next to Jonn's ear. "Until then, either die or get well. It makes no difference to me, but one way or the other, I want you the hell out of my hospital."

"You son of a bi..." Jonn felt his arms restrained as he attempted to reach for the major's throat. "Let me go! Damn you! Let me go!" He wrestled the orderly but his weakened state provided very little in usable strength. "No! Please, let me go." Watching the major return down the aisle, spouting words of the eleventh hour charge to the lifeless bodies lining both sides, he fell beaten into his bed and closed his eyes. "Oh, Sarah... Why?"

"I believe the wind is picking up a little. Other than that, it sure is a pleasant afternoon." A voice spoke through the overhead rush of leaves fluttering with the steady breeze.

"Huh? Oh, I'm sorry. Yes. Yes, it is very nice." Jonn attempted to stand as he rubbed his eyes in focusing on Mrs. Sweeney's approach.

"No, please sit. I hope I'm not intruding again." She stopped and rested her hand upon a granite marker.

Jonn hesitated for a moment. This could be his chance to speak with her about A.J., about their experiences in France. He could count on one hand the number of times he has spoken with her since his return. Each time he wanted to confess what he did, but the words would never fall into the proper alignment. In his heart he understood she deserved to know the truth.

"Mrs. Sweeney, I...I..."

"No, Jonn. I want to apologize to you. It was not right of me to ask you to visit Albert when you are here, tending matters of your own."

"But, but..."

"At times, I become too focused on Albert, and forget that others bear concerns to deal with as well." She straightened the purse around her arm. "You deserve a little privacy, Jonn. Albert is your friend and I'm sure he understands. If you get a chance, please stop over to the house for lunch sometime. It would be a nice change to cook a meal for more than one again."

"Yes ma'am. I'll do just that."

"If you feel up to it, maybe you could share some stories of Albert in the war. I only know that he was...that he was..." She placed her fingertips against her lips, and closed her eyes for a moment. "It was in the letter that Captain Anders sent after his death. You boys were gone an awful long time. I'm sure some good things happened over there. It would be nice to know that."

Jonn nodded.

As he watched her step around the graves in moving toward her automobile, Jonn could feel her pain in lacking closure. Except for the letter from the commanding officer, the army did not provide her with anything in which to remember A.J.'s service to the country. They do not give medals to the dead, only the living. A lighthearted story or two would help in easing the pain, but he may not be able to bring himself to stop. Once he began to talk, he may spill his guts, leaving Mrs. Sweeney with more questions than answers. For the moment, killed in action is most likely the best explanation.

Beyond the wrought iron fence, at the edge of the cemetery's boundary, two German sentries stood motionless. With frayed, partial uniforms fluttering in the light gusts, they stared at Jonn through tired, hollow eyes.

"Looks like you boys got what you came for, and then some." Jonn watched as the soldiers slowly turned toward the entrance road, placed one foot in front of the other, and faded away. "You always do."

Chapter 10

THE needle dragged. Scraping against the bottom of the record's groove, the steel point vibrated a crackling hiss through the phonograph's horn, as it skipped against the center wax. Nearing the end of the main spring's tension, the motor slowed, and the turntable's rotation ceased.

"Lunch soon!" Aggie called out through the screen as Sophia pushed the door open and they stepped onto the front porch. A series of quick cranks set the portable phonograph back into motion. Changing the record, she dropped the needle at its edge and waited for the first notes to begin before returning indoors.

Kettie poked her head from the Jenny's rear cockpit. "I'll be in shortly, to help."

"Just listen to that trumpet growl." Roman swayed his head to the off-staff, guttural timbre. "Sounds like it's readying to chase the devil – chase the devil and bite him in the ass." He pulled on the flying wires in testing the tension against the wing's struts. "Ah, now that's hot jazz. Jazz like we knew back in Chicago."

"I'm impressed." Kettie chuckled. "I pictured you as preferring more of a sweeter, softer style of jazz. Maybe even a waltz."

"Are you kidding me? Sophie and I spent many a night at the Friar's Inn on East Van Buren. Hot jazz and hard liquor, there was plenty of both. The best was on the South Side, though. Ain't no one can play jazz like the colored bands." Roman's fingers fluttered above the valves of an imaginary cornet pressed to his lips.

Jacob pulled his steel brush from the engine hood and rested it on the cowling. "Roman and Sophia were Chicagoans for a few years before returning to the farm."

"You mean you tasted the excitement of the Windy City, and you came back here?" Kettie furrowed her brow. "I find it difficult to believe anyone would do that."

"The Windy City," Roman snickered, "it's an ill wind that blows no one any good, or so the saying goes."

Jacob wiped the grease from his hands. "This engine won't take much but maybe a good cleaning and a tune-up. We'll still need to replace the propeller. It took a beating when it hit the ground – split it on both ends."

"It may be best just to order one." Roman opened the hood on the opposite side. "Be sure you know what you're doing with this engine, Jacob. Even the good ones are known for quitting in mid-flight, as well as just after take-off." He pushed the spark wires in seating their connections. "Those are the risks of flying." He closed the hood and ran his hand along the leading edge of the lower wing. "Once I patch the holes in the fabric, I'll mix up a batch of home-made dope to coat what needs sealing. Other than that, a little grease and oil, and she's ready to soar with the eagles."

Shifting through an assortment of pry bars in the corner of the garage, Jacob reached to catch the barrel of a falling rifle. "What do you have here?" The dust rolled into the air as he blew upon its blued steel. "Looks like a neglected Model 94 Winchester. You should take better care of your firearms."

"I forgot that was even there. I used to keep it handy for coyotes, or maybe a wolf."

Jacob stood the rifle in its corner. "I thought Grandpa killed the last wolf in these parts, when he was a kid?"

"So he says, but it's the strayed wolf you don't think will appear that is the dangerous one. He can suddenly materialize out of nowhere, and take a lethal nip before you even realize what's happening."

"Hey, Look! The previous ace left you a gift." Kettie tossed a balled up piece of leather at Jacob as she crawled from the cockpit. "It was under the seat. Try it on."

"An aviator's helmet." Jacob's finger poked through a cut along its side. "I wonder what caused this." He handed it to Roman.

Roman peered at the light through the hole. "They most likely pulled this off his head when they found him in the wreckage." He dropped it back into Jacob's hands. "You could ask him, if he wasn't dead."

The flight headgear bounced off the workbench and rolled next to the rifle's stock as Jacob shuddered and moved away.

Kettie searched through the box of phonograph records. Placing a disc on the turntable, she wound the spring tight and set the needle at the edge of the spinning wax. "I'll check on Sophia and Aggie, and then be back to help." The screen door popped against the frame as the piano introduction lead to the sweet, feminine vocals of a smooth melody.

Sorting through the toolbox, Jacob retrieved a wrench and approached the fuselage. "Uncle Roman, when will you teach me to fly the Jenny?"

Roman pointed at the work in progress and shrugged his shoulders. "She's got to fly before we get to fly."

Jacob nodded. "Was France the first time you took to the air?"

"Actually, Fort Omaha, Nebraska – learning to fly balloons. Once we crossed the pond, I spent most of the war in an observation balloon company near the front lines."

"Balloons, huh." Jacob smiled. "What was it like to fly one of those?"

"As tranquil as they may seem, it was very fast-paced. When the conditions were right, headquarters would request a look-see. The balloons were tethered with a steel cable to a truck on the ground. We would rise up some 3,000 to 4,000 feet." Roman's head tilted as he looked upward. "There, my partner and I would look out and over the lines, and see what the Huns were up to. Other times we would spot for the field artillery – tell them where to aim their cannons. We were so busy relaying what we saw to the ground crew that we really didn't have time to absorb the pleasures of flight."

"How did you manage to go from balloons to planes?"

"The balloon was nothing more than a big gasbag filled with hydrogen. They were easy pickin's for balloon buster pilots and their incendiary bullets. I watched many kites along the front lines burst into flames, and then one day it happened to me."

Jacob stopped and stared at Roman. "What did you do?"

"Nothing I could do, but jump over the side and ride my parachute to the ground. My partner wasn't so lucky."

"He didn't make it?"

"No. That's when I started having second thoughts about roasting in a ball of fire. The air service needed airplane pilots, so I volunteered to fly. I thought it was a good opportunity to get some payback for all of the times the Hun tried to burn my kite out of the sky, and the one time he did."

"And then the war ended."

"Yep. I trained in France and flew some ferrying duties, but like I've said, the war ended before I was able to fly my first combat mission." Roman stepped away from the plane and stared out into the pasture. The soft, gentle croon of the singer's voice filled the speechless void, as the world stood still for the moment. "Jacob, I need to be honest with you. I don't know if I can do this."

Jacob's wrench dropped to the ground. "But you just said the structure repairs were minor. If you don't want to patch the holes, I..."

"No. It has nothing to do with repairing the Jenny and making her flight worthy." Roman hesitated. "It's just that..."

"Just that what?"

Roman turned and looked at Jacob. "I don't know if I can fly the Jenny."

"You said they were basically all the same." Jacob pointed at the airplane. "You said any dumb idiot could fly one."

"It's not that I don't know how." He looked at the plane and then back at Jacob. "I...I don't think I can fly."

A puzzled look contorted Jacob's blank expression.

"I haven't slept one night through since we pulled this thing into the yard." Roman grasped the strut and looked beneath the upper wing. "The flaming balloons of the war have returned to my dreams. I wake up in a cold sweat, and crawl from my bed to the front porch, as though it's calling me. I sit on the steps and stare at the damned thing until the sun rises."

Jacob hung his head. "Uncle Roman, I'm sorry. I didn't know."

"It's no one's problem but my own." He shrugged his shoulders. "Years ago, I used to drink heavily to try and drown the nightmares from my mind. It helped some, but didn't always work. It wasn't until I quit the booze and moved back here, before the horrid visions eventually ceased their nightly visits." He patted his hand against the bowed, wooden brace. "Now, they've returned."

Jacob circled the plane as he absorbed Roman's troublesome disclosure, and contemplated a remedy to the dilemma. "We should sell the Jenny. Get rid of it."

"No." Roman shook his head. "That's not an option."

Jacob paused. "Then, what should we do?"

"Well, we shouldn't give up now. I said I couldn't fly the Jenny. I didn't say anything about you not flying her."

"Me fly the Jenny?" Jacob laughed. "Just how are you going to show me, if you can't even sit in the cockpit for a training flight? I don't see how it can be done."

"It's not that difficult, Jacob." Roman grabbed the padded cockpit rim. "Here, put yourself in the seat. I'll show you the controls. We'll begin working it from the ground and see where it goes. At least it's a start."

Jacob climbed into the rear, single seat compartment and grasped the control stick located before him. As Roman explained the coordinating of the stick movement with the foot bar in producing the pitch, roll, and yaw of the biplane, thoughts of coursing through billowy clouds and tracing the woven pattern of contiguous fields eclipsed absorbing the relevant instruction.

"You got that?" Roman rocked Jacob's shoulder in pulling his attention back to the cockpit. "Let's go over it again."

"No. No, I got enough of it." The wing ailerons and rear rudder waved in a harmonized movement as Jacob worked the controls. "How fast does this thing go?"

"Normal cruising speed is most likely around sixty miles per hour. Remember, always be aware of a good place to land. If that engine quits, and it will, you're going to need to bring it down safely, without wrecking the aircraft or killing yourself. One more thing to keep in mind, the most dangerous place for engine failure is just after leaving the ground. Slow speed, no control, and more than likely no place to land is a sure recipe for disaster."

"Are my partners waiting for my help in getting our flying business off the ground?" Kettie approached and handed each a glass of lemonade. "Maybe this will help, or would you prefer something with a little more of a kick."

Roman rolled the cool glass across his forehead. "You don't know how tempting that sounds right about now."

Lifting the glass to his lips, Roman noticed the trailing dust swirl of a dark automobile advancing up the long, dirt driveway. Racing through its gears, the vehicle accelerated within the staggered broken screams of its roaring engine. Reaching the edge of the yard, its spoke wheels seized, spinning the car to a sliding halt, as the ending hiss of the phonograph crept to a stop.

The car showed no signs of life, with only the low, purr of the engine's idle to indicate otherwise. Its soil coated windows concealed the occupants from view. Hesitant to approach, Roman glanced at the Winchester, propped in the corner, and then stepped toward the vehicle. "Can I help you with something?" He circled toward its front. "Do you need assistance in finding where you may be heading?"

The engine killed as the front passenger door unlatched and swung open. A black oxford shoe, draped with a pearl button white spat, planted itself upon the ground. The fine threads of an expensive suite followed. "If you wouldn't mind helping my driver, he tried a few shortcuts, and well, here we are." The man pulled the hat from his head and spun it onto the car seat. "We could use a little water, too."

"Water's over there." Roman nodded toward the pump perched above the stock tank. "Do you need help with bringing it up?"

The man shook his head. "No. He can use the exercise." A sudden snap of his fingers brought the driver from within. As both stared back, down the long driveway, a feminine voice returned their attention to the vehicle.

"Is someone going to help me out of this thing?" She yelled as she attempted to unlatch the back door. Two solid kicks sent the door swaying upon its hinges. The beads of her dress sparkled in the sunlight as she stepped out and straightened her hat. "For Christ's sake, are you both deaf? I've had to pee since we left, and do you think either one of you two, so called gentlemen, could take the time and pull your heads out of your gold-plated asses and remember how you treat a lady?"

The man looked at the driver and then nodded toward the vehicle. The driver made quick steps to its rear and pulled two glass containers from the trunk. Spinning the caps from their necks, he rested the bottoms on the bumper and waited as the clear liquid poured out upon the ground.

"Excuse me, sir." The woman approached Roman. "Do you mind if I use your john?" She pointed a beaded purse toward the house. "I've got to iron my shoelaces."

"You sure can, but our john is located over there." Roman pointed to a small building located at the end of a narrow path.

"You're kidding me. That's it?"

The man shook his head. "It's an outhouse, stupid. Go."

"If I could hold it, I would." She hurried down the pathway.

"Stay away from these men." Roman whispered to Jacob.

"But why?"

"Trust me, we want them out of here," he watched the woman give multiple slams to the outhouse door, "and all of their trash, too."

As Roman helped the driver fill the containers at the pump, the man wandered over to the Jenny. Looking up at the top wing, he rubbed the beard stubble upon his face. "Looks like you've got yourself some kind of aeroplane here. You barnstormers or something?"

"No, not barnstormers." Jacob stood next to him. "If we can get it to fly, then we may take a go at offering rides."

"It doesn't fly?"

"Not in its present condition."

Jacob followed the man back to the automobile. "Your car has got a healthy layer of dust covering it. You must have been driving for some time."

The man pulled out a half-pint of gin from is pocket. Removing the cap, he glanced down the driveway, and then pressed the bottle to his lips.

Jacob looked down the road as well. "Whereabouts were you coming from?"

The man's thumb pointed to the north as he swallowed the liquor. Lifting the legs of his trousers, he sat down upon the vehicle's running boards, and took another good sized gulp from the bottle. "We're on our way back to Chicago."

Jacob sat down next to the man, with Kettie sliding in at his side. "Chicago? You're a long way from home."

The man swirled the bottle toward Jacob. "It's not too bad of a jaunt."

Jacob grimaced as the gin burned its way down his throat. He passed the bottle back to the man, who in turn offered it to Kettie. "The guys make this trip a couple of times a year." He pulled it back as Kettie waved it away. "I never ride along, but the boss didn't want any screw ups on this one, so I got the lucky draw." He took another drink.

"Jacob was on his way to Chicago, that was, until we got the airplane." Kettie pushed her shoulder into Jacob's. "Instead of living there, it will now become just a stop on our way to somewhere else."

The man looked at the plane and then at Jacob. "You really know how to fix that thing?"

"I've never worked on one before, but the way I see it, an engine's an engine." Jacob pointed at the Jenny and then at the automobile.

"If anyone can get it off the ground, it's Jacob." Kettie added. "I can vouch for him – I'm actually a recipient of his work."

"I like that attitude. You don't see much of that in the city." The man twisted the cap onto the gin bottle and tucked it into his pocket. "It's too bad you're not coming to Chicago, we could use a man like you. If you ever change your mind, look me up. There's lots of work available if you know the right people."

"I had a job lined up. It paid good and it was steady work."

"Steady work? Doing what?"

"I'm not exactly sure, but it had to do with paint in a factory."

"Paint?" The man laughed. "Hell, forget paint. I'm talking about real work paying real dough. On top of it all, lots of respect. People will part the way when you walk down the street, and you never wait in line for anything. Those you do business with will go out of their way to make sure you are satisfied with everything. I mean everything."

"What would he do?" Kettie asked.

"Like I said, there's lots of work." He pointed at the Jenny. "You like pulling wrenches?"

"If something's not working, I guess you could say I enjoy the challenge."

"There you go. We've got vehicles that need looking after. The boss was even talking about getting one of those areoplanes. If you prove your worth, things could be good. Things could be very good."

Jacob looked at Kettie. "How about Kettie? Could she come, too?"

"There are plenty of dolls in the city, but you can do what you want."

The liquid splashed out of the narrow opening as Roman dropped the water on the ground next to the driver's brimming container. Standing at the vehicle's edge, he caught Jacob's attention, and nodded him toward the Jenny, and away from the man, but Jacob's head shook in defiance. The sudden unfolding of a map summoned Roman to the driver in fulfilling his previous offer of assistance in determining their whereabouts.

"Chicago is a big city." Jacob continued. "How would I go about getting a hold of you?"

The man fumbled through his pocket and produced a silver dollar, and then felt again, this time displaying the shiny copper-nickel plating of a pistol cartridge. Pressing the shell against his knee, he carved about the casing, using the coin's reeded edge. "Here." He flipped the round high into the air. "Show this around. Someone will point you in the right direction."

Jacob reached out to grab the tumbling piece. "What is it?"

"It's my card." He shoved the coin back into his pocket.

Before the shell hit Jacob's palm, Kettie snatched it out of the air. She pulled her thumb across the scratches and read the inscription aloud. "Jacob." She held it out so he could see. "He wrote your name on it."

"Hang onto it, kid. As long as it's never chambered, you're safe."

Jacob chuckled. "You mean, like an amulet – it protects from evil?"

"I've never been into that hocus pocus hooey, but I do know one thing, those who have kept theirs close to their person, are all still above ground."

The screen door slammed. Pushing Aggie to remain on the porch, Roman hopped down the steps with a brown paper bag crumpled in his hand. "My missus made some sandwiches for you to eat on your way. Sorry you can't stick around."

The man glanced at the driver and nodded. "Fill it."

"Now?"

"I said fill it. We need it functional and ready before we get there."

The vehicle's trunk lid bounced against the hinge stops as the driver reached inside the dark opening. A series of short grunts rolled a water cooled machine gun into his lap. Sitting on the rear bumper, he removed the plug and began filling the barrel's jacket with the water pumped from the well.

Roman handed the sack to the man, and then froze at the sight of the military weapon. "M1917?"

The man remained silent as he observed the water pour into the plug hole.

"How did you come about that?" Roman asked.

"The National Guard."

"I didn't know they were giving out water cooled machine guns." He looked at the man. "You enlist?"

The man laughed. "A soldier had two guns, but the company paperwork said they only had one. Now the paperwork's correct, the soldier has a little extra veteran's pay, and the boss is extremely pleased. Everybody won. It's not often that happens."

"You know they tend to need those things in case of war, don't you?"

"If I remember right, we just finished the war to end all wars. Hell, it was in all the newspapers. If the paper's print it, then it must be true. If it's true, then the army doesn't have a need for it, does it."

"Here, little girl." The woman placed a quarter on the porch railing before Aggie. "The john was all out of paper, so I had to tear pages from the Sears and Roebuck catalog you left sitting on the bench. I apologize if I ruined your book. That should cover your troubles in getting a new one."

"Come on, let's go." She approached the man. "I told you before. I'm tired and hungry, and just want to get back home."

"Here, eat this and shut up." He shoved the paper bag into her hands.

"What's this?" She unfolded the sack and pushed the sandwich to his face. "You promised me fine dining, expensive wine, and dancing till dawn." The bread slices slid from his shirt and bounced off his shoes. "I haven't had anything decent to eat in the last three days, and you give me this?"

The man stared at her. "Be polite to our hosts."

"I've got nothing against these people." She pointed the sack at Roman. "I'm tired, and I just want to leave and go home, damn it." The remaining contents of the bag emptied as it flew through the air and tumbled across the yard.

"The lady has a valid request." Roman asserted. "You should leave now, otherwise you may end up driving in the dark. I wouldn't trust any of these twisted and pothole filled roads past sunset."

"We're in no hurry to go. We'll stay, maybe catch some sleep."

"There are much better places along the main roads to sleep."

The man stepped toward Roman. "Your ears must have separated from your brain. We'll go when we're good and ready."

The quick mechanical movement of a rifle's lever action sounded from the garage doorway. "My husband's ears are just fine." Sophia's aim encompassed all three visitors. "He's just a little concerned you might be close to wearing out your welcome."

As heads turned toward Sophia, the driver's hand slowly crept up his suit jacket, released the top button, and disappeared beneath the lapel.

Crack! The Winchester responded, followed by an immediate ejection and reload of a fresh cartridge into its chamber.

Roman spun around. "I wouldn't do that, mister. She'll send you to God, and we both know where he'll drop you."

Receiving a conceding nod from the man, the driver gently lowered his hand along his trouser seam.

"I know you, don't I?" The man's head tilted. "Sure, the both of you."

"You are mistaken." Roman shook his head. "We're just a couple of dirt farmers trying to scratch a living in the sticks of the Dakotas."

The man glanced at Sophia and then back at Roman. "Sure, okay. If that's what you want, I'll buy it."

"Let's get out of here." The driver pressed. "This wasn't part of the plan. We got the water. We're done."

"Not so fast, wheelman." Sophia placed the front sights on the driver as her finger applied pressure upon the trigger.

"Let them go, Sophie." Roman sidestepped toward her.

"But Roman."

"No, let them go." The corner of his mouth pulled into a half smile.

"We don't want no trouble, miss." The driver pleaded. "Like I said, we just came for the water. Really."

Roman nodded at the man. "Go. Start your car and get back on the road." He glanced at the sun. "It's too damned hot to bury three gunny sacks in the coolies, today."

The man squinted as he looked up. "Or four...or five." He returned the nod. "Okay, we'll leave. You never saw us...and we never saw you."

The driver yanked the back door's handle and swung it open as the woman reached the vehicle. She stepped her foot inside. "I guess I should have eaten the sandwich."

"Just get in the car and keep your mouth shut." The man warned as the woman slid across the seat, and the door latched.

The Winchester's aim held steady before the vehicle's dust trail. Following the car's path, Sophia continued a firm tightness upon the trigger.

"You can put it down, Sophie." Roman moved toward her.

Sophia maintained her firing posture.

"They're gone, now." Roman reached up and peeled the rifle from her hands. "There's no need to worry." He squeezed the trigger, while gently lowering the hammer. "We're safe."

"Damn it, Roman," a tear rolled down her cheek, "you said they would never come. You said they would never find us."

"It's not them, Sophie." He nestled her head within his shoulder. "Nobody's coming. I promise. Nobody will ever come."

The tender sentiments drew in Jacob, Kettie, and Aggie. They watched as the vehicle turned from the driveway and shifted gears in accelerating up the road.

"Uncle Roman, did you know those people?" Aggie asked.

"No. I don't know who they were, but I do know what they are – products of an ill wind."

Jacob reached into his pocket and revealed the pistol cartridge to Roman. "He etched my name into the casing of this shell." It rolled down his fingers and spun into his palm. "He wanted me to look him up if I would ever get to Chicago."

Snatching the round from Jacob's hand, Roman flung it across the yard, burying the gangster's invitation within the manure and mud of the hog pen. "I told you to stay away from those men, Jacob. Now, you understand why."

"But it was just a keepsake." Jacob stepped toward the wooden confinement fence. "I would never go there and work for them."

Roman grabbed his shoulder. "Leave it be, Jacob. It's a tease, a draw, something to gnaw at your senses when life takes an unexpected turn. Just remember, even a good man can be easily wiled from what he truly knows is right."

As Jacob returned to the task of readying the biplane, Kettie followed behind, while maintaining a darting eye on the shell's last observed whereabouts. A tiny sparkle emerged from the shadows. She glanced over her shoulder at the others entering the house, and then at Jacob sorting through the tools on the workbench. Allured by the enticing flash, she rushed to the pen and slipped between the wooden boards in search of the copper-nickel cartridge. Sifting through the hog excrement with the tips of her shoes, she freed the shell from a dung pile, and wiped its surface clean.

"Jacob." She slipped behind him and smiled as he turned. Cupping the round within his hand, she reached up and pressed her lips against his.

Hearing the phonograph needle dance on the record's edge, he returned the smile and quickly dropped the amulet back into his pocket.

Chapter 11

SNAP! A quick spark ignited the match's head into a sudden burst of light. While permeating a pungent, sulfur stench throughout the room, its narrow, blue flame quickly faded with each successive flicker. Growing impatient, Hugh inverted the matchstick and pulled the fragile glow over his pipe's chamber. Drawing a few steady puffs through the bore, the flame completely vanished before the tobacco had time to catch fire.

"For Pete's sake, Em." He tossed the smoldering splinter of pine into a glass ashtray. "Where on Earth did you find these matches? I couldn't light gasoline with these, if I struck the whole box at once."

"They may be a touch damp, Dear. It's been an awful sultry day." Emma wound a remnant of wool string into a small ball as she maintained the steady motion of the wooden rocking chair.

Hugh pulled another matchstick from his shirt pocket and pointed it at her. "I don't believe it has anything to do with the humidity. It's these matches. Poor quality. They just don't make them like they used to." Noticing a partial knitted cap resting on Emma's yarn bag, he raised an eyebrow. "We've just finished with spring. Aren't you pushing things a little?"

Emma chuckled. "It's for our study club's winter clothing drive. We're sending hats, scarves, and mittens to the children in Europe. They're still having a difficult time recovering from the war. It's always the children who end up suffering the most."

"I admire your enthusiasm, but you seem to devote an enormous amount of time and effort into these things. I think they purposely take advantage of you." Hugh tossed another chard matchstick into the ashtray and bounced his pipe against the holder. "That sounds like an ambitious project. Who's running ramrod on that operation, anyway?"

"Betty Tucker. She's asking that all donations be submitted by this weekend for bulk shipment overseas."

"Betty Tucker? Why, that's Ray's wife, isn't it?"

Emma nodded her head while looping single stitches across one another.

"She can't keep her hands off of anything." Hugh shook his head. Taking a quick look over each shoulder, he leaned toward Emma. "You know what I heard?"

"No Dear. What's that?"

Hugh glanced a second time in both directions. "I heard that Ray joined the Klan."

The rhythmic motion of the rocker stopped dead. "Hugh, you know I don't want you talking of such things in this house. It scares the children."

"Ah, the children have gone to bed." Hugh sat back in his chair. "I'm just saying that I didn't think he was that way – you know – a Catholic hater. He's always been friendly and pleasant to you and me."

"Stop it. Just stop it. I don't want to hear any more."

"But we can't keep ignoring it. We need to talk about it. We can't just…"

"I said stop it!" Emma slammed her knitting on top of the bag. "Little Willie is scared to death of them. Sure, we try our best to shield the children when we can, like pulling them from the parade route before the Klan marches by, but that doesn't stop him and his school friends from teasing each other about ghost coming to snatch them in the middle of the night. He has bad dreams! Nightmares! He wakes up screaming they are burning him." She stood up and wiped a tear rolling down her cheek. "Don't you understand? He's afraid…*I'm* afraid. And what sickens me most, is everyone knows they are planning this big meeting to be held right here, in our very own town, and there is nothing that anyone is willing to do to stop this madness."

Hugh pushed himself from the chair and stepped toward Emma. Taking her into his arms, he brushed away a tear stream moving down her face. "Please don't cry, Dear. I'm trying my best. I really am. The priest, and those in the church I've spoken with, are worried that attempts to stop the meeting will only result in harsh retaliation. It wasn't that long ago the Klan shattered the stained glass windows and vandalized the Saint John's Catholic Church in Groton, and that's just a few miles down the road. With that still fresh in their minds, they fear the Klan will follow through on their threats to set fire to the school, or worse yet, they may even take their frustrations out on our parishioners."

"But what about the mayor? He can put a stop to this. Why doesn't he do something?"

"Well, when Ralph and I attended the city council meeting the other night..."

"Ralph? You didn't tell me you took Ralph with you."

"I called Ralph to explain why I would not be in attendance at the Oddfellow's meeting that night. It really surprised me when he asked if he could come along. Especially when I spoke with others and none were willing to go with me. Actually, when all was said and done, I was glad he was there."

"Why is that?"

"When it was my turn to address the council, some in the audience began tapping their rings against the wooden armrests of their chairs."

"Tapping their rings against the chairs? Why would they do that?"

"Oh, I believe it was a subtle reminder to the mayor and some city council members as to where their allegiance should align. I don't know if it was fear or favoritism, but when the tapping started, the council refused to take up the matter, stating the Klan meeting location was planned just outside of the city limits. The mayor had a look of relief on his face and quickly suggested it was a county matter, and moved to the next order of business. It seems the people in this town are either frightened of the Klan or they support them."

"What did you do?"

"Well, I'm not proud of myself. I said a few things I probably shouldn't have, but there was not much we could do. Ralph evened the score though."

"How did he do that?"

"When the next person addressed the city council, Ralph smiled at me and winked. I thought he might not have understood what just happened until I heard his wedding band tap against the armrest."

"No." Emma giggled. "Ralph did that?"

"Yeah. As he tapped, some of the others in the audience began tapping as if to counter. The council members looked like lost sheep. They didn't know if they should agree on the issue at hand or not. Ralph continued the little game throughout the remainder of the meeting. They tabled everything – probably the least productive meeting of the year. I swear, I don't believe some of those people could even get off the toilet without someone telling them which hand to use."

The creaking of loose oak boards, echoing within the open staircase, cast a silence upon the conversation as both heads turned. Standing quietly on the landing, a few steps from the floor, one of the children politely waited.

"Susie, what are you doing out of bed?" Emma cleared her throat as she hurried toward the steps.

"I need to tell Daddy something." The little girl smiled.

"Tell Daddy something? Why, you should be in bed. And what are you doing wearing your Sunday best? You will be in big trouble, little lady, if you dirty those clothes."

"But I need to tell Daddy something."

"What is it, Honey?" Hugh spoke up. "Go ahead, tell me, but then you need to change back into your pajamas and go right to bed."

"I wanted to tell you I borrowed a penny from my piggy bank." Susie opened her purse and held up a shiny coin for Hugh to examine. "See? Just one penny, and I will pay it back, right after I do more chores for Mommy."

"A penny?" Hugh scratched his head. "Why do you need a penny?"

"I want to give it to Jesus. You know, an offering."

Puzzled, Hugh looked at Emma. "This isn't making any sense. Do you suppose she is sleepwalking?"

"No. No, she looks fine."

"How about a fever? Check her temperature, but be careful, she might be sleeping."

"I haven't heard of anything going around." Emma placed her hand on Susie's forehead. "No, she doesn't feel feverish."

"Jesus is coming." Susie continued. "And I just wanted to give him an offering."

"I knew it. I knew it." Hugh tossed his newspaper into the chair. "It was only a matter of time. It's those Protestant kids. Some of her friends have got her all worked up about Jesus returning."

Emma knelt down and grasped the little girl's shoulders. "Susie, what would make you think Jesus is coming?"

"The angels are here." Susie smiled and pointed through the flowing window curtains at the movement of white cloaks roaming about the front yard. "See?"

Hesitant to look, Emma felt a wisp of cold brush against her back as the fine hair on her arms began to lift. Understanding completely, but refusing to accept, she hung her head, closed her eyes, and prayed whatever intrigued her young daughter would no longer be there when she looked up.

Slowly raising her head, she opened her eyes to the unsteady flicker of fire dancing from the crown of one rag-bound torch to the next. Watching in horror as hooded figures struggled to erect a large, wooden cross within the confines of her fieldstone-encircled, flower garden, her silent screams went unheard as paralyzed vocal folds constricted her airflow. As a burly man lifted a steel sledgehammer, the shock building within Emma's system finally released as the large head connected with a wooden stake aimed at the cross's base. "*Hugh!*"

"Ah!" Hugh echoed the distress of horror, having discovered two sets of dark eyeholes peering from white hoods through the narrow side window.

"Mommy, Daddy." Susie hopped down the remaining few steps and darted for the front entrance. "Don't be afraid of the angels."

Hugh grabbed Susie's hand as she turned the doorknob, and pulled her away. "Em, get Willie and take the children out the backdoor to the neighbors."

Hypnotized by the surreal images of hooded men transforming the front yard into an Abaddon of their desire, Emma could not bring herself to look away. Through social gatherings, she heard of the Klan's disturbing actions, but never thought she would ever experience firsthand the terror induced by their presence. This could not be happening. No, not to them.

"Em! Em, please listen to me." Hugh pulled her face towards his in breaking the trance.

"It's not for us, Hugh. It can't be. They made a mistake. Go out there and tell them they are at the wrong house."

"Listen to me. You need to get Willie and run the children next door."

The handbrake on the old Ford truck forced a series of high-pitched squeals as the vehicle slowed to a sudden halt. Pulsating behind a short row of cars parked along the dark, side street, a set of yellow headlights dimmed before cutting out completely when the rough idling engine choked to a stop.

"Quinn, I see them! I see them! You see them?"

"Yeah, Toad, I see them. Looks like we aren't too late. Just remember, don't take your hood off and don't say a thing to anyone unless asked. If you listen and do what you're told, they just might start taking you along on more of these burnings."

"Okay, Quinn. Okay, I'll listen and do what they tell me to do. Can we go now?"

"Settle down, Toad." Quinn shook his head. "Boy, I've never seen anyone so anxious."

As the two men stepped from the truck, the light, reflecting from the partially covered full moon, summoned a brilliant glow from within the white threads of their robes.

"You must have stitched some fancy needlework on this." Quinn knelt down and shifted Toad's robe into place. "It looks like the entire bottom half is missing."

"Mrs. Sweeney sewed it for me. You know, A.J.'s mom."

"Yeah, I know. I don't think they actually intended for you to wear it though. You're not an official member."

"I'll soon be. Wes says they are still waiting on special word from the Atlanta Headquarters, you know, because of...because of my size."

"Yeah. Yeah, I know."

"I miss A.J., Quinn. He was my friend. He never let people say bad things about me. Do you miss A.J.?"

"Yeah, I think we all do a little. Come on now, let's get going." Quinn looked up the street at the small crowd beginning to assemble. "We're already late."

Slamming the pickup door, the two rushed to join the others.

"Oh no! I forgot something." Toad shouted as he stopped midway and made a quick dash back to the truck.

"Toad, wait." Quinn slowed, threw his hands into the air, and continued toward the group.

The steel head of the sledgehammer splintered the jagged edge of the final stake as the shim penetrated the soil and stabilized the large, wooden cross. Tugging at its tightly wrapped, kerosene saturated burlap, the Klansman located a loose fold in preparation to set the structure ablaze.

"It's nice that you could join us." One of the Klansmen spouted as Quinn approached. "Can we start the meeting now, or would you prefer we…" Surprised at the sudden appearance of a half-sized ghost stepping from Quinn's shadow, the man recoiled in protest.

"It ain't Quinn's fault, it's mine." Toad patted an irregular wound coil draped over his shoulder. "I almost forgot the rope."

The man stopped and stared. "Rope? We don't need no rope, you idiot. What do you think this is, a hanging?"

"Who brought the Toad?" Another spoke up.

"He showed up at my house, ready to go. I couldn't say no." Quinn explained.

"He ain't worth two pinches of coon shit in the daylight." The man continued. "How much help do you think he's gonna be out here, in the dark?"

"He doesn't mean any harm. He's just a little slow to catch on at times, that's all. I couldn't say no."

"It's too late now. You brought him. You babysit him." The man poked a boney finger into Quinn's chest. "If he causes any problems, just remember, there are two ends to that rope, and I'll drag one of you from each."

Quinn helped remove the rope from Toad's shoulder and set it out of the way. "You need to stay next to me. Don't say or do anything unless I tell you. Do you understand?"

"Yeah, I understand. I just wanted to help."

"Is everyone here?" Wes asked as he looked over the group in estimating the attendance.

"Yeah, I believe so." The man answered. "All who said they'd make it. I sent a few around to watch the back."

"That's good. Gather the rest of the men and we'll get this meeting started."

Hugh blotted the sweat from his brow as he listened to Emma's footsteps hurrying the children down the staircase, and toward the backdoor. Feeling somewhat relieved they were safely on their way to the neighbor's, he reached up and pulled the double-barreled shotgun from the wall rack and cracked the breach open.

Retrieving a box of shells from the drawer, he watched in disbelief as the cardboard split open, spreading the contents, like marbles, rolling across the hardwood floor. Dropping to his knees, he quickly snatched a handful of shells as they spun under the desk, and out of his reach. Juggling them in his hand, each slipped, one by one, from his sweaty grip and bounced out of sight. Frustrated, Hugh plopped himself upon the floor, and tightly clenched the last remaining shell in his hand.

"Calm down. Just calm down." He spoke quietly as he stared at the shell in his hand. "You can do this. You just need to calm down and steady yourself."

He drew in a deep breath, looked down at the shotgun, and exhaled. The forced movement of air lifted a light covering of dust from the barrel. As the particles slowly drifted about, he thought of the pheasants and grouse gliding through the seasonal warm air during last fall's hunt. Walking side by side with his friends and neighbors, through the cornfields and grasslands, they flushed numerous upland game birds from the dense cover, dropping many at shoulder height. With the breach of his shotgun open, and a shell in hand, he now prepared to defend himself from some of those same people. How could he do it? Pull the trigger and possibly injure or kill someone he knew, or thought he knew. His stomach began to churn as the notion gnawed at his mind.

"Hugh Langley!" A deep voice called from outside of the house. "You are hereby summoned to present yourself in whole to the Knights of the Ku Klux Klan."

Hugh looked up at the rolling shades of orange light projecting against the sheer, window drapes and shook his head. "May God help us all." Fumbling the last shell into one of the open barrels, he snapped the breach shut.

Hugh planted the butt of the shotgun on the floor and pushed himself to his feet. The room slowly tipped on end. With his guts stirring uncontrollably, he steadied himself along the furniture, while staggering to the front door. Multiple beads of sweat rolled down his glistening face. Feeling a sudden fullness occupy the back of his throat, he dropped the shotgun next to the door, grabbed the lip of a nearby ceramic planter, and heaved the contents of his stomach across the potting soil.

"Come on, Susie. We need to hurry." Emma pulled the puzzled, little girl along by her arm as they rushed through the house. Shifting Willie from hip to hip, she let go of Susie's hand and lightly nudged the backdoor curtain to one side. Peering into the moonlit, shrub-encircled backyard, she attempted to define a clear path – an escape route leading to the house next door.

"Ah!" Surprised by the sudden appearance of a hooded Klansman walking up the steps, Emma screamed before catching herself as the man attempted to look into the window. With her back against the door, she slid to the floor, and pulled her children close in her arms. "This isn't happening. This can't be happening. No, not to us. What have we done to deserve this?"

"Mommy, why can't we just invite them in, you know, and talk?"

"Shhh...Susie, you don't understand." Emma whispered. "They aren't who you think they are. Please be quiet."

"But Mommy..." Susie's small voice muffled as Emma cupped her hand over the little girl's mouth. "Shhh!"

"Hugh Langley, you are hereby summoned to present yourself in whole to the Knights of the Ku Klux Klan." The voice called once again.

The blued steel, twin barrels of the shotgun inched their way through the widening gap between the front door and its frame. As the brass door handle tapped against the plaster of the inside wall, Hugh stepped to the threshold, and gazed across the front porch at a dozen white robed men carrying burning torches at the edge of his yard. Fending off the waves of nausea, he hoped they would not notice the uncontrollable tremble of his gun barrel.

"I suggest you all..." Hugh hesitated for a moment as he cleared his throat and wiped the burning sweat from his eyes. "I suggest you all get back into your trucks...and leave...leave before someone gets himself hurt."

Resembling marble statues, the men remained steady with only an occasional flutter of white cloth to indicate otherwise. Unsure if the strength of his voice carried across the lawn, Hugh prepared to reissue the warning as he stepped through the doorway. "Leave now...leave before..." A hand reached from just beyond the doorway, grabbed the twin barrels of the shotgun, and pulled Hugh out of the house and onto the front porch. *Boom!* The pulled trigger fired a circular pattern of lead shot into the air, ripping a hole through the porch roof.

In a swift, precise movement, the Klansman pried the smoking shotgun from Hugh's hands, swung the wooden stock around, and cracked its butt against Hugh's face. The force of the blow knocked Hugh from the porch and sent him rolling across the lawn, and into the fieldstone-encircled flowerbed.

"Leave now?" The Klansman cracked the breach open and ejected the smoldering shell. "Why, the meeting hasn't even started yet." He threw the shotgun into the leaved shrubbery bordering the house.

"Hugh! Hugh!" Emma rushed onto the front porch clutching Willie beneath her arm. Discovering Hugh's motionless body straddling the flowerbed stone, her knees weakened as she watched a stream of blood beginning to trickle from his nose and mouth. "No! No! You shot him! You killed my husband!"

"Ah, he's not dead." The Klansman forced her down onto the porch decking. "He's just a little knocked out. That's all." He gave a quick signal, sending two of the others toward Hugh. "You can thank us for stopping him. The damned fool just might have hurt someone."

Hugh felt his body break contact with the ground as a sharp tug upon his arms pulled him to his feet. With each successive beat of his heart, a general numbness about his face gradually transformed to an agonizing pain. Rolling his eyes, his lids blinked repeatedly in an attempt to focus his vision on one approaching white figure, passing the two departing.

"Mr. Langley," the form stopped directly in front of him, "it's so nice that you could honor us with your presence on this beautiful star filled evening." A scattering of laughter erupted from beyond his view.

Sporadic vapors of kerosene penetrated Hugh's nostrils. Its mild irritation gradually slowed the wild spinning within his head. As Hugh watched the man tug upon the cross's saturated burlap cloth, he suddenly realized the bleak situation at hand, dropped down upon his knees, and hung his head. "No, God. Please, no."

The Klansman grasped a handful of hair in cocking Hugh's head back, and stared nose-to-nose into Hugh's watering eyes. Swinging a second hand through, causing Hugh to flinch, the man retrieved a matchstick from Hugh's shirt pocket, and struck it against the wooden base. Foom! The cross burst into flames. Raising his arms into the air, the man addressed his fellow Klansmen. "This special meeting of the Knights of the Ku Klux Klan will now come to order."

"No, you've got the wrong house. We've done nothing wrong." Emma pleaded from the porch, but her cries fell upon deaf ears as the group's members repeated versus spoken by their leader. Tears welled in her eyes. Noticing light radiating from some of the surrounding houses, she attempted one last time to rally support for her family. "Help us! Alice, Bob, Fran, someone please help us!" A feeling of hopelessness overtook her as she watched a cascade of vanishing lights and drawn curtains ripple down the street.

Abandoned by those she once called friends and neighbors, Emma pulled Willie closer and suddenly realized, during the terrifying events of the dreadful night, she misplaced one child. "Susie! Where's Susie?" She felt the Klansman's heavy hand against the back of her head as she attempted to stand. Lying helpless upon the porch, she began to weep. "Oh, please. Please don't hurt my Susie."

Standing quietly on the back stoop, Susie extended her index finger and poked it against the Klansman's white rode.

"Ah!" The man leaped from his seated position, and spun halfway around in midair, before landing on his feet. Grasping his chest, while catching his breath, he discovered the little girl, startled by his unexpected reaction. "What are you trying to do young lady, give me a heart attack? Don't you know it's not polite to sneak up on someone and scare them half to death?"

"I'm sorry. But I wasn't trying…"

"You weren't trying? I'll tell you what you weren't trying. You weren't trying to put me in a coffin. That's what you weren't trying to do, I'll bet." The man tilted his head slightly as the little girl displayed a shiny penny for him to take. "What's this for?"

"Can you please give this to Jesus for me?"

"Jesus?"

"Yes, it's okay. I asked my dad."

The man scratched his head. "Oh, I really think you should take it to church on Sunday and give it to him, yourself."

"But, aren't you an angel?"

"Huh? Angel?" The man looked down at his white robe. "Oh. Oh, no. No, I'm no angel." He pulled the hood from his head and chuckled. "If I were, I would most likely be a lost one at best."

Susie wrinkled her face. "If you're not an angel, then what are you doing here?"

The man sat back upon the stoop and hung his head. "To tell you the truth, young lady, I've been sitting here trying to figure that very thing out, myself."

Susie hopped down a step and sat next to the man. "What's your name?"

"Name? Oh, my name's Ray."

"My name's Susan Marie Langley, but everyone just calls me Susie. My mom says I was named after one of my grandmothers. She drove a covered wagon. She's dead now. I wish I could have known her, you know, because we have the same name. Do you have any children?"

"Huh? Children? Yeah, three. Oh." Ray laughed. "And one on the way."

"Do they go to school?"

"Raymond Jr. does. The others are still too young."

"I have a friend named Raymond. He doesn't go to my school. He goes to the big school. He said I can be the first to join his tree house club when he builds it."

"That sounds like junior. He's been asking about that tree house for some time now, but I just haven't the time to sit down and talk with him about it. Seems like every time I turn around, there's always some darned meeting to attend."

"Why do you need to attend meetings?"

"It's a requirement of the fraternal organizations I belong to."

"Fratnal..."

"Fraternal organizations. Clubs. People coming together to support the communities they live in. One or two are fine, but it seems that just about every month, someone is coming up with a new club to join. It's almost ridiculous."

"Why do you want to join all the clubs?"

"My boss says it's good for business, but to tell you the truth, I'm thinking it has more to do with my wife. She says I need to be involved in all of these clubs. I'm not sure if it's for her benefit of joining the auxiliaries, or if she just wants me out of the house."

"How many clubs are you in?"

"Oh, I lose track." He chuckled. "Probably all of them. I suppose I shouldn't blame it all on her. The members put a lot of pressure on each other to join the other clubs, too. The last one now has been the Klan. I made the mistake of telling my wife about it and she told me I needed to join. I tried explaining to her that all of these clubs consist of the same members. Sometimes I go to meetings and I'm not actually sure which club I'm attending until someone breaks out in song or recites a verse."

"What did she say when you told her that?"

Ray pinched the white cloth of his robe and then threw his hands in the air.

"If you help Raymond build the tree house, you wouldn't have to join his club, unless you wanted to."

"Oh, young lady, that's one club I would be very happy to join."

"Are you sure you don't want the penny?"

"You place that shiny coin back into your purse. I'm sure the Klan has enough. They practically bled me dry when I joined this outfit."

Hugh glanced at the solidified tar painting the side of a five-gallon, steel bucket standing beside one of the Klansmen. Even from that distance, its heavy, petroleum stench cried out a declaration of the doom to come. Beaten, both physically and emotionally, Hugh's thoughts remained on the safety of his family. How could he ever forgive himself if something happened to them, and all because of him? His friends warned him not to add to the trouble that already existed. He did not listen. The priest said that it would all end in time. He refused to wait. His wife, Emma, asked him not to speak of the Klan. He chastised them, both publicly and privately. Now, the invisible monster whom he taunted without imprudence, prepared for its long awaited vengeance in Hugh's own front yard.

"I know I've said some things," Hugh cleared his throat, "some things that I should have just kept to myself." He looked up at the man in white. "Allow me to apologize…apologize to anyone that I offended. Please, stop all this from happening, and I swear, I swear I will never speak against the Klan for as long as I live. So help me God. I swear."

The man chuckled. "A confession to the hangman may benefit the soul, Langley, but the noose squeezes just as tight."

"No, no, please." Hugh wiped the tears from his face with folded hands. "My family, please spare my family from any harm. I'll do anything…anything you ask. Just don't hurt my family."

The starched cotton snapped as the hooded man threw his arms to the moonlit sky. About to speak, he felt a quick tug at his robes from another Klansmen in pulling him to the side. "Your Excellency."

"What's going on? What the devil do you want, Reverend?" The hooded man pointed back at Hugh Langley. "As you can see, we are kind of in the middle of things here."

"That is what I need to speak with you about, Wes." The Reverend Woodard placed his hand on Wes's back and walked him a few additional steps away. "This may be an excellent opportunity that we should at least explore."

"Opportunity? I'm not following." Wes pulled from the reverend's shallow hold. "Let's just get this thing over with. It's been a long time coming."

"Just hear me out. As you can agree, for some time now, Langley has been quite a large thorn in the Klan's side. He is most undeniably our biggest adversary."

"Yes, and after tonight, he'll think twice before shooting his big mouth off again."

"This is true, but suppose…just suppose we take it one step further. Suppose we actually bring him over to our side. Make him a member."

Wes pulled his head back. "You mean, petition for Langley to join the Klan! Are you out of your mind? He's a Catholic. We don't want his kind. Sorry, Reverend, but it's like they say – the only way to cure a catholic, is to kill him."

"Wes, it's been done before." The reverend stepped in and placed his hand on Wes's shoulder. "He meets the criteria of being white and native born. We just need to see where his allegiance lies."

Wes shook his head. "No. No. It will never work. Not for him or us."

"Think about it." The reverend squeezed his shoulder. "You can hurt this man and continue to scare his kind away from the Klan, or you can bring him in and provide a gateway for others to follow. For the benefit of the Klan, I do believe we should at least try."

Wes glanced at the shell of a man whimpering on both knees, and then back at Woodard. "Alright, Reverend. I know I'm going to regret this, but you've got the stage for five minutes." He shook a finger into the reverend's face. "If he's not making plans to attend the next Klan meeting by the time you're through, the tar comes out and we finish this thing."

Snap! The sharp flick of Wes's fingers summoned two Klansmen in aiding Hugh to his feet.

"Unfurl the Colors!" A cry emanated from the crowd as the remaining men stiffened to attention.

As the star filled blue field appeared from within the red and white stripes and danced about the flicker of the burning cross, Wes's right hand raised to cover his heart with his fellow Klansmen mirroring his movement.

"I pledge allegiance to the flag," all voices cried out as they removed their hands from their hearts in pointing their arms toward the flowing colors, "of the United States of America, and to the Republic for which it stands, one nation, indivisible, with liberty and justice for all."

The reverend approached Hugh. "Mr. Langley, in considering your dire request for leniency in this difficulty that you brought upon yourself, it has been decided that we just may be able to offer a resolution that would spare you from any remaining...displeasure."

Woodard began to circle Hugh. "First, you must agree to enroll your children in the local public school."

"Take my kids out of the Catholic School?" Hugh's head turned in following the reverend.

"Are you an American, Mr. Langley?"

"What?"

"Are you an American?"

"Yes, of course I am."

"Prove your loyalty to this great nation by supporting the public school, and the values and patriotism that it instills in our young. Trust me. Your children will thank you for it."

The Reverend Woodard stopped before Hugh, and then looked down into his befuddled expression. "We as Klansmen understand that America is a protestant country. It was protestant in the beginning, has been protestant in its history, and is protestant in its destiny. You must therefore renounce the Catholic Church and all its traditions."

The reverend placed a hand on Hugh's shoulder. "Agree to these requests and you will be naturalized into the order. You will be allowed to recite the Oath of Allegiance and become one of us – a Klansman."

Hugh looked at the heavy determination set deep within the eyes of the hooded men. "So that's it? Place my children into public school, renounce the church, and join you. I do that, and this all ends?"

"Don't forget about the klectoken!" A Klansman approached from the group.

Hugh turned with a puzzled look.

"The $10.00 initiation fee, the klectoken." The man continued. "Also, there is a $6.50 uniform fee. We'll send that off to the Atlanta headquarters, and within two weeks, you'll receive your official Klan robe and helmet. They've been busy, so they've generally been running a week longer."

"I got mine in ten days." Another voice spoke up.

"Bill!" Wes gave a stern shout.

"Yeah, yeah that's right. Albert got his in ten days. But I wouldn't expect to receive it that soon. He wears an odd size, so they probably had extras on hand."

"Bill!" Wes tried once more to quiet the discourse.

"Also, there's an annual membership fee of $5.00, an imperial tax of $1.80, and we highly encourage you to take advantage of the life insurance offered."

"*Bill!*" Wes screamed. "Please."

"Oh, I'm sorry, Wes." Bill tipped his head toward Hugh. "You know I get excited when we are about to bring in someone new."

"That's alright, Bill. It's all important, but the timing is just a little off."

Wes stepped toward the Reverend Woodard. "Your five minutes are up. What's the decision?"

The reverend slowly extended a hand toward Hugh, and then moved to the side.

Propping his fists upon his hips, Wes leaned over. "So, Langley, what's it going to be?"

"It's not that simple. I...I can't. It's my beliefs. My...my life."

Wes's backhand rolled Hugh to the ground. He glared at the reverend. "See. What did I tell you."

"Gentlemen!" A figure emerged from the shadows in following his wandering dog. "Let's not be too hasty in our actions."

Surprised, the Klansmen turned one by one and faced the intruder appearing within the flickering light cast by the burning cross.

"I'm quite sure Mr. Langley has done nothing to harm any one of you, at least not in deserving of this harsh treatment."

Wes stepped from the crowd. "Reverend Thomas, you don't know what you're getting yourself into. It would behoove you to stay out of this. I suggest you turn around and find another street to walk your dog."

"First, I would like to know who I am speaking with. Please remove your hood."

The group stood eerily silent.

"Come now. Why don't you *all* take off those ridiculous masks so we can discuss this like civilized men?" The reverend pushed his way into the group and stared into the eyes of those he passed. "I'm sure

I know some of you. Is that what you're afraid of? Is that why you feel the need to hide?"

Wes grabbed the reverend's arm and swung him around. "You are interfering with official Klan business. Leave now."

Reverend Thomas pulled away and continued toward Hugh. "I request that you show your faces. No. No, I demand it. If you're about to prosecute, condemn, and pass sentence on an innocent man, you could at least have the decency to show him who the judge, jury, and hangmen are."

Wes took long strides in attempting to catch the reverend. As the reverend reached Hugh, Wes shoved his index finger into the reverend's chest. "The only thing you need to know, Reverend, is that we are all good men. Every damned one of us. We come together to protect all that is right in this community, and this great nation. On these hoods are the faces of untold millions – the jury, if you will, who could not be with us tonight. So, in respect to them, the hoods remain on."

"Huh!" Hugh laughed. "Good men you say?" He wiped the blood from his face with the back of his hand. "Good men have nothing to hide. Only evil thrives in secrecy."

The reverend scanned the glistening eyes of the darkened hoods silhouetted by the burning cross. "Yes, it would appear so."

"That's it." Wes grabbed the reverend's throat and launched his body into the air, landing him next to Hugh. "My patience has run out. Grab me that damned rope!"

"Wes, no." Reverend Woodard stepped in front of him. "You can't…"

A white robed figure, carrying a young girl in his arm, emerged from the side of the house. Stopping by the edge of the front steps, the man hesitated for a moment and observed the disorganized array of wandering sheets before standing the girl on the front porch.

"Susie!" Emma screamed as she reached out and pulled the young girl next to her son. "Oh, Susie, where have you been? I was so frightened something might have happened to you."

"I was okay, Mom. I was with my new friend, Ray."

"Ray," Toad spoke up, "you're not supposed to take your hood off."

Ray walked past the group of puzzled Klansmen without saying a word.

"Bye, Ray!" Susie shouted.

Toad looked at Quinn. "But he's not supposed to take his hood off."

Quinn shook his head and lifted a finger to his lips.

"Good night, young lady." Ray called back as he stepped into the street.

"Where do you think you're going?" Wes watched in disbelief as Ray opened the door of his vehicle. "No one leaves until the meeting has officially adjourned."

"It's late. I'm going home." Ray adjusted the engine's choke rod and inserted the hand crank. "I've had my fill."

"You can't just leave. Get back here!"

A Klansman broke from the group and rushed toward Ray.

"Now, where are you off to?"

"I rode here with Ray."

As the automobile's engine sparked to life, another robe darted to join the second.

"And you?"

The Klansman pointed at the vehicle starting into motion.

Wes looked at the crowd, shook his head, and threw his hands in the air. "What the hell is going on here!"

As one of the men slowly approached Wes, he waved a pointed finger at the man. "You better not tell me you rode here with Ray, too."

The man paused briefly. "No, I came here by myself, but if the others are leaving, I'd like to go, as well. It's getting late and I've got to be at the train station early tomorrow morning to pick up my freight shipment for the store."

With his finger still pointed in the man's face, Wes's vision focused directly behind him on the group of hooded Klansmen who waited silently in anticipation of his next decision. The meeting did not proceed as planned. One more surprise would certainly topple the increasing unsteadiness of the evening. He reached his hand up and patted the man's shoulder. "You make a good point, Charlie. I believe we are all through here."

"Gentlemen," Wes addressed the group, "for the most part, we have accomplished our objective this evening. Under these unusual circumstances, let us dispense with the formalities and adjourn the meeting for tonight. Our next meeting will convene at the regularly scheduled time and place."

As the Klansmen trickled toward their vehicles, Reverend Woodard turned toward Wes. "Wise decision."

Wes shook his head. "We would have had this all wrapped up and been on our way home if it wasn't for that meddling preacher." Wes looked back at the Reverend Thomas who lay upon the ground, nursing his throat. "Nobody does that to me. Nobody does that to the Klan. I promise you, he won't get away with this. When I'm through with him, he'll wish he never set foot in this town."

"Not to worry, Wes." Woodard rested an open palm on his back. "We'll take care of him, but on our terms, and when the time is right."

"You and your boy share a lot in common, Langley." One of the Klansmen noted as he passed. "Looks like he pissed himself, too."

Another Klansman laughed as he followed. "He pissed himself, too. That's a good one. Let this be a warning to you." He stopped and placed the heel of his boot on Hugh's collarbone. "If you stir up trouble again, you won't get off this easy next time." He shoved Hugh onto his back.

Free of the Klansman's confinement, Emma sprang from the porch, with both children under her arms, and rushed to Hugh's side. With tears in her eyes, she attempted to clean his seeping wounds.

Angered by the barbarous humility inflicted upon him, Hugh winced from the pain as he pulled himself to his knees. "This is insane!" He cried at the departing Klansmen. "How can you do this to another human being? How can you do this..." He fell onto his hands and wept.

Flaming fragments separated from the burning cross and fell upon the turned soil of the trampled flowerbed. Its pulsating, orange glow gradually faded as the fire extinguished itself within the darkness of the night.

Chapter 12

CRACK! Jacob felt the angry pop of the ice snap against the sole of his boot. The handful of early winter, subzero nights, provided a substantial firm covering of the lake that continued to expand and contract with the varying temperatures.

"Come on, Stach." He gave a sharp tug at the sled's rope in an effort to wake his bushy tailed companion, and coax him from the boxed platform. "Are you even trying to find them? They just didn't disappear from the lake. They were in this area last time."

Stach pried open a lazy eye and peeked through its closing lid. The soothing combination of the warm afternoon sun, and the sound of the ice and snow compressing beneath the tin covered, pine runners of the old, wooden sled, trounced the annoying sporadic attempts to rouse him.

Avoiding the loss of traction when walking on the slick ice surface, Jacob maneuvered from one snow patch to another, while paralleling the long, unstable ice heave from a safe distance. Caused by the continual expansion and contraction of the ice, the heave split the lake with its jumbling of thin ice sheets, pillared over dangerous hidden open water.

The load suddenly lightened, causing Jacob to lurch forward and nearly lose his balance. "Here?" He steadied himself, as he dropped the rope, and allowed the sled to skid past. "Did you finally find them?" He pulled his mittens from his hands and threw them to the ice. "It's about time. I was getting a little tired chauffeuring you around the lake."

Stach stood motionless, peering across the heave. With his ears turned toward the shoreline, a quiet whine resonated from his throat.

"What's the problem, Stach?" What do you see?"

Studying an eerie silhouette of a lone coyote sitting stationary on the ice, Stach gave another quick whine, and stepped toward it.

"No!" Jacob warned.

The dog stopped, glanced at Jacob, and then back at the coyote.

"Is that what has you all worked up?" Jacob slapped his leg, directing Stach to return. "She's just a tease – a decoy. I'll bet the rest of the pack is hiding nearby. As soon as you approach to say hello, they'll jump out and tear you apart."

Jacob scanned the shoreline. The pack most likely hid in the tree line or just below the upper lip of the raised ice sheet. "It's in their nature, Stach, so forget about her." He knelt down and patted the dog's neck. "Let's keep moving." Jacob noticed a tint of dark clouds filling the western horizon. "Maria just might be right. Looks like a storm brewing. Come on. Jump back on the sled. Or would you prefer to walk?"

Stach gave a quiet whine, retrieved one of Jacob's mittens, and stepped back onto the sled.

"That's what I thought." Jacob picked up the remaining glove. "You know, dog? If you weren't so good at sensing what's under the ice, you'd be walking like me, instead of enjoying my efforts in providing a ride."

Jacob quickened his pace. He passed the frozen remnants of chiseled holes from past rewarding trips, and thought of how the fish practically jumped out of the water. Tempted to stop and reopen the ice, he trusted in Stach's unexplainable ability, and continued on his way.

The tension of the rope went limp, and the front edge of the sled bounced against the back of Jacob's boot. "It better not be that coyote again. We don't have that kind of time to waste." Jacob turned and discovered his dog scratching its paws at the slick ice surface. "Oh boy! Fish!"

Stach gave a sharp bark as he stamped his front feet from side to side on the lightly etched markings.

Jacob wasted no time in piercing the center of the mark with the point of his steel, ice bar. As large, clear chunks scattered about, and their accompanying fine shavings drifted to the side, he continued to hurl the heavy spear into the deepening hole until it penetrated the frozen membrane, and freed the icy water from beneath, flooding the jagged, square opening to its top.

Wiping the sweat from his brow, Jacob shed his coat, and knelt onto his mittens placed next to the hole. Unwinding the spool of dark fishing line, spun tightly on a notched scrap board, he prepared its attached, barbed hook with a small piece of leftover cheese. Lowering the bait through the hole, he watched as it disappeared from sight, stopping some twenty feet below, near the bottom of the lake.

"The cork. I forgot to bring the cork." As Jacob patted his chest pockets, a solid tug on the line, drew his hand into the water.

"Already?" Jacob challenged the resistance with a steady pull, as the finned opponent on the opposite end of his line exhibited a great displeasure in leaving its world. "Stach, I take back any doubt that I had in you. You're definitely worth your salt."

With long, slow draws, Jacob countered the creature's side-to-side movement, and delivered it to the bottom of the ice. "I'm going to lose him." Jacob became concerned. "He's not going to straighten out and come up through the hole."

He bounced onto his chest and reached his hand deep into the icy water. "Ah!" He screamed as the extreme cold shocked his fragile nerve endings and sent a burning sensation through his arm. Snagging the fish's gills with two fingers, he pulled it up through the hole and rolled it across the ice.

"I got you!" Jacob laughed as the walleye flopped in the splash water created by the catch. As it struggled to reenter the water, its olive and golden hue glistened in the sun. Securing the hefty fish against the ice with his hand, Jacob pulled a needle nosed pliers from his pocket to remove the barbed hook from its mouth. As he pried the lower jaw open, the hook fell from inside.

"What luck." Jacob scratched his head. "He could have spit it out and swam away at any time."

Jacob reformed the portion of cheese on the end of his hook, and dropped it back into the hole. Finding a splintered piece of wood on the sled, he knotted the string around it in substitution for the missing cork. Feeling a sudden coolness mix with the air, he noticed the encroaching clouds covering the sun and stealing its warming rays.

"Maria said she could feel a storm brewing on in her bones." Jacob wrung the water from his sleeve. "It took us long enough to find this spot. We'll catch a few more and then leave for home before it hits."

Stach raised the ridge above one eye and stared at Jacob.

"I know. I've tried calling her Ma, but I just can't do it." Jacob confessed. "My ma died when I was a kid. I feel that if I call Maria, Ma, I'm abandoning my real one."

Jacob knelt upon his mittens, and lifted the line up and down attempting to attract another fish. "You know, Stach. Sometimes I feel scared that I might forget what Ma looked like. I mean, I still remember her face, but each time, it seems that her image fades a little more." Stach moved next to him and laid his head upon Jacob's leg.

"Pa keeps an old picture of her hidden in his dresser drawer." Jacob continued. "Don't tell anyone, but sometimes I go in and sneak a look at her. I'm sure Pa wouldn't care if he found out, but maybe it would hurt Maria's feelings. I don't know. I just don't want to forget the way she looks. I would feel bad if my son forget me."

Stach jumped to his feet and peered once again across the heave. Eyeing the returned coyote, he began a series of quiet whines.

Jacob glanced at the troubling distraction. "Looks like she's back. Remember what I told you. If you go to her, you might not come back."

The wood splinter darted through the water to the bottom of the ice hole. Jacob grabbed the line and began his graceful waltz in an effort to land another catch. Pulling a slightly smaller walleye onto the ice, he removed the hook from its mouth, and laid it next to the other.

"It's not as big as the first one, but we'll take it." Jacob dropped his line down the hole and rubbed his hands together for warmth. Noticing light snow flurries beginning to drift upon the breeze, his concerns turned to the darkening western sky.

"We'll catch one more, and then we'll leave." He patted Stach's back. "We certainly don't want to get caught out in the open when the storm hits."

"And there we go." The wooden cork disappeared under the ice. As Jacob began to pull the line from the water, Stach gave a loud bark and darted for the teasing coyote seated on the shoreline.

"Stach! No!" Jacob threw the gathered fish line from his hands and took off in pursuit of the confused hound. Within two steps, he found himself facedown upon the ice. Feeling a slight tug at his leg, he discovered the fish line wrapped and knotted around his boot. The fine line cut deep into Jacob's hands as he attempted to break loose. Reaching for his pliers, he snapped the line and tossed all to the side as he jumped to his feet and rushed after Stach.

Driven to see the coyote, Stach ignored numerous commands to stop. Leaping over the heave, he continued on a dead run with Jacob trailing farther behind with each step.

Reaching the heave, Jacob leaped over the jumbled ice pillars, and landed squarely on the opposite side. *Crack!* The ice sank from beneath him as the dreadful sound echoed across the shoreline. Observing the edge of the fractured ice sheet rise before him, he felt himself sliding backward toward the opening water near the heave.

"Stach!" Jacob screamed, as he clawed at the tilting mass to avoid entry into the freezing water and the ensuing entrapment beneath the ice.

Deciphering Jacob's distressful tone, Stach stiffened his front legs in an attempt to return, but his forward momentum carried him on an uncontrollable skid. Tumbling through a snow drift, he spied the lone coyote standing on its feet, and to its rear, a dozen sets of aggressive eyes peered with anticipation from the upper ridge of the shoreline's ice sheet.

The water's freezing burn instantly consumed every nerve ending in Jacob's lower legs as he caught a glimpse of his dog's appearance at the zenith of the fractured ice piece. "Go! Get out of here!" Jacob screamed, but his warning came too late. Thrown off balance by the ascending sheet, Stach tumbled over its edge and began a slide downward toward the open water as Jacob disappeared beneath the heave. Clawing and biting at the ice, Stach managed to slow his descent. As his hind legs entered the water, the ice mass returned to level and pinched his body between the two sheets.

Suspended within the dark, frigid water, Jacob felt its mind-numbing, painful freeze penetrate deep within his body's core. The only chance for survival laid in somehow finding the ice break, in which he entered, and hoped it did not close, or search for a narrow opening along the jumbled heave. Time became the impartial foe. The lake's freezing temperature and the lack of oxygen would consume his life in a matter of minutes.

He followed the light upward to the bottom of the ice. Smooth to the touch, he could not pull himself along its slick undersurface. He reached into an empty pocket and remembered his pliers lay tangled in the fish line above. Unaware of an accurate direction, he searched frantically as he kicked his feet and pulled himself through the water. A sudden resistance bound his arm within the winds of a dark fishing line, which he followed to the underside of his chopped opening.

He reached up through the narrow hole, continuing to grasp at the fish line, and felt the ice bar lying near the water's edge. Ignoring his body's response to breathe, he began to tire. Unable to determine a direction to his adverse entry, he debated whether the best alternative was to hold onto the bar and hope his arm froze with the ice. At least his family would find him in a day or two. If he attempted to locate the heave, he would surely drown trying, and his family would be fortunate if they found his body rolled up onto the beach some time in the early spring. He felt his mind drifting. It was time to breathe the water and end the pain.

Ouch! He felt a sharp bite on his hand. Stach? His ears picked up the muffled barks and yelps of multiple dogs. Coyotes! They're after Stach. He saw shadows through the ice, possibly moving in a direction of Stach and the ice heave. He would never make it there in time. His weakened strength prevented swimming and the bottom of the ice was too smooth to pull himself along. He reached around the upper edge of the ice hole hoping to snag one the coyotes and if possible, pull its snout into the water and drown it as a last effort to help Stach.

Grasping around the circumference of the hole, Jacob felt the roughened jaws of a metal device. Pliers! The pulled fishing line carried the tool near the hole's edge. Knocking it into the water, he caught the apparatus before it drifted from sight. Opening the lever, he stabbed it into the bottom of the ice, dragging himself along the underside as he followed the movement of the hound's shadows.

Discovering Stach's tail and legs pinched between the ice sheets, Jacob pried the crevice open and stabbed the pliers onto the sheet, freeing him from the icy tomb.

"Ah! He screamed as the abundant, cool air sucked into his burning lungs, and the choking lake water coughed from the back of his throat. As the coyotes scurried away, he scooped Stach from the water with his free hand, swung his legs onto the ice, and rolled off the leveling sheets.

The contents of Jacob's stomach painted the slush and snow as he gagged and heaved on all fours. Wet and shivering, he turned his head toward a low toned growl near where he last set Stach. The lone coyote remained. Attempting to drag Stach's lifeless body into the heavy snowfall, she snarled at Jacob's unwelcome presence.

"Stay away from him you goddamned bitch!" Jacob leaped up and drove the pliers downward, ripping a deep gash along the coyote's narrow spine. A haunting yelp sounded throughout the ice sheet as the wounded predator disappeared into the falling snow.

A mass of blood soaked fur and torn flesh lay motionless before Jacob. With a trembling hand, he stroked the tattered coat, attempting to reposition the detached skin, and stop the bleeding. "Oh, Stach. What have they done to you?" A faint whimper wheezed with each exhale. Missing a paw, Stach raised his front leg in an effort to thank Jacob.

"Oh, Stach." Jacob lifted the dog into his arms. "You're going to be okay, boy. Just you wait and see. I'll carry you home. We'll fix you up as good as new."

An eerie cascade of barks and howls approached from beyond Jacob's sight. The aggressive exchange was like none he heard before.

"We've got to get out of here." He pulled Stach close to his chest. "There's absolutely nothing good about their intentions. We've got to try to make it home."

With Stach in his arms, Jacob climbed to the top of the jumbled ice heave and slid down the opposite side. Staggering around the scattered fishing equipment, he stopped and squinted through the heavy falling snow against the certain darkening twilight. It was the direction he guessed as home. Placing one foot in front of the other, he ventured into the blindness, assured he would eventually reach the shoreline somewhere along the edge of the ice.

As the temperature dropped, Jacob's stiffening clothing began to snap and crack with each step as it peeled away from his bare skin. The firm embrace with his dog provided both only a negligible amount of warmth, but he knew they could not maintain it for much longer. Stach lay still in his arms. If it were not for the occasional feel of his weakened heart beating against Jacob's chest, he would have thought his friend gone.

A dialogue of muffled yips and barks waxed and waned to his rear. Jacob maintained a steady pace fearing the coyotes may try to snatch Stach right out of is arms. If he did not stumble upon a recognizable landmark soon, both may freeze to death in the storm, providing the coyotes an opportunity to feast on two.

A jagged flash of lightning speared above Jacob's head. Its bright streak dulled by the heavy falling snow. Stopping, he attempted to focus his ears on the phenomenon, but no thunder followed. "Did you see that, Stach? I've heard stories of thunder sounding during winter snowstorms, but never lightning, and especially lightning without thunder."

The strange flash appeared once again, emerging from his right and fading to his left. "What do you think, Stach?" Jacob hesitated. "We don't seem to be having any luck on our own. We could use a little guidance, whether it's meant for us or not." Forcing his legs to follow, Jacob readjusted his course and continued on.

Within a few steps, Jacob felt a series of sharp barbs scratch against his frozen trousers. "A fence! Will you look at that? We were only ten feet away, and would have walked into nothing if we hadn't turned." Jacob pulled on the taut wire. "I'm not sure if this is ours, but it's got to lead to a building somewhere down the line."

With his eyelashes frozen closed, he bounced his hip against the barbed wire, keeping to the rhythm of bumping into one fence post after the next. His pace slowed with the deepening snow, until his shoulder grazed against the chipped paint on the corner trim of the barn.

Lifting the barn door's handle, Jacob stepped inside and dropped to his knees. He brushed the heavy snow from Stach's fur, and laid him upon the floor. In the fading light of a kerosene lantern, Jacob confirmed what he feared for most of the journey. Stach was dead.

He gently ran his hand back and forth over the stained and torn coat. "Heavenly Father. Please accept my good friend, Stach, into your divine kingdom. He has truly earned it." He laid his head upon Stach's midsection, as he did so often before, and closed his eyes.

Chapter 13

STEP and jab. Sparring through a feathered, cigar haze, the boxers' exhales hissed with each attempted blow. Step and jab. Sweat beads rained from their foreheads, dotting the stretched canvas below. Step and jab. Bobbing and weaving, they continually slipped each other's punches until one fighter's glove connected with the other's jutting jaw line. The elevated ring echoed a loud thud as the southpaw collapsed onto the scuffed mat with the snickering of a few seated spectators.

"Tuck your chin, damn it! How many times does your dumb ass need to end up on the damned floor before you learn to tuck your chin?" The vertical boxer offered his opponent a glove. "Come on, get up, let's try it again."

Musical notes mixed with the shuffling of boxing footwear, as a piano's hammers began to knock out a tune's measures upon its spring steel wires. The score's tempo dramatically increased and then slowed until the melody stopped. Its pages shuffled back and forth upon the piano's music shelf, as the outside sunlight suddenly stretched upon the maple wood floor. An elongated shadow filled the rectangular light and then disappeared with the clunking of the door's catch.

"Wes, you're early." Ossy shifted his hat across the table in opening an adjacent seat. Straightening papers within a folder with one hand, he pointed at the empty chair with the other.

The worn floors creaked as Wes moved his way to the table while watching the exchange of punches on the elevated platform above. "I see they assembled the ring."

"Yeah, they put it up last night."

"Is that Rick?" Wes stopped to watch a series of well placed rotated jabs.

"Rick and his younger brother, Pauley." Ossy took a puff from his cigar and returned it to the ashtray. "They asked if they could spar for a while. I figured as long as the ring was open, someone might as well get some use out of it."

The voices raised from those parked in the front row, as they began to argue over comparisons of professional boxing matches fought in the past.

Wes chuckled. "Did they bring their fans with them, too?"

"No. Just the usual morning drifters killing time."

"Tom, come sit with me." The feminine, French accent turned all heads toward the piano, and then rotated to Wes.

Wes glanced at the pianist and then stared back at the half dozen sets of eyes affixed on his reddening face. A stern nod toward the boxing ring returned the echoes of conversation back into the room.

"What the hell is she doing in here?" Wes's hat landed next to Ossy's as he pulled a chair from the table.

"Who, Miss LaFae? She asked if she could use the piano to practice."

"Practice? Practice what?" He sat down. "That's no song I've ever heard of."

"That's because it's not supposed to be a song, it's the film score for the cinema."

"Then why the hell doesn't she practice at the cinema?"

"She said it's too quiet over there. She gets spooked when no one else is around." Ossy blew a slow, steady stream of smoke into the air as he listened to the notes form the tune. "Besides, we could use a little something to liven up the joint."

Wes opened the folder and scanned through the pages. "I guess men fighting just isn't as exciting as it used to be." He turned the papers right side up. "What does the inventory look like? We set for the weekend fights?"

Ossy pulled a page and placed it on top of the stack. "Booze looks good. All except for the gin, which we're expecting our shipment from North Dakota to arrive sometime this afternoon."

"How about the fight match-ups? Rick on the list?"

"Yeah, he and Pauley are both on there." He placed another sheet on top of the previous. "Pauley's first official bout."

"Looks good." Wes scanned the list to the bottom. "Wait, I don't see Cy Pierce's name anywhere on here."

"I couldn't find anyone willing to fight him. The boys say he's awful rough."

"Awful rough? This is boxing not dancing. There's always going to be a little blood."

"They know that." He shrugged his shoulders. "It's not the blood they're worried about. It's the broken bones."

Wes tossed the list back to Ossy. "Broken bones or not, we need a Pierce match-up to fill the house. How about Rick? He always seems to hold his own."

"I already tried. Rick won't fight him."

Wes watched as Rick demonstrated the proper stance once again to Pauley. "Then stick him with Pauley."

"What! Are you out of your everloving mind?" Ossy's cigar bounced in the tray. "Pauley would be lucky to last sixty seconds with Pierce. Even then, he would look like he got stomped on by an angry bull."

"Of course he would." Wes smiled. "That's why big brother is going to step in and take his place on the card."

"Ah." Ossy brushed the eraser debris from the list and penciled in the corrections. "Genius. Genius."

"You don't have to be afraid of me, Tom." The cinema score softened to a moderate sweet jazz. "You can take my word for it. Isabelle LaFae has never bitten anyone." She began to croon the soothing lyrics.

"Who does she think she is, Vaughn De Leath?" Wes turned his back to the tease of the flirtatious vocals.

"I don't know, Wes." Ossy closed his eyes and tilted his head back. "She sounds pretty damned close."

Wes rolled his eyes. "Is that it? Anything else we need to cover?"

Ossy opened one eye and nodded toward the glimmer of a tin star, pinned on a man sitting at the end of the bar. "You've got a visitor."

Wes glanced up at the police officer, who took short punches into the air as he watched the sparring opponents jab at one another. Wes anchored his elbow on the table. Covering his mouth with one hand, he turned toward Ossy. "Isaac Hess?"

Ossy closed his eye. "The one and only. He's been waiting here about an hour. Said he stopped by the hardware store, but you weren't around."

"Did he say if he was here in his official capacity, or is he just one of the boys today?"

Ossy leaned forward with the ending of the song. He looked at Wes. "Sounds like a good question to break the ice. Everyone's been a little stiff since he walked through the door."

The scattering of wooden chairs turned curious heads as Ms. LaFae caught herself while stumbling through the aisle in approaching the table. "Tom, I get the feeling you are deliberately trying to ignore me." She waved a scornful finger in Wes's direction.

Ossy hopped from his seat, and quickly gathered the papers into his folder. "I was just about to leave."

"Oh, please. I hope it's not on my account." The table shimmied as Ms. LaFae steadied herself with one hand.

"No ma'am, not at all. I've got business to attend to in the back that I should have finished long ago." He retrieved his hat and tipped it as he hurried away.

"It's pleasing to know there is still *one* gentleman left in this world." She plopped herself onto the empty chair.

Wes grumbled. "Belle, isn't it a little early in the morning for whatever the hell it is that you're taking?" He stared at her. "What is it this time, cocaine, heroin?"

"I've never been too concerned about too early for anything. It numbs the jagged edge of realization that I may be stranded in this purgatory, and never gather the courage to escape."

"What's so bad about this town that makes it any worse than any other city?"

"I suppose it's not so much about leaving here," Belle struck a match and lit a cigarette, "as it is about traveling to somewhere else."

"Where is this somewhere else that you think is so much better than here?"

She blew a smoke stream away from the table. "New York City, of course. Back on Broadway – The Great White Way. I need to find

Rich Pennington." She tapped her finger upon the table. "You know, he once told me I was the best thing that ever happened to theatre."

"Oh, right. Your famous producer friend. Last I remember, your letters to him all came back marked return to sender." Wes laughed.

"He is a very busy and important man. He is someone who prefers to be spoken to *en personne*."

"I see. Well, then we better get you on the next train to New York." He extended his arm. "I'll walk you to the depot."

"Do not ridicule me." Belle shoved his arm away. "It does not become you."

A long silence encircled them as their eyes darted about the room. Each glanced at the other for an instant in an attempt to rekindle the conversation, but the words strangled one another at the tip of their tongues, and suffocated before birth. Sensing the needless impasse he engendered, Wes pushed himself from the table.

"So, where have you been keeping yourself?" Belle drew in a long puff from her cigarette. "I don't see you around anymore. Not like before." Smoke exhaled through her nostrils as she squashed the half used butt into the ashtray. "Not like before, when we were...you know..."

Wes slid back into his chair. "I've been busy. I've had a lot going on lately. If you haven't heard, we've got an important Klan meeting about to land right before us. We were very fortunate to have those of influence, in key positions, to secure this event. It'll be the biggest thing that's ever happened to this town."

"Oh, yes, I've heard something about that, but it doesn't concern me." She turned her head from side to side.

"Doesn't concern you? Well it should. You just don't understand how important an affair like this is for all of us."

"Me, not understand?" Belle smirked. "I would say that it is the Klan who doesn't understand – a bunch of frustrated, supposedly adult men, who do not understand what a good, clean, white sheet can be used for."

"I wouldn't say that too loudly if I were you." Wes looked over his shoulders. "You just may find yourself sporting a coat of feathers, with your rear end parked on the outside of the city limits."

"Like I said, it doesn't concern me." Belle slapped her hands upon the table. "Oh, Wes, I didn't come over here to quarrel with you.

Why can't it be like when we first met? You do remember, don't you?"

A half smile formed on Wes's face as his mind displayed minute glimpses of the past.

Belle placed her hand on Wes's forearm. "I remember vividly. My theatre troupe made a stop to perform at the Webster Opera House. Stepping from the train, I tripped on the boarding dock and broke a heel. You were there to help me to my feet. You told me I was the most beautiful woman you had ever seen." She smiled. "Then you carried me to the cobbler and asked him to repair my shoe immediately." A small giggle danced from her lips. "Oh, I was a big city girl awestruck by a handsome, charming knight of the prairie."

Wes nodded. "Come to think of it, I never did pay Henry for his work. I guess I couldn't think of anything but you at the time."

Belle nudged closer as her eyes smiled at his. "You managed to convince me to stay. Everyone in the troupe thought I took leave of my senses. Rich pleaded with me to go on with them, but my heart said otherwise."

"You, in that blue dress. I still remember how you looked. There wasn't a woman within a thousand miles of here who could hold a candle to you." Wes grinned. "I'll admit. Life was good, wasn't it?" His eyes gazed into hers. "Whatever happened to us, Belle?"

"Whatever happened to us?" Belle stiffened her posture. "I ran out of excuses trying to explain the bruises and black eyes. One minute you were kissing me with great passion, the next, you had your hands around my throat, chocking me to unconsciousness."

"I don't have to listen to this." Wes pulled his arm from Belle's hand as he shifted to leave.

Belle clenched his arm in prompting him to stay. "I'm not blaming you. I understand it was the war." She pulled him back. "I still have it…the drop waist dress with the loose, straight fit." She ran her finger down his arm. "Wes, let me come over and see you tonight. I will wear the dress. We can go out on the town and dance the devil away. It can be like it was before. And, I promise I'll be careful to not upset you."

"You don't have another date lined up for this evening?" He snickered. "I've heard you've been chasing the devil with quite a few others around town, and some just passing through."

"A girl's got to eat." She pulled away and crossed her arms. "Besides, why should it matter to anyone at all, if a gentleman wants to treats me like a lady."

Wes reached into his pocket. "If that's your definition in being treated like a lady," he shoved a few folded bills down the front of Belle's shirt, "there, go buy yourself a steak."

The money rolled across the table as Belle dug the currency from her brazier. "I'm not a whore, damn it." Light tears began to trace lines through her makeup.

"Then stop behaving like one. For Christ's sake, do you know how many wives would like to see you run out of town?"

"They don't have to run me out." She wiped the streams away. "I will be content to leave on my own accord. Back to New York. Back to my stage family. I will find Rich, and then tour the country again with the theatre troupe."

"You'll never do it. Deep down you know there is nothing back there for you. Those you once knew are no longer there, they washed out with the times. Like you, their stage appeal has long gone. Yes indeed, the best thing that Pennington probably ever did for himself was to ditch you along the trail."

"Liar!" She slapped at his shoulder as she pushed him away. "Take it back. Take it back." The tears continued to flow.

Wes stood up and watched as Belle hid her face in the crook of her arm and sobbed. He shook his head at what she had become. The beautiful woman he met years ago by accident at the train depot no longer existed in the pathetic tramp weeping before him.

"I'm leaving, Wes." She dried her face as she caught her breath. "I'm through with you. I'm through with this whole damned town."

Wes grabbed his hat from the table. "Then go." He turned and walked away.

Belle dropped her head back onto her arm. Wiping an occasional tear, accompanied by quiet sniffles, she projected a blank stare toward the silently waiting piano.

"Give me a glass, Bert." Wes leaned against the bar. "This day has taken a sudden turn and I'm going to need a little help to straighten it back out."

"You sure, Wes?" Bert nodded toward the far end of the counter where Isaac Hess sat watching the sparring bout. "He's been here about an hour."

Wes glanced at Hess. "So I've heard." He tapped his finger upon the countertop. "I'm not going to sweat it. Give me a glass."

"All right, Wes, but if anyone asks, I didn't see a thing." He chuckled as he felt his way along the row of snifter glasses and stopped when his hand fell on top of the short tumblers. Turning one over, he strained through thick lenses as he struggled to identify the correct whiskey decanter.

Incoherent bits and pieces of disparaging comments caught Wes's attention as he spun around and watched Belle gather the cash from the table. Steadying herself as she made her way back to the piano, she gathered the sheet music and left.

Sliding two fingers over the rim of the glass, Bert rubbed them against the bottom, and then tipped the bottle in pouring, until he felt the level reached his second knuckle. Wes turned to find his glass containing a good shot of whiskey with spilled droplets leading to the decanter. "Bert, you know I like to pour my own."

"Sorry, Wes." He felt for another tumbler and set it on the bar. "I guess I'm just in the habit of pouring once I turn the glass. I'd better go check on Ossy." He moved toward the backroom.

"Cy on the card for this weekend?" Hess walked over and stood next to Wes.

Wes nodded. "It took a little manipulating, but I think we can expect to see him here."

"Good." He planted his elbows on the bar. "Should be an exciting night of boxing. I'll be here."

"I understand you were wanting to see me."

"Yeah." Hess lifted his hat and wiped the sweat from the band. "The mayor is a little upset about the Klan meeting the other night at Langley's."

"He's not the only one." Wes shook his head. "I'm thinking we should meet and do that one again – show Langley we mean business. He got off too easy. The message may not have set in deep enough."

"That's not why the mayor's upset." Hess pulled the hat back over his head. "It should not have happened at all. The mayor is receiving complaints from the citizens – mostly Catholics. And, unless you forgot, they enjoy casting votes, too."

"It had to be done. We need to seize on these opportunities to show our strength, to demonstrate to ourselves as well as the community the power that the Klan possesses. That was the largest attendance we ever assembled at a cross lighting. You should know. You were there."

"Yeah, I remember. It was very impressive, but what we didn't know is that the mayor directed you to hold off on Klan activity until after the big meeting. People are upset, Wes. Instead of increasing our numbers, that little demonstration is causing the opposite. Those who are anti-Klan are threatening to put ghosts in the sheets. Something like this could damage Whittson's chance for reelection."

"No one got hurt. It's just the typical anti-Klan rumblings from the Catholics we always hear about after a meeting like this. In fact, this was good for our membership. It bolstered excitement and enthusiasm for the upcoming klonverse."

"Well, be that as it may," Hess pulled a hand down his face, "the mayor has given me a new job."

"What else is he having you do," Wes chuckled, "besides keeping his ass clean so he can pull votes out of it, when he needs them for the next election?"

He pointed a finger at Wes. "He wants me to keep an eye on you."

"Well, Isaac, I would never have taken you for a spy."

"I'm no spy, Wes, but I'm no damned fool, either. I can't afford to lose my job, so I told him I would do what was needed."

"Does he really think he can stop the Klan from performing its civic duties?"

"No one's stopping the Klan, Wes, especially not Whittson. You know that. Hell, if it wasn't for the mayor, we wouldn't be putting all this effort into preparing for the klonverse next month." Hess reached over and grabbed the poured shot. "Just remember, we're all working together to make this happen. Klansman or not, I would hate to be the poor son of a bitch who fouls it up." He raised the glass above his head. "Here's mud in your eye." The whiskey hit the back of his throat as he slammed the glass upon the counter. A contorted look rushed over his face, and then he shook his head. "Why the hell don't you buy that man a bar of soap?" He turned and walked out.

The decanter stopper rattled against the countertop as Wes filled his tumbler. He lifted the glass and stared at the golden brown swirl of liquor within. "Mud in your eye," he gulped its contents down, "and blood on your edge." He inverted the glass and rested it upon the bar as the thud of a body striking the ring's canvas echoed about the room.

Chapter 14

THE snorting echo faded. As the chestnut and white pinto mustang stepped forward, Samuel pulled lightly upon the bridle's reins in coaxing the stallion back into line. Looking to his left and then to his right, he estimated a total of one hundred painted faced warriors joining him on the long, narrow hilltop ridge.

A broken down train of horse drawn wagons circled below in forming a defensive arrangement to thwart the impending attack. As the settlers propped their rifles behind the wooden spoke wheels, a small delegation mounted their horses and rode outside of the wagons' protective cover, positioning themselves as an invitation to parley.

"We go down now?" The native on his right pointed his lips toward the contingent.

A light breeze pushed up the gradual slope. Sensing the cool morning air upon his face, Samuel closed his eyes and slowly shook his head. His thoughts drifted back to when he was a young boy. Back to when there were very few white men upon the plains. He hunted the land and fished the many lakes. The pioneers he did meet were friendly and helpful. How was he to know the sheer numbers who were not long to follow? Now, the whites have consumed the land. It's time to change. All things change. Change or die.

Samuel opened his eyes. The expectant stares of the men in his party rested upon him. He hesitated as he looked down at the small group waiting to discuss terms. Raising his staff high into the air, its feathers shifted in the downward thrust as he pointed its tip at the distressed caravan of unfortunate trespassers.

Ululating war cries followed the thunder of hoofs beating against the earth. As the renegade band approached the enclosed ring, the sharp sound of rifle fire exploded from beneath the wagon beds. Warriors fell from their steeds, and women and children cried out in terror.

"Cut! Cut! Cut!" The command resonated through a large megaphone.

As the action gradually slowed to a stop, the director stepped from his chair, and waived to one of the painted braves. "You, over there!"

The man's eyes widened as he pointed to himself.

"Yes, you! Weren't you briefed before the scene? Indians didn't wear wristwatches. Lose it." He turned toward the others. "That goes for the rest of you wearing them as well."

The man nodded. "Well, that explains why they're never on time." He snickered as he unbuckled the leather strap.

"An Indian does not need a watch to know what time it is." Samuel spoke up.

"Oh, is that a fact?" He tucked the timepiece within his clothing.

Samuel gave a slow nod.

"Okay, smart guy. Without using a watch, I'll bet you a greenback you can't tell me what time it is right now."

Samuel stared at the man. "Let's see the money."

Feeling through his clothing, he produced a wad of paper, which he straightened into a one dollar bill.

Samuel raised his hand above his head in shading the sunlight from his eyes. Squinting through the cracks between his fingers, he glanced at the horizon, and then back at the sun.

"Take thirty! The catering truck is here." A voice called through the large megaphone.

Samuel looked at the man. "It's lunch time." He snatched the money from the man's grip, smiled, and walked away.

"Oh, very funny. Very funny." The man gibed. "There's always got to be a comedian in the bunch."

A sparse laughter erupted from the members of the wacipi committee on the Lake Traverse Indian Reservation, and then quickly withered as Samuel finished recounting the wittiness of his wristwatch tale.

"After that, he never asked me for the time again." Samuel smiled as he drew in a puff from his cigar.

Following a brief moment of silence, one of the men spoke. "Tell us, Samuel," he grinned at those beside him, "how long have you and the others worked in moving pictures?"

Samuel thought, and then spoke. "We didn't start out in Hollywood. The Miller Brothers Wild West Show is where we entered show business. As the public grew disinterested in that type of entertainment, we moved our teepees to California, and stayed on at the Bison Ranch studio where we transitioned into moving pictures. It was a new and exciting time. I worked alongside Bill Hart, and Francis Ford and his little brother Jack."

The stillness of the room accommodated many expressionless faces, with eyes careful as not to cross paths.

Sensing the slight ridicule behind the question, Samuel rose to his feet. "Since we have accomplished our intent in deciding not to change the scheduled date of the wacipi, you will excuse me, as I have business to attend to elsewhere."

"Yes, I will say again." Another added. "If the Klan meeting now occupies the same day as the pow wow, then so be it. If they are there, they are not here."

"But they do not bother us." One spoke. "Around here, they are only concerned with persecuting the other whites."

"There is no one left for them to conquer," another chuckled, "so they have turned on themselves."

Samuel smiled at the comments. "One day, when receiving my costume, I looked at the odd pieces and asked – what Indians wear this? The man said Plains Indians. I told him that I was there. This is not how my people dressed. He shook his head. I asked the others who were standing in line for their hides and feathers – did the Blackfoot, Crow, or Pawnee wear this? No one knew. So I told the man, no Indian wore clothes like this. He looked at me and said, yes they did. I asked, then who? He said, the American Indian." Samuel looked about the room. "It was at that moment, I understood. We are American Indians. That's how we are looked upon – as one people, but we are not. We know we are many different tribes."

"But the white man is one people. They do not come from tribes."

Samuel nodded. "If we are American Indians, then you could consider them as American whites. Although they like to believe they are one people, in actuality, they are many tribes as well, with different religious and ethnic beliefs. We, as tribes, are separated by our beliefs, to a certain degree, onto reservations. The whites, on the other hand, are not, and therefore will always be in a state of unrest."

After a short period of silence, another spoke up. "I hear that you are recruiting more of our people to return with you to join the others in Hollywood."

Samuel glanced toward both sides of the room. "I am recruiting no one." He drew in a quick puff. "I am seeking. My good friend Bill Hart asked that when I return, I should bring with me some good reel Indians. He said that in the western moving picture business, a good, reel Indian is hard to find."

A silence floated through the small room as Samuel glanced around the group. "I will go now." He returned the cigar to his mouth and moved toward the door.

"Back to California?"

A scattering of laughter quickly arose and faded.

Samuel stopped and turned toward the group.

The man spoke up. "I don't think one day has passed since you returned to the reservation where you haven't said you were going back to California. So tell us. Today? Tomorrow? Next week? When are you leaving, if at all?"

"When I find some good, reel Indians, I will go back." Samuel retrieved his derby and opened the door.

"Well?"

Samuel stopped. "Well what?"

"Well, what about me?"

"What about you?"

"You said you were looking for good, real Indians. What about me and some of the others in here?"

Samuel glanced at the staring faces. "I'll keep looking." He adjusted the bowler on his head, and closed the door behind him as he walked out.

The man turned toward the others. "Every year is a grievous repeat of the one before. We endure his arrogant demeanor while listening to the same stories over and over again. I don't care if he is an elder. He does not live among us. He does not experience life as we do. What does he know?"

"He sees the visions." Another spoke up. "He can converse with those of the spirit world. At times, our people need the reassurance of an ancestral guidance."

"What about the young boy? He has the gift as well."

"Yes. But he is frightened of it. As he grows and matures, he will come to understand its importance. Until then…"

The man shook his head. "Until then."

Chapter 15

THE skipper raced. From petal to petal, the petite, tawny butterfly sailed the hillside yellow and purple coneflower maze. Darting across a plaid blanket, it alighted upon the brass, tone arm of a tiring, portable phonograph as the turntable slowed to a stop. In the shadow of a lone elm tree, taken root near Pickerel Lake, at the summit of Day County, it brushed its hooked antennae and then captured the next gust in pursuit of another.

Kettie pulled her lips from Jacob's and looked out and over the countless rolling hills. "It's so beautiful up here." Her finger pointed to a blur on the outer horizon. "There it is. I see it." She squinted as she rolled to a seated position. "How far away are we?"

Jacob sat up and rested his chin over the back of her shoulder. "Roughly fifteen miles, as the crow flies." His teeth gently tickled her earlobe.

A short giggle erupted as she flinched away. "Who would have known you could see the city of Webster, all the way from Pickerel Lake. How did you find this place?"

"The property belongs to a friend of mine. He doesn't allow anyone up here. I guess he just doesn't want to put up with the trespassers." Jacob lifted his knee and rested his arm over the top. "He was having a difficult time finding a spot to dig a well, so I helped him with a little water witching. By chance, we found a good source, so he kind of lets me come and go."

"Water witching, is dowsing another one of your talents?" Kettie teased. "I can see you now, walking along while holding a set of magic sticks in your hands."

"Magic sticks?" He chuckled. "Sure. I'll bet I made at least a dozen rabbits appear before we actually found the water."

"Jacob the *Magnifique!*" Kettie quipped.

As the laughter faded, Kettie reached for Jacob's hand. "I want to thank you for sharing this special place with me. It's a perfectly wonderful view." She scanned beyond the distant skyline. "This must be how the world looks when you're flying in the Jenny."

Jacob raised an eyebrow. "I never thought of it that way, but I imagine it's very similar."

Kettie shook her head. "That propeller seems to be taking its own sweet time in getting here."

"It should arrive any day now." Jacob sorted through the records. "Roman said he would let us know when it does."

"Then the adventure begins?" Kettie smiled.

"Then the adventure begins." He slid the disc's center hole over the turntables spindle. "Traveling, offering plane rides, picking up a mail run here and there, it's all so close, and to think I actually settled to wilt my soul in a dank, stagnant factory." Jacob turned his head away. "That life wasn't for me. I would have suffocated." He looked at Kettie. "Are you ready for the adventure?"

"The hospital asked me again to stay on and work as a nurse. My aunt and uncle were very disappointed when I turned the doctors down, but if you're leaving, I see no reason for me to stick around here."

"Then, come with me." He squeezed her hand.

"I don't know, Jacob. I see the excitement in your eyes, and everything inside of me says I want to be a part of it. We've only known each other for a few short months, but the world has come alive. I've never felt like this before. And as much as it invigorates me, it also terrifies me, because it's uncharted territory, I guess I don't know what to do."

A trio of skippers fled from the dark brown head of a black-eyed Susan as Jacob plucked it from its slender stem. Leaning across the blanket, he brushed its long petals against Kettie's cheek. "Is this so terrifying?"

Kettie closed her eyes as she felt the light touch. "No, it's refreshing." She took the flower from Jacob's hand, and pressed her lips against his. "Thank you."

"A wildflower for a taste of your sweet lips?" He smiled. "I got the better deal out of that trade. If that's the going rate, I'll make sure I never run out of flowers."

"So, you'll plant a flower garden just for me." She giggled.

Jacob stared into Kettie's eyes. "I will, and it'll be so large they'll feature it in the *Believe it or Not* column of the newspaper." As they angled toward each other to embrace, a skipper shot between them and landed on the alluring, bright yellow coneflower.

"Oh my, looks like we have a guest." Kettie lifted the flower away, careful not to disturb the insect from its nectar.

"They call them the gem of the prairie." Jacob attempted to coax another into his hand. "They emerge at this time every year, but only for about three weeks – three weeks to mate, lay eggs, and then die."

"Three weeks. They don't have the luxury of indecisiveness do they?"

"I'm sure they do. They just don't understand how much of their life it's actually costing them."

Kettie scooted the skipper onto the side of her finger and lifted it into flight. "When I was a little girl, my grandmother once told me that a promise made in the presence of a butterfly can never be broken."

Jacob raised his eyebrows. "Why is that?"

"She said the words of the promise are inscribed upon the butterfly's wings. As the butterfly floats upward, it carries the vow to Heaven where angels read the words before God."

Jacob nodded as he watched the skipper chase another, and then disappear into the shortgrass tufts.

Kettie nudged her elbow into his side. "So, do you still want to make that promise about a flower garden?"

"This requires some serious thought." He rubbed a hand over his mouth. "I wouldn't want to send a butterfly to Heaven before its time. Three weeks is short enough for these little guys."

"I believe some can come and go as they please, you know, like in the blink of an eye."

"More of grandmother's wisdom?" He smiled.

"No. That part's mine."

"All right." Jacob squeezed her shoulder and laughed. "Looks like you've got me in a corner." He stood up and reached for her hand. "First, I want to show you something special."

Assisting Kettie to her feet, he escorted her just beyond the blanket's fringe. He wound the phonograph spring to its near limit, and set the record free on the rotating platter. As the steel needle drifted on the wax's edge, Jacob lifted Kettie's hand into his, and wrapped his arm around her waist. The notes of a waltz escaped the brass horn. Soothing the hilltop with an enchanting ambience, the music prompted the young couple into motion.

Staring up into Jacob's eyes, Kettie began to grin. "I just realized something. We are dancing at the top of the prairie."

"I guess we are." Jacob concurred. "How does it feel?"

"It feels new…fresh…it feels wonderful." She closed her eyes momentarily as their soft flowing movements lulled her senses.

"I'm glad you like it. I wouldn't want to share this dance with anyone else."

As the music continued, their bodies swayed, and rose and fell with each step, to the moderately slow beat.

"This has been a most perfect outing, Jacob." Kettie stepped around him in a full turn.

"I'm pleased you are enjoying yourself, but I still have something to show you. Like I said, it's very special."

"Oh, now it's *very* special." She glanced about the hillside. "Would you like me to close my eyes?"

"No, believe me." He nodded. "You'll want to see every second of this."

"You certainly have my undivided attention. Continue your lead and I'll follow."

Gliding through the wind-sewn weave of yellow black-eyed Susan and purple Echinacea coneflowers, the air began to imbue a bright orange tint as a kaleidoscope of countless butterflies engulfed their graceful movements. The music played on, inducing a surreal splendor, as Jacob and Kettie's heads swirled with the twirling wave.

"Oh, Jacob. I could never have imagined." A tear rolled down her cheek. "It's…it's so breathtakingly beautiful."

"Did you really mean what you said?" He looked into her eyes. "You know, about the Jenny. About being unsure in coming with me?"

"If traveling with you is even half as exhilarating as this, I believe you could talk me into going just about anywhere with you."

"Then, marry me."

The orchestral instruments dampened as Kettie turned a partial ear toward Jacob. "Please say that again. I want to be sure I heard you, correct."

"I have never felt this way about anyone before. I don't want to lose you. Please, marry me, and I promise I will pick flowers for you the rest of my life."

A smile turned upon her lips. "Do you butterfly promise?"

"Yes. Yes, I butterfly promise." Jacob laughed. "I butterfly promise I will love you forever."

Kettie nodded. "I love you so much, Jacob." She stared into his eyes. "Yes, I will marry you."

The music strengthened in full and then arrived at its final note, as Jacob and Kettie touched their lips together. Embracing within the whirling mass of ten thousand messengers, their everlasting promise to each other began its ascension to angels in wait.

The thunderous roar of a biplane engine broke the celestial silence. Appearing from the meadow below, the aircraft barely cleared the hilltop while scattering the butterfly swirl within the vortices' churning wake. Veering to the side, it gained altitude as it turned to conduct another pass.

"It's the Jenny!" Jacob screamed. "Look, it's the Jenny. Roman got it off the ground...and he's flying!" Both leaped into the air while waving their arms as Roman sailed a pass above them, and returned the gesture.

Peter's hammer bounced upon the ground. "Maria! Maria, come quick!" He rushed to the house while observing the airplane approaching above the horizon.

"What is it, Peter?" The screen door cracked against its frame as Maria stepped out onto the front porch. Squinting beneath a shielding hand toward the nearing sound, she spotted the aircraft to which Peter pointed. "Oh, no."

"Oh, no, is right. Somehow, that damned fool brother-in-law of mine got that worthless contraption off the ground. He's going to put himself or someone else into a pine box."

The sky tractor rumbled along, hurdling the cottonwood treetops of the winding shoreline and dispersing the pelicans over the rippling waves of Pickerel Lake. Pulling the control stick and pressing the foot bar, Roman tested the machine's constraints in an attempt to locate the source of an occasional shudder. Coming upon Peter's farmstead, he reached into his leather aviator coat and retrieved a half-pint of gin.

"Here's to my brother-in-law, Peter." He raised the bottle. "My sister married a good man, God rest her soul." As he gulped from the opening, a severe vibration shook the liquor from his hand. Juggling the dancing bottle, Roman watched over the side of the cockpit as it jumped from his fingertips and plummeted toward a running Peter, who dove for cover at the plane's passing.

"Sorry, my old friend." Roman gave a half salute to the tumbling bottle. "Looks like drinks are on you today, Peter." He chuckled as he observed the glass shatter upon impact with the ground. "You sure are limber for an old man. I'll give you that much."

Gliding through a climb in a left-hand turn, Roman felt the fuselage shake once again. Concerned for his safety, he maneuvered the controls to gain additional altitude as he began a desperate search to find a suitable location for an impromptu landing. Returning over the farm site, the plane shook violently, causing a landing wheel to lose its grip from the axle, and target a small poultry building below.

Peter watched the chickens scatter as the plunging disk crashed through the coop's pent roof, rolled out the door, and bounced down the pleated ramp. He threw his hands up and screamed. "You damned lunatic. You'll pay for that."

The plane's engine sputtered and coughed. Roman leaned from the cockpit and surveyed the damaged to the building, and then the bare axle that once supported the missing wheel. Nursing the failing engine with the dashboard controls, he set a course for the incline below the summit where Jacob and Kettie picnicked.

"Roman's flying this way." Jacob shaded the bright sky from his eyes. "Something's not right." He turned an ear toward the engine's rough operation. "He's having problems. I hope he makes it back."

Clearing the hilltop, Roman slowed the Jenny's ground speed by braking against the slope's updraft. As the remaining landing wheel touched the ground, the bare axle of the opposite side pulled into the meadow's sod. The biplane spun and cartwheeled, collapsing the wings onto the fuselage. Rolled into a disfigured ball of wood fragments, wire, and cotton fabric, the Jenny lay completely destroyed.

Jacob and Kettie rushed to ascertain Roman's unknown fate as a plume of dark smoke began to drift above the wreckage. Finding him unconscious within the confines of the crushed frame, they freed his body, and dragged him from the debris as the flames began to grow. A small explosion forced the three to the ground, followed by a secondary detonation that devoured the remains of the Jenny.

"Did I land it?" Roman slid his goggles upward, and supported his head with both hands as he slowly regained consciousness. "Did I land the Jenny?"

Jacob rolled to his seat. He sat motionless as he watched the smoke swirl about the taunting flames. "It's on the ground." He sighed. "So, yeah, yeah, in a sense, you landed it all right."

Roman spun around. "Oh, my god!" He leaned forward and reached toward the fiery pile of rubble. "I'm sorry. I'm so sorry. I wrecked the Jenny." He fell back. "I should have never taken it up. I should have waited and checked for more repairs."

"Forget the Jenny." Jacob looked at Roman. "It was never meant to be. You're alive, and that's all that matters."

"No. No, it's my fault." He shook his head. "I'll make it up to you. I swear, somehow, I'll set things right."

"Listen to Jacob." Kettie paused while examining Roman's wounds, and pointed at the burning mass. "You are very fortunate to be alive after what you've just been through." She wiped a trickle of blood from his forehead. "We can find another Jenny, but we could never replace you."

Jacob chuckled. "You were flying, Roman." He pushed on his shoulder. "You were actually soaring through the sky, like an eagle."

"Yes. Yes, I guess I was." He grinned. "Oh, it was just as I remembered – the power, the excitement, and the adrenalin rush. It...it..."

"Look," Jacob pointed at Roman's aviator cap, "you're bleeding from the exact same place where the previous pilot was cut."

Roman flinched as he felt his wound through the old gash in the leather. "What in the hell..." He ripped the helmet from his head and threw it into the fire. "I was right. It was nothing but a death plane."

Brushing the side of his pant leg, Jacob felt the copper-nickel pistol cartridge within his pocket. His thoughts drifted to the three strangers who happened onto his aunt and uncle's farm, and the words of the well-dressed man who visited with Kettie and him.

"What do we do now?" Kettie moved next to Jacob and stared at the fire while holding his arm.

Jacob shrugged his shoulders. "What can we do, but hope for something better."

The flames continued to reach into the sky, spewing a tall chimney of dark smoke directly above them. Both pushed themselves to their feet and stood watching as their plans to travel the country in the biplane disintegrated into ash. The dreams, the adventure, the excitement, slowly vanished before their eyes. Reaching for each other's hand, they held tight to one another as the popping and cracking of the blaze perforated the quelling silence at the top of the prairie.

Chapter 16

PROVINCE of West Prussia, 1886. Pious silhouettes darkened. As the late evening horizon absorbed the remaining orange and violet hued half-light, the shadowed, jagged structures, perched above a small village, hinted at a provisional sanctuary to the passing weary.

Stepping within one another's footsteps, two Prussian soldiers stared upon the heels of their leader in following his quick pace as they arrived at the town's outskirts, just before dark. The vacant streets carried a fresh emptiness. The stagnant smell of settling road dust and laboring draught animals irritated their nostrils and watered their eyes. Loosening burdensome knapsacks, they patted empty, linen, bread pouches, while searching for the light of a local inn, where rumbling stomachs could find temporary relief.

Black soot clouded the cooling air above the torched foundation of a once consecrated place of worship. Rummaging through the ash and scorched cedars, an old man and his nephew stockpiled a partial cord of fragmented rafters and beams.

"You won't find anything of value there." A soldier cupped his mouth as he called out in passing. "What the Catholics didn't take, thieves did."

"We're not looking for treasure." The old man responded. "Just finding timber pieces for a fire. The chard ones catch easier."

The leader pointed for his men to take note, and chuckled. "The church is of better use now than when it was whole." The two followers joined in laughter as they continued on into the village in search of food and rest.

With a cautious eye on the soldiers, the scavengers continued sifting through the debris. As the three turned out of sight, the young

191

man kicked into the stacked pieces, scattering them about the ruins. "Uncle Karl, I don't understand why you dragged me with you to dig beneath this pile of ash. This is too dangerous. We were almost caught."

The old man extended the long handle of a shovel. "Just keep your voice down, Leo, and dig. I wouldn't ask for your help if I wouldn't have twisted my arm here last night. I can no longer do it by myself."

"Foolishness." Leo shook his head as he stepped the shovel's blade into the soil. "That's what this is, foolishness that will get us both beaten and thrown into prison like the priest and the others. I should be on my way to Hamburg with my wife and son," he stopped and stretched a hand toward the rubble, "instead of this." He looked toward the east. "I should be on my way to America."

"Settle down. Settle down." The old man struck a match and lit his pipe. "America is not going anywhere." He extinguished the flame with a quick wave. "Trust me. There will be plenty of time to travel. Steamships leave the docks from Hamburg every day."

"But my days here have ended. I sold my farm to the Prussian Colonization Commission and must vacate by tomorrow." He looked at his uncle. "Why don't you sell like I did, and come along with us? There's plenty of good, fertile land to buy overseas."

"I'll stay. This has always been the land of the Poles, the home of our ancestors." The old man patted his chest. "This is my home as well."

"Home? Home is where you are welcomed. Do you think that ruthless monster, Chancellor Bismarck, wants you here?"

"I'm not concerned with what Bismarck wants." He blew a puff of smoke into the air, and looked away.

"Well, I'll tell you what he wants. He wants us dead…all of us. He said that Poles are like wolves. You shoot them if you can."

"Ah. I'm still alive. You're still alive. He can't kill us all."

"And my land. Do you actually think the Commission is going to resell it to a Pole? No! The whole program is designed to relocate Germans to Polish lands, and push us out for good."

"If you don't approve of what they are doing, then why did you sell to the Commission?"

Leo speared the shovel into the ground. "The same reason other Poles sold their land." He threw a heap of dirt onto a pile. "I've had enough."

The old man nodded in agreement.

Leo stopped and leaned upon the shovel handle. "It's not that I've given up. It's just that I don't want my son and his children to live like this. Everything Polish, including our language is forbidden in schools and public offices. Catholics have been thrown out of civic positions, and they've even confiscated our Catholic newspapers. The list goes on and on. Basically it comes down to Bismarck wanting to eliminate our Polish national identity by forced Germanisation."

The young man bent down and turned a few more shovels of dirt. Lifting a portion of a blackened crucifix, he pried the severed arm of Christ from the wood crossbar. "God is not here. He never was. If he were, this church would still be standing, not burned to the ground." He threw the carved limb to the side. "We would all be safe in our homes instead of hiding in them."

A sharp slap silenced the young man's tongue, as Karl's hand swatted his mouth. "Don't you ever talk like that again!" He waved a rigid finger. "God is here, oh yes, he certainly is here."

Leo wiped the drivel from the side of his mouth. "I mean no disrespect to the Heavenly Father," he traced the sign of the cross upon himself, "but if he were here, would not this church still be standing? Would we all not be attending Mass instead of running from the Protestants?"

"God did not build this church, man did. It was built by man, and it was destroyed by man. Do you think God cares about a bunch of sticks and mud? Nonsense." Karl pushed the back of his hand against the young man's shoulder. "That's free will."

Leo smiled and threw a shovel full of dirt. He stopped and wiped the sweat from his forehead as he pointed toward a dried pile of earth. "Looks like you dug a deep hole last night. If I'm not mistaken, that's where the altar was, right?"

"That's right. And I found nothing there. I felt like a damned fool, thinking the stories I heard told over the years were just that, nothing but stories. Then while walking home, I happened to remember when I was a boy, my grandfather speaking to another village elder about the sanctuary being moved years before." He pointed at the spot where they were currently excavating, and then to the hole of the previous night.

"Uncle, you still haven't told me what we are digging for."

"I'm not exactly sure, myself, but I'll know when we find it."

Leo shook his head. "I should have never agreed to this. If we don't find anything here, you won't be the only one feeling like a damned fool. I'll be second on that list."

A loud crack echoed from the base of the hole as the shovel bounced off the bottom.

Karl's eyes widened. "That's got to be it."

Leo lifted the shovel. "It's either that, or we just unearthed a grave. One of the early villagers, I would guess."

Karl stared at Leo. "Now who's being foolish?" He pointed at the hole. "Just clear the dirt away."

Leo's shovel encountered little resistance as decayed wood crumbled with each and every strike. "It's getting too dark out here to see anything down there, but whatever it is, we busted a hole through it."

Pointing down into the blackness, Karl looked up and scanned the building shadows for possible encroachers. "Reach down in there and tell me what you feel." He glanced around once more. "And be quick about it. I'm starting to get an uneasy feeling."

"Me? Reach in there?" Flipping a small pebble into the air, both watched as it passed through the hole's rim and disappeared from sight. "You must be joking. I agreed to help you dig, but you said nothing about sticking my hands down into a box of dead man's bones. For all we know, it could even be the opening to the gates of hell."

"It's not the gates of hell!" Karl restrained his voice. "It's not a grave, and it's not the gates of hell. Please, just reach down in there and tell me what you feel."

Leo hesitated, and then slumped to his knees. Rolling onto his side, he slowly reached down into the darkness. His eyes closed as he began to grope about.

"What do you feel, Leo?" Karl leaned forward.

"I feel…I feel…Ah!" Leo lurched about the hole as he cried out in pain.

"Leo! Leo!" Karl collapsed upon the ground and tugged at Leo's arm in an attempt to set him free.

A burst of laughter erupted as a smile pulled across Leo's face.

"You idiot. What the hell is wrong with you?" Karl wiped his forehead with a trembling hand. "Do you think this is some sort of game?"

Leo continued a quiet laughter. "It serves you right, Uncle." He began to probe the cavity with his hand. "Reach into the hole," he mimicked the words of his uncle, "huh."

Pulling a handkerchief from his pocket, Karl sat up and blotted the sweat beginning to bead upon his face. His neck stiffened as he looked over the foundation's edge in scrutinizing the movement of wandering shadows.

"Wait, I found something." Leo stretched his reach.

"Stop it with your nonsense." Karl poked the cloth back into his pocket.

"No. I mean it. I can feel it."

Karl rotated to his knees. "Can you grab hold and pull it up?"

"Wait." A series of low grunts muffled in the hole as his reach deepened. "There's too much debris in there to pull it through. Wait." Gritting his teeth, he maneuvered the rotted wood around the object and wrenched it through the opening. "I've got it!"

Karl sparked a match and ignited the lantern wick. Its light reflected off the dull tarnish of an intricately embossed miniature chest. Brushing the loose soil from the surface, Leo pried his thumbs upon the lid.

"No!" Karl smacked Leo's hands away. "No, don't open it."

"But, Uncle…"

"I understand the curiosity is strong, but neither one of us has a real need to actually look at, let alone touch, what's in there." Karl pulled a thin strip of leather from his pocket and tied it around the box. "Trust me. You'll sleep better not having opened it."

Leo stepped back. "I don't understand. We were almost thrown into prison for searching for something you weren't even sure existed, and then when we do, by pure luck, find the thing, we can't even examine what it is that we took the risk for."

Karl traced his finger over the recessed image of a pierced wing, etched within the designs of the tin. "This is our family crest." He lifted the chest and placed it before him. "Hundreds of years ago, one of our ancestors participated in the crusades. Before engaging in the northern clashes, he traveled on a pilgrimage to the Holy Land in protecting and serving the King of Jerusalem. While there, he unintentionally discovered the artifact within this case and presented it to the king. The king in turn entrusted it to him for safe keeping. It seems he felt there was a purpose that God revealed it to the knight, and the piece should stay with him. Upon his return to Poland, the opportunity presented itself where he secretly buried it beneath the church altar, and it has remained until now." He smiled at Leo. "Its existence here is only known by our family, with the knowledge passed down generation to generation, from father to son."

"But, Uncle, I'm not your son."

"I have no sons." He placed Leo's hand upon the tin. "And the altar no longer stands. It's under your charge now."

Leo pulled his hand away. "What are you saying?"

"Tomorrow, when you leave, you must take it with you." Karl placed it in Leo's hands. "Take it to America. You must follow the tradition of our ancestors in adhering to the wishes of the King of Jerusalem."

"How do I do that?"

"Find a good safe place for it."

"But it's just an old tin box with who knows what's inside." Leo rattled the contents. "It's a good story, but you keep it." He shoved the chest toward Karl. "I have enough to worry about with Basia and little Peter. I don't want to take anything along that may beleaguer our trip." He stepped onto a pile of rubble and strained to peer into the darkness. "How about we find a nice safe place around here, and replant it?"

Karl stared at Leo. "We can't trust it here any longer."

"What? Weren't you the one telling me earlier about God not being concerned with man-made wood and mud structures?"

Karl nodded. "Yes." He pushed a finger into Leo's face. "And you're right. This could have been made by man, but then again, it may have been forged by angels. Either way, it was most certainly touched by God."

Rocks scattered from a debris pile as a Prussian soldier stumbled into the church's foundation. "We are needing to start a fire as well." He picked himself up and leaned over to gather a handful of chard wood pieces. Noticing the lantern's dull reflection off the tin covered box, he dropped the kindling and stepped forward. "What is that you have there?" His eyes widened. "Papist treasure?"

As the corporal lurched for the chest, Karl grasped the shovel handle and swung it over his head, knocking the man unconscious. A bright flash lit the shadows with a bark of thunder, dropping Karl to his knees. Leo grabbed the wooden crucifix limb, and threw it at the approaching soldier, knocking his rifle from its aim. Losing his balance, the man tottered on one foot, and then fell backward upon the remnant cross, its metal spike piercing his back and protruding through his sternum.

Leo rushed to Karl's side and placed the old man's head in his lap. "Uncle! Uncle!" His hand patted listless cheeks.

Karl's eyes fluttered open. "Looks like Bismarck has added another wolf pelt to his collection." He coughed, producing a flow of blood from the corner of his mouth. "At least he felt the sting of my bite before he stole it."

"You're going to be fine, Uncle." Leo noticed lanterns exiting from nearby homes, and voices mixing with the yap of dogs. "I'll take you to help."

"No. I'm afraid it's too late for me. You must leave. Leave now. The remaining soldier surely heard the gunshot. He'll be upon us soon." Karl reached his arm out and laid his hand upon the tin chest. "Please, take it. Take it with you."

"But, Uncle."

"You'll know what to do with it when the time comes." Karl drew in a deep breath, and slowly exhaled.

"Uncle?" Leo shook the lifeless body that lay before him. "No, this can't be happening. Uncle!"

"I believe it came from over there." Distant voices grew louder. "Check the church ruins."

As the approaching lights flickered through the piled timbers, Leo quickly plopped back down next to Karl's side. Closing his uncle's eyes, he whispered a small prayer as he turned his sight toward the star filled sky above. "Goodbye, Uncle." He kissed the old man's forehead, and extinguished the lantern's wick.

The S.S. Rugia's bow dipped beneath the wave. As the ocean water reached over the railing and danced upon the steamship's deck, young Peter wiped the salty spray from his face with the sleeve of his coat, and wrenched the tin chest beneath his arm. Stalking a scavenging gull, he climbed the outer railing and shimmied along its top beam. While slowly reaching for the teetering bird's legs, the boat suddenly dropped from beneath them. Striving to scream, a hand clenched the back of his coat before a shriek could escape the bottom of his throat. Peter looked at his feet dangling above the sloshing ocean current. As his eyes widened, he felt a labored yank return him to the deck side of the outer railing. Glancing upward, he watched the gull float on a wind current and veer to the port side of the ship.

"Unlike your prey, you haven't quite developed the ability of horizontal flight." The stranger tugged at the brim of his hat in deflecting falling rain droplets. "Vertical is the best you could manage, and I'm afraid downward is the only option."

"There you are young man!" Leo rushed to the railing and pulled Peter next to him. "Your ma and I have been searching everywhere for you." He looked at the stranger. "Thank you, mister." He extended his hand.

"The name's Woodard." He shook Leo's hand. "Reverend Thaddeus Woodard."

"Thank you, Reverend. Your selfless action saved my son's life. I am in debt to you. Please let me know if I can ever be of help."

He looked up at the falling rain. "Can you do anything about this?" He chuckled.

Leo glanced at the heavy clouds and shook his head. "Yes, my wife and I are ready to be through with this voyage. The dreary weather hasn't made it any better."

"It won't be long now." The reverend pointed to a dark gray blur upon the horizon. "New York Harbor is not far away. Once there, you'll move through immigrant processing at Castle Garden on a little island off the southwest tip of Manhattan. They'll assist you with searching for work in the New York area, or purchasing tickets for transportation elsewhere."

"You've been through the processing before?"

"No. I've done my share of traveling though."

Leo nodded. "Once again, thank you." He guided Peter by the base of his neck and turned to walk away.

"There may be one thing." The reverend followed. "That's a most interesting design etched into the tin on that box your son is carrying."

Leo stopped, glanced at the box, and then placed his arm on Peter's shoulder in moving on.

Woodard followed at their heels. "Please, sir, I mean you and the boy no harm. As I said, my name is Reverend Thaddeus Woodard. I work in the study of religious relics for a church sponsored university. I'm only interested in the tin your son is carrying. Actually, I know of two in the world just like it. Neither one of them are in as extraordinary condition, such as this one."

Leo stopped once again and smiled. "You are mistaken. The box contains children's toys. The design was stamped by my son. It is of no importance to anyone but him."

The reverend laughed. "Hiding in plain sight. How ingenious. You have no need to worry. I can assure you I am the only one aboard ship who could identify the symbols."

Leo stared at the reverend.

"May I ask what the box contains?" Woodard pointed as Peter pulled the chest tight beneath his arm.

"I told you, children's toys."

"You can call it a coincidence or you can call it Divine Providence. Either way, I am a man who can provide proper placement of the box's contents within the safekeeping of the church."

"And which church is that?"

"Does it really matter? As long as it's Christian? As long as it recognizes the position of the bishop of Rome as supreme pastor?"

"No, the box stays with us."

"Maybe you would be more inclined to accept a monetary offer in exchange for the enclosed contents. I assure you, it will remain in Christian hands. It will be cared for with the utmost respect for Divine relics. Please, sir, our meeting was meant to be. God would want it placed where it can remain safe and secure."

"God made his decision. It stays with us." Leo pushed Peter along as the reverend followed.

"I understand. Please, sir, then may I ask a small favor of you?"

Leo stopped.

"It's a personal request, nothing to do with the church, just my own private indulgence. You see, I have spent most of my professional life searching for religious antiquities. As you can imagine, they are few and far between, so when I do happen upon one, the excitement sets my soul to dance like nothing else in this world." He smiled. "Would you be so kind as to allow me to at least touch the box?"

Leo looked down at his son and nodded toward the reverend.

Peter cradled the chest tightly within both arms as Woodard knelt before it. Reaching out, the reverend's hand began to tremble. His eyes closed, and his lips moved in silent prayer, as his palm hovered inches above the tin etchings. Resting his hand upon the box, his body fell limp and an expression of peaceful contentment appeared within his face.

"Come along, son." Leo pulled upon the young boy's shoulder as they turned and walked away.

The reverend struggled to his feet. "I wish you and your family safe travels." He called out. "God is with you."

The train's boarding whistle blew loud and long. Safeguarding the smaller luggage, Basia stood on a bench seat and scanned the station crowd of immigrants, in search of Peter. Her repeated calls absorbed into the deafening babble of voices. In waving her white handkerchief, she eventually drew the attention of her approaching husband.

"It took longer than expected to load the trunks into the baggage car." Leo helped her down from the bench. "Is everything all right?"

"No. It's Peter." She tucked the small cloth within her sleeve. "I can't seem to find him. He wandered off. He was with me one second, and then gone the next."

The mass surged as the steam whistle blared the command once again.

"That boy." He caught a glimpse of the conductor opening the doors of the passenger cars. "Just when they're beginning to board." He shook his head. "You stay here with our bags. I'll find him."

"Peter!" Leo's call was interrupted by a slight tug on his hand. Looking down, he discovered the young boy at his side, wiping tears from his face. "Why, there you are." Leo knelt down.

"Oh, Peter." Basia dried his eyes with her handkerchief. "You had us worried."

"Pa, I went looking for you to help, but the man took my chest."

Leo held his shoulders. "Which man was that, the baggage clerk?"

"No. The man on the Rugia. The man who wanted to touch it."

Leo jumped to his feet and studied the passing faces. Some were of those they met aboard ship, others of strangers, but the reverend was no where to be found. "Do you remember in which direction he went?"

Peter pointed with an outstretched arm. "I tried to catch him, Pa, but I got lost."

"Don't worry son, you stay here with your ma."

He turned to Basia. "I've got to try and find that man."

She clenched his coat sleeve. "But the train is about to leave."

Leo watched a blast of steam escape from the whistle as it cried once more. "I have to try, Basia. I must go now. You and Peter board the train. I promise I'll be back before it leaves."

"I'm afraid. We should wait and take a different train."

"No. We were fortunate to purchase tickets for this one. The Castle Garden clerk said there are a large number of new arrivals expected again today. If he's correct, we wouldn't be able to leave for maybe another week. We can't afford to pay for one more night of these ridiculously high prices they are charging immigrants, let alone a week. We must leave now."

Leo disappeared into the crowd. Forcing himself against the flow of traffic, he spun and bounced within the compressed pack of boarding immigrants. A familiar brown, bowler hat moved toward the exit. Just beyond his reach, he leaped into the flow of bodies and clenched onto the man's arm.

"Not so fast, Woodard." His grip loosened as the pull of the crowd separated him from the thief.

Yanked from his balance, the reverend caught the tin chest as it slipped from his hands. He turned to look, and saw Leo's outreaching arm vanish within the swirl of woolen coats and dark leather baggage. Alarmed, he continued to fight his way toward the station entrance.

Leo struggled to follow, careful not to lose sight for too long. Reaching the entrance, he scanned the street and spotted the reverend scurrying down the sidewalk. A hasty leap from the steps sprawled Leo onto his back as he collided with a stranger. Rocking to his seat, his eyes came within inches of an oval shield pinned to a dark blue uniform.

"Say! Just who do you think you are!" The policeman freed his baton in attempting to push himself from the pavement.

Leo sprang up and lifted the officer by his arm. "I apologize, sir. It was an accident."

"An accident? I've got a good mind to run you in." He suddenly realized the heavy accent in Leo's voice. "Oh, you must be one of them. Well, you've got a lot to learn about manners. A night's stay behind bars will educate you quite quickly."

"Yes sir." Leo swiped his hat from the ground and sprinted off as the officer shouted demands for him to return.

The Reverend Woodard hastened his step with the thinning of the sidewalk traffic. Brief glances over his shoulders calmed his nerves with every turn of his neck. A glimpse down at the tin chest beneath his arm produced a half smile and a curt chuckle.

Blinding stars engulfed the daylight as the reverend felt a tackling blow to his side. Hurtled from his feet into the adjacent alley, he toppled a stack of wooden crates, scattering its refuse about the entrance.

As his eyes reformed the city's image, he found himself staring up at the countless rows of drying wash swaying upon the clotheslines connecting the multistory buildings. A sudden realization as to the reason he lay there, sprung his hand patting about his side. The chest was gone. Rolling onto his knees, he discovered Leo, retrieving the box from beneath the trash and wrapping it with a soiled rag.

"Please." The reverend held his head while attempting to rise. "You must understand, it is best if the tin stays with me. I can provide for the safekeeping of its contents."

"As I told you before, it belongs to me."

"It does not belong to you. It is given for all of mankind. It should be kept under the watchful eye of those who understand its importance, and not by those who are biblically illiterate."

"Stop right there!" The policeman's voice screamed from the walkway. "You steamship rats are all alike." He pulled the baton from his belt. "It's bad enough that we put up with you people bringing sickness over here, but I'll be damned if I'll let you get away with disrespecting the law."

Leo looked at the box and then held it out for the officer to see. "Sir, I was only getting back what this man stole from my son."

The reverend reached into his coat. "The name is Reverend Thaddeus Woodard. You can examine my credentials if you wish." He extended a leather bound pocketbook. "I demand that you arrest this immigrant."

The muffled sound of the train whistle swirled in Leo's ear. As the policeman reached for the papers, Leo wrapped the soiled rag around the officer's head, and shoved him into the reverend, sending both tumbling to the ground.

Dashing through the street congestion, Leo maintained a steady lead on the series of shrill police whistles signaling an eagerness for his immediate apprehension. He leaped up the train depot steps, stopped, and turned toward the roadway. A single file of dark blue jackets speared through the crowd with the offended officer in the lead, and the reverend at his side, pointing toward Leo. "There he is!"

Leo felt a hand clutch his arm. He spun around to discover a fellow steamship passenger he met during the transatlantic voyage on the Rugia.

"Ah, a familiar face in the crowd." The man spoke in their native Polish language.

The train car couplers clanged in succession against the steam engine's struggle to break friction with the tracks and accelerate. Looking over the man's shoulder, Leo watched as the final car crept from the dock.

"I'm sorry, my friend," Leo shook his hand, "but I must be on that train with my wife and son."

The man glanced at the departing observation car. "Then you must go, and go now."

Leo nodded toward the policemen ascending the steps.

"Go." The man nudged Leo. "I'll slow them the best I can."

Spinning through the waves of compressed bodies, Leo suddenly tumbled out and onto the clearing next to the tracks. Angry shouts erupted at the depot entrance from where he left his friend. Leo hesitated as he looked back, and then jumped onto the tracks, skipping from timber to timber, closing the distance between himself and the departing train cars.

As Leo grabbed onto the wrought iron railing of the observation car's platform, the train engine lurched forward, causing him to lose his footing from the steps. Dragging along the aggregate and wooden ties, he kicked frantically to regain his hold. Finger by finger his grip gradually weakened. He glanced at the chest beneath his arm and contemplated whether to drop the tin box and pull himself on board with both hands, or release himself from the platform and hope to outmaneuver the police while venturing to meet up with his family somewhere down the line. Outstretched arms unexpectedly appeared over the side. Reaching down, Basia and Peter grasped Leo's coat and pulled him to safety.

Feeling Basia press upon his shoulder, he looked up and saw her pointing back toward the train station. He turned his head and watched as numerous batons, pointing skyward, poured down upon the remaining helpless immigrants waiting upon the dock. At the edge of the savage chaos, the Reverend Woodard stood and stared at them, as they accelerated down the clackity tracks upon the departing train.

Enticed by the federal government offering of plentiful land available in the Dakotas, Leo and his family traveled the line and settled on a claim near Pickerel Lake and the Polish village of Grenville. Talks of expanding and rebuilding the local Catholic Parish church caught his attention. He approached the priest with his unique request, and the tin chest was subsequently buried beneath the new altar. Its presence there known only to the present priest and those who would succeed him in the years to come.

Early summer, 1925.

A long exhale faded. Lying upon the hardwood floor below the altar, Father Majer's body remained motionless. The early morning sunlight crept its stained glass colored rays up the side of his face, as a small housefly set foot upon the tip of his nose. A loud snore growled from his throat. Lifting a hand from his side, he swiped at the pest and then fell back into his previous state of slumber.

Knock! Knock! Knock! A rap on the front entrance doors echoed about the church walls. His left eye partially opened. The sparkle of the large glass candelabra, suspended from the ceiling above him, teased at his weariness. His pupil rolled beneath his lid and his eye closed once again.

Knock! Knock! Knock! The beat grew louder with each blow.

"Klan!" Father Majer sat straight up. His heart raced as he looked about the room. "Daylight. Yes, daylight. No Klan in the daylight. I must have been dreaming." He rubbed his eyes and lay back down. "We made it through one more night." He traced the sign of the cross upon himself. "Thank you, Heavenly Father."

Knock! Knock! Knock! The priest sat up once again. "That's no dream."

The steel bar rang out as Father Majer pulled it from the entrance door in disassembling the makeshift locking brace. Propping the bar in the corner, he opened the door with his free hand.

"Father Majer?" Jacob peered into the widening crack.

"Jacob, it's good to see you." The priest squinted at the incoming daylight.

"The sisters said you were..."

"I apologize for not being ready. I forgot there was a game scheduled for today." The priest stepped outside the church doorways and glanced about the parking area. "Ask the others to wait while I get ready."

"We don't play today, Father."

"What, no game?"

Jacob laughed. "No. I'm not here to play baseball." He turned toward the girl at his side. "I wanted to introduce you to Kettie."

"Oh, so this is the young lady I've heard about." He took her hand. "Maria has been saying that Jacob had a new friend. She said they know little about you, but Jacob has not quit smiling in weeks. It's a pleasure to meet you."

Kettie nodded. "Thank you. And you as well."

"I have not had my coffee this morning. Come with me." He placed a hand on their shoulders and began walking them down the steps. "The sisters will enjoy the company as well."

Jacob stopped. "Actually, Father, we were hoping to speak with you in private. I apologize if we were supposed to contact you beforehand."

"Nonsense. You know you don't need to schedule an appointment to see me. Besides, coffee can wait." He looked toward the rectory and rubbed his hand over the dry corners of his mouth. "Don't ever tell anyone I said that. To some around here, coffee time is tantamount to church time. It wouldn't surprise me one bit if some parishioners actually drank their morning brew while bent on both knees." His boisterous laugh brought quick smiles. He patted Jacob's back. "It's a beautiful morning – a good time to stroll through the garden."

The subtle scent of lilies swirled within the sweet aromas of iris and peonies, and drifted about the freshly cut grass along the cobblestone walkway. Chortles and croaks echoed within the leafy elm treetops as a flock of steel blue colored swallows ruddered their forked tails through the maze of braided limbs and into the open flyway. Perched upon the miniature porch edges, some nourished young occupants of the elevated multi-cavity birdhouses.

"Ah, the purple martin colony has returned in great numbers." The priest pointed toward the staggered houses.

"I remember cleaning the houses as a young boy in school." Jacob tugged upon one of the lift ropes, and then tested the tightness of its knot. "The sisters would pay me with pieces of hard candy."

"Yes, it's good to teach young people these things." The priest reassured him.

"I was fortunate. One of the boys, Iggy, tended to the flowerbeds." Jacob knelt down and matched the broken ends of a crippled peony's stem. "He disliked it so, and the others taunted him relentlessly for it. One day, he became so upset over the teasing that he decapitated all the tulips from the stems with the garden knife." He snapped the cherry red flower at the break and presented it to Kettie.

"All of them?" Kettie touched the soft petals against her lips as she drew in a long easy breath.

Jacob stood up and nodded.

"How awful he must have felt to do such a thing."

"Yes. The sisters were not pleased one bit with any one of us."

"Poor child." The priest shook his head. "Sometimes, children act more like adults than we prefer to think." He glanced at Kettie's hand. "I noticed your ring finger wrapped in platinum, my dear. Is that what you two have come to discuss?"

"Yes, Father." Jacob looked deep into Kettie's eyes. "We would like to be married." Both smiled at the priest. "And we would be most pleased if you would perform the ceremony for us."

"I think we could arrange for that." Father Majer chuckled. "Tell me Kettie, did he ask for your hand on a baseball field?"

"No. Not a baseball field. More like a butterfly field."

"Butterflies? Ah, yes, written on the wings. Then we must not disappoint." He pressed his eyelids closed and thought for a moment. "On the wings of thee I do write. A promise made while ye take flight. To the heavens ye will flow. To the angels who will know." His eyes popped open. "There is more to it, but it slips my mind." He shook his head and laughed. "It's been many many years since I read that poem."

Jacob smiled. "Then, you know of this?"

The priest nodded. "Yes. Something from my youth. I thank you for helping me find that memory, my dear." The priest extended his arm in resuming their walk through the garden. "During the past year that I've been here, I've come to know Jacob's family quite well. Please, Kettie, would you mind sharing with me a little about yourself?"

Kettie folded her hands behind herself. "My family is in Minneapolis, but I am living with my aunt and uncle in Webster while I attended nursing school at the Peabody Hospital."

"I'm familiar with the St. Otto's Parish in Webster. Which parish in Minneapolis were you a member of?"

Kettie hesitated. "As in Catholic?"

"Oh." Father Majer raised an eyebrow. "You're not Catholic?"

"No. I'm Protestant. You see, my aunt and uncle are the Reverend and Mrs. Woodard."

The priest stopped. "Ah, yes, I met the Reverend Woodard on a number of occasions – a very outspoken individual."

"Then you'll understand if I tell you he would not be in favor of our engagement."

"And that is why you chose me and not him to perform the ceremony."

Jacob looked at Kettie and then at the priest. "You make it sound as though we are being deceitful."

"No, not at all. Although, you should let your families know as soon as possible. It will lessen any hard feelings, if they will exist at all."

"We'll do our best." Jacob conceded.

"I'm sure you will. Well, there is much to prepare for over the coming months. Do you have a specific date in mind for the wedding?"

"As soon as possible." Kettie exclaimed.

"Yes. We would marry today if we could." Jacob added.

"Oh." The priest smiled. "I believe today might be a little short of notice."

"Well, within the next few weeks, that is." Jacob looked at Kettie. "We are just anxious to start our new life together."

"I understand you are anxious. All couples feel that way. I would suggest waiting while you get to know each other even more than you do now. This will provide time for you and your families to prepare for your union. Any anticipated adverse feelings will fade in the time and allow your marriage to be truly honored by all.

Jacob shook his head. "I'm sorry, Father. We can't wait. We have plans to leave and start our new life together elsewhere."

"You two will make a fine couple. I can tell. Give it time. Let it grow. You will be pleasantly surprised at what will blossom – a strong, prosperous marriage."

Jacob turned away for a moment and then back toward the priest. "Then, you won't perform the marriage for us within the next few weeks? Fine, we'll find someone else."

"Please, don't become angry, Jacob. Think about what you are doing. Remember your childhood friend Iggy. His imprudent action might have worked in his favor, but many felt the pain because of it. I'm only considering what's best for the both of you, so believe me when I tell you it's for your own good."

Jacob glanced into Kettie's eyes. The glowing excitement no longer lit her face as before. Taking her hand into his, they turned and hastened back down the garden path from which they came. Pausing for an instant by the peonies, Jacob scooped the red blossom from Kettie's hand and dropped it within the flowerbed, where it bounced, and then rolled against the stem from which it was severed.

Chapter 17

THE graphite tip snapped. Arch wiped away the carbon fragments from the paper, and pried a single blade free from his pocketknife. Whittling the cedar pencil to an irregular point, he continued where he left off in calculating the lumber quote.

"Here you go, Vernon." Arch circled the estimated total. "Once again, I appreciate the opportunity for business the Klan has provided over the years."

"We take care of our own whenever possible." He scanned the list. "That should do. I'll notify the others to stop by and pick it up."

"Oh, no, Vernon. This isn't available now. I can place the order today. Should take about three weeks to arrive here, two if all goes well."

"Three weeks!" Vernon stared at the paper. "The Klan meeting will be over by then. No. No, that won't do. No, that won't do at all. They need the lumber now. We have to begin building platforms for the speakers and tables for the guests."

Arch slid the pencil behind his ear. "Sorry. There's nothing I can do about the shipping schedule. Two weeks is the quickest they can have it here."

"I thought I saw a shipment of lumber sitting at the depot yesterday. What do you have in stock now?"

"That lumber belongs to others. I couldn't possibly let you take that."

"Considering the circumstances, I'm sure you can persuade your customers to wait. They will certainly understand that the lumber is needed to benefit the community as a whole." Vernon turned the diamond centered fraternal ring about his finger. "Wouldn't you agree?" He looked at Arch.

"Most of it belongs to Gust. He's…" As the light reflected off the clear stone's multiple facets, the glare of the sparkle caught Arch's eye. He pulled a hand down his face. "No, please. Don't do this to me, Vernon. I beg you. These are good, honest people. I can't lie to them."

"If you're unwilling to convince them the lumber is needed elsewhere, business might become a little sparse for you. How long can you keep your doors open if you have no customers at all?"

The overhead bell rang as the door swung open and quickly closed. Gust gave a slight wave as he followed the worn path to the peanut barrel and scooped a handful, cupping it close to his chest.

"Well, Gust." Arch struggled to maintain a welcoming smile. "We were just talking about you." A nervous laugh withered within his throat.

"My ears were itching this morning. Now I know why. You must be telling wild stories about me, again." He stepped up to the far end of the counter and dropped the nuts onto the top. "I swear, if it weren't for me, I don't know what you'd do to entertain these people around here." He chuckled.

"Excuse me for a moment, Vernon." Arch pulled a clipboard from the wall. "I'll start Gust in the right direction, and then we can talk more about the order." He slid Gust's paperwork down the counter as he moved toward the end.

"I saw the lumber being unloaded from the train car, yesterday." Gust flipped the nuts from its half shell into his mouth. "I'll pull the truck inside the alley, and load. Just show me where to sign, and you can get back to your business."

A slow, steady knock haunted the room, as Vernon struck the diamond stone against the countertop with the back of his hand.

Gust looked up at Arch, and followed his frozen stare to Vernon, who sat motionless at the far end. He quickly spun back. "Arch?"

Arch did not move. His stare shifted to an empty gaze, while the pink tone vacated the flesh color of his face.

"Arch!" Gust pushed his hand into Arch's shoulder. "Is there a problem with my order?"

Arch's head whirled back as his eyelids fluttered. "Ah. Your order? No, Gust. There's no problem."

The grim knock returned. Its rhythm matched that of the wall clock's pendulum. When Vernon's hand ceased the motion, the controlling sound continued to intensify within Arch's head.

Gust glanced at Vernon and then back at Arch. Raising a finger, he opened his mouth.

The counter shook as Arch's hands smacked its edge and gripped tight. "I'm sorry Gust." His head fell below his shoulders. "I'll have to reorder your lumber."

"What are you talking about, reorder? It's here. I just told you I saw it arrive yesterday."

"I'm sorry, but it's my mistake. That belongs to someone else." He looked at Gust. "Why don't you let me reorder your lumber? It'll be here in a few weeks."

"But I've got work to complete. People are counting on me. How am I going to get paid if I don't finish the jobs?"

Gust nodded toward Vernon. "I know what the hell is going on here, and you don't have to do this, Arch. This is wrong and you know it."

"There is nothing I can do about it, Gust." He shook his head. "The Klan will boycott my store. They'll shut me down. I'll go out of business."

"This is bullshit. I've been a good customer of yours for many years," he swung a backhand in Vernon's direction, "long before the Klan was ever around." He pounded his fist upon the counter. "You've never had any problems with me, Arch. I've always paid my bill on time. Always!"

"Please, Gust." Arch raised his hands in an attempt to calm him. "Don't make this any harder than it has to be."

Gust turned toward Vernon. "You goddamned ring knockers! You're all alike. Expect everyone to bow down and kiss your ass at the drop of a hat."

"Gust, please." Arch reached across the counter and rested a hand on his shoulder.

Ignoring Gust's remarks, Vernon retrieved a cigar from his coat pocket. He bit off the end, struck a match, and puffed it to life.

Gust shoved Arch's hand to the side and stepped toward Vernon. "You must think you're some kind of big shot, pressing your thumb on the little people in this town, but not me. I'm not afraid of you."

A long, steady stream of smoke swirled from Vernon's mouth and filled the air above his head.

Gust advanced another step. "Look at me when I'm talking to you." He pulled away from Arch's attempts to hold him back. "It's about time someone stands up to you bastards. It's... It's..." Gust braced himself against the counter. His face contorted as he clenched his chest. "I'm not afraid of you. I'm not afraid of any of you." He dropped to his knees and sprawled upon the floor, unconscious.

"Oh, my god!" Arch leaped around the corner and knelt next to Gust. "Gust! Gust! You okay?"

The wooden stool creaked as Vernon stepped down upon the floor. He stood above Arch and blew a puff of smoke into the air. "See, Arch, sometimes these little problems end up working themselves out. I'll send some of the men over to retrieve that lumber." The overhead bell rang as he adjusted his hat and walked out the door.

Chapter 18

THE reed note bent. Blowing and drawing air through the square holes of the harmonica's mouthpiece, the player wound a deep moving tone through the stave of a familiar song. As Jonn approached the man and his elderly companion, resting on the oversized porch of the communal farmhouse, the rhythm slowed and the tune faded away.

"Hey Sig." Jonn waved his hand as he placed his foot upon the first step. "And well, look who that is. If it isn't old Joe. I thought you were dead."

"No, the devil ain't caught me yet." Old Joe smiled as he evened the tobacco across a sheet of rolling paper.

"Devil ain't caught him yet." Sig laughed as he pushed the mouth organ into his shirt pocket and fastened its button. "No, devil ain't caught him yet."

"You'll have to forgive me. My eyes are a bit weak." Joe wet the paper's edge with his tongue, rolled it into a cigarette, and pinched it near the corner of his mouth. "Who would this be talking?"

"It's Jonnie. It's Jonnie." Sig bared two remaining teeth as he nodded his head.

"Sig remembers, don't you?" Jonn smiled. "It's me, Jonn Reese. Gust and I put up that big shed in the back a few years ago."

"Jonnie Reese. Why yes, I do remember. So what brings you way out here, are you working another project, or visiting this time?"

"Just visiting."

"We don't get too many visitors out here. Mostly preachers." He touched a lit match to the end of the cigarette and coughed on the first drag. "They come parading around here all noble-like, acting as if they were Jesus visiting the lepers."

"Jesus and the lepers." Sig laughed. "Jesus and the lepers."

"You come here to see Gust?" Joe picked a shred of tobacco from his tongue.

"Yeah, he asked that I come out. I wanted to see how he and Mae are doing anyway. See if there is anything they need."

"That's too bad, what happened and all. He sure is a good fella, but he should have left the Klan alone. You can't argue with the big shots. Money will win every time."

"Every time. Every time." Sig laughed.

"You see," Joe coughed, and then raised a coffee can sitting next to his chair leg, and spit, "those of stature allow others to have only what they feel other's deserve, nothing more...nothing less. Keep in mind that it's still just scraps off the table, because if it were worth anything more, they would have it for themselves, or find a way to take it from ya."

Jonn's eye caught the motion of a resident tending the farm's large garden. "And I suppose there's nothing we can do about it?"

"Never was...never will be, but the jokes on them, because we're aware of this, and they're not. We see this happening day in day out to us and folks like us, but they're completely ignorant to what they're doing. They're blind. Blinded by their undue generosity, and that's why there is nothing we can do about it...ever."

"Joe, they're just doing their best to be what we consider good people."

"Good people? They don't know anything about being good people. They've spent the decades painting a beautiful portrait of themselves with the acts of a meager few. Truth is, if they would ever look into a mirror, the actual reflection they see would scare the hell right out of them."

"Scare the hell out of them. Scare the hell out of them." Sig laughed.

Jonn smiled and nodded. "How is Gust holding up since they brought him here?"

"Not good. They said he's paralyzed down half his body. Can't walk. Needs help to eat and take care of his daily duties. Spends most of the day crying."

"And Mae?"

"She's up all night singing. Sounds like Swede to me. If she ain't singing, she's screaming at people who aren't there. They can't have that here, Jonnie. It upsets the residents. I hear they are going to send her away."

"Send her away? Where to?"

"Ain't no other place can handle someone like that but the state hospital at Yankton."

Sig flinched, and then looked away. "Straighten up or go to Yankton. Straighten up or go to Yankton."

Joe pulled the last drag through the cigarette and blew the smoke above his head. "Of course, Gust'll stay here. He still has all his marbles."

Jonn noticed movement through the screen door and grabbed its handle to enter. "Thanks fellas for filling me in on Gust and Mae. I appreciate it."

"Appreciate you stopping by and chatting. To tell you the truth, if it weren't for Sig blowing a song through that mouth organ once in a while, most of the time I wouldn't know whether I was alive or dead."

Sig laughed as he placed the harmonica against his lips and threaded a series of cheerful notes into a short, playful tune.

Jonn gave a light push upon the half-open, bedroom door, as he poked his head around its edge into the dimly lit room. Sitting in the window's light, the silhouette of a sleeping man in a wheelchair, rocked with the movement of each labored breath. As Jonn's eyes adjusted to the shadows, he was taken aback at the sight of an elderly woman, in dress and shoes, with purse in hand, lying motionless on the neatly made twin bed.

"Gust?" Jonn called out as he tapped on the door's panel.

Gust's head popped up. "Jonnie!" He struggled to turn his chair with one arm. "Jonnie, I wasn't sure if you got my message." He wiped the drool from the side of his face with his shirtsleeve. "Glad to see you made it."

Jonn placed his hat upon the dresser, and with a slow step, moved across the bedroom floor toward the ratcheting chair. "It's good you're out of the hospital. Sorry I didn't stop and visit. I don't care much for those places."

"That's perfectly fine, my boy. I don't remember much about being there, myself. Just overly thrilled to be out."

Discovering a wooden, folding chair leaning against the wall, Jonn opened it and seated himself in front of Gust. "So, you decided to take up residence out here in the country?"

"I don't know what's wrong with those idiot doctors. When they discharged me, they said I needed help, but couldn't go home. You know, I've got a little money. I don't need to be here. I'm not poor. I don't know why they put me here."

"I'm sure their intentions are for the better, besides it's only for a short while."

"I don't know, Jonnie. Things aren't good." His eyes began to well up. "They're talking about sending Mae away. They can't do that. She's my wife, damn it. I warned them, there will be blood if they take her away from me."

"They haven't sent her anywhere yet, Gust. I'm sure everything will work out fine. Just be patient and give it some time."

"Jonnie, I can't control my bowels anymore. Half the time, I'm sitting in my own filth. I can't do it." A tear rolled down his face. "I just can't do it."

"No. No, Gust. Things are going to be all right for you and Mae. Just wait and see. You'll heal up fine and we'll be right back to working carpentry, just like before. Until then, you have lots of good friends and neighbors who will visit."

"Tell me Jonn." Gust wiped the tear away. "How many of these folks living out here are people you actually know?"

"Well, in one way or another, all of them, I guess."

"Other than the one time we built that shed a few years back, how often have you been out here to visit them?"

"Well, to be honest. This is the first."

Gust glared at Jonn.

"That's not important." Jonn shook his head. "You and Mae are the closest I have to family around here. I would never abandon you."

"I know you wouldn't, Jonn. I know you wouldn't. And that's why I asked them to send for you. You see, I need you to do me a favor."

"Sure, Gust. Anything. You name it."

Gust pivoted his wheelchair toward the window and gazed out. "I'm not going to last much longer."

"Sure you are, Gust." Jonn pulled the wheelchair back around. "You'll be up and hard at it in..."

"Listen!" Gust interrupted. "Please. Just listen to what I have to say."

"All right." Jonn sat back and crossed his legs. "Go ahead. Talk."

"The doc says things don't look good for me, and I've accepted that. With my heart condition, I have always known I've been living on borrowed time. I'm asking you to help Mae and me. I don't know whether it's because I'm selfish, or just a plain coward, but I should have done it myself long before now."

"What's that, Gust?"

"I'm asking you as a trusted friend. No. No, I'm begging you." His eyes began to fill again. "Please. Please send Mae and me home."

Jonn tilted his head toward Gust. "Send you home?"

"Yes...to God."

Jonn stared at Gust while attempting to replay the absurd request within his mind. "You can't be serious. You're asking me to take your lives?" He laughed. "I think that stroke did something to your head."

"Please. I wouldn't ask this of any other man on earth. I trust you, Jonn. I'm asking, I'm asking because it has to be done now. They are going to take Mae away. I've spoken with her and we are both ready. Please do this for us and accomplish what I failed at so many times before."

"You really are serious about this?" Jonn stood up and walked to the dresser. Reaching for his hat to leave, he glimpsed the mirror's reflection of two fragile shells, tarnished and beaten by many years of a well-lived life. Thoughts of Sarah and himself came to mind. How they might have aged over time. How their love for one another would not consent to the other's suffering and pain. He walked over to Mae, stood above her, and gently touched her shoulder. "Mae, what Gust is telling me, is it the truth? Do you want to end your life?"

Mae's eyes rolled open and blinked as she attempted to focus on Jonn's face. She reached up and grabbed his forearm. "Do you know who my sister Ellen is? Can someone tell her that I am here? She is supposed to give me a ride home."

Jonn shook his head. "No, I won't do it." He pushed her hand away and stepped back. "I must have been crazy to even think it possible." He turned toward Gust. "Let me send a preacher out to talk with you. This just isn't right. You need help. Help I can't give."

"No, you're the only one who can help us, Jonn. I need someone who knows death. You were in the war for Christ's sake. You know what death is all about. You're a soldier, damn it. Don't think about it. Just do it."

"No, I said I wouldn't and that's my final answer. How could you even think I would do such a thing?"

"Come on. You're no stranger to this, so stop acting so damned high and mighty. I know what you did in France, how you killed that Sweeney boy. That's right, I've always known. No matter how hard one tries to keep a secret, there is always someone out there willing to give it up. It gnaws at them, eats them from the inside out. Until one day, someone asks the question and sets them free. So, I did both of us a favor and kept them from shipping you off to Yankton. The way I see it, now it's your turn to ante up. You can't back away from this. You owe me."

Jonn stared at Gust in disbelief.

"All right, that wasn't fair." Gust wiped the drool seeping from the corner of his mouth. "I apologize. Please, forget what I said. I'm just a crippled, desperate, old fool. At least send Mae home. Put a pillow over her face and end her suffering. I'd do it myself if I could, but I've proven many times that I am not the man I thought I would be."

Jonn hesitated as he looked at Mae lying quietly on the bed. This wasn't the life either one of them envisioned for their final moments. But what could he do about it. It was the lot they drew. No one gets to choose. "I can't do it. No, absolutely not." He turned and hurried out the bedroom door.

"Where're you going, Jonnie!" Gust screamed. "You can't leave us now. We're running out of time. It'll soon be too late."

Making big strides, Jonn rushed down the hallway in an effort to reach the entrance door. Looking back, he heard Gust's desperate pleas wane with each step. "Go to my house. Get my Bible. Please, I beg you, Jonn. Bring…"

Jonn shoved the screen door open and stood motionless on the front porch as it slammed against the frame behind him. The absurd conversation persisted to run wild within his head.

"Thanks again for stopping." Old Joe smiled. "Come back soon."

With a trembling hand, Jonn pulled his hat onto his head, leaped from the porch, and landed on the brick pathway. Catching himself, he continued to accelerate his pace until he reached the parked truck.

"Most people just can't handle reality." Old Joe lifted his can, and spit. "They prefer to live in their own little dream world where the image of death doesn't exist. That's all life is for them out there. Just a dream."

"Just a dream." Sig laughed. "Just a dream."

The truck motor idled as Jonn slumped over the steering wheel in front of Mae's and Gust's home. The words of the sobering conversation, and the reflection of both slowly drifting from life, whirled within his thoughts.

Thump! Two hands slapped against the vehicle door's window frame. "Have you been out to see Mae and Gust?" Bill asked.

"I just came from there." Jonn switched off the ignition and waited while the engine shuddered to a stop. "Gust wants his Bible. I thought I would stop by and pick it up, in case I get a chance to go back out there."

"The wife and I knew it was only a matter of time before something like this would happen. He was beginning to have difficulties keeping an eye on her, so when they admitted him to the hospital, we notified the police of what was going on. I guess everyone pretty much knew about it. I suppose this was the only way it could end."

"I don't know much about that, Bill." Jonn yanked on the door latch, startling Bill, who sprung away. "Things seemed to work the best they could."

"We said we would help put the house up for sale, and hold an auction for their belongings. Just being good neighbors." Bill accompanied Jonn as he walked to the house. "Besides, it'll give us a chance to scrutinize possible buyers. You know, pick someone like ourselves, people with good character and strong moral values."

"You seem to be pushing things a little fast, aren't you, Bill? They're coming back, and when they do, they'll need their house to live in."

Bill turned in front of Jonn. "You're going to have to face the facts. Mae and Gust are not coming back. You've seen them. There's no way they can take care of themselves, alone. All of their property has to be sold to pay their bills. Any remaining proceeds will more than likely go to the county to help cover the costs of their stay out there."

"All of their property?"

"Every single piece, which I'm sorry to inform you, includes the truck."

"Bill, why are you doing this? I've been trying my damnedest to finish up the projects that Gust and I had been working on."

"And that's why I'm allowing you to use the truck for another week. I tell you what, we'll set a price on the truck, and if you come up with the money before the auction, it's yours."

"Yeah, sure." Jonn shook his head. "I'd better get the Bible and keep moving before you ask me to be a pallbearer at their funerals."

"You'll need these." Bill tossed a set of keys to Jonn as he walked up the steps. "Lock it up when you're through, and just leave them in my mailbox."

The door pushed opened with a smooth, steady swing. While standing in the living room, Jonn sensed an eerie but welcoming quietness about the house, almost as if Mae and Gust personally invited him into their home. Careful in his search, he lifted an odd pile of outdated newspapers, and overturned various stacks of old magazines in an attempt to locate the Bible.

An assortment of ornamental dishes, along with photographs set in decorative frames, adorned the display shelves that bordered the living room walls. Prints of Mae and Gust, family and friends, at various locations and events, told the many rich stories of their time together.

An elongated group picture caught Jonn's eye. Removing it from the shelf, he read aloud the inked inscription. "1st South Dakota Volunteer Infantry. Manila, Philippines – 1898." Within the numerous rows of light, straw hats, a graphite circle centered on one particular soldier's face. "I'll bet that's Gust." Jonn chuckled as he returned the photo to the shelf.

A pair of worn, stuffed chairs, separated by a wooden, lamp table, stood empty along one of the inner walls. "Ah, there it is." Jonn identified the black book's gold embossed title, printed across its thick spine, sitting upon the narrow, walnut top.

Retrieving the book from the table, Jonn noticed small lengths of rope scattered about the floor below one of the chairs. As he knelt down to examine the fine cut ends, a heavy stench of urine drifted from the chair's seat cushion. His stomach knotted as thoughts of Gust's request flooded his mind. Looking down at the Bible, gripped tightly within his hand, he sat upon the floor and opened the cover. "Please, God. I need your guidance. Show me something, any-thing...anything that will help me understand what it is that I should do."

Grasping at generous portions of the bound pages, Jonn stopped at various underlined paragraphs with accompanying handwritten notes scribed within the narrow margins. Skimming a verse or two, he quickly flipped back and forth through the chapters, pausing at random marks. "I don't understand any of this. Why does it have to be so damned confusing?" He rubbed his forehead. "It's just words in a book. Why doesn't it make sense?"

Jonn held the book out in front of him and looked through tum-bling sheets as he fanned the pages before his eyes. "It's all just bull-shit. What the hell good is any of it, if you can't understand what it says?"

Decorative plates shattered, and picture frames crashed to the floor as the Bible slammed against the living room, display shelf. Slid-ing down the wall, the book bounced off the baseboard and landed on its spine. As the front cover slapped against the maple hardwood flooring, a cascade of tumbling pages followed, from the first through the last.

As the back cover gently tapped the wood, Jonn noticed multiple lines of black, cursive script marked upon the final page. Curious, he dragged himself through the broken shards of porcelain and splinters of wood, and focused his eyes on the cracked and faded, inked words.

Laden with intense passion, the paragraphs revealed an unspeak-able promise made to one another, and an assurance of eternal for-giveness upon its completion. Wiping a teardrop from the yellowed page, Jonn closed the back cover, and walked out the door.

Chapter 19

WELCOME Knights of the Ku Klux Klan. The ominous banner flapped on its perch above the width of the Yellowstone Trail. Its bold lettered, double entendre scrutinized passing guests in embracing as well as cautioning the arrivals to the transformed carnivalesque city. Bumper-to-bumper, the two-way traffic crawled through a seemingly endless cycle of slowing, rushing, and stopping. Horns and shouts mixed with the engine clatter in both the acknowledgment of the streamer's subtle ovation, and the prevention of unintended scraping and gouging of automobile finish.

Peter mouthed the stenciled words as he passed beneath the sign. "They sure as hell didn't hang that damned rag up for us." He applied the brake and fell in line with the entering row of vehicles. "Or maybe they did."

Jacob nodded as his attention left the stream of traffic before them, and followed the erratic movement of a red-winged blackbird flock chase itself over the adjacent grazed pastureland. His vision focused upon a distant hill, where a group of laborers placed the finishing touches on a platform erected just below its summit.

"The streets will be full today, son. It's hard to tell what we may run in to, so we'll need to pay attention and stick to why we came." Peter adjusted the accelerator in minding the position of the vehicle they followed. "You can exchange your books at the library, and then we'll stop at the sheriff's office and ask if they've seen Ben. Before we leave town, we mustn't forget to pick up a list of groceries for Maria."

Jacob cleared his throat. "And the train station."

"The train station?"

"I won't be returning to the farm with you, Pa."

223

Peter's eyes darted toward Jacob and then back on the road. "Yeah, I noticed your bag seemed a little light for books."

"Kettie and I are traveling to Minneapolis this afternoon." Jacob attempted to steady a nervous smile. "We're getting married."

"That's a long way to go to get married, son."

"We talked with Father Majer, but..."

"I know. He shared your visit with me."

"We know Kettie's uncle certainly would not perform the ceremony, let alone, allow any of the other clergy in town to do it either."

"These men mean well, but sometimes they're just out of touch with the times." Peter chuckled. "Your mother and I were once young and restless like you two."

A grin appeared on Jacob's face. "Really? You and Ma?"

"Why sure. When we decided to marry, nothing was going to hold us back. Everyone told us to wait, but they didn't understand how we felt," he looked at Jacob, "you know, about each other." He clenched his fist. "I swear, I was that close to hauling off and hitting the priest. I think that's when they realized we were serious, and here you are."

Jacob broke into laughter, with Peter joining. Staring at the tail of the vehicle they followed, Jacob thought for a moment, and then turned toward Peter. "We can wait, Pa. You, Maria and everyone should be there."

"No. You get yourself married before the girl changes her mind. If you two have a plan, stick to it."

Jacob nodded and looked through the windshield. "Do you like her, Pa?"

"She is a wonderful girl," Peter affirmed, "a wonderful girl. She reminds me a lot of your mother. God rest her soul." He smiled. "With that one, you'll enjoy a good, strong life together."

"I feel bad about leaving you without someone to help with the chores on the farm."

"Don't worry about the farm, Jacob. The farm will always be there, besides, it's about time the younger ones take on more responsibilities. I feel myself fortunate that you stayed on as long as you did. Not so much for the work, but I was able to witness you becoming the man that you are today."

Jacob braced his hands against the dash as Peter braked the vehicle to an abrupt stop. Standing before the radiator, a white robed

Klansman stretched out his arms and cursed beneath a pointed hood, while his companions crossed the street behind him.

"Yeah, yeah, rot in hell, you bastards." Peter waved through the glass and smiled. Inching his way between the constant streams of pedestrian traffic, he pulled to the side of the street and parked outside the train depot. "Damned my fast reflexes." He throttled the engine down to a quiet murmur.

Jacob scanned the small group waiting outside the station. "Kettie must be running late. I wanted you to see her before we left. Can you wait for a bit, Pa?"

"I wish I could stay and see you both off, son, but I really need to get over to the sheriff's office." Peter dug into his pocket and placed a roll of bills into Jacob's hand. "Here, take this. You may need it."

"No, Pa. I don't want to take your money."

"Take it." He squeezed Jacob's outstretched hand and pushed back. "When you think you don't need something, that's when you soon find that you do."

"Thanks Pa. I'll never forget this." Jacob extended his hand.

"No. No need to thank me. I just want you to remember two things." Peter grabbed his hand. "Don't forget where home is, and don't ever change who you are." His arms wrapped around Jacob's shoulders and held tight.

Peter wiped the corner of his eyes with his sleeve, as he looked into the rear view mirror and watched Jacob enter the train depot. The piercing sound of an automobile horn pulled his attention back to the city streets, and those moving about it. A quick glance back into the mirror showed the depot's image without Jacob. He was gone. "Good luck, my son."

Discovering a note on the sheriff's office door directing all those needing assistance to contact the local police department, Peter coasted the auto in front of the city jail, and stopped behind the police car. Examining the building's main entrance, he stepped from the vehicle and walked inside.

Steam ascended and disappeared from a full cup of coffee sitting within the scattered paperwork of an unoccupied desk. "Is there anyone around!" Peter nudged the chair beneath an open drawer as he sidestepped through a maze of stacked file boxes.

"I'll be with you in a minute." A voice responded from an open door labeled with the words *Authorized Persons Only*.

The chair's wooden legs vibrated against the maple floor as Peter slid it next to the desk. Stepping over the file boxes, he sat down and placed his hat on his knee.

"What can I do for you?" Officer Hess closed the door to the jail cells and spun the key in its lock.

"I was looking for the sheriff, but the notice said to come to the police station."

"That's right. The sheriff has been out of town all week. He's attending a meeting at the state capital in Pierre. He won't be back until tomorrow morning." Hess pulled the chair from beneath the drawer and sat down. "The chief's around, but he's out assisting the mayor with the Klan celebration. Looks like you're stuck with me for now. I'm Isaac Hess." He blew into the coffee cup and drank a sip.

"Well, Officer Hess, you may be able to help. I'm looking for my hired hand that may have passed through here on his way to Yankton a few weeks back. I haven't heard a thing from him or his family since he left, which is not like them."

"What's his name?" Hess set the cup on the desk, and pulled a blank notepad from between a stack of papers.

"Benjamin Green. He goes by Ben."

Hess thought for a moment. "No. That name doesn't sound familiar. How would you describe him?"

"Well, he's a black man about..."

"Oh, him. I think I know who you're talking about."

Peter straightened his posture and leaned his arm on the desk. "Then, you've seen him?"

"Yeah, we had one of them pass through here about that time." Hess laid his pencil on the pad. "That's all I know. Wish I had more to help you with." He stood up. "I've got to make my rounds now. You know...the Klan celebration and all."

Peter pushed himself from the chair. "Why am I getting the feeling that there is more to the story than you're telling me?"

"Listen. You know all there is to know. No reason to make any more of it than there is. I'm sure you'll eventually hear from him." He nodded toward the entrance. "Now, if you'll excuse me. I'm very busy."

Peter glanced at the door. "Yes, I see you are." He smiled and extended an open hand. "Thank you for your time."

As Hess reached down to shake, Peter shoved his fist into the officer's groin, and clenched tight. An agonizing scream emerged from deep within the man's throat, and grew louder with Peter's increasing pressure.

"This is just as uncomfortable for me as it is for you. Well, maybe more for you, but consider yourself very fortunate." Peter asserted. "I've already completed my chores for today, so my hands are not as strong as they could be."

As the cries died to short whimpers, Peter slid the officer in front of his chair. "I'm going to let you go, now. In exchange, I want you to answer my questions. I want you to tell me everything you know about Ben."

A painful grimace spanned Hess's face, while struggling to provide two quick nods. Collapsing into his chair, he slumped forward onto the desk producing a series of gagging coughs and gasps. "You crazy lunatic." He wiped the drivel from his mouth. "Who the hell do you think you are? I could throw you in jail for that."

Peter leaned over the curled up officer. "You could, but you won't." He pulled his chair closer and sat down. "The longer I'm here, the more questions will be asked by others, and you don't seem to be the type wanting to provide answers."

Hess lifted a hand. "Okay. Okay, a few weeks back, a colored man came beating on the police station doors in the middle of the night. He said he was hitchhiking up in your neck of the woods. A truck pulled up and he jumped in the back. They took him away and beat him unconscious. When he came to, he found himself locked in shed. Not knowing where he was, he peeked through a crack in the boards and sees they're butchering a hog, and talking about doing the same to him. They're boozing and get to arguing about who gets what of his body parts. First chance he gets, he kicks the side out of the shed and doesn't stop running until he ends up here."

Peter closed his eyes. "So, that's when you helped him."

"No." Hess coughed. "We don't want to mingle in what you people do to the blacks. What you do is your own business."

"You people?" Peter shook his head. "Just tell me where he went."

Hess raised his hands. "I don't know."

Peter's fist struck the corner of the desk. "Where did he go!" Coffee and files flew across the room as his arm swiped the top clean.

Wincing in his chair, Hess lifted his hand in protecting his face. "I don't know! I called a few of the boys, Okay. They hauled him to the county line and got rid of him."

"Got rid of him?"

Hess shrugged his shoulders. "I don't know, you know, got rid of him. I don't care as long as he's not around here stinking up my jail."

Peter shoved his finger into Hess's face. He opened his mouth and hesitated as he stared into the officer's eyes. Shaking his head, he pushed himself to his feet and stormed out.

Jacob stretched his neck to the sound of an approaching motor vehicle. Its late model and unfamiliar operator lowered him back onto the wooden bench. Watching the second hand chase the Roman numerals around the train depot's clock face, he wondered as to what may have pulled Kettie late for their intended departure. Turning an ear toward another engine sputter, he jumped to his feet once again.

Rubbing his hand down the side of his pants, he felt the small bulge of the bullet nestled within his pocket. He pulled it out and wiped his thumb over the letters carved upon its side, and thought about the well dressed man who etched his name, and the offer of big money if he went to Chicago.

"Can I help you with something, sonny?" The depot clerk called out from beneath the ticket office window as he struggled to open the sash.

"There you are." Jacob shoved the bullet back into his pocket and stepped up to the booth. "Is the Eighteen running on time?"

"Like an expensive watch." The man smiled. He adjusted his glasses as he pointed to a list of cities and corresponding times. "The sheet indicates it left its last stop on schedule. Are you waiting for an arrival?"

Jacob leaned his arm against the wrought iron window bars. "No, I'm planning on leaving, that is, my girl and me."

The clerk looked through the glass and scanned the platform. He pointed to an approaching woman, who seated herself on the bench near Jacob's bag. "Ms. LaFae?"

Jacob shook his head. "No, she hasn't arrived yet."

"It'll pretty much be an empty passenger car." He arranged a stack of tickets near his inkwell. "Most people seem to be arriving here for the Klan meeting – very few are continuing on. I suppose the next day or two will be hectic with all wanting to leave at the same time." He pulled two cards off the stack, dipped his pen into the ink, and touched its tip against the brass well. "Would you like to purchase your tickets now?"

"Not at the moment." Jacob's attention darted toward a passing vehicle. "I'll wait until she gets here."

Jacob took his seat and pulled his bag to his side. His thoughts turned to Aggie. He questioned the secrecy of his proposal to Kettie, and not telling Aggie or the others of their planned trip to Minneapolis. He knew Aggie enjoyed Kettie's company, so she would certainly approve of their union. His only comfort was in the explanation he wrote in a letter he left upon her pillow. Once she read it, she would understand why they chose to do things the way they did.

"Are you not traveling far?" The waiting woman's French accent sang as pleasant notes in Jacob's mind.

Lost in the intrigue of her foreign spiced tone, the question slipped his mind. "I'm sorry, ma'am. What did you say?"

"I asked if you were not traveling far." She aimed the tip of her lace parasol at his single bag. "I see you do not have much for luggage."

He looked at his bag. "No, just to Minneapolis."

"Minneapolis? Oh. No farther?"

Jacob shook his head.

She rested her hand on the parasol as she placed its tip upon the platform. "Do you travel often?"

"This is my first time on a train." He smiled. "I've always dreamed of traveling, but never really had the chance to go anywhere."

"I'm sure you'll enjoy it." She laid the parasol across the bench seat. "At one time, I practically lived on trains, traveling up and down the East Coast and into the Midwest." She sparked a laugh. "Trains and hotels, oh, what a life it was." She extended her hand. "My name is Isabelle LaFae. You may have heard of me."

Jacob's head turned from side to side. "No, ma'am, I'm sorry." He reached for her hand. "My name is Jacob."

"Jacob? I once knew a Jacob. He was a brilliant vaudevillian performer, and then went on into the cinema." She tugged the fingers in removing her white gloves and draped them over the parasol. "Since we are on a first name basis, you may call me Belle."

Jacob hesitated, then smiled and nodded.

"Don't feel bad that you do not know who I am. That's quite all right. You see, I am an actress. I've performed in many musicals on Broadway, in New York City." She stared at Jacob. "You have heard of Broadway, no? The Great White Way?"

Jacob laughed. "Yes, everyone has heard of Broadway."

"Then maybe you've also heard of *The Night Boat, Poor Little Ritz Girl, Sally*?" She raised her hand. "Oh yes, *Sally*, I'm sure you remember the song – *Look for the Silver Lining*? It was very popular."

Belle's voice carried across the platform as she sang through the first verse. The pleasant tune reached out and grasped Jacob's ear, as well as that of the depot clerk. Upon the final note, the complete silence begged for more.

Jacob straightened his posture and leaned forward. "That was very beautiful."

"Thank you." Belle bowed her head. "You may be wondering why a professional actress, such as myself, is not still performing in the bright lights of the big city."

Jacob listened attentively.

"A good friend of mine and producer, Rich Pennington, convinced me to join his New York theatrical revue. They were to spend a season traveling the country in a series of scheduled performances. It was a spectacular tour with mostly luxury trains and expensive hotels. One of our performances was at the Webster Opera House. It was there that I met and fell madly in love with the man of my dreams." She unfolded a decorative hand fan and waved the air about her face. "Oh, it happened so quickly. I was young and never felt that way before. Rich and the others begged me not to stay and to continue on with them, but like I said, I was young."

Jacob acknowledged with a slight nod.

"It has taken time for me to understand that Rich and the others were right. I should not have stayed. Oh, the wasted years." She collapsed the fan. "Yes, it's time to leave, time to start anew. The white lights are awaiting my return."

"You're traveling back to New York City?" Jacob's face lit up.

Belle smiled. "Yes. I'm on my way to find Rich Pennington. You know, he once told me I was the best thing that ever happened to theatre. I've written him several letters, but the postman returns them marked unable to deliver. He is a talented producer and very busy. I will have to talk with him *en personne*."

"I wish you the best in your renewed career. I can tell you will do very well."

"Thank you, Jacob." Belle leaned forward. "You do not think it is a crazy idea? To start again?"

Jacob shook his head. "You will never know until you try. I would only think it crazy to never attempt a new start, when that is where your heart truly is."

"Thank you for your generous words of encouragement." Belle looked into Jacob's smiling eyes and felt his true sincerity. "Did you say you were only going as far as Minneapolis?"

"That's right. On the number Eighteen."

"Would you allow me to ask a favor of you?"

Jacob's head tilted toward Belle.

"I know we have just met, and I don't want you to think unkindly of me, but would you consider traveling farther, say to New York, and possibly accompanying me to Broadway?"

Jacob felt at a loss for words.

"It's that you seem confident of yourself, and it would be a great help to me to have someone along to provide a reassuring support. It would only be temporary."

"I'm sorry, but…"

"Please, we can escape this town together. I have enough money to pay for your ticket as well as mine. When in New York, I can show you the city. You will see for yourself the magnificent lights." Belle took hold of Jacob's hand. "You see, I'm afraid. I'm afraid that without help, I may never leave this place. Please, Jacob, will you come with me?"

Jacob covered her hand with his. "I'm sorry, Ms. LaFae. Your offer is most enticing, but I'm not the one who can help you. I'm waiting for my fiancée. We are traveling to Minneapolis together to be married."

Ahooga! Ahooga! The cry of an automobile horn pulled their attention to the street, where a vehicle slowed to a stop before the train depot.

"Jacob!" Brina waved from the driver's seat. "The Reverend Woodard found out about you and Kettie. He's very upset."

Jacob leaped to his feet and rushed toward Brina. "Where's Kettie? Is she all right?"

"Yes, she's a little shaken up, but fine. She sent me to let you know she couldn't be here. If you get in, I can take you to her."

Jacob grabbed his bag from the bench. "Have a safe trip, Ms. LaFae. I wish you the best of luck on your return to Broadway." He dashed to the waiting motor vehicle and jumped in.

Belle watched the dust churn behind the auto as it accelerated down the block, around the corner, and disappeared behind the long row of buildings. Her head dipped as a tear rolled down her cheek. Looking up at the depot clock, she followed the ratcheting second hand, while her thoughts raced to piece together an acceptable arrangement for travel.

She blotted the tear stream from her face, and approached the clerk. "Excuse me. Is the Eighteen running on time?"

"One moment, please, and I'll check." The clerk turned to his assistant entering the booth. "Ralph, do you know offhand if the Eighteen is still running on time?"

"It just left Andover, with a stop in Bristol and then Holmquist, before arriving here."

He nodded his head to Belle. "Yes, Ms. LaFae. As far as we know, the Eighteen is right on schedule." He ran his finger down the passenger manifest. "You purchased your ticket in advance and your baggage is ready to load. We can assist you in boarding the passenger car when the train rolls in."

"Thank you." Belle unfolded her hand fan. "I am on my way to New York City. I'm an actress. You may have heard of me."

"Yes ma'am." The clerk smiled. "I remember watching you perform at the Opera House a few years back. You have a beautiful voice. I will never forget your performances."

"So, you have seen me on stage."

"Yes ma'am."

Belle glanced around the nearly vacant platform, and then turned toward the clerk. "I hate to trouble you, but I have changed my mind. I will not be traveling to New York today." She collapsed the fan into her palm. "May I receive a refund?"

"Refund, again? Why certainly."

As the clerk pulled the money from the drawer, a loud thud shook the ticket booth walls and rattled its windows.

"Excuse me," Kettie attempted to catch her breath as she hung onto the countertop, "can you tell me if there was a tall, dark haired man waiting here?"

The clerk ignored the question as he counted aloud the bills, aligning each in a stack before Belle.

Belle leaned toward Kettie. "Would you be looking for Jacob?"

Kettie looked at Belle. "Yes. Jacob. Have you seen him?"

"He was waiting here to meet his fiancée. I assume that would be you?"

"Yes, that's me. Please tell me where he went."

"There are very few like him, young lady. Very few. Don't ever let him go."

Kettie stared at Belle, and then smiled.

The change toppled as the clerk placed the last coin onto the bills. "Bob Martin's daughter picked him up a short while ago. They drove off that way." He pointed down the street.

"Brina? Oh, she has caused me more trouble today." Kettie ran to the road's edge and peered in the direction indicated by the depot agent.

"Can you store my luggage for a while?" Belle asked the clerk. "I'll have someone from the hotel stop by and pick it up later."

"Yes ma'am. I'll place it back into storage where it was. It'll be safe there until you need it again."

"Thank you." She slid the money into her purse. "You are a true gentleman." The parasol's canopy popped open as she rested its shaft upon her shoulder and strolled away.

Ralf snorted. "I don't understand why you put up with her." He moved behind the clerk and stared at Belle as she stepped from the depot platform. "She does this every time." He shook his head. "She buys a ticket, waits for the train, and then refunds the ticket before it even arrives." He rested his hand on the clerk's shoulder. "She'll never leave this town, although, I'll bet there are a dozen wives who would certainly pay her fare if she actually did board that train and never came back."

The clerk watched as Belle crossed the street and faded into the crowd. "Maybe it's not her fare they should be paying for." He crossed her name from the passenger list. "All I know, as long as she is here, their straying dogs won't be sniffing around my Ruth." He looked at Ralf. "Or your Cora, either."

"Ah." Ralf threw his hands in the air and walked away.

Chapter 20

DING! Ding! The overhead doorbell chimed Jonn's entrance into the store. Walking past the wooden, nail kegs and bundles of shake shingles, he made his way to the unattended back counter. A quick glance down the vacant aisles confirmed he was alone. With the morning city streets filled to capacity with out-of-towners joining in the Klan festivities, the unexpected moment of solitude felt refreshing.

Noticing a shadow float past the office doorway, he leaned to catch a glimpse of its possessor. "Arch, you around?" He called out.

A pork sandwich jutted out from the office, followed by the lumberyard's manager. "Jonnie." He patted a napkin across his mouth and swallowed. "I had a lull in customers, so I thought I'd grab a bite from the barbeque the city organizations are putting on."

"You go ahead and finish. I'm in no hurry. It feels nice in here, away from the congestion."

"How are Gust and Mae? I feel bad not visiting them, but I haven't had a chance to get away." Arch flipped the last chunk of bread into his mouth and reached for his cup of coffee.

"Doing the best they can." Jonn nodded.

"I heard Gust's truck is up for sale."

"I heard that, too."

Arch shook his head. "Yeah, I don't like the way it's being handled any more than you do. Some people have a bad habit of over-stepping their bounds. The only thing you can do is to stand aside so their foot doesn't land on you."

Jonn shrugged his shoulders.

"Have you been taking in any of the festivities or entertainment today?"

"No, I try to steer clear of it all. It works best for me, and I think others as well. Besides, I'm trying to finish up a few repairs for Gust. That's why I stopped by, to pick up a couple of pine boards"

"With the exception of the scrap bin pieces, I'm out. Between the benches, picnic tables, and anything else you could possibly think of to host a celebration, they used it all. It was a good thing I discovered extra, beyond what they thought they would need."

"Completely Out?"

"Oh, there's a small stack of knotted wood material behind the scrap bin. It's in poor shape, but if you can use it, go ahead and help yourself. If not, a new order is scheduled to arrive at the depot at the beginning of next week."

A ratcheting entrance handle precipitated the sounding of the overhead bell. Closing the door behind them, three of Wes's boys shuffled over the creaking floor, enticed by the salted shells of a newly filled peanut barrel. They trailed one another to the wooden drum, each digging down in and scooping out a handful.

"I'll be with you fellas in a moment." Arch's wave gleaned a half nod from the impassive trio. He nudged Jonn toward the door. "Frank, Quinn, and Boyle, besides no good, I think I know what they're here for. You'd better grab what lumber you can, before the Klan commandeers it all."

"Thanks, Arch. I'll pull the truck inside the lumber alley and load up."

The board slid up the truck's flatbed and bounced against the back of the cab. "Just one more like that and I'm on my way." Jonn gathered another plank from the stack, and sighted down its edge in his elimination of those with an overly curved warp.

"Put that back, Reese." Quinn's voice approached from his rear. "It doesn't belong to you. It's now the property of the KKK."

Jonn snickered. "They can find something else to burn today. I've got work to do."

"It's not for burning. The town's guests are in need of additional seating. We have orders to take all that's left. Frank's coming out with the bill of sale in a minute."

"If there is no place to sit, maybe they'll all go back to where they came from." Jonn leaned on the board's end. "They've taken enough from Gust. I'll be damned if I'll give up even another splinter."

"You've been nothing but a wart on this town's hind end since the day you returned, Reese. People want you the hell out of here. Especially after the rumors of what you did in France – what you did to Sweeney."

"That's right." Boyle joined in as he stepped up.

"You don't speak for anyone." Jonn shook his head. "If there's a problem, let them tell me to my face."

"They're not going to tell you a damned thing." Quinn snapped. "They're waiting – waiting to hear you're gone or dead – preferably dead. That way they're sure you'll never come back."

The board flopped against the flatbed flooring and landed next to the first. "I'm tired of watching your lips flap." Jonn peeled the gloves from his hands. "Like I said, I've got work to do."

"Are you deaf?" Quinn stepped in Jonn's path. "Or just not understanding what I'm telling you."

"No! *You're* not understanding." Jonn stopped and poked a finger in his face. "Your big shots put Gust in the poor farm. He's given up enough for you idiots. Now, I'm taking this wood, and there's not a damned thing you, or any one of them other cowards hiding under a yellowed sheet, can do about it."

Out of the corner of his eye, Jonn spotted Boyle reaching across the flatbed and grasping the two planks. Grabbing a shovel propped against the wall, Jonn whirled its handle over his head and crushed the man's fingers between the shovel's edge and the board. A painful cry echoed within the alley. Moving back, he swung at Quinn, splitting the extended columella between his nostrils.

Stepping forward, in preparation for a follow up stroke, Jonn's head heaved forward from the sudden impact of a timber piece striking at the base of his skull. Observing the daylight drain from his vision, he dropped to his knees, and fell onto his face.

A suffocating squeeze tightened around Jonn's neck. The choking pain shocked him to consciousness. Clawing at his throat, he attempted to pry loose the frayed twine, which pinched his access to air. Looking down, past his swinging feet, he watched as one of his attackers knotted the rope's end to a post, and then rushed to catch up with the other assailants.

"Bastard broke all my fingers." Boyle extended a swollen hand, with mangled digits pointing in all directions but straight. "He damned near cut 'em right off my hand."

"What are you whining about? I almost lost the nose off my face." Quinn pointed at the blood trailing from the open wound beneath his nostrils.

"Both of you quiet down." Frank caught up with the two. "This town is done worrying about Jonnie Reese, and if they actually knew what happened, they'd thank us for it."

"If they knew? What if they ask questions?"

"The only question anyone is going to be asking is, did you hear about Jonnie Reese?" He smiled. "Yeah, I heard it was a suicide." They burst into laughter as they fled the building.

Jonn lurched outward as he tugged himself up the rope. His fingertips scratched upon the rafter's bottom edge, but his weakened state denied him the inches needed to grasp over the top of the beam. He fell back to the rope's end. Grimacing from the sudden snap, he lashed out into the open air. A split second fracture of his neck would end his life, now he will endure the suffering of a slow strangulation. Absorbing the unbearable pain of the rope burning his neck and crushing his windpipe, he began to drift with the slow deprivation of oxygen to his brain.

A blinding flash transported him to the floor of the lumber house. "The rope broke," he said to himself.

Feeling for the twine remnant cinched around his neck, it was nowhere to be found. He speculated it separated at the noose, and remained draped over the rafter. As the brightness subsided, his vision stretched beyond himself. He was not alone. Encircling him, stood a band of men dressed in German, field gray uniforms.

"Welcome!" A powering voice emerged from the group.

Jonn identified the tall man as one of the soldiers who continually haunted him during the past years. Unlike before, he now bore no wounds or dismemberments. In fact, there existed not a scratch about any one of them. Sharp creases and highly polished leather detailed their fresh clean uniforms.

Jonn grinned. "So, you do sprechen sie Englisch after all."

"English? No, no English. I speak German, just like you."

"No, I don't sprechen sie Duetsch." Jonn asserted. "I never had the desire."

"And I don't speak English either, but nevertheless, we converse."

Jonn nodded. "Why have you been harassing me all of these years?"

"Harass you?" The soldier laughed. "We haven't been harassing you. We've been waiting for you."

"Waiting for what, for me to go completely insane from staring at your mangle corpses day in, day out?"

The Soldiers laughed.

"No." The man replied. "We must forgive you. We cannot go on until we accomplish that task. There are no hard feelings. Life is life. We all pass through it on our way to the eternity."

A puzzled expression pulled down Jonn's face. "Go on? Go on to where?"

A small white oval appeared behind the soldiers, and expanded in diameter to the size of the group. Its glow radiated a warmth he never experienced before. He stepped toward it, and then stopped.

"You've got me confused, Fritz." Jonn turned and looked at them. "I don't understand what you are forgiving me for."

The soldiers glanced at one another. "It is we who are now confused. Do you mean that you do not remember?"

Jonn shook his head. "I think you may have mistaken me for someone else." He chuckled. "All these years of making my life a living hell, and you've been haunting the wrong sap. You know, if it wasn't such a damned dreadful ordeal, it would actually be quite funny."

"I believe he has not completely crossed." One of the soldiers spoke up.

"What do you mean he hasn't completely crossed, he's here isn't he?"

The man stepped forward. "Yes, but I would reason that he is not fully here. Part of him is still in his flesh body. Part of him is still wearing that rope." The soldier lifted his arm and pointed toward the rafters. "Look."

Jonn turned his attention overhead and stared with the others. Hanging above him, his lifeless body spun and swayed as it floated at the end of the rope.

"Ah yes, that could be." The soldier lifted his hand. "Let me help you remember." He extended a finger and touched Jonn's forehead.

Jonn screamed as the pain returned and encircled his neck. Dropping to his knees, the blinding light ferried him back to a previously forgotten time and place.

"Do you see them, Jonnie?" A.J. whispered through the final belt of ammunition draped over the feed tray of the Hotchkiss machine gun.

"No, I can't see a damned thing, but I know they're out there. I catch a waft of their stink every now and then."

Blindfolded by the darkness, the invisible veil covered their eyes, hiding the slow but sure German troop movements. The moonless night offered little but a hint of assistance from the spackling of starlight through the pinholes scattered above. A damp, cool breeze drifted over the pockmarked and smoldering section of no-man's land spread out before them, forcing the bitter taste of sulfur onto their tongues, and the putrid stench of rotting flesh seared into their nostrils.

Cut off from the main road during an unexpected Hun rush, they squirmed slowly in the mud behind a machine gun entrenchment, straining their eyes in an effort to distinguish the countless dancing shadows continually mocking them. On occasion, they shifted hands in scratching the skin under their wet, soiled clothing in a futile effort to deaden the irritation caused by the colonies of lice crawling next to their hide.

"It's too quiet." Jonn turned an ear toward the open field. "I can't hear anything but the ringing in my ears from the gunfire. I wish someone would throw up a parachute flare so we could at least see if anything is actually out there."

A.J. ran his fingers down the length of the ammo belt. "We're almost out. Where's Wes with that ammo? He should have been back by now."

"No idea, something must have happened, otherwise he would be here."

"I don't know, Jonnie. He's okay to pal around with, but there is something quite different about him. He's not like us. I guess I've never really trusted the guy. I know he's going to get someone killed. I just know it."

"You and I go back a long way, A.J. I know he's a little different, but you can't expect him to jump in and seem like..." Jonn snapped his head to the side and pushed his ear forward.

"What is it?" A.J. whispered, hoping it to be just the eerie settling of the beaten field before them, or even the general scrounging of a half-starved rat.

"I don't know, probably nothing. If it gets busy again, you'll have to run back and bring up all the ammo you can carry. I'll do the best I can until you return."

"We're out of the belts. All we have left at the ammo point is the 24-round strips." He looked toward Jonn. "I'm not going. I can't leave you alone up here."

"You've got to go, A.J. If the Huns attempt another rush, neither one of us is going to make it out of here. Grab whatever is back there. If we need to, we can piece the short strips together. That should give us a little longer firing time before reloading."

A.J. pulled a soiled, trembling hand over his face. "Yeah, you're right." He turned his head back and peered down into the darkness of the trench. "I hope that little girl is doing all right back there. She's just a kid – can't be more than thirteen."

"How you were able to talk her into riding along with us, I'll never know."

"What else was I to do? The poor kid was wandering the roads near the front line, looking for food. She's got that nasty cut down her forearm. I'm sure the aid station can bandage it up for her."

Jonn chuckled. "Small animals, and now little girls, you're just not satisfied unless you are caring for something."

A.J. shook his head. "She trusted us to help her. Now, we are all caught up in this mess together."

"Like the other French in this country, I'm sure she has seen a lot since this war began. She knows how to take care of herself. She'll be fine."

The thunder of a lone artillery piece echoed over the treetops. Moments later, a glowing candle, suspended from a small parachute, lit the sky as it drifted slowly back to the earth. The light reflected off the eyes of a dark silhouette frozen in its tracks less than fifteen feet from the barrel of the Hotchkiss gun. Without hesitation, Jonn pulled the trigger. The soldier toppled backward as the heavy gun barked.

Another appeared and then another, with some firing, and others barely standing, before the dotted line of sizzling lead cut them down.

"Get the ammo A.J.! Go now! Get the ammo while you still have light!"

Mud splattered against the clay walls as A.J. scrambled back through the trenches. Sprinting across the boards laid out over the muck and stagnant water, he slid to a stop next to the ammo point. "Wes! Wes! Where are you?" His calls went unanswered.

Bending over the ammunition stack, A.J. grunted as he lifted the heavy ammo cases and tucked one under each arm. As he turned to leave, he spotted Wes in the dim glow of the small firelight. Propped in the entrance of the small earthen room carved from the clay bank, Wes stood with the back of his coat facing A.J.

"Wes! Wes, we need your help! Grab two cases and follow me!"

Wes's head dropped as he emitted a low groan.

The cases fell from A.J.'s arms and rolled back onto the ammunition stack. He rushed over and tugged on Wes's shoulder. "Wes?"

On the table before him, lay the beaten, naked body of the young French girl. Barbed wire bound both of her hands, and a muddy rag protruded from her open mouth. She remained motionless as wide glassy eyes stared off into space.

"What did you do to her?" A.J. screamed. "She was just a helpless kid."

Wes buttoned his trousers and stepped away. "She's a whore. A dirty whore just like the rest of them. Besides, she was dead. I found her that way." He shrugged his shoulders. "What does it hurt?"

Wes's head bounced against the dirt wall, as A.J. choked him by his jacket collar. "Naked, and with her hands wired together?"

A muffled gag erupted from the girl's throat as she began to stir.

"She's alive!" A.J. shouted. He dragged her off the table and into his lap while digging the rag from her mouth. Gasping and coughing, the little girl began to whimper and cry.

"Take two cases of ammo to Jonnie!" A.J. screamed. "Hurry, he's close to being out by now. I'll follow you with more." He wiped the dirt, tear marks from the girl's face. "I'm bringing her with me once I get her dressed."

Crack! Crack! Crack! A quick series of shots rang out as the girl jumped and then folded in A.J.'s arms. Blood streamed from a tight pattern of bullet holes sunk within her chest.

"I told you, she was dead when I found her." Wes pressed the barrel of his .45 caliber semi-automatic pistol against A.J.'s temple. His finger applied pressure upon the trigger. "There, now it's your turn. Go ahead, while she's still warm. I won't tell anyone."

The young girl's head drooped back as A.J. gently placed her body upon the wooden plank flooring and stood up. "You filthy animal!" He looked at Wes, and then back at the girl. "Why? Why would you do this?"

As Wes lowered the pistol, A.J. reached up and knocked it from his hand. Grabbing Wes's throat, he shoved him backward, causing both to fly through the air. Mud splashed and sludge rolled as they plowed through the thick puddles. Unsheathing his bayonet, Wes drove the blade's point deep within A.J.'s ribcage.

The machine gun continued to fire in multiple bursts as Jonn carefully aimed at the approaching Hun. A disheartening metallic click of the firing pin striking an empty chamber signaled the weapon was no longer functional. Shoving the heavy gun to the front, he crawled through the mud to retrieve his rifle. In single shots, he emptied its shells at the remaining Germans, who dove into nearby craters in taking cover.

With his face to the ground, Jonn crawled back into the mud-filled trenches to warn his two companions. Arriving at the ammo point, he found Wes wiping a bayonet along the seams of his trousers while hovering above A.J.

"What happened to A.J.?" Jonn pushed Wes from his path.

"It was an accident." Wes explained. "We had a little disagreement. He came at me. It was an accident, I tell ya."

Jonn's weapon dropped into the muck as he fell to his knees and cradled A.J.'s head upon his lap. "You're going to be all right. Hang on. We'll get you to the aid station."

"No, Jonnie. This is it." A deep cough forced blood through the corners of his mouth. "Promise me you'll keep an eye on my mother. Tell her the good things we did here."

"You can tell her yourself, A.J. Just wait and see. You're going to be fine."

"I was right." He grinned. "Wes did get someone killed. It just happened to be me." His eyes widened as determined lungs pulled in a deep breath. Accompanying a long exhale, his body fell limp.

"No, this can't be happening." Jonn muttered to himself. "This isn't real." A.J.'s head wobbled to the side as Jonn shook his shoulders. He placed an ear against the still chest in hopes of finding at least a faint spark of life – anything to indicate A.J. continued to be with them, but nothing presented itself. A.J. was dead.

"I tell ya, it was an accident." Wes slid the bayonet into its sheath. "Besides, he wasn't much of a soldier anyway, too soft. We'll do better without him. You'll see."

Jonn stared into Wes's eyes. "You killed A.J. you son of a bitch." Prying his rifle from the mud, he jumped to his feet.

Wes tumbled to the ground as the rifle butt stroked the side of his head. The world spun around him. Perched on his hands and knees, he waited while attempting to regain his bearing.

"You'll hang for this." Jonn's fist waved in Wes's face. "With God as my witness, I swear you'll hang for this."

"It was an accident. It wasn't my fault." Wes wiped the blood oozing from a cut next to his ear. "Come to your senses, Jonn. This is a war. These things happen."

"Like hell they do!" He stepped toward Wes.

A dull shine within the mud caught Wes's attention, as he recognized his pistol half buried next to his leg. Snatching it from the muck, he shoved the barrel at Jonn. "Get away from me. I told you it was an accident. Get away, or I swear you'll sure as hell be next."

Jonn stared up the gun's sights and into Wes's eye, whose squint tightened with his gradual squeeze upon the trigger. Jonn hesitated, if he were out of the picture, Wes could walk away a free man. No one would suspect his actions in either's death.

Jonn lunged at the pistol as its hammer struck down upon the pin. The gun barked. Its bullet left the barrel and traveled on a direct path toward Jonn's head. As he closed his eyes, a strong scent of fresh, spring lilacs overwhelmed his senses. Envisioning an image of Sarah within his mind, a sensation of their entwined spirits flowed through him and briefly soothed his being. A sudden pressure nudged upon his shoulder. Its slight movement pushed his body from the direct course of the lead projectile. The bullet tore the flesh from Jonn's head as it grazed the side of his skull, knocking him onto his back, unconscious.

Directly behind Jonn, upon the berm, a German soldier dove for cover as the bullet separated the shoulder strap from his field gray overcoat.

Startled by the Hun's presence, Wes fired his remaining shells into the darkness where the soldier once stood. He listened for a moment, praying for a sign he hit his intended target.

A German Stahlhelm rose from behind the berm. As the rifleman pushed himself on to two legs, he stepped to the edge of the trench, pulled his rifle to his shoulder, and took careful aim at Wes.

"No! No! Please, I beg you. No…" Wes screamed as he crossed his arms over his face.

Crack! The echo of a single shot reverberated above the trench and out into no-man's land. Wes opened an eye and peered through the space between his arms. The German rested on his knees with a hole drilled into his forehead, and bounced onto his belly. A sharp silence held the night. Wes lowered his arms. Nothing existed above him but the billions of bright stars twinkling in the black sky. He patted himself in searching for a wound to his skin or a bullet hole through his clothing. Somehow, he escaped death's calling.

The serenity quickly ended with a thundering boom of an artillery cannon in the distance. A parachute flare lit the sky. Within seconds, men in kilts appeared overhead. Hundreds of British soldiers leaped the trenches with the gracefulness of deer, landed on the far side, and continued the charge.

Lying in the mud, Wes watched in wonder. It did not seem real, until a splash of mud flew up next to him and splattered his face.

"Are ya hurt, laddie?" A stretcher bearer asked as he knelt beside Wes. "I see you've got a cut by your ear."

Wes shook his head.

"We weren't sure who ya was at first." The soldier pushed a cloth bandage over the cut. "Ya Yanks are supposed to be miles down the line."

"We were transporting a cannon back to our regiment, and then the road exploded."

"It don't matter. Anyway, we saw everything ya Yanks did. Yes sir, we saw it all." He spoke as he checked A.J. and Jonn's condition.

"We tried to get to ya sooner but them Hun bastards would not let up. This is definitely going into the report."

"You…you saw everything?" Wes pushed himself to a seated position.

"Yes we did. Our boys were pinned down on the right. Ya kept that machine gun screamin'. Ya saved 'em. I don't know how many of them ya laid out. You're a hero, laddie."

"A hero?"

"Sorry about your buddy." He nodded toward A.J. "The other doesn't look like he's gonna make it either. It's a bad head wound. We'll carry him back to the medical officer. If there's a chance, he'll know."

A quick yell summoned three additional bearers down into the trench. They rolled Jonn onto a canvas stretcher and carried him off as soldiers continued the jump in following the charge.

Wes rested his head against the crossed boards supporting the trench wall, as thoughts of the German soldier about to steal his life flashed vividly in his mind. By all rights, he should not be alive. In fact, considering the recent events taken place in the trench that night, it would be better if he actually were dead. Dead like A.J. Dead like Jonn. A trembling hand wiped tears from the corners of his eyes as he curled into a ball and wept.

"Jonnie! There you are." Arch patted Jonn's cheeks. "That's a good boy. For a moment there I thought we lost you." He lifted the noose over Jonn's head.

Jonn gasped. The world came into focus as his heaving chest inflated air into his lungs. Watching the sparrows dart through the above rafters, he felt the sting of the raw rope burns encircling his neck, and considered himself fortunate the rafter remained vacant while he sat alive upon solid ground. The forgotten memories the German revealed replayed vividly within his mind, as though he just stepped from the mud-filled trenches of France. Wes was a murderer. He killed A.J. and the little French girl. All of these years Wes has been concealing a lie, unknown to anyone, until now.

"I won't even ask how it happened, Jonnie, because I'm sure it had something to do with them troublesome idiots." Arch shook his head. "Rest here." He stood up and rushed toward the office. "I'll get you something to drink."

Officer Hess exited the Wesley Hardware Store on south Main Street, and disappeared into the sidewalk stream of visitors. Within the red bricked establishment, the boys licked their wounds as they seated themselves around a worn, oak card table.

"What was Hess all worked up about?" Frank questioned, as Wes appeared from the back storeroom.

"One of the Polacks, from up north, was in asking about that missing colored." He knotted an apron around his waist. "Nothing to worry about."

"Fifteen cents for the three of you." Toad set a round of soft drinks upon the table. "I'll put it on your tabs as usual." The legs rumbled as he pulled a chair up to the table and seated himself next to the others.

"He asked about the extra benches, too." Wes continued. "Did you find anything left at the lumber yard?"

"Warped, knotted, and no good, otherwise, they had a special on rope today." Frank laughed, with the others joining.

Wes leaned his head over the counter and stared at Boyle's blue, swollen hand. "What happened to you?" He spotted the blood trickle from Quinn's nose as the cola bottle pulled away. "And you!"

"Well, we kind of had a run in with…"

Wes spotted Jonn through the store windows, pushing his way through the crowd to the entrance. "What did you get yourselves into, now?" He stared at the boys.

"I don't believe it." Frank pushed himself to his feet as he watched Jonn approach. "Lazarus has returned."

Wes stripped the apron from around his waist and threw it to the side. "Damn it! I've told you to leave Jonn Reese alone. You were just supposed to pick up the lumber and haul it out to the hill. Why the hell can't you listen?"

The door chimed as Jonn pushed against the glass and stepped through. Scanning the merchandise, he pulled a baseball bat from a wood box and stepped back to the doorway.

"I'm sorry, but the store is temporarily closed." Jonn strained to speak as he pushed an entering customer back onto the outside steps. "Please come back later, after I've had a chance to clean things up a bit."

As the lock clicked, nervous laughter arose from the table. "Damnedest thing I ever saw." Frank leaned back in his chair. "Reminds me of an old, mangy dog I just couldn't get rid of. I don't know how many times I..."

The wood bat connected with Frank's jaw. As broken teeth tumbled onto the tabletop, quick footsteps brushed the floor as Toad darted for the back room.

Jumping to his feet, Quinn dropped the rag from his face. "Now, just wait a minute."

A crack echoed against the tin ceiling, as the man fell over backwards and rolled across the floor.

Bowing his head, Boyle held up his inflated, discolored hand. "Please, Jonnie, I don't want any of this. It wasn't my idea. I beg you." He folded his hands together.

Ready to swing, Jonn hesitated as he stared at the cowering man. Glancing toward the counter, he noticed Wes shrug his shoulders as he lit a cigarette, and then pulled a stool up to sit.

Jonn dropped the bat to his side. As a smile stretched across the man's face, Jonn poked the bat's end between his eyes. The quick snap tumbled him over the back of the chair and onto the floor to lay with his two partners.

"Next time you kill someone," Jonn hovered above the three unconscious bodies, "make sure they're dead." He looked at Wes. "Did you hear what I said?"

Wes's eyes grew big as Jonn pointed the bat in his direction, and then approached the counter. "Why did you kill A.J.? Why? He never did any harm to anyone."

Wes stared at Jonn. "So this is the day, huh?" The cigarette's ash glowed bright orange as he drew in a quick puff. "Every time I saw you on the street, I always wondered – Is this the day? Is this the moment he walks up and questions what happened in the trench all those years ago?"" The smoke exited his nostrils as he pressed the butt into the tray. "I almost came to believe that as far as you were concerned, it was over and done with."

"This is A.J. we're talking about. It will never be over and done with. I just don't understand how you could do such a thing. And then you had the gall to manipulate the story to your own benefit. I thought we were all friends."

"I don't expect you to understand, but this hasn't been easy for me, either. Not a day has gone by where I haven't thought about what happened that night. You see, I had no other choice. A.J.'s death was an accident. Why should I be punished for a mere accident when defending myself?" He pointed at Jonn. "And if I remember correctly, it was you who attacked me. Once again, I had no choice but to defend myself." He lifted his shoulders. "They all said you weren't going to make it, and treated me as though I was royalty. I guess I kind of liked the attention, so I did what was best for me, and what was best for the regiment. Was it my fault you pulled through?"

"Your twisted story has even you believing you did no wrong. Tell me. Was it a mere accident that you raped that little girl as well?"

"You don't seem to understand, Jonn. You can't blame me for that. You can't blame me for any of what happened. It was a war. These things happen. Actually, in the sum of it all, you could say she was just a casualty. Both of them were. Make that the three of you."

"Are you out of your mind?" Jonn cracked the bat against the countertop. "I'll see you hang for what you did."

"Hang? War is war and people die. Good, bad, young, old, guilty, innocent, soldier or civilian, it doesn't matter. People have, and always will die in war, and that will never change. The average person understands and accepts that. Why don't you?"

"What you did to A.J. and that young girl was outright murder. There is a great difference!"

"Is there? What about the Eleventh Hour Charge? What about those boys who were sent out onto the battlefield in the final minutes before the clock struck eleven, and the war ended? Thousands were killed or seriously wounded, and there was no blame placed whatso-ever. Like I said, people understand, war is war."

"Representative Johnson's Subcommittee Three's investigation determined otherwise. They established it as unnecessary slaughter and wrote it in their report to Congress."

"And the politicians and newspapers shut them down faster than a barn cat pouncing on a field mouse. The war was over, and we won. They weren't about to let anything or anyone taint that victory. Even Johnson retracted his statement." A grin pulled across his face. "Yes indeed, politics and patriotism, they can pull the wool over many an unsuspecting eye, and intimidate the hell out of the rest."

"Then we'll skip the trial." Jonn rubbed his hand down the bat's barrel, flicking off an embedded tooth fragment, and grasped the handle. "There are other ways to set this right."

"Be my guest. Go on, end this misery." Wes leaned his head toward Jonn. "Come on. Do it now. Hit me. Split my skull."

Jonn gritted his teeth as he cocked the bat over his right shoulder.

"What are you going to tell the people?" Wes continued. "How are you going to justify this? You've spent the last six years proving to everyone in this town just how crazy you are." He looked up at Jonn. "Do you think they're going to believe you?" He turned his face down toward the counter. "Come on, let's get this over with. Go ahead and do it."

Tightening his grip, Jonn pulled back farther. His scream echoed within the store as the bat twirled through the air, and shattered the glass in a corner display cabinet. "I swear, I won't let you get away with this. You may have everyone in this town fooled. There is nothing I can do about that. I'll set things right though." Jonn backed to the entrance and turned the deadbolt from the frame. "With God as my witness, you'll pay for what you did." The door chimed as he walked out.

Wes struck a match against the register and lit a cigarette. From behind the counter, he watched as Jonn crossed the traffic and faded into the flow of the crowd. His thoughts wove a tattered fabric merging the tainted past with the distorted present – the deaths of A.J. and the French girl, accepting another's Silver Citation, appointed Exalted Cyclops of the Klan, and directing the upcoming night's klonverse. Sure, Jonn could talk, but would anyone really listen. Deep down, he hoped someone would.

The shuffling of two feet in the back room pulled at Wes's attention as he continued to watch the crowd move along the far sidewalk.

"Toad, why don't you throw some water on those boys and wake them up. There's work to be done. Last time I checked, the sky looked a little dark toward the west. We may need to be prepared for a possible rain shower during the klonverse tonight." He blew a stream of smoke into the air as he crushed the whole cigarette into the ashtray. "Then grab a broom and clean up that broken glass."

Wes buckled to his knees as a sharp blow cracked against the side of his head. Bright specks of light danced upon a dark background to

the inflection of his moans. Reaching to examine the point of excruciating pain, another jolt laid him flat on the floor.

"A.J. was my friend." Toad raised the bat above his shoulder. "He
never treated me wrong. He was always good to me." The bat continued to swing.

Chapter 21

CLICK! Click! Click! The empty cylinder ratcheted within the revolver's frame. "See if you can make him squeal." Casey tossed the handgun over the car's hood and watched it disappear into the shadows. Reaching for a Mason jar perched on the fender, he plopped himself onto the vehicle's running boards, and inhaled a sip.

A silhouette appeared within the headlamps. "I don't know, Casey. We've been at this for a couple of hours, and he just lays there." The corn whiskey rolled over the rim as Milt grabbed the glass jar from Casey's outstretched hand. "I'm getting bored out of my mind." Milt squinted down the handgun's aligned sights and pulled the trigger. Snap! The hammer fell on an empty chamber. "Bang! You're dead." A mixture of laughter and giggles erupted from the small gathering.

A streak of lightning ignited the night sky. Its bright burst reflected off the glossy tar coating of a naked figure, huddled motionless upon the ground. Sensing the luminous glow, Jacob's eyes suddenly appeared within the tacky, black glaze. He held his breath, as he listened in wait, for the crack and subsequent rumble. Nothing followed.

A second jagged vein materialized overhead, and darted into the northeast. Still, no sound trailed the flash. Lightning without thunder. He remembered how this occurred during the snowstorm, and how the familiar phenomenon saved his life. When all seemed hopeless, it took him by the hand, and guided him to where he needed to be. Home, Jacob thought. Once again, it's directing me home.

Milt winced as the alcohol ran through the split in his lip. "Ouch! Damn it." He puckered his eyebrows, and kicked into Jacob's ribs, scraping a flesh colored patch into the black coating that unmasked numerous bruises and cuts, acquired from the evening's hard-hitting opening act.

He rolled the cool glass over his open wound, and aimed the revolver once more at Jacob's head. Snap! "You're dead again." Snap! "And again." He pressed the barrel to his temple. Snap! "I'm dead." He threw the handgun into the shadows. "There, can we go now?"

Brina and Ron approached from around the rear of the vehicle. "Yeah, we agree with Milt. There's still a lot going on in town, and we're missing it." Ron placed the handgun on the fender.

"Soon." Casey pushed himself to his feet. "We need to wait for the Klan's klonverse to begin. Then we can parade this Polack's tarred ass through the crowd for all the big shots to see." He laughed. "Won't they be surprised?"

"Oh, you're just trying to impress the judge." Ron snickered. "Win daddy's approval."

"What the hell is that supposed to mean?" Casey stepped toward Ron.

"Isn't that what this is all about?" Ron spun around while waving his hands about the immediate area. "Hasn't it always been?" He looked at Casey. "You can ask any of the guys. Every time you've gotten us together for one of these wild escapades, somehow it always turns into a production to please your old man."

"Bullshit!" Casey shoved Ron against the vehicle. "You take that back, or there will be two tarred assholes paraded in front of the Klan tonight."

"Break it up, girls." Milt stepped between them. "We've got company."

A set of headlamps flickered within the trees, as the engine chatter of an approaching automobile accelerated. Winding through the final segment of the dirt path, the two bright beams spotlighted the group, and then faded to a glowing orange filament as the motor choked to a stop. The side doors creaked and banged, as the two occupants stepped from the vehicle.

"It's Dob." Casey smiled. "I knew he would show." He tilted his head. "And who is that with him?" He took a step forward. "Why, if it isn't the missing bride to be."

Ron chuckled. "It looks like this humdrum of an evening has taken a fortuitous turn for the better."

"Oh Ron." Brina attempted to restrain a series of giggles. "You are the worst."

"Where is he?" Kettie shouted as she rushed toward Casey. "What did you do with Jacob?"

"Easy now." Casey struggled to deflect wild swings as her fists beat down upon him. "I said, easy now. We've taken good care of him." He nodded at the balled up resemblance of a man, lying in the flattened tallgrass. "He's just taking a little rest before the main event."

"Jacob!" Her screams absorbed within the congestion of elm and cottonwood trees. "Oh, what did you do to him?" She attempted to force her way to his side.

"It was for your own good, Kettie." Brina explained. "I had to tell the reverend. You didn't know what you were doing. Trust me, you'll thank us later for saving you from what would be the biggest mistake of your life."

"The biggest mistake?" Kettie reached for Brina. "The only mistake I made was confiding in you. You have no right to interfere with anything in my life." She stepped back and glared at the group. "None of you do."

Brina pulled back. "Well, pardon me for trying to help, but I think you're just being selfish. You should be thinking of Reverend Woodard and your aunt, and what others will say about them. Everyone knows that Protestants and Catholics don't mix. Besides, when I picked him up at the train depot, he was holding hands with that quiff, Isabelle LaFae. So, you see, he's no good."

"Ah!" Kettie lunged at Brina, her hands sliding across the girl's face, and toppling both to the ground. Feeling the pull of an arm against her waist, she twisted and jerked to free herself from the grasp.

"Hold it. It's just me." Dob lifted her to her feet and away from Brina. "Go see how bad he's hurt." He nodded toward Jacob. "I'll make sure no one bothers you."

Shooting a cold stare in Casey's direction, she moved to Jacob's side as Casey indicated a halfhearted consent.

"I knew you would show." Casey placed his hand on Dob's shoulder. "You said you didn't want to be any part of this, but I knew you would eventually change your mind."

Dob turned toward Casey. "Don't get any false ideas. I'm not here to participate. You've had your fun. Now it's time for everybody to sober up, and go home. This is over with."

"Over with? Over with?" Casey laughed. "Why, it's only just begun." He retrieved the Mason jar and pointed it toward a faint orange glow on a nearby hilltop. "Do you see that?" He sipped from the glass and stared at the pulsating gleam. "That's where we are heading. There are thousands of people attending the klonverse there tonight, and we are just minutes away from making a grand appearance, and introducing our guest of honor to the Knights of the Ku Klux Klan." He tipped the glass to Dob and smiled. "Consider it our little contribution to the day's festivities."

"That's not right, Casey. That's not right at all. None of this is. You might have your indifferences with Jacob, be it baseball, girls, or whatever it is that he does better than you, but this is no way to settle it. Kettie and I are taking Jacob, and we're leaving."

The corn liquor spilled across the fender as Casey reached for the revolver. "Looks like someone thinks they're a big man. Is that what you think you are, some kind of big shot? You think you can just walk on up and tell us all how it is going to be?" He waved the gun about the group. "After all the preparations we went through, and the klonverse we are about to attend, you think you can take it all away, just like that?"

Dob stared at the revolver in Casey's hand. "Is that my old man's revolver?"

Casey smiled. "Yes it is. We thought that if you were unable to devote your time in joining us tonight, then you would at least want to provide a little something to support the cause. Although, I can't believe he's still hiding the shells. It almost makes one feel as though he thinks we are...criminals."

Dob extended an open hand. "Give it to me, now."

"Sure, all right." Casey flipped the gun and extended it to Dob. As Dob reached for the handle, Casey pulled it from his grasp. "Under one condition. We'll call it a test."

Dob wrinkled his brow.

"You know what my old man always says." Casey smirked. "If you're afraid to pull the trigger on an empty chamber, at a worthy man, you can't be trusted to pull the trigger on an opposing man when it counts. You're basically worthless."

Dob shook his head. "Knock it off, Casey. As far as I'm concerned, that's a load of crap. Besides, your old man never saw combat. He never even went to France. He was stationed in Arizona with the others."

"That wasn't his fault!" Casey's grip tightened upon the revolver. "He wanted to go to France. He couldn't help it they sent him to Arizona. There was nothing he could do about it. He had to follow orders, and then the goddamned war ended before he had a chance to go." His face met Dob's, as he swung the revolver's barrel through the air. "You can damn well bet, if the idiot generals would have sent him to France to begin with, the war would have been over a lot sooner, and he would be a hero."

"That's right, Casey!" Milt concurred. "The judge would be a great hero."

Casey glanced at the handgun, and then back at Dob. "So, how about it? Do you think you are man enough to pull the trigger? Do you think you have the guts to kill a man when it counts? Or are you just a worthless piece of shit?"

"Damned right!" Milt threw his fist in the air. "I'd do it. I'd kill a man."

The revolver slid across the crest of the fender and spun about itself. Retrieving the glass jar, Casey tilted it toward Dob. "You decide."

"Jacob, I'm so sorry about all of this. I didn't know." Kettie attempted to scrape the tar from his face. "The reverend became furious when he found out about us, and locked me in my room. I couldn't get away until they left. By the time I arrived at the train station, you were no longer there, so I got really scared. The clerk said you left with Brina, so I knew something wasn't right. I found Dob, and we went looking for you. We were lucky we finally ended up here. Oh, Jacob, what have they done to you?"

"I love you." The weak, raspy words passed through stiff, swollen lips.

"I love you, too. You know you are my world." She pulled a hand-kerchief from her pocket. "We need to get away from here. Can you walk?" She pushed the thick coating from Jacob's hand.

An agonizing groan reverberated through his larynx, as he displayed a set of mangled fingers protruding from an enlarged hand, and contorted arm.

"My god! Why would they do that to you?"

"Collected on the homerun." He muttered.

Kettie looked over her shoulder at the others, who continued to argue with Dob as they challenged one another. "I don't think those idiots are going to let us leave. I can't believe them. Dob said they've been boozing on corn liquor all day. They must be out of their minds."

A quick streak of lightning split the night, and then faded to a distant point in the northeast. As Jacob stared at its diminishing flash and listened for the trailing sound, thoughts of home, and the picnic with Kettie on the hilltop, flowed within his mind – dancing with her through the swirls of flickers, and holding hands, while lost deep within her eyes.

"Did you see that?" Kettie pointed to the sky. "No thunder. What happened to the thunder?"

"Butterflies."

"What?" She looked at Jacob and a smiled appeared upon her face. "I was worried that after all of this, you may never want to see me again."

"Written on the wings of butterflies." He gently touched her face. "Forever."

Tears welled within her eyes as she sensed the love and beauty from beneath the tarred surface. Through all that happened, it was still she and Jacob, now, and to the end of time. Nothing would ever change that.

The sound of the escalating argument pulled her back to the central matter at hand. "We've got to get out of here. You need a doctor." She recognized his clothing scattered within the tallgrass. "They're intent on parading you around, while making fools of themselves. I won't let them do that to you. No, I would never let that happen."

The long, green stems toppled against one another, as Kettie crawled upon her hands and knees through the switchgrass bunches. Keeping an eye on the others, she gathered Jacob's shirt and trousers, balled them together, and then returned to his side. As she straightened the clothing, a small object tumbled from the trouser pocket and bounced beside her knee. Reflecting in the vehicle's headlamp glow, the shiny copper-nickel jacket of the pistol cartridge sparkled within the turned soil and trampled grass.

Kettie snatched the shell from the ground and stared at it. Cupping it in her hand, she looked around to see if anyone noticed. "Jacob!" She displayed it before his eyes. "It's the bullet that the gangster gave you." She spotted the revolver sitting on the fender of the automobile. "Be ready to move. I'm getting us out of here, right now."

As Kettie leaped for the handgun, Jacob attempted to pull her back. Throughout the evening, he was severely beaten, tarred, and humiliated. Enduring a tremendous amount of undeserved pain and cruelty, he knew eventually, the night would end, he would heal, and life would go on. He watched as they teased and taunted one another with the unloaded handgun, and at times, even laughed to himself at their foolish misbehavior. Adding a potent piece to their sadistic game, such as the cartridge, would only turn matters worse.

Nudged by Kettie's reach, the revolver slid from the fender and disappeared within the darkness. Glancing at the others, to see if they noticed her failed attempt, she patted upon the ground with both hands in a frantic effort to locate the missing piece. Feeling a firm lump beneath the folded grass, she pried the handgun free from within the tangled blades and clicked open the cylinder.

Kettie hesitated. The shell's copper-nickel jacket reflected the dim glow of the headlight's beam. As she suspended the cartridge above the open cylinder hole, her mind raced with the beating of her heart. Was this the only solution to their dilemma, or had she become just like them?

A high pitched giggle rose above the bickering. "What are you up to, Kettie?" Brina pushed on the others as she pointed.

Snap! Kettie rolled the cylinder into the frame, as the others turned to look.

"Well, I do believe she wants to play." Ron laughed. "You must allow her a turn. You simply must."

"No!" Jacob attempted to push himself from the ground. "No…"

"Hold it! Everyone, just hold it right there." Kettie pointed the revolver at the group as she knelt upon the ground. "We're leaving right now." She looked at Dob. "Help Jacob to the car. Hurry!"

Dob moved forward. "Kettie, what are you doing?"

"Just do what I say, Dob. We're getting out of here."

"She appears to be more of a man than you, Dob." Casey chuckled. "Now, tell me, just how does that make you feel?" He reached for the handgun.

"Stop right there!" Kettie shoved the barrel, halting Casey's advance. "I'm not kidding around. Just let us go, or I'll shoot. So help me God, I'll shoot."

"This is beautiful." Casey looked at the others. "See. This is how it's done. This is how you pull the trigger on a man." He turned to Kettie. "You, by far, gave the best performance. I think a round of applause is in order." He began to clap his hands.

"Hear, hear!" Ron joined in, followed by laughter.

As Casey moved toward Kettie, she jabbed the barrel at him once again. "Stop! Stop! Stop!" Her eyes pressed shut. With her finger squeezed upon the trigger, she let out a denouncing scream. Snap! The hammer dropped on an empty chamber.

"Nice one, Kettie." Milt pulled the revolver from her hands. "You get an A plus."

"So help me God, I'll shoot. So help me God, I'll shoot." The others laughed and mimicked Ketties words, as she collapsed upon the ground and lay motionless.

"No, no, no…" Tears streamed from her eyes.

Casey grabbed the gun from Milt's hand and stepped over Kettie. Stopping next to Jacob, he leaned down and scraped a round circle in the tar on his temple. He wiped the barrel clean with Jacob's shirt, and then aimed for the center of the circular mark. A smile appeared on Casey's face as two eyes disappeared from the black glaze.

"Stop that!" Dob screamed. "Look around you, Casey. The game is over. By the look of Jacob, you've gotten more than enough out of him. You won." He moved toward Casey. "Everyone's right, let's call it a night, and go home."

Casey pointed the gun at Dob. "No, I don't think so. You haven't proven anything to us tonight. Ron has, Milt has, why even Kettie joined in, but you haven't even attempted to step up to prove yourself." He pulled the hammer back. "Would you like me to show you how it's done?"

"No!" Jacob screamed. As he pushed himself to stand, Milt rushed over and kicked him to his back. Trapped beneath the sole of Milt's shoe, he struggled to break free. He tried for Kettie's attention, but she remained distraught and inconsolable.

"That proves absolutely nothing, Casey." Dob laughed. "Point a gun and pull the trigger?" He shook his head. "This is pure lunacy. I don't even know why I call you a friend."

"We've been wondering the same of you, Dob." Casey snickered. "A friend would be here. A friend would take part in a great endeavor, such as this. A friend would pull the trigger." He dropped the revolver to his side. "But, not on another friend."

Dob stared at him. "All right. All right." He grabbed the gun and stood over Jacob. "Is this all you want, huh?" He looked at Casey, as Milt stepped away and grinned. "Is this what all of you want — for me to prove my friendship?" He glanced at each as they remained motionless in awaiting his likely move.

Casey stretched a hand toward Dob, as he looked at the others. "See, I told you it might take a bit of convincing, but he would do it. He would shoot a man. Dob is just like us."

Dob pulled the gun up and aimed it directly at Casey. As his finger pressed upon the trigger, a smile slowly appeared upon Casey's face. The small assembly of friends suddenly doubled in size with a cast of dark shadows, as a streak of lightning fractured the sky. As Dob closed his eyes and squeezed the trigger, a tarred body leaped from the ground and descended between the aimed barrel and its intended mark. The thunder followed.

Chapter 22

THE earth trembled. As the thunder's echo stole the revolver's crack, and carried it off with its dispersing rumble, a blinding flash ignited the towering clouds of a passing front, and relit the night sky. The luminous reflection trounced a countless series of automobile headlamps stretching from Webster to the Klan's klonverse forming at the top of the hill, which overlooked the town.

"Ten cents each." A teenage boy collected the admittance charge, as the white robed and plain clothed participants entered the gate in following the burning torches, aligned to the stage.

"Say, where are they serving the special refreshments tonight?" A gentleman asked as he nudged his wife through the entrance.

"See Charlie or Bob." The boy nodded into the crowd. "They can take care of you."

"What about you?" The man flipped a quarter from his thumb. "Didn't you brew anything for the big event?"

The boy snatched the coin from the air. "Twenty jars. They sold out early this afternoon. I've never seen this many people in town. Must be thousands." He held out an Indian Head nickel as the man followed after his wife.

"Don't you want your change?" The boy asked. "You gave me two bits."

"Keep it." The man nodded.

"Thanks!"

A lingering ribbon of light split the sky, and splintered into a fade. Gathering in Hugh Langley's front yard, a small group speculated as to the Klan's possible actions once the meeting adjourned later in the evening. As they monitored the orange glow emanating from the hill, the group grew in numbers as close neighbors wandered in.

"Hugh, I can't believe that two-faced mayor and his city council cronies allowed this to happen." A man spoke up. "There are people hiding in their homes, behind locked doors, and afraid of what may happen when that meeting ends tonight."

Hugh lifted the pipe from his lip and blew a steady stream of smoke into the air. "I can. Actually, I wonder how many of our town officials are up there, cloaked in white sheets and hoods. It wouldn't surprise me if they all were."

"That's not right." Another protested. "That's not right at all."

"What are you worried about, Adams? You're not Catholic."

Adams glanced at the man, and then returned his attention to the orange glow. "The Catholics may be feeling the direct sting of the Klan, but the pain is felt by all who aren't supporters."

"He's right." One agreed. "It doesn't matter who you are, if you end up on the list, the consequences are all the same."

"I swear, if I see a white sheet standing in my front yard tonight," a man cracked open the bridge of his shotgun, "it sure as hell is gonna have holes in it when I get through."

"I don't want to hear talk like that." Hugh turned to the group. "I understand that many are afraid of what's going on, but if you shoot one of those men, you could be killing a family man, with a wife and kids. How would you feel then? Do you want to be a manufacturer of widows and orphans?"

"I think I would feel just fine." The bridge snapped shut. "The way I see it, if they're wearing sheets, the only family they care about is the Klan."

A low roll of thunder carried across the sky, and spread a nervous silence over the group, as they drew closer together.

"Maybe it'll rain." One finally broke the stillness with a quick laugh. "The sky will open up, and a downpour will drown out their meeting. That would certainly place a damper on any plans they have afterwards."

"That's were you're mistaken." Hugh chuckled. "It's not gonna rain. Nope, no matter how hard you wish for it. It will never rain tonight."

"Why is that?"

"You see," Hugh drew a puff from his pipe, and exhaled a dissipating breath of smoke, "it doesn't rain in hell." He patted the man on the shoulder and walked away. "No, it will *never* rain in hell."

Crack! A blinding white flash carried forth a legion of dark shadows upon the swarming hilltop. With harmonic voices in unison, hymns sang out in praise to the heavenly realm, as bodies scurried to commence the delayed opening ceremonies.

"Where in the dickens have you been?" The judge snapped as he stepped from the staging area and glared at Wes's boys. Limping nearer, they struggled in carrying the missing master of ceremonies himself, Wes, the Exalted Cyclops of the local Klan. "You were to have been here hours ago to help with the crowd." The judge stared into each face, as one by one they quickly turned in concealing their cuts and bruises. "There are thousands of people out there waiting for this klonverse to begin. Almost two hundred will be receiving the ceremony of naturalization to become new members."

The long bench sagged as they sat Wes upon the wooden plank. Moaning, they pulled their robes over their heads, and adjusted the cloth around their waists. The bench dropped deeper and deeper as each planted themselves next to him.

"What happened to him?" The judge wiped a blood trickle oozing from a split bump on Wes's forehead. Rubbing the deep red fluid between his fingers and thumb, he plucked a handkerchief from his pocket and wiped his hand clean. "And look at the rest of you." He hovered above them. "It looks like you were in some kind of automobile accident."

"It's nothing, sir." Quinn spoke up.

"He's right." Added Boyle. "It's nothing to worry about. Just a few scratches, that's all."

"A few scratches my rear end." The judge returned the cloth to his pocket. "Wesley!" Tom's shoulder gave way to the judge's sharp jab. "Wesley! Damn it! Are you still alive in there?" He stared into a set of dark, glazed eyes.

"What?" Wes shook his head as he pulled away. Attempting to focus on the clearing image of those standing near, he popped his head back and squinted at the judge. "Yeah. Yeah, I've never been better." Each word slurred upon itself.

"Well, you better hope so. Klansmen and aliens alike are waiting for you to set this thing into motion." The judge leaned closer. "I'm sure you had a chance to review my introductory speech I sent over earlier this week. You remember, the one I prepared specifically for the special announcement this evening?"

Wes's hands patted empty pockets within his robe. Glancing up, his eyes met folded sheets of paper suspended by the judge's out-reached hand. "I expected as much," the judge smirked, "so I brought an extra copy."

As Wes reached up, the judge pulled the documents from his attempt to grasp, and hesitated. "Are you sure you're well enough to direct the klonverse tonight?" He stared at a silent Wes. "Don't you forget, a tremendous amount of effort has gone into assembling the extensive list of high profile guests who are scheduled to speak." He softened his voice. "Now listen, and listen good. So help me God, if you foul this up, I'll see to it that you are crucified on one of those blazing crosses, for all to see."

The wooden bench sprung as Wes jumped to his feet. "Don't worry about me!" He poked a finger into the judge's chest. "I'm here aren't I? I'll give the goddamned speech, just like I promised." Wiping the crusted blood from his eye, he focused on a water bucket, and staggered through a small group of Klansmen, while reaching for it. The liquid splashed above the rim as he forced the tin ladle deep below the surface. Wincing, as a poured scoop ran over his head and washed through his open cuts, he cried out. "When I get my hands on that sawed-off runt, he'll wish he had never been born!"

Wes scanned the crowd and established eye contact with another Klansman. "Charlie!" He twisted his hand above his mouth. "See if you can scare me up a pull from somewhere!" As Wes bent down and dropped the ladle into the bucket, the world began to spin. With flailing arms, he grasped at the open air, as he spiraled to the ground in a dead heap.

"No. No, I don't think so." The judge shook his head as he watched others scurry to administer aid. "Pullman!" He stopped a Klansman in his tracks, who followed to help. Taking the man by his arm, he guided him away. "It's evident that Wesley is out of the picture now. He's not capable of conducting any type of meeting in his current condition, let alone the klonverse this evening. You're the

Klaliff, you're the vice-president. You need to take the initiative and begin the ceremony. We've waited long enough."

"Gee, I don't know, Judge. I should talk with Wes first." Pullman stopped and peered over his shoulder as Wes lost consciousness for a second time.

"Just look at him." The judge continued. "We certainly don't need this happening when he's out there in front of God and the world. It will only upset the crowd." He rested his hand on Pullman's shoulder. "As you know, Tom Wesley was to provide my introduction tonight. Do you have anyone with a little fire in his belly, who can take his place in introducing me?"

Pullman rubbed the back of his neck. "Well, we've got that new guy. With the right motivation, he just might be aggressive enough to accommodate your expectations."

"Well, go find him." A brief flash of light preceded a heavy crack of thunder. "And make it quick." The judge tugged at the brim of his hat and raised his shoulders, as he traced the fading glow across the dark, low hanging clouds. "I don't want these people to disperse before I accept my turn to speak."

"Bullshit!" Wes snatched the speech from the judge's hand. "You're not going to cheat me out of a chance at becoming the Grand Dragon. No one will notice anything. My helmet will cover this." He pointed at the gash on his forehead. "Now, move the hell out of my way." The judge and Pullman stumbled to the side as Wes pushed through.

The clear Mason jar sparkled in the dim, amber, torch light as Wes's unsteady hand rippled the last swallow of corn liquor over his lips. "Thanks Charlie." He tossed the jar to the side and pulled the white hood over his head. Swaying in an elliptical motion, he stared into the open field and its surrounding multitude.

"You're making me dizzy just looking at you." Charlie grabbed Wes's arm and steadied him. "Are you sure you're going to be okay?"

"Do me a favor, Charlie, would you?"

"Sure thing, Wes. You name it."

"When it's time, would you give me a push in the right direction?"

The crowd quieted, as a lone Klansman, the Night-Hawk, crossed the field, and with the assistance of two others, raised one large, burlap wrapped cross on each side of the main platform.

"Wes, I believe that's your cue." Charlie gave him a slight nudge.

Striding a half-dozen quick, overly large steps, Wes paused, located the platform on the field, and then corrected his bearing. Reaching the structure, he grasped the stair, hand railing to steady himself. With a muffled moan at each step, he pulled himself to the top. His vision blurred and refocused, as he scanned over a sea of plain clothed aliens, with twice as many white robed Klansmen. Crack! The gavel struck the hardwood sound block, and dropped to the floor, bouncing over Wes's feet.

Red and white stripes flowed behind the forward movement of a star-filled, blue field, as Pullman marched the massive flag and posted it next to the platform.

A steady applause disseminated through the body of spectators, as a stream of fire raced up the two wooden posts and danced about their crossbars. Leaning down into a shallow ditch, freshly cut within the earth, the Night-Hawk dropped a glowing torch onto a bundle of kerosene soaked burlap sacks and cut timber. The crowd gasped when a burst of flames overflowed the trench and touched the sky. As the flare subsided into the shape of a massive burning cross, a deafening cheer arose from the crowd, and echoed within the rolling prairie coteau.

Monitoring the preceding actions, the Klokard Klansman moved toward the platform and aligned himself with Pullman and the Night-Hawk, in facing Wes, the Exalted Cyclops. He touched his forehead and extended his open hand toward Wes, before lowering it to his side. "Your Excellency, the sacred altar of the Klan is prepared. The fiery cross illumines the klonverse."

Wes stood motionless, with empty eyes fixed above the horizon.

The Klansman cleared his throat, and again touched his forehead and extended his open hand toward Wes, before lowering it to his side. "Your Excellency!" He hesitated. "The sacred altar of the Klan is prepared. The fiery cross illumines the klonverse."

The white cloth of Wes's robe swayed on a light gust within the flame coaxing shadows of his lifeless stance.

"*Psst! Psst! Wes!*" Pullman kept his voice low, as he provided a discreet motion for a response.

Detecting the slight hand movement, Wes's attention returned to the ceremony. He shook his head in focusing his concentration, and stared at Pullman.

"*The fiery cross illumines the klonverse.*" Pullman nodded.

"Oh, yes." He turned to the Klansman. "Faithful Klokard, why the fiery cross?"

The Klansman bowed slightly. "Sir, it is the emblem of that sincere, unselfish, devotedness of all Klansmen to the sacred purpose and principles we have espoused."

Wes raised his arms and looked out into the crowd. "My Terrors and Klansmen, what means the fiery cross?"

"We serve and sacrifice for the right!" Thousands of voices called out in unison.

With the fading of the echo, Wes closed his eyes and dropped his arms, ensuing in an uneasy silence over the crowd.

"*Devotions!*" Pullman attempted once again to gain Wes's attention.

Wes's eyes popped open. "Devotions?" He looked down at a nodding Pullman. "Yes, ah, devotions." He extended his hands. "Klansmen all, you will gather for our opening devotions."

The Klansmen filled the field with cascading ranks surrounding the burning trench, as the Reverend Woodard ascended the platform in preparation for his invocation.

"Wes," the reverend opened his Bible and removed his notes, "are you feeling all right?"

"Yes. Tip top." Wes growled. "Just sing the opening klode, and lead the prayer. I'll leave you to do your part...you leave me to do mine."

As the Klansmen sang of honor, country, and home, the judge corralled Pullman in the staging area. "This is not going well at all. He's spoiling what has been an exceptional day for the Klan as well as the community. You need to pull him off that stage, and you need to do it now, while there's a break in the ceremony."

Pullman shook his head. "But Judge, I don't have the authority to do that."

"In view of his current actions, or inactions, it appears you have no other choice. He's going to fall hard out there, and take everything we've built with him."

"But it's Wes!"

"I'm not going to say another word. You know what you need to do, so do it." The judge turned, and walked off.

A deep red blotch appeared on the side of Wes's forehead, and dipped downward as the blood seeped through the white cloth. With the finish of the song, Wes continued his silence as the Reverend Woodard raised his hand for all to bow their heads in prayer.

"Our Father and our God. We, as Klansmen, acknowledge our dependence upon Thee and Thy loving kindness toward us…"

A strange sensation moved through the flicker of Wes's soul. Raising his head, he looked up and over the countless number of inclined hoods. Within the sea of white robes, he discovered a dark skinned man roaming through the edges of the ranks. Straining his eyes in assurance of what he saw, the moving image faded away, and all was white again. He rubbed his eyes and returned to his bow.

"…remember always that the living Christ is a Klansman's criterion of character…"

The odd feeling strengthened. His guts began to churn. Peeking through one eye, Wes glanced up to check once more. The trespasser reappeared and approached from the center of the Klansmen in moving toward the platform. Wes lifting his head, stepped forward, and then clutched the railing with both hands. The man vanished once again.

"…God save our nation. And help us to keep a nation worthy of existence on Earth. Keep ablaze in each Klansman's heart the sacred fire of a devoted patriotism to our country and its government…"

As Wes lifted his foot to back away from the railing, the dark man reappeared below the platform.

"What do you think you're doing here!" Wes screamed as he shoved his finger toward the man.

The prayer halted as the reverend stopped and glared at Wes.

"You sure are a brave son of a bitch." Wes continued. "Night-Hawk, grab that black bastard, and drag him the hell out of here, before he tarnishes the purity of our sacred gathering."

The reverend snagged Wes's arm and surveyed the area where he pointed. "Are you mad? What are you talking about? I don't see anyone out there who's not supposed to be here."

A low murmur resonated within the klonverse as all searched in an attempt to identify the detected intruder.

Wes leaned over the railing. "I told you to.." A teenage girl emerged from the forward line of Klansmen. Stopping to reposition her beret, she glanced up and down the row, and then skipped toward the black man.

"Stop right there, young lady." Wes warned. "Stay away from…" Dried cuts materialized around her wrists and filled with blood, as her blue dress shredded away, revealing a bruised and broken torso. "It can't be you. No, it can't. I left you dead in France."

He glanced at the Negro. Mud covered clothing ripped and tore before Wes's eyes. Flesh and skull fragments exploded from the back of the man's head, as a long jagged slit appeared around his throat. "No. No, you can't be here. I buried you deep." Wes reached out to those in attendance. "This can't be happening. Make it stop. It's not real. It's got to be some kind of trick."

Wes fell to his back, as a group of Klansmen rushed the platform and wrestled him down. Recognizing the olive drab uniform of a young doughboy approaching from the rear, Wes pushed the men away and crawled forward. "A.J.? A.J.? No, go away. Leave me be. I'm sorry, A.J. I'm sorry I killed you."

The judge stepped to the podium as the Klansmen pulled Wes off the platform. "Folks, please excuse our great Exalted Cyclops. He was in an automobile accident earlier today, but didn't want to let his fellow Klansmen down. Now it appears his injuries are more than he can bear. Not to worry though, with a little medical care and some rest, he should make a full recovery. Please, let's give him a well deserved hand for his noble, selfless effort which epitomizes what we hold true as a model Klansman."

As the crowd burst into applause, the Klansmen carried Wes to the staging area. "A.J.! A.J.!" He continued to scream. "You shouldn't be here. None of you should be here. I killed you. I killed you all!"

The judge scurried down from the platform and stood before the small group. "Not to worry. Not to worry. We can still salvage this."

The Klansmen toppled over as Wes broke their grip. Leaping over benches, he darted off, crying into the dark of night. "Stay away from me. Please, stay away!"

"Let him go." The judge waved the Klansmen back. "We've got a ceremony to conduct. He'll be all right. He's heading in the general direction of town."

Woodard's eyes widened as the judge pointed a cigar his way. "You, get back up there and finish the prayer. That should buy us a little more time to reorganize." He turned around and cupped Pullman's shoulder. "You're in charge now. You pick up where Wesley left off, but first, did you locate that new member to give my introduction?" He struck a match and puffed the cigar to life.

"That won't be necessary, Judge." Woodard spoke up. "You don't have to look any further. I'd be honored to introduce you."

Blowing a stream of smoke into the air, the judge smiled. "I appreciate the offer Reverend, but you're not quite what I had in mind."

A puzzled look formed upon Woodard's face. "Why is that?"

"Well, you're a good man Reverend, but the fact of the matter is, your singsong voice could put a clock to sleep. Not one Sunday has gone by where I haven't left church with a stiff neck from bobbing my head up and down like a sewing machine needle."

The reverend hung his head as the judge stepped toward the field and scanned the white robes reorganizing into ranks. "No, what I need is someone with a fierce, damning spark, someone young and full of energy." He turned. "Where in blazes is that new guy Pullman promised? Why isn't he here?"

A Klansman approached with another straggling behind. "Here he is, Judge. I'd have been here sooner, but with everyone wearing the same white hood, it's nearly impossible to tell who is who out there."

"Excellent!" The judge extended his hand to the approaching member. "I understand you gave quite a performance at the Langley Klan gathering a few weeks ago. That's just the mettle I'm looking for. I would like you to do something special for me tonight. I guarantee this will benefit you just as much as it will me."

The Man dipped his head in acknowledgement as he listened.

"As you witnessed, Tom Wesley has unexpectedly taken ill. He agreed to introduce me as a speaker during the ceremony, but those plans have now changed. What I am asking of you is to go up and onto that stage and take Wes's place in introducing me. No need to worry. The introduction is prepared." He produced the copy of the written speech. "I know this is an extremely short notice, but I trust you will provide the enthusiasm normally portrayed during such an important occasion."

The linen snapped as the man ripped the hood from his head. "No, I refuse to do that." Pastor Thomas protested. "I don't agree with any of this. I'm only here by coercion and force."

"My offer is still on the table, Judge." The Reverend Woodard tried once again. "Why don't you let me do this? I feel like I've earned it. If you…" He stopped and backed away, as the judge's hand raised in answer to his question.

The smoke stream weaved through the air as the judge directed his cigar at the pastor. "Correct me if I'm wrong, but didn't your church take a generous donation from the membership during last Sunday's services, whereas you became a member of the Klan?"

Evan laughed. "That was well played, but not *all* of my congregation is interested in siding with the Klan. A good number feel as I do. There wasn't enough time to convince the others, so I agreed to attend your gathering tonight, but that's all I agreed to, nothing more than to attend."

The judge chuckled. "I don't believe you have grasped the gravity of the situation. You see, as the preacher of your church, you are one of us now. Whether you like it or not, you will continue to be one of us. If you refuse my request for assistance with an introduction, you just may find yourself out of the Klan, and subsequently out of a job." He drew another breath through the cigar and blew a cloud of smoke. "Now, I don't believe your special skills will transfer very easily to many of the other occupations offered in this town. We already employ a pretty good soda jerk, so chances are you'll be penniless in a week."

"You can't do this to me."

"Oh, I believe you would be doing this to yourself. Also, if I may add, if you're planning on looking elsewhere to preach, keep in mind the Klan's invisible membership is spread far and wide." The judge extended the copy of the speech and smiled.

The pastor stared at the folded paper fluttering in the light breeze. Hanging his head, he reached up and grabbed the sheets from the judge's hand.

The judge patted Evan on the shoulder. "We are not bad people. On the contrary, the Klan is composed of those who are entrusted with the responsibility to steer this community for the benefit of all. You will see for yourself. Once you've attended a few meetings, you will consider yourself fortunate to be among the town's elite." The judge nodded toward the platform. "This is an opportunity for you to establish yourself. When it's time, go up there and give them a speech as though you were introducing the Almighty himself."

Evan pulled the white hood over his head and stared into the dancing flames of the cross trenched within the earth. Shaking his head, he walked to the platform steps and waited in silence.

* * * *

The drums beat steady. As the wacipi ceremonial fires burned bright on the Lake Traverse Indian Reservation, swirls of dark smoke escaped the flame's grasp and funneled into the night sky, reflecting the vivid flash of a distant thunderhead. Shifting their weight from foot to foot upon the trampled tallgrass, the Sissetons and Wahpetons danced to exhaustion, invigorated by the strength of the singers' piercing falsetto descents.

Sitting with those encircling the fire, Samuel closed his eyes, and drew a long puff through a stone pipe, before passing it to his side. The exhaled smoke floated before him. His hands formed around the white cloud, in rhythm to the drum's beat, as he cupped the smoke and gently pulled it back over him.

His thoughts flowed through a spiritual diary of a lifetime of events. From childhood to the present, scenes flickered in random disarray. A vague shadow suddenly appeared within his mind's vision. The warmth of a familiar presence followed. Opening his eyes, he recognized a friend's silhouette against the burning flames. A smile appeared upon his face, and then faded. "Jacob, is that you?"

Chapter 23

PETER tightened his squint. Blocking the rising sun with the back of his hand, he peered through one eye in a search of fishing boats afloat on the reflective, lake surface below. One, lone vessel ripped the mirrored finish in spearheading two trailing wakes, before cutting the throttle and coasting to a dead halt.

"No! Don't stop there." He spotted an anchor splash above a little known deep hole. "Damn it! There won't be any left by the time I finish chores. Now the others will pull in there like vultures. Clean out all the big ones."

Peter swallowed a gulp of water and flung the remaining liquid upon the ground. Hanging the tin cup on the wire hook, he glanced through the windmill's angle brace and noticed the shape of a single traveler walking the quiet, dirt road adjacent to the far side of his pasture. He wiped the sweat from his brow and speculated as to where the stranger originated from, and possibly where they may be bound for.

The light straw spread across the dirt floor. Pulling from the partial mound of dried wheat stalks, Peter rolled his pitchfork in building a fresh, soft layer of bedding throughout the open barn stalls. Lost in his work, his thoughts churned regarding the son he left at the train station the day before. He questioned himself as to whether the young man was ready for the realities of the fast moving, and sometimes chaotic world such as it was. He thought of the countless things he should have said but was unable to. Foremost, he wondered how he should break the news to Maria that Jacob would not be returning home.

"Would your horse mind if I scooped a tin of water from his tank?" Samuel blotted a stream of sweat from his forehead with a folded handkerchief.

Peter turned toward the barn door opening and chuckled. "He just might. He's kind of fickle that way." The pitchfork handle bounced against the top stall board as he made his way to the windmill. "How about we not take the chance in upsetting him, and pull a drink straight from the pump?"

The water sparkled in the sunlight as it flowed over the cup's rim and rippled the surface within the half full stock tank. "Will this do?" Peter set the cup in Samuel's outstretching hand.

"Yes, that will do very well, thank you." The overflow ran down his cheeks and erased the white salt marks in the corners of his mouth. "In the film, *Wagon Tracks*, the studio gave me a somewhat strange animal to ride. No matter how much you coaxed him, it seemed he just would not eat in the presence of others." A smile spread across his face. "Come to think of it, I don't ever remember seeing him dropping manure, either."

"Animals and people are more alike than some care to admit." Peter laughed. "Jacob mentioned you were looking to take a few others back with you to work in the movie business. Were you able to convince anyone to go?"

Samuel shrugged his shoulders. "Some had interest, but none were qualified. I'm traveling back the same way I came – by myself. As a matter of fact, I'm on my way to Waubay now, to board a train." He shook his head. "I have been away from Hollywood for far too long."

"If it's Jacob you are here to see, I'm sorry but you missed him by a day. He left on the outbound train heading east to Minneapolis, yesterday."

"Actually, I'm here to see you." He pointed his chin at Peter. "I'm here to deliver a message."

"Deliver a message? From who?"

"I saw Jacob at the wacipi late last night."

"I don't see how that could be. He and Kettie were going to take the train, which should have been off by mid afternoon at the latest."

"He had not yet left when I talked with him. We walked, and he allowed me to journey with him, but he said he was not ready to cross through the valley. I had never been there, on the edge, before." Samuel closed his eyes and slowly shook his head. "It is like no other place I have known." He looked at Peter. "He understands why things are the way they are. You have always been a good father, and he wishes he could have spent more time with you. He knows he will see you and the others again one day. He gives his love to all."

"That's odd he would ask you to tell me that." Peter removed his hat and rubbed his forehead. "I probably should have stayed with him longer. He may have wanted to talk, but I'm not good with those words." He looked out over the expanse of the lake. "I'm sure he and Kettie will do just fine." He hesitated, and then turned toward Samuel. "Thank you for delivering Jacob's message. You have always been a good friend of his." He rested the hat on his head and stared at the farmhouse. "Now, I just need to figure out how I'm going to tell Maria."

"I must be going now." Samuel returned the cup to Peter. "When the steam whistle sounds, you mustn't stand around. A train waits for no man."

The remaining droplets of water dripped from the turned cup as Peter watched Samuel walk down the long driveway.

"The letter! Peter, did you see the letter!" The screen door cracked against the frame as Maria hopped from the steps and rushed to Peter's side. "I didn't find it until this morning." She noticed Samuel leaving. "Oh, I didn't know we had company. What did he want?"

"I'll tell you in a bit. First, what's all this excitement about a letter?"

The paper stiffened as Maria pressed upon the folded creases. Pushing her glasses up the bridge of her nose, she read the handwriting and interpreted its contents. "It's a letter from Ben. He writes that he made it home safely…His wife is doing fine…He looks forward to returning in the fall for the harvest…He says he met another negro on the road looking for work, and sent him our way…He sends his regards." Maria folded her glasses and slid them in her apron pocket. "So, he's been home all this time."

"That's good news." Peter nodded. "At least he's safe and unharmed."

"The man Ben sent here for work – he didn't show up." She pointed at the writing. "Do you suppose he went somewhere else?"

"I've got a good idea as to what happened to him. When I get back to Webster in a couple of days, I can talk with the sheriff then. He might be a little more willing than the others to check into things for me."

The rapid clatter of an approaching automobile slowed as the vehicle reduced speed upon the dirt path bordering the property. Pulling a cloud of dust from the road, the car accelerated as it turned up the long driveway.

"Now, who do you suppose is coming to visit?" Maria took a step toward the nearing auto.

A slow grin pulled across Peter's face. "Well, speak of the devil." He took the letter from Maria's hand. "It's the sheriff."

As the sheriff's vehicle met Samuel, Samuel caught the look of the front seat passenger, Father Majer. Both locking eyes, they stared at each other until the auto passed and Samuel disappeared into the road dust.

* * * *

The Klan smoke lingered. A scattering of smoldering kerosene rags and glowing pine embers were all that remained of the prior evening's white robed dignitaries and their fiery rhetoric. From a scar cut deep within the earth for all to see, long wisps drifted below the hilltop and settled upon awakening homes and stirring streets. Pursuing the darkness across the morning sky, the sun pried its light beneath the translucent blanket in an attempt to liberate the town from the suffocating hold.

Jonn loosened the quilt from around his shoulders as he felt the warming rays penetrate the patch-stitched fabric. Watching the sunrise peek through the trees, he repositioned his seating within the swaying swing, and then stopped. From the porch, he studied the front yard. Something felt different. Something appeared missing. He pushed the swing into motion, and then stopped once again. The field grey coats, with mangled limbs, no longer roamed about. How could this be? They never missed a morning. Even during the harshest weather, Jonn could look out his window and find at least one German soldier pacing through the extreme conditions.

"I'm here!" Jonn called out. He scanned the yard in expectation of a disfigured ghoul to materialize. The brief silence gradually disappeared as an orchestra of crickets increased their chirps within the light sways of the dewed, uncut grass.

Jonn pushed against the tender burns encircling his neck. The quick sting of the wounds, and the throbbing ache of his muscles, provided an absolute reminder of the attempt to end his life the previous day. Had the rope not separated, he would surely be dressed in a secondhand, ill fitted suit, stretched out in a cheap, pine box in the back room of the undertaker's furniture store, with a final stop scheduled for potter's field.

His subsequent interaction with the ghost soldiers, and the hidden memory they freed from within his mind, seamed almost but a dream. Was this the sole purpose they tugged at his sanity for all those years, to deliver a message? Perhaps they continued to walk about, unseen, invisible to those of us still living, pursuing a penitence in a purgatory of their own choosing.

"Are you still here?" He called out once again. "I'm sure you're well aware that it's a grievous offence for a soldier to quit one's post before being properly relieved of duty." His taunts went unanswered. The yard, street, and adjacent properties remained vacant of wandering souls. Jonn pushed the swing into motion. For the first time in many years, he truly felt alone.

A familiar scent escaped from the quilt fibers. As Jonn pulled Sarah's patchwork to his nose in an effort to catch a hint of her fragrance, he heard a thud upon the swing seat. Reaching within the cloth folds, he felt the cool, steel barrel of his .45-caliber pistol.

The chatter of a gasoline engine accelerated as the city police car turned the far corner of the block and picked up speed in reaching a forced full throttle. The brakes screamed as Officer Hess pulled the hand lever, bringing the black Chrysler to a jumping halt in front of the weathered bungalow. As Jonn watched the street dust overtake the stopped vehicle, he clenched the concealed pistol's wooden handgrip, and cocked the hammer back, exposing the readied shell's primer to a willing firing pin.

Through a rant of obscenities, the policeman wrestled with the door handle. A blow from his elbow finally sent the door adrift on its hinges and the officer stumbling from the seat.

"Jonn, you're just the man I was looking for." He hurried up the sidewalk toward the front porch.

With a hidden, blind aim, and a firm tightness on the trigger, Jonn hesitated. A long sigh prompted a slight pressure to the trigger, and a controlled release of the hammer with his thumb, whereby he rested the pistol, unnoticed, back into the quilt's folds.

Hess lifted his foot onto the top step and laughed. "You must have had a pretty rough night. I see you didn't even make it through the front door."

Jonn tilted his head and gave a slight nod. He glanced up and down the street. "Where are the others?"

"Others? What others?" Hess stared at Jonn. "You're not making any sense. You still drunk?"

Jonn shook his head. "I haven't touched a drop. I just thought there would be more, after…"

"After what?" Hess lifted his cap and scratched his head. "You're still not making any sense. There seems to be a rash of that going around this morning. It's like the whole damned town went nuts last night. Must have been the Klan meeting stirred folks up. The mayor estimates a crowd of over 5,000 people. Can you imagine that? Like he said, it brought a lot of well deserved recognition to this town."

Jonn stared off into the distance. "I suppose it doesn't matter, Isaac. I promise I won't be any trouble." He extended both wrists with palms up.

Hess reached over and slapped a folded handkerchief into Jonn's hand.

Jonn lifted his head in eyeing the faded cloth in his outstretched hand. "What's this?"

Hess shrugged his shoulders. "Wes gave it to me before the meeting began last night. He said I was to deliver it to you." He shook his head. "Ya know? It's kind of funny. Damned fool just disappeared before it ended. No one has seen hide nor hair of him since." He glanced down the street. "Ah, hell, he'll show up sooner or later. He knows those poor boys are lost without him."

Jonn pulled the handkerchief before him, and then rested it upon the swing.

"What's that on your face?" Hess squinted through one eye.

Jonn looked at him.

"Right there." He grasped Jonn's jaw and turned it from side to side in examining a scattering of dark specks. "Looks like dried blood."

Jonn pulled his head away and brushed his cheeks with the back of his hand.

Hess smiled. "Oh, that's right. I heard you took on the boys yesterday." He shook his head. "Oh well. Some of them bastards had it coming for a long time now, for one reason or another. It might have done them good. Put them in their place, for a little while that is."

Jonn gave a slight nod.

"Well, I've got to be going." Hess stepped from the porch. "I'm on my way to the poor farm. The sheriff returned from Pierre this morning and he's heading out to Pickerel Lake. Sounds like one of the Polacks got himself killed last night. Chasing around with that preacher's niece. You know, the wild one. I'll bet the reverend will have her on a train back to Minnesota before the day is through." He chuckled. "Anyway, the sheriff asked if I would check on an incident at the poor farm."

Jonn watched as Hess set the police car in motion and sped off in a cloud of road dust. Looking down at the handkerchief, he carefully lifted the first layer and laid it to one side. The sudden bark of a stray dog shifted his attention for a moment as he drew a quick look about the yard. Repositioning the cloth on the swing, he raised the last fold. The object, hidden within, slid from the cloth and rolled off the seat. Jonn's attempt to catch the piece sent it bouncing across the porch with a metallic ring at each strike.

Jonn knelt down. Leaning against the edges of two uneven boards, sat a bronze medallion with a winged figure of victory covering its front. He gently cupped the medal within his hands and straightened its shiny silk rainbow suspension ribbon between his fingers. Positioned above its two battle clasps, rested a small silver star. He looked up and took a quick glance around the yard. Rewrapping the medal within the handkerchief, he gathered the pistol within the quilt, and then hurried into the house.

The sink drain pulled the remaining lather and shave stubble from the bowl with a loud burp. Jonn dried his face and threw the damp towel over the rack. Walking past his opened footlocker, he retrieved the olive drab, wool coat from the wooden hanger suspended on the four-panel door. Repositioning the puttees around his lower legs, he donned the jacket and stood near the window. Staring out into the yard, a half smile appeared as he shook his head.

Jonn grabbed the pistol from the dining room table, and released the encased magazine from the handgrip. Ejecting a .45-caliber round from the pistol's chamber, he paused for a moment as he watched it fall and bounce upon the table's surface. "One." He called out. Picking up the magazine, he pressed his thumb down upon the shells stacked one on top of the other within its confinement. With a quick thumb-flicking action, he counted aloud as he began ejecting the cartridges, in succession, directly onto the tabletop. "Two, three." As each time before, the shells danced on the hardwood surface before rolling in random directions. "Four, five..." He hesitated for a moment as he looked into the cleared magazine. With his free hand, he reached up and set two empty, .45-caliber shell casings upon the table. "...six...seven. All accounted for. All seven."

The screen door cracked against the frame as Jonn left the house and stood on the front porch. Fastening the top button of his uniform, he contemplated the long walk before him. He scanned the jackets attachments, giving a slight pull to the freshly stitched honorable discharge red chevron sewn onto his left sleeve. Reaching into his trouser pocket, he pulled the folded handkerchief from within, examined it, and then quickly shoved it back inside. Sliding his fingers through his hair, Jonn donned the overseas service cap, and took the first step on his way.

Vivid reflections of a young man arriving home from France absorbed his thoughts, whereby he did not notice those along his route, who stopped and stared or conveyed a favorable comment. The front door of his destination was suddenly before him. As he raised his hand to knock, he hesitated inches from the door's frame. The tremble in his hand had vanished.

"Is someone out there?" A call came from within. "I'll be there in just a minute."

A familiar scent of baked cinnamon and pastry flowed on a light breeze through the screen door.

"Why Jonnie, what a surprise." The door's hinges squeaked as Mrs. Sweeney pushed upon the crosspiece. "You're in your uniform. Is everything all right?"

"Yes ma'am. Everything is just fine. I have something for you that belongs to A.J."

She pushed the door open. "Belongs to Albert? Oh, dear, do come in. You arrived at the right time. I have a pie cooling, fresh from the oven."

Jonn caught the door as she turned and walked inside. Thoughts of hearing A.J.'s laughter formed a smile on his face. Memories of the Mexican border, France, and palling around town on a Saturday afternoon flooded his mind. Pulling the service cap from his head, Jonn stepped through the doorway and followed Mrs. Sweeney inside.

* * * *

The snowmelt roared. Surging through the lake's narrow spillway, the frigid, spring runoff swirled upon the dry grass creek banks, and facilitated an effortless exodus for a profusion of olive green and reddish brown dorsal fins. Striking against one another, the aggressive pike battled for space in a territory of shrinking boundaries, as their prey lured them into the vast unknown.

Sitting on a fallen tree, Aggie picked upon the limb's bark as she stared into the rolling currents. Her scattered thoughts darted endlessly, from the nauseating kerosene smell that filled the house when her father attempted to clean the residual tar from Jacob's body, to the refusal to prosecute due to the official determination that the incident was more or less an accident, and unopened letters from Kettie that Maria burned in the kitchen stove.

She looked down at a curled sheet of paper clenched within her hand, a note left on her pillow by Jacob last summer. The frayed and worn page disclosed an apology for leaving, a hope for a more fulfilling life, and a promise to see her again one day. Over the year, she read each sentence countless times in hopes of discovering something new, something she overlooked, but the words never changed.

The limb rocked slightly as Aggie stood up. She walked to the creek's edge and looked into the water at her drifting reflection. Wiping the welling of tears from her eyes, she released the letter into the stream, and watched it disappear within the moving currents.

"Goodbye my beautiful brother. You belonged to the coteau. You were a part of it, as much as it was a part of you. Now, you've finally escaped...you belong to the angels." She hesitated as she felt a slight brush upon her cheek. Turning her head, she noticed nothing but a light swirl of the midmorning air pull itself up and through the leafless treetops.

As the horse nudged against Aggie's shoulder, she scooped the bridle's reins into her hand, and then pulled herself into the saddle. Unbuttoning her pocket, she retrieved a worn notebook. The pages danced within the breeze as she thumbed her way to Jacob's last written entry and added her notes. With a slight squeeze of her legs and a thrust of her seat, she set the horse into motion in following the creek's edge. Moving through the budding branches of the bordering cottonwood trees and burgeoning shrubs, she heard the hollow echo of a great horned owl fade within the downstream rushing waters. *Hoo-hoo-hoo! Hoo-hoo!*

www.ingramcontent.com/pod-product-compliance
Lightning Source LLC
Chambersburg PA
CBHW030628110726
47901CB00002B/364